DOSED TO DEATH

DOSED TO DEATH

A KENZIE KIRSCH MEDICAL THRILLER #3

P.D. WORKMAN

ISBN: 9781774681176 (IS Hardcover)

ISBN: 9781774681169 (IS Paperback)

ISBN: 9781774681183 (IS Large Print)

ISBN: 9781774681138 (KDP Paperback)

ISBN: 9781774681145 (Kindle)

ISBN: 9781774681152 (ePub)

pdworkman

Brewing Death

Coup de Glace

Sour Cherry Turnover

Apple-achian Treasure

Vegan Baked Alaska

Muffins Masks Murder

Tai Chi and Chai Tea

Santa Shortbread

Cold as Ice Cream

Changing Fortune Cookies

Hot on the Trail Mix

Recipes from Auntie Clem's Bakery

Parks Pat Mysteries

Out with the Sunset

Long Climb to the Top

Dark Water Under the Bridge

Immersed in the View (Coming Soon)

Skimming Over the Lake (Coming Soon)

Hazard of the Hills (Coming Soon)

Stand Alone Suspense Novels

Looking Over Your Shoulder

Lion Within

Pursued by the Past

In the Tick of Time

Loose the Dogs

AND MORE AT PDWORKMAN.COM

*To those strong enough to face their fears
and those who aren't*

H ow's it going?" Kenzie asked Zachary, poking her head into the bedroom to see whether he had finished packing.

Zachary was sitting on the bed looking at his duffel bag. It didn't look as if he had made much progress since the last time she had seen him. She cocked her head to the side.

"Tired?" she asked sympathetically.

Zachary raised his head to look at her. His face was painfully thin, eyes dark hollows. He attempted to hide how sunken his cheeks were with the dark stubble, but she could still tell. The antiviral protocol that the two of them had been through had been much harder on him. Kenzie was feeling pretty much her old self. She just tired a little faster than usual. But Zachary had already been sinking into his annual depression and didn't sleep or eat well, so it had really taken its toll on him.

But better thin and tired than dead.

"I just don't know if I can do this," Zachary said.

Kenzie had already taken care of everything else. The only thing left for Zachary to do was to pick out the clothes he wanted to wear for the holiday and throw anything else he wanted to take along into the bag. Once they were at the resort, he could rest and sleep as much as he needed to. They had a cabin to retreat to that was separate from anyone else, so they didn't have to worry about thin walls or people being aware of their comings and goings. They would have both the privacy they needed and socialization activities to boost their spirits.

Rather than criticizing him or telling him to just focus and get it done, Kenzie entered the bedroom to see if there were anything she could do to help.

"Do you know what you want to wear?"

He looked at his flat bag listlessly. "No."

"Does that mean you don't care? Can I just pick some stuff out for you?"

Zachary rubbed the back of his neck. "Yeah. Sure."

Kenzie went through Zachary's drawers and his side of the closet to pick out a few outfits, folded them neatly, and set the piles into his bag. "There. What else? Do you have your meds?"

"Yes."

Kenzie opened the toiletries case to see what was in it. Comb, toothbrush, razor, and a few bottles of pills. She checked the names on the sides of each, and didn't think he had everything he needed. She left the bedroom and went down the hall to the main bathroom, which was the one that Zachary usually used, leaving the ensuite bathroom to Kenzie. She opened up the medicine cabinet and looked through the remaining pill bottles, picking out a couple more that Zachary probably couldn't go without for a week. She grabbed his deodorant and toothpaste and glanced over his toiletries for anything else he might need that the resort wouldn't have on hand.

She returned to the bathroom and added the items she had picked out to his toiletries bag. Zachary watched her and didn't comment.

"What else are you taking? Your computer and phone? Anything else?"

"Computer," Zachary echoed.

"It's in the living room? Let's go grab it and you can tell me if there is anything else you need."

She picked up the duffel bag. Zachary took a few extra seconds to consider this, then pushed himself to his feet. He took the bag from her as they walked to the doorway, and Kenzie let him. She didn't know whether he was being chivalrous or just didn't want someone else touching his stuff, but it didn't matter. It was good he was taking some part in the preparations, however small.

In the living room, he put his bag down on the couch and picked up his laptop computer, which was sitting closed on his mobile desk, and put it into his soft-sided briefcase beside the couch. He picked up the cord, unplugged it from the wall, and carefully coiled it up to add to his gear. Kenzie stayed back and watched him gather the peripherals he wanted. An external drive and mouse. A couple of notepads. He stood there looking at his desk, again grinding to a stop.

"Is that it?" Kenzie prompted.

"I don't know if I can do this," Zachary said again.

"Do what?" Kenzie had assumed that he meant he couldn't do the packing on his own, but since he was now packed, she wasn't sure what he meant.

"Just... this whole thing. Going to this place. Being around other people. Leaving my business behind when I've already been neglecting it because of this virus protocol..."

"You wouldn't be able to do it if you were here anyway. You still need more time to recover. Just because you're out of the hospital, that doesn't mean that you are one hundred percent better. What about after your car accident? You couldn't go right back to work a couple of weeks after that, could you?"

"No. But that was different. I had a lot of rehab to do... I couldn't physically do the work."

"And how is that different from now? You're not being weak or lazy. You're recovering from a virus and treatment protocol that could have killed you. Just like that car accident. Your clients will understand that you can't service them right now. They will wait, or go to another private investigator, or Heather will help them out with what they need. And when you're feeling better, you can get back to it."

"Heather can't do everything. She's not trained. She doesn't do field work."

"I know. I said that they could go to another PI if they need to. If they just need backgrounds or skip tracing or other computer stuff, Heather can do that."

He scratched his head. "Yeah."

"You can't work like this. And if you're out of town, people will get that. Everyone takes a vacation now and then. It's not healthy to work all the time. Most jobs will wait a couple more weeks, until you're ready."

"I thought this vacation was only a week."

"Yes, the vacation is only a week. But I don't think that's going to be enough time for you to recover enough to work cases again."

"I can do some. Maybe not everything, but I can start doing some work, can't I?"

"I'm not the one dictating it. That will depend on your body."

Zachary started to sit down on the couch. Kenzie stepped forward and picked up the duffel bag. "Don't get comfortable. Let's get the car loaded up."

He took the bag away from her firmly, then bent down and picked up the laptop bag as well. "Which car are we taking?"

It was always a fight to see who got to drive. Zachary enjoyed driving, especially on the highway, where he was able to zone out and let go of his usual anxieties. Kenzie loved getting out in her baby, a sporty red convertible. But she had decided they would take Zachary's nondescript white compact instead. It was better in the fall weather in Vermont, which was supposed to be taking a turn for the worse in the next few days. And she wanted to give Zachary that time to drive, to get out of himself and be in the zone for a while. It would help him as much as any vacation. She also preferred not to have her baby sitting outside unprotected when they were at the resort. It was safer in her garage.

"Yours. But you have to watch the speed limit."

Which meant that he'd better not go more than ten miles or so above the speed limit. Zachary preferred to drive way too fast for Kenzie's comfort. At least, when they weren't racing against time to stop a viral outbreak.

Zachary brightened a little at this news. He hefted his bags higher and headed to the front door. Kenzie grabbed the food bags from the kitchen and her suitcase from the hall and followed him out to his car.

Zachary had the trunk open and carefully stowed his bags, then took Kenzie's from her and fit them in.

"You aren't taking a computer?" he noted.

"I'm on vacation. I've got my phone and tablet for simple emails or looking things up, I've got some books I intend to read, and I'm going to participate in some of the group activities and spend time with you. No work."

He considered this. "They *do* have Wi-Fi, right?"

"Yes, they have Wi-Fi. I don't know how fast their internet service is, being up in the mountains like they are, but there is internet. And you could always hotspot to your phone."

"Maybe I should have bought some extra data..."

"You can do that later if you need to. You don't have to be home to do that. Now, is there anything else? Last chance."

Zachary gazed back at the house, but his eyes were far away. She didn't know what he was seeing or remembering. "Yeah. I'm fine. Got everything."

Kenzie kept an eye on Zachary as he drove out of the city and settled into highway driving. He gradually became more relaxed, the lines in his face softening and his hands loosening on the steering wheel. Kenzie gave him a while to enjoy the drive before trying to start a conversation.

"Now are you happy to get out of town?"

Zachary nodded. "Yeah. You're right. Some time away from work will be a good thing, even if I have already been off for a couple of weeks. There's money in the bank and I don't think I would be able to do much in the shape that I'm in right now."

"I think you'll feel a lot better once you've been able to relax for a while. Lorne says this resort is really nice."

"Did Pat take him there?"

Kenzie grinned. Patrick Parker had previously taken his partner, Lorne Peterson, to a day spa as a Christmas gift. While Lorne had said that he enjoyed it, it really wasn't his type of thing. Pat was far more concerned about healthy living and taking care of his body. Lorne was more of a pizza and beer guy. Zachary was clearly trying to set his expectations of the resort based on which of the men had first suggested it.

"No. It's run by an old friend of Lorne's."

Zachary nodded, understanding it was more of an indulgence than a health spa. Somewhere he wouldn't be expected to be fit or to eat clean.

"Sounds nice... Do you think..." Zachary trailed off.

Kenzie gave him some time to rethink his question and tell her what he wanted to know, but he fell silent and didn't finish the question.

"Do I think what?"

"It's just stupid."

"It's not really fair, deciding you know my answer without asking the question. How do you know what I'm going to say?"

"I don't. I just decided it was a stupid question and I don't want to ask it."

"Ask me anyway."

Zachary pulled out to pass a few cars. Kenzie watched the speedometer to make sure that it settled back into place once he pulled back into the right-hand lane.

"Okay. But it is stupid. I was just wondering if we could *not* tell people what I do for a living. People find out I'm a private investigator, and suddenly they're telling me their whole life story and asking my opinion about cheating spouses and Poirot and Monk and if I could help them find a long-lost family member..."

Kenzie laughed and nodded. "Like when people find out I'm a doctor and want to know what I think of their mole or if there really are untraceable poisons."

Zachary smiled. "Exactly like that."

"Well, I'm game. What do we want to tell people we do instead?"

"I can be unemployed. Then no one will ask me any questions requiring my expertise in any other area."

"Okay. Then I'd better be something that makes money. But something really boring. How about... an accountant. Hmm... not just an accountant..."

"How about an IRS agent?" Zachary suggested. "No one will

ask you for your opinion on any creative accounting if they think you might turn around and audit them."

Kenzie nodded, pleased. "Great! I'm an IRS agent. An auditor. If anyone starts a conversation, I don't want to be a part of, I'll just start asking them questions about their income and whether they have ever been the subject of a detailed audit."

Zachary chuckled. "You are evil."

"It was your idea. I'm putting the blame on you."

Despite the fact that Zachary enjoyed driving, Kenzie suspected that driving the whole way would be too much for him. He was blinking a lot and his forehead was lined with concentration.

"Are you getting tired? I think maybe we should switch drivers."

Zachary blinked and used the heel of one hand to wipe his eyes. "I'm okay."

"I know you're used to long hours on surveillance, but there's no reason we can't divide up the driving. I'd like to do at least part of it."

"I'm not tired, though."

"Then say that you're tired so that your girlfriend can get a chance at the wheel," she urged, appealing to his caring nature. There was no need for him to admit that he didn't have the strength to do the whole trip on his own. Not when she really wanted to drive partway herself.

Zachary blinked slowly a couple more times, and Kenzie caught an infinitesimal head bob. If he waited much longer, he was going to be asleep at the wheel.

"Zachary. Pull over here. My turn."

He glanced at her, then sighed and pulled to the shoulder. The highway was quiet, so they didn't have to worry about the traffic whizzing by them as they got out. Kenzie made sure that Zachary had shifted into park, then got out. They crossed paths as they circled the car, and Kenzie gave Zachary a quick kiss. "Thank you."

He nodded, ears getting a bit red, then went around to the passenger side. Kenzie pulled back into the lane, and within five minutes Zachary was fast asleep, his head against the door.

"Not tired, my foot!" Kenzie said softly and shook her head.

She let herself relax. As much as she loved Zachary, it was stressful trying to look after him while he was sick. She was constantly trying to monitor his depression to make sure that he wasn't a danger to himself. Being human, she couldn't help but feel more down when he was depressed and didn't want to talk or to do things with her. She wanted to lift him up, but it was a struggle not to be pulled down instead.

A vacation would help. Getting him away from work to somewhere he was allowed to relax rather than moping around about not being able to do his job. They hadn't ever taken a holiday together. She hoped to be able to get his physical and mental health on track before December, so it would be easier to get him through to Christmas, when his anxiety and depression would start to return to their normal levels.

And it wouldn't hurt Kenzie, either. She had been through the same antiviral protocol as Zachary and, although it had been easier on her system, she still found herself tiring more easily than usual, dealing with brain fog, and just being generally out of sorts. She wanted to be one hundred percent when she went back to her job at the Medical Examiner's Office. Or at least, as close as she could get to it.

Zachary started to move around as they were making their way up a winding mountain road. At first, Kenzie thought he was awake, but he started to moan and mutter under his breath, and she realized that he was dreaming. He must have been really tired to not only be able to sleep in the car, which she had never seen him do, but to actually be in a deep enough sleep to dream while he was there.

He moved his head back and forth. Kenzie said his name a few times to try to rouse him gently, before the dreams turned into nightmares. She should have known it was already too late.

"Zachary. Zach. Wake up." She shook his arm. Then she put her hand back on the wheel. She didn't want to risk an accident because she was trying to wake him up.

He grunted and made a gesture of pushing something away in his sleep, but there was nothing there for him to push away.

"No. No," Zachary insisted.

"Zachary. It's okay. You can wake up."

"No!"

Kenzie tried shaking him once more when she was on a straight portion of the road. He startled suddenly and went rigid, hands out protectively in front of him. It would have been funny if Kenzie didn't know how terrifying his dreams could be.

"It's okay," she told him. "Just a dream. You're safe."

Zachary blinked a few times and looked at her. He looked around him, looked out the window, looked at the interior of the car. Maybe wondering why she was driving instead of him.

He blew his breath out in a puff and took a few deep breaths to try to calm himself. He rubbed his eyes and relaxed back into his seat.

"I fell asleep."

"Yeah. Have a look at the scenery, this is gorgeous."

He looked out the window again. "It is," he agreed.

The Vermont autumn was spectacular. She knew Zachary didn't like snow and Christmas card scenes, but the beautiful reds and oranges of the leaves were stunning. As a photographer, he had to appreciate them.

"Did you bring a camera with you? You might want to take some pictures while we're out here."

"I have my phone. Other gear is in my bag in the trunk."

"Good. I hadn't even thought about you being able to do photography while we're up here. That will be a nice break, won't it?"

Though she had seen a little of his artistic photography, he was mostly confined to surveillance photos while he was working. He hadn't had much time to do any hobby shooting lately. That was one thing they could plan to do together. Kenzie wouldn't mind going for some scenic walks, both at the resort and when they got back home. It would be a nice way to unwind together.

"Yeah," Zachary agreed. He sat up and watched out the window with more interest. "Are we getting close?"

"I think we're about ten or fifteen minutes out."

Kenzie was glad they were at the end of the road trip. It had seemed like an easy drive when she had mapped it out, but she hadn't been taking their lack of energy into account. Zachary was wiped out, and Kenzie was nearly as bad, yawning and fighting a fatigue headache.

"What were you dreaming about?" she asked, trying to keep a conversation going, which would help to keep her awake and alert.

Zachary didn't answer right away. He kept looking out the window, acting as if he hadn't heard her. Eventually, he glanced over at her and, seeing she was still waiting for an answer from him, shrugged.

"I dunno. Just something."

Not his usual nightmare, then, of the house fire he had been trapped in as a ten-year-old. The last straw that had broken his family up. Zachary was the only one injured in the fire. A fire that he had accidentally set with Christmas candles and decorations. Which explained why he still hated Christmas even now, decades later. It had been traumatic and a defining point in his life. He could never leave it behind, even when he slept.

"You don't remember what it was?"

Another shrug. And another evasive answer. "Not really."

Kenzie was silent, thinking it over. She had been wondering lately how often he dreamed about Bridget, his ex-wife, and the twins she was expecting. He had told her about a few dreams, mostly when he had first found out that she was pregnant. After that, he had stopped talking about it. But the babies would arrive any day now, and it had to be on his mind. Another reason Kenzie wanted to get Zachary out of town and focused on something else. He didn't need to be worrying about his ex and her babies on top of everything else.

And she suspected that he had been doing more than just worrying about Bridget, a suspicion that gave her a sinking, heavy feeling in her gut every time she considered it. He had previously monitored Bridget's comings and goings, putting a GPS tracker on her car so that he would know where she was at all times. He had managed to shake himself free from that compulsion, under threat of stalking charges, by a med change and returning to therapy.

But Kenzie feared that he was back up to his old tricks. When he wasn't home when she expected him or when he was vague about where he had been or what he had been doing, she couldn't help wondering.

5

There was a sign pointing right for The Lodge, the resort they were booked at. Kenzie slowed and looked for the turnoff, eventually finding a narrow gravel road that led into the trees. She slowed some more and turned onto it. As they bounced and crunched through the gravel, Kenzie was glad that they were in Zachary's car instead of hers. She hadn't even thought of gravel roads and what they could do to her paint job. And as she thought about it, there were probably other dangers too. Not just birds leaving evidence of their presence, but the possibility of goats or horses licking or munching it. Or stray shotgun pellets slicing holes through the panels. Tractors and machinery rolling right over it as if it weren't even there.

Of course, none of that was going to happen. But she was glad she didn't have to worry about it.

Kenzie hoped that no one would come down the road in the other direction. She wasn't sure there was space for two cars to pass each other. Especially if one of them were a truck or jeep, or some kind of farm machinery.

They made it to the end of the road without incident. Kenzie looked around at the painted fences, the pretty farmhouse, and the cottages nestled down the hill among the trees.

"Well, this is it."

Zachary opened his door and stepped out of the car. He looked around. "This is it?"

"Yes. You don't need to sound so disappointed."

"No... I'm not. I just thought... I don't know. I pictured a hotel, a town, stores, and maybe a lake..."

"There is a lake. But it's a resort, it's away from other settlements so that people can come here to regenerate without all of the interruptions of city life. Just... nice and quiet. Relaxing."

Kenzie got out of the car. Zachary started to pace restlessly. Kenzie had told him all about the Lodge, but little of it appeared to have actually stuck. Or he had heard the words but not understood that she was being literal about how isolated they would be. It was a retreat. Somewhere for them to just be themselves and not have to worry about work. Or exes having babies. Or viruses.

"Try to relax," she advised. "You're going to love it."

"It's fine," Zachary said quickly. But it was clearly going to take some time for him to adjust to the place. "We should... find out where our room is."

"Yes," Kenzie agreed. "Let's go into the main office and find out."

She gestured to the farmhouse. Zachary looked around, checking to see if there were, perhaps, a more obvious office, more modern or hotel-ish. But there wasn't. They walked up to the house together. Kenzie knocked on the door and entered.

It was quaint. Charming. It was not a city hotel. Zachary looked around, and looked back at Kenzie.

"Isn't it great?" she enthused. "You should take some pictures. I bet there are lots of good subjects here."

A man came out of one of the back rooms to greet them.

He was an older gentleman, well past retirement age. Probably the original owner of the farmhouse. Or maybe the son of the original owner. He smiled at them pleasantly but, having done so, his mouth fell back into a creased, unhappy-looking state. He had a head of gray hair and was thin, though not as thin as Zachary.

"Welcome to the Lodge," he told them in a gravelly voice that attested to many years of cigarettes or scotch. Or both. "I hope you will enjoy your stay with us."

Kenzie nodded. She stepped forward and put her hand out toward him. "It's nice to be here. You have a lovely place. I'm Kenzie, and this is Zachary. I guess we should get checked in and find out where our cabin is...?"

He returned the handshake, but it wasn't really a grip and a shake. He just barely touched her and then let go. One of those men who didn't think ladies should shake hands or take the initiative, she supposed.

"Stuart Dewey," he said shortly. "Why don't you come over here to our registration table," he invited. "I have your reservation here already, printed out, you just need to sign it. Fill in your license plate number. I think that's everything. We already have your credit card on file."

Kenzie nodded and followed him to a small writing table. He showed her the printouts, which were identical to the ones Kenzie had printed out for herself, and had her sign a form.

"There's no smoking in the rooms. If you want to smoke, you have to do it in a safe area. Not out in the woods with all of the dry leaves. There is a sort of a compound behind the groups of cabins. You can smoke there, if you are so inclined."

"We don't smoke," Kenzie assured him.

"Good. Darn place is as try as tinder this year. Whole thing could go up in a blaze."

Kenzie's gaze immediately went to Zachary. He had been hanging back, letting her handle everything, and hadn't moved from the space he had occupied since stepping in the door. His hands went out blindly to steady himself against the wall. Kenzie could see sweat on his face, and his skin turned a shocking white.

"Excuse me. Just a sec," Kenzie told Dewey.

She went over to Zachary and took him by the hand. "Come sit down. You're all right. Tell me five things you can see," she suggested, beginning an anchoring exercise.

Zachary's legs moved automatically when she tugged him over to an inviting couch. But his mind was far away.

"Five things, Zachary," Kenzie said, keeping her voice slow and reassuring.

He collapsed into the sofa. "The... books," he said faintly, looking at the bookshelves that lined one wall, filled with Readers' Digest Condensed Books. "The light. The... windows."

"That's three things. Give me a couple more."

Zachary's head turned. His face relaxed slightly. "The stairs. Something green."

The "something green" was some sort of macramé wall hanging. Kenzie wasn't any more sure than Zachary what it was supposed to be.

"Five things you hear?"

"Your voice. Mine."

"I think that's cheating. What else?" Kenzie strained her ears to listen and identify sounds around them.

"Outside... voices. Horses." Zachary thought about it. "Birds."

His color was starting to return as he pulled himself out of the flashback. "Good. How are you feeling?"

He put his hand over his heart, which was pounding hard and fast. Kenzie had her fingers over his pulse and was paying attention to the pace.

"Out of breath."

"Yeah. But you can breathe freely. And it will be back to normal soon."

"Okay."

Kenzie released his wrist, rubbed his shoulder for a few seconds, then went back to the registration table.

"What's wrong with him?" Dewey asked, a little too loudly. Zachary would be able to hear him clearly.

"Nothing is wrong with him. He had a bad experience with a fire. It's best not to talk about it."

The man eyed Zachary for a moment, then turned his attention back to the registration process. "License plate here. Initial here and here. There is a damage deposit of five hundred dollars. You get that back if everything is clean and undamaged at the end of your stay here. If the room smells of smoke or you have... remodeled... you lose your deposit on top of the rental fee. Understood?"

Kenzie nodded and initialed the spots he indicated. "Zachary, what's your license plate number?"

He recited it for her, his voice steady. Kenzie wrote it into the space provided.

"There is dinner at the house every day at six," Dewey advised. "There are no restaurants within an hour's drive. Every Thursday in November is Thanksgiving dinner. It's all included in the package you paid for."

Kenzie nodded.

"Here is a brochure setting out the various events that will be taking place over the next week," he handed her a flyer printed on an inkjet printer. "We have bonfires," a covert glance at Zachary, "Don't suppose you'll be going to those. Hayrides. Fireworks. Live entertainment at nine."

"It sounds like it's going to be great. I'm really looking forward to it."

He nodded dourly. "If you go walking, stick to the trails. They will bring you back here. If you get turned around, just keep taking right turns. There are wild animals. Most of them are not out during the daylight. I'd advise you to stay out of the woods at night. They're more afraid of you than you are of them, but don't be stupid and try to feed them or get your picture taken with them."

"I don't plan to!"

"No one ever plans to get mauled," he snapped. "But people are still all-fired eager to get themselves et. The Lodge isn't liable if one of you goes off into the forest molesting the wildlife."

Kenzie tried to keep a serious expression, nodding her agreement. "No sir. We'll be careful."

"Good. Welcome again to the Lodge. I'll see you at supper."

He handed her a key with a large plastic square with the number five on it. "Out the door, down the hill, and to the right. You can't miss it."

"Thank you."

Kenzie went over to where Zachary was still sitting on the sofa. The owner disappeared back into a back room. Kenzie thought he was probably going to the kitchen. She looked down at Zachary.

"Good to go?"

"Yeah." Zachary stood up. He stayed still for a moment, getting his legs back. Then they walked together toward the door.

6

H e didn't say anything at first. When they left the house, he took one look back over his shoulder. He raised an eyebrow at Kenzie.

"Molesting the animals?"

Kenzie snickered. "Bothering them. Trying to get too close. Throwing sticks at them or trying to get them to eat out of your hand."

"Why would anyone want to do that?"

"Some people see wildlife and lose their minds. They want to show everyone back home how brave they are, or how cute the animals are. So they do something stupid."

"If I ever get the idea of taking a selfie with a bear, please just shoot me and get it over with."

Kenzie grinned. She looked around. The road continued down to the individual cabins, so they didn't have to walk their luggage all the way there.

"You'd better be careful what you say. You are the one with problems with impulse control."

Zachary nodded, letting out a low chuckle. It sounded forced, but she was glad that he was at least trying to enjoy himself.

"Still. I've never had an impulse to cuddle with a wild animal."

"That's good. I don't want to wake up one morning and find out that you've wandered off with Yogi."

They got back into the car, Kenzie in the driver's seat, and she coasted down to the parking pad in front of cabin five.

"Well, here we are. Let's take the bags in."

She popped the trunk and they each took out the bags they had put into the trunk back at the house and carried them to the cabin. Kenzie put hers down to unlock the door and push it open. Zachary grabbed her bags as well as his own and stepped in.

Kenzie took a look around. She had looked at all the pictures on the website, so she had a good idea of what to expect. The cabin felt larger than it had looked in the picture. Not a cramped little place like her great-grandparents might have built with ventilation cracks between the logs, but a spacious, well-sealed modern building. She flipped the switch beside the door and the lights went on. Not that they needed them in the middle of the day, but it was nice to know that they worked.

"Electricity," Zachary observed. "I was worried for a few minutes."

"They have all the amenities. Electricity. Indoor plumbing." Kenzie grinned at him. "Including a hot tub."

He considered this thoughtfully. "Would that be a hot tub big enough for two people?"

"I believe it seats eight."

Zachary nodded slowly, smiling. "We'll have to test it out."

"I agree."

He looked around again. "Heated. Forced air."

"Yes." No need for them to light a fire in the fireplace. They would be comfy cozy without the need for an open flame.

Zachary wandered farther into the cabin. The living room and kitchen were together in the right side of the cabin. He went through a hallway to the left to check out the other rooms. Kenzie followed.

There were three bedrooms. Lots of space for them to spread out. They wouldn't be right on top of each other for a week.

Zachary picked one of the bedrooms and put their clothing down. He took the bags of food back out to the kitchen.

"You brought a lot of food with you. He said that they have dinner every night in the main house."

"I know. And there is a continental breakfast, and sandwiches and cold cuts for lunch. But I wanted to make sure that you had familiar food that you like. I know how hard it is for you to eat when your meds make you nauseated."

She had packed chocolate chip granola bars, one of the only things he could get down in the morning. And the various other snack foods that he subsisted on when they didn't have meals together. She didn't want him to have any excuse for not eating. The vacation was to fatten him up, not to let him waste away any more.

"Thanks," Zachary said, sounding surprised, like he was amazed that she would have considered such a thing.

"We take care of each other," Kenzie said simply.

It wasn't just her looking after Zachary when he ran into problems. He helped her too, when she was working late, when she had run into trouble at work and needed help with a case.

When he had jumped in between her and a crazed killer at the masquerade ball. He'd only needed a few stitches, but it could have been much worse.

They were both tired from the packing and the drive, so they ended up napping most of the afternoon. Kenzie was up before Zachary, which, if he weren't recovering from his treatment, would have been remarkable. Even just sleeping during the day was unusual for him, despite how little he slept at night.

Kenzie got up slowly, careful not to wake him up. She got out one of her paperbacks and curled up to read it on the couch. Zachary was up in another hour, rubbing his eyes sleepily.

"How are you doing?" Kenzie asked. "Good nap?"

"I'm sorry. I didn't mean to sleep the whole afternoon."

"You're still recovering. Don't worry about it. We're here to rest."

"Rest, yes, but not to sleep the whole vacation away."

"You won't. I slept a lot of the time too. You weren't the only one. Are you getting hungry?"

Zachary shrugged. "I could eat something."

For him, that was about as good as it got. He usually said he didn't want anything, so Kenzie took it as a good sign.

"Great. They'll be serving dinner at the farmhouse pretty soon.

Do you want to go up and meet the other guests and have dinner together?"

Zachary hesitated, then nodded. "Yeah, sure. That sounds good."

"You sure?"

"You don't want to stay in the cabin all day, do you? And you'll want a good dinner."

"Yes, but we don't have to rush into it. If you want to just have dinner ourselves tonight, we can do that. I brought plenty of food."

"No. Let's go have dinner with the others."

Kenzie smiled. She was looking forward to meeting the other vacationers. It felt like going to camp as a kid. She'd never gone to any that were real wilderness experiences. Lisa, her mother, had only selected camps with modern facilities. But Kenzie had enjoyed being closer to nature, making new friends, and trying new things. It was always an exciting time. Maybe that was why she had been drawn to the Lodge.

"Great. Give me a few minutes to freshen up, and then we'll head up and join the others. They have cocktails before dinner, so we can meet everyone and mix a little."

Zachary's eyes followed her as she got up and headed back to the bedroom. "I guess... I should change and shave."

She stopped in front of him and laid her hand over one whiskery cheek. "If you have the energy. If not, there's no dress code. You can go looking like a mountain man, I don't think anyone will object."

He put his hand over hers for a few seconds, his fingers warm and his touch light. "I'm not sure this rises to the level of mountain man, but it could use a trim."

"Okay. I'll see you in a few minutes."

Kenzie changed into a blouse and slacks. She didn't want to be overdressed. She would see how everyone else was dressed before going to dinner in a dress. She applied fresh red lipstick and touched up her makeup in front of the mirror in the bedroom. She could hear Zachary's razor buzzing in the bathroom.

They met back in the living room. Zachary had managed a trim, and she supposed he had probably run a comb through his close-cropped dark hair, though it was impossible to tell. Which was exactly why he kept it that short. Kenzie touched her own spiraling dark curls. Her hair looked pretty good for having slept on it half the afternoon. Zachary hadn't changed his clothes. Shaving had probably used up most of his available energy.

"Looks good," Kenzie approved. "Let's go meet the other campers."

They walked up to the main house together, Kenzie's hand through Zachary's arm. The sky was dark and the stars out, shining brightly overhead.

"Wow. It's beautiful," Kenzie breathed.

Zachary raised his head and looked up at the stars. "You never see them like that in the city. I've seen photographs, but this is... amazing."

"How do you take pictures of stars? Do you need special equipment? Because you're taking pictures in the dark?"

Zachary went into a detailed explanation of what he would need to do to capture the brilliance of the stars, what equipment he would use and what camera settings. Kenzie didn't pay much attention to the details, just listened to his voice, relaxed and passionate about his hobby. By the time he was done, they were to the door of the farmhouse.

A young woman was walking up at the same time, and Zachary opened and held the door for her and Kenzie. The other woman barely acknowledged his existence. She was blond and, Kenzie had to admit, absolutely gorgeous. She probably had all kinds of men running to open the door for her with regularity. Zachary's eyes lingered on her as she walked away from him. Kenzie wondered whether he was thinking of Bridget, also blond and beautiful.

But he didn't watch her for long. He took Kenzie's hand again and walked with her into the main living room area where the guests were gathering for drinks.

It was an intimate group, not too noisy and overwhelming. It was a relaxed, peaceful atmosphere rather than a party with music blasting. The blonde went directly to the drinks at the side table and she poured herself a glass of wine before looking around at the other vacationers.

"Do you want something?" Zachary asked.

"A glass of wine would be nice."

He let go of her and went to the sideboard to pour her one. She watched him pour a glass of ginger ale for himself.

He returned with her wine.

"Thank you." Kenzie looked around, smiling at the others. One man smiled back and approached them, reaching out his hand to shake with them. He had round apple cheeks that made him look very young despite his beard, which Kenzie thought was an obvious attempt to look mature.

His grip was firm. "Redd Flagg."

Kenzie blinked and looked at Zachary to see whether he had heard the same thing as she had. He looked just as bemused as she felt.

"What?" Kenzie asked.

"My name. I'm Redd Flagg. That's two D's, two G's."

"Oh, well that's unique. I'm Kenzie, and this is Zachary." Using their first names only would help to preserve their anonymity.

"Nice to meet you! It's a pen name, actually. I'm a thriller writer."

Kenzie nodded and smiled pleasantly. It sounded like a good name for a thriller author, but was not one that she recognized. "Would I have read anything that you've written?"

"Not unless you're a time traveler. Right now I'm... in the drafting stage."

"I see. Just starting out."

"I decided to go on my own little writer's retreat. Just me and my computer, in a room, until I get my manuscript written."

"Wow, sounds intense."

"How is it coming along?" Zachary asked politely.

"Well... not as much progress as I would hope. But I'm getting words down on the page. That's the main thing."

"You can't do much without them," Kenzie agreed. She looked around the room. "So is this everyone?"

"Uh," Redd looked around. "Yeah, most of us. Do you recognize her?" He nodded toward the blonde who had entered the house with them.

"No. Should I?"

He nodded vigorously. "Brittany. Brittany 'the Bombshell' Blake. You've heard of her, right?"

Kenzie recognized the name of the celebrity, but didn't know what she was actually famous for. An actress, probably, but backwoods Vermont was a strange place to find a famous actress. If she were a Hollywood starlet, shouldn't she be living on the west coast and holidaying in a spa? "I know the name," she said, "but I have to confess... I don't keep up with a lot of pop culture."

"She's a really big thing. Has her own website and this following that call themselves The Bambas."

Kenzie wasn't much more enlightened. But she supposed she could go search the Bombshell up on the internet any time she pleased.

"Interesting. What's she doing here?"

"Getting away from the paparazzi is my guess. Trying to stay under cover. We'll see how long that lasts. All it takes is one person posting where she is, and we'll be surrounded by The Bambas."

"Well, I hope that doesn't happen."

"Don't we all," Redd agreed, but his tone and expression suggested otherwise. Kenzie guessed that nothing would thrill him more than to be able to be caught in the middle of a media frenzy.

"Who are the lovebirds?" Zachary asked, looking at a young

couple cuddling and occasionally smooching on the couch, in danger of spilling their drinks during their amorous activities.

"The newlyweds," Redd advised, rolling his eyes. "Mr. and Mrs. Andy Collins. And no, I don't know her first name at all. She's just Mrs. Andy Collins, she is so smitten with him."

Kenzie chuckled and felt about a hundred years old. She had dated a lot of guys before Zachary, but had she ever been so cow-eyed and dumbstruck over any of them? Not even secret crushes. She'd been out to have her fun, but didn't think she'd ever been quite that silly.

"We have another bachelor," Redd continued, indicating a dark-haired man with a smile Kenzie instinctively distrusted.

Seeing that they were looking at him, the man approached them. He raised his eyebrows and didn't offer to shake hands. "Jack Fowler. And you are our newest arrivals."

"Kenzie and Zachary," Redd introduced them. "Just filling them in on everyone's details."

"So you've already met our writer in residence," Jack said sardonically, managing to make it sound like a writer was the most ridiculous career ever. "Be careful or he'll write you into his story."

"It's a *thriller*," Redd pointed out. "Lots of military and spy types. Not..."

Kenzie suppressed a smile. If he only knew some of the cases that they had been involved in! Redd was just the sort of person they wanted to keep from knowing their actual jobs.

"I'm a forensic accountant for the IRS," Kenzie said, making it sound as boring as possible. "And Zachary is..." she trailed off.

"Between jobs," he contributed.

Redd shrugged at Jack and rolled his eyes as if Kenzie and Zach couldn't see him. "You see?"

"You think spies would actually tell you that they are spies?" Jack challenged. "You think you would be able to tell just by looking at them? Kenzie and Zachary are exactly the type of ordinary, boring people that a spy would be masquerading as."

R edd looked speculatively at Kenzie and Zachary and shook his head. "I don't think so," he dismissed.

Kenzie waited until Redd looked away, then smiled at Zachary, enjoying their shared secret and how wrong Redd was.

Stuart Dewey, the gray-haired owner, entered the room and called for everyone's attention. "Dinner is served. If everyone could adjourn to the dining room, we will partake."

Everyone started to move toward the dining room, some faster and some slower. Zachary was looking back at something behind him when Kenzie caught sight of the set table, and her heart dropped to her stomach. She moved quickly to Dewey's side.

"We need to get the candles off of the table," she told him urgently. Her mind spun as she looked for an explanation. "You realize they're against fire codes, don't you? Like you said, it's been dry as tinder this year. One accident and everything could go up in smoke."

He looked at her. "I've been running this facility since you were learning your ABC's. I think I know the rules."

"Can we please get them out of here? They're not safe."

"They're perfectly safe. We've had them on the table for decades of dinners."

"Please." Kenzie put her hand on his arm. "You saw earlier... Zachary has a fear of fire. Can you please dispense with them while we're here?"

He rolled his watery blue eyes, raising his brows. "Your boyfriend is afraid of candles."

"His house burned down in a fire started by candles when he was ten. Please, have some compassion."

"Seems like he's had long enough to get over it."

"Some things you never get over. It's still really traumatic for him. Can we please?" Kenzie looked back at Zachary. He had seen the candles as well by now, and was standing back in the living room, face pale and sweaty. He was doing pretty well to be able to hold it together, when a bad flashback could send him crashing to the floor, curled up with his arms over his face. The same position he had assumed as a boy, trying to keep the smoke and flames away from his eyes and to make a pocket of breathable air.

Dewey relented. "Fine," he said gruffly. "We'll take the candles off the table."

Kenzie helped to blow them out and remove them from the table. She tried to do it unobtrusively, but her actions were out of the ordinary, so people were watching and wondering what was going on.

"Just need to get these out of the way," Kenzie said lightly, not trying to explain to the rest of the observers, though some of them had undoubtedly heard Kenzie's words to Dewey and were looking back at Zachary speculatively.

When they were all cleared away, Kenzie went back to where Zachary stood. "All clear. Can you do this? Or do you want to go back to the cabin?"

He swallowed, Adam's apple straining. "I'll be fine," he assured her. They walked together back over to the dining room table and found seats. There was another woman Kenzie hadn't noticed before. She had apparently joined them while Kenzie was taking care of the candles.

She was a slim black woman with an afro. She had the effect of studied calm, moving slowly and deliberately and watching everyone around her carefully. She seemed serene, but at the same time, watchful. Kenzie ended up sitting down next to her.

"Hi. We haven't met. I'm Kenzie and this is Zachary."

"Raven." The woman nodded at Kenzie and looked past her to Zachary. "Everything okay?"

"Fine," Zachary said tersely. "Thanks for asking."

"You... had an accident? Your house burned down?"

"We really don't like to talk about it," Kenzie said, raising her voice so that everyone would hear. "Okay? It's not something that's easy to talk about."

Raven paid no attention to Kenzie's protest. "Did you get burned?" she asked curiously.

Zachary was already breathing heavily. Had he brought any of his anxiety pills with him? Kenzie figured they were going to end up going back to the cabin before dinner was even underway.

But he pushed up his sleeve in response, showing off one of the worst scars from the fire. Despite the skin grafts, it was still a deep, ugly scar. Everyone stared at it, some openly and some covertly, pretending that they had no idea what was going on across the table from them. Zachary gave Raven a good look, then pushed his sleeve back down again.

"Kenzie's right," he said in a flat, unemotional tone, "I don't like to talk about it."

Raven nodded and turned her attention to her plate and to a fork that apparently needed polishing. They all waited, but no one else posed any questions about the fire.

Dewey extended a welcome to the newest guests, who had already become the center of attention, and Kenzie and Zachary quietly accepted the good wishes of the other guests.

"We will have one more guest arriving tomorrow," Dewey informed them. "Or at least, I assume he will get here tomorrow. Then that's it for the rest of the week. This will be our group."

Kenzie looked around at the others. It was a nice sized group. Most of them seemed friendly enough. She wasn't sure how big the staff for the lodge was, but she was pretty sure that Dewey was not doing everything himself. Not if they were having "Thanksgiving" dinner every Thursday. There had to at least be a Mrs. Dewey or a cook.

As she considered this, two women came in, bussing the dishes to the table. An older, white-haired woman who might very well be Dewey's wife. And a slender, Slavic-looking blond of around twenty-five who gave everyone big smiles as she helped with the table.

It was a roast beef and potatoes dinner, with several sides of vegetables available. A nice hearty meal for people who had been hiking, horseback riding, or doing whatever other activities the Lodge offered. Kenzie was careful not to take too much. She could always have a snack later in the evening if she wanted to, but if she stuffed herself, she would be uncomfortable all night. And she knew she needed to watch her portions to keep her figure, especially when she spent most of her workday sitting at a desk.

Zachary's servings were scanter than hers, but even so, she doubted he would eat everything he had taken.

"Is that all you're going to have?" Jack questioned, staring at Zachary's plate as if fascinated. "That wouldn't feed a bird. It's no wonder you look like you do."

Everyone else was shocked into silence. But they looked at Zachary to see what his answer would be.

"I just finished a round of chemo," Zachary said, "In case that means anything to you."

"Oh." Jack rubbed his upper lip, thinking about it. "Okay then. I guess that makes sense."

It was the truth; Zachary had been on chemo drugs as well as antivirals. They hadn't known for sure what would get rid of the virus, but from what they knew of its deadly effects, they knew they had to throw everything on it that they could without killing the patients in the process. There was no room for error. So Kenzie and Zachary had both been on the chemo protocol.

Kenzie took a couple of bites of the roast beef and gravy,

making appreciative noises. "And who is the cook? This is wonderful."

"That would be Mrs. Hubbard," Dewey said, making a gesture to the older woman. "She has been cooking here for quite a number of years now. She does a very satisfactory job."

The compliment fell a little short. Kenzie nodded politely and repeated her praise. If that was the kind of gratitude that Mrs. Hubbard got from Dewey after quite a number of years, it was a wonder she had stayed.

"My late wife hired her," Dewey muttered, mostly to himself, "She was always good with the staff."

"Your late wife?" Brittany the Bombshell chimed in. "That means that she died? That's so sad. How long ago?"

Everyone's eyes turned back to Dewey.

"Couple of years now," Dewey said, looking down at his feet. "An eternity."

9

They learned a little more about each of the guests and
what kind of behavior to expect from them over the
next hour, and then Kenzie begged off, noting that
Zachary was nearly falling asleep in his plate and had long since
reached his limit as far as food went.

"There's a bonfire later," Jack offered. "Maybe we'll see you
there."

Kenzie stared at him. "I don't think so," she said pointedly.

He laughed. "Oh yeah. Forgot about your *problem*," he said
to Zachary.

Zachary paid no mind. They walked down to their cabin arm
in arm. Kenzie didn't make any comment about the stars this
time. The weather had cooled and there was a bite in the air.
Kenzie cuddled closer to Zachary. They kept their heads down
against the wind and hurried to the cabin.

"Whew!" Kenzie removed her coat and hung it on a peg next
to the door. "I'm not sure anyone will want to be out there
tonight, bonfire or not."

"Maybe they won't light one." Zachary removed his jacket as
well. He rubbed his arms briskly. "Nice inside. I'm happy to just
stay in."

"Me too. That was a bit of an ordeal... sorry about the candles and everything."

"Sorry?" his tone was surprised. "For what? You took care of it."

"Well... yeah. But I'm sorry they were there in the first place. Maybe I should have asked about candles when I was booking the holiday. I never even thought about it."

"Why would you? Most places use those little lights now. Live candles are dangerous." He choked up a bit over the word. "People reaching across them, around them, they could..."

He was sweating again. Kenzie rubbed his back and ushered him over to the couch.

"Everything is fine. Disaster averted. And he won't put them out the rest of the week, so you don't need to worry about it. How are you feeling, do you need another nap?"

"I slept most of the afternoon. I shouldn't sleep more now. I'll just stay awake... until I can't anymore, I guess."

"You don't have to push yourself. Whenever you want to sleep is fine."

Zachary shook his head. "No... you remember how bad my sleep got messed up before. I have to be careful, I don't want to end up sleeping during the day and laying awake nights."

"I don't think you need to worry about that. Your body is still trying to heal, and you need to sleep when it tells you to."

"I'm going to stay up for a while." His voice was determined.

"Okay. Great. Shall we put on a movie? Or did you want to test out the hot tub...?"

Zachary considered this offer. "Do we... have time for both?"

"I don't see why not. We don't have to be anywhere in the morning. Which do you want to do first?"

***

Kenzie supposed that Zachary would have ended up asleep on the couch while they watched the movie no matter which order they picked. The hot tub was great for soothing muscle aches from the drive and holding herself tense during the dinner. And for a little couples time together, just enjoying each other's company without any expectations.

Zachary had been dealing with intimacy problems ever since his kidnapping a year before and, while they had been going to couples therapy regularly and working on communication, they were not yet back to where they had been before the kidnapping. But Zachary had made a lot of progress, dissociating far less and enjoying intimate moments more.

One day, they would be back to where they had been. Kenzie was glad to be past the days when she couldn't even touch him without his flinching or pulling away.

She watched him sleep on the couch beside her, head tilted all the way back in what looked like an uncomfortable position, snoring slightly. She wasn't sure what movie they ended up watching or what it was about. She just enjoyed sitting there with him, watching him sleep.

Kenzie awoke to a thumping noise and was disoriented at first, thinking that someone was knocking on the door. Or maybe the window. She turned her head and tried to pry her eyes open.

"Who is it?" she asked Zachary. "Can you get that?"

He moved beside her, sliding his feet out of the bed and walking over to the window. He looked out, shading his eyes against the bright morning light. They had slept late.

"It's a helicopter. What would a helicopter be doing out here?"

"Really?" Kenzie squinted at him. "Are you sure I'm not just dreaming?"

"Looks pretty real to me."

"Mmm." Kenzie rolled over, turning her back to the window and the intrusive sunshine. "Come back to bed."

Zachary stood at the window for another minute. "No, I think

I'm going to get up now. You go ahead and sleep as much as you need to."

"If I still need more sleep, then you need more sleep."

Zachary didn't argue. He just walked quietly out of the room, leaving her to sleep alone. Kenzie tried to get back into the comfortable, drowsy space that she had been in, but it was no use. Now that she'd been awakened, she couldn't get back to sleep. She got up and wandered out to the living room, where Zachary had pulled out his computer and was staring at the screen.

"You'd better not be working," she warned.

"Just checking email."

"Work email?"

"Uh... no."

Clearly, he was. "Do you want to hit the hot tub again this morning?"

Zachary grimaced. "My stomach is pretty rocky this morning. I think I'd better not. I might get seasick."

"Seasick? Really?"

He shrugged. "I can't help it. The water sloshing around..." He looked a little green just thinking about it.

"Okay, okay." Kenzie held up her hands. "No morning hot tub for you, then. As for me, I am going to have a soak for a few minutes. Then we can have breakfast."

He was studying her face intently. "Do you mind? Is it okay?"

"My morning would not be enhanced by you throwing up on me in the hot tub. So no. I would rather you refrained."

He let out his breath in a little laugh. "Okay, good."

"Did I just dream the part about the helicopter, or was there really one there before we woke up?"

"Yeah, there was. Some guy in a pinstripe suit and dark glasses. Like he's the president traveling incognito or something."

"Maybe it is."

"No. Not the president. But somebody... wealthy. Someone who thinks he's important and wants to make a statement."

"Why would someone like that stay here? It isn't exactly an

expensive resort. I mean, I paid enough for it, but it's not a millionaires' retreat."

"Maybe he wants to meet up with someone else. Brittany Blake, maybe."

Kenzie nodded. "Yeah, that would make sense, I guess. Do you know anything about her? Brittany Blake? I know the name, but I really don't know anything about her."

Zachary moved his hands up and down like a scale. Maybe he knew something, maybe he didn't. "She's one of those famous YouTubers. But I don't really know what she does that is so special. I don't think she actually *does* anything."

Kenzie shook her head. "I guess if you look like her, you don't need to."

"I'd rather be with someone like you. Real. *And* beautiful," he said quickly, in case she took his words the wrong way. He gazed at her. "And real."

Kenzie gave Zachary a kiss, even though she hadn't yet brushed her teeth. "You're sweet. Thanks."

She went off to have her solitary soak in the hot tub.

After what was not exactly a short soak in the hot tub, Kenzie dressed and made herself presentable. She looked at the time on her phone and joined Zachary again in the living room.

"Do you want to eat here or up at the house? The continental breakfast should still be on."

"I'll stay here, I think. But if you want to go up to the house…"

"I can eat here with you."

"They might have something good. Fresh fruit and pastries. Stuff that you don't usually get."

"There's a reason I don't get fresh pastries…"

"But this is a holiday. Calories you eat on holidays don't count, do they?"

Kenzie laughed. "No. Okay, if I'm going to go up to the house you have to tell me something to grab for you. Just humor me and pretend that you're going to eat something other than a chocolate chip granola bar."

Zachary shook his head. "Okay… a muffin."

"I'll get you a muffin. What kind do you like?"

"Anything. It doesn't really matter."

"Pick something."

He gave her a mischievous smile. "A chocolate chip muffin."

"Perfect. If they have chocolate chip muffins, I'll bring you one back. That's my mission."

Kenzie gave him a kiss before heading up the hill to the farmhouse again.

There were not as many people around for breakfast as there had been for dinner. Or maybe it was just because they came at different times, spread out more. As Kenzie browsed over the offerings, she could hear raised voices in the back of the house. A woman's voice that might have been Mrs. Hubbard's, and a man's voice that she didn't recognize. Certainly not Stuart Dewey's voice. Someone much younger.

Kenzie raised her eyebrows at Raven, who was sitting at the table eating a muffin and looking at something on her phone. Raven looked back at her phone without reacting. Kenzie picked out some fresh fruit and a small danish for herself. And there were muffins, including a chocolate chip one, for Zachary. Kenzie put it in a napkin and sat down at the table.

"How is everyone this morning?" she asked pleasantly.

Raven glanced at her again, and again didn't have any answer. Redd Flagg, the author, was sitting down at the other end of the table. "As well as can be expected, considering how we were all wakened up early this morning," he grumbled.

"How you were wakened up?"

"By that darn helicopter. You didn't hear it?"

"Oh, yes, I did. I just figured I slept in later than the rest of you. Later than I would normally sleep."

"It's vacation. No one wants to wake up at nine o'clock. Why do you think they serve breakfast until eleven?"

"So did you get an early start on your book this morning?" Kenzie asked. She didn't hear her answer, distracted by a man who came striding from the back of the house to the front, looking as if he were ready to shoot someone.

"I guess I shouldn't expect good service in a backwoods little rat hole like this," he snapped, to no one in particular. "I suppose Mama's home cooking means that Mama cooks whatever she pleases, and there's no way to get what you want."

Kenzie glanced toward the kitchen, then back to the man, who was obviously the "millionaire" that Zachary had seen getting off of the helicopter.

"I don't think we've been introduced," she told him frostily. If he was going to act like they were friends, or in all of this together, then he could at least have the courtesy to drop his name first.

He stopped short and looked at Kenzie in astonishment. "I am Vance Stiller," he said, so haughty it was clear that she should have known him on sight. Or she should at least know who Vance Stiller was on hearing his name. But she didn't. She had no idea.

"Nice to meet you," she drawled. Though, of course, it was anything but nice. If that was the way Vance Stiller treated the people around him, then she was glad that Mrs. Hubbard had turned down whatever outrageous requests he'd made. "I take it you're the last guest for this week."

"I wouldn't know anything about that. I just arrived this morning and I don't have the lay of the land yet. And you are?"

"Kenzie."

Kenzie didn't dare give her full name in case he happened to know her or one of her parents. Their names were fairly well-known in Vermont. Though she didn't know if Stiller was a Vermonter or just vacationing there.

Raven looked at Stiller and decided that he wasn't asking her for any of her details, so she went back to whatever she was reading on her phone.

"So that was your helicopter this morning," Redd piped up. "It was a little noisy first thing in the morning, don't you think?"

"I wasn't aware that there were any rules about noise way out here in the boonies. I certainly wasn't going to waste my time driving in." He tapped his wrist. "Time is money, you know."

"Oh, time is money," Redd repeated mockingly. "I'm so glad that you told us. So why would you come vacation somewhere like this, if you don't like it and don't like to waste your time? Wouldn't you be better off in New York? Wall Street? Why would you want to be here?"

Stiller waved this comment away as if he were wiping something off of a whiteboard. "I can work anywhere. Even here. My computer and internet access, and I can make money wherever I am."

He waited for one of them to ask what it was he did. No one obliged him. Stiller looked over the various foods available for breakfast and shook his head with disgust. "I don't know what you call this, but it's not breakfast where I came from. The brochure said that there was a professional cook on staff. This stuff isn't even cooked in-house. It's obviously store-bought."

"Mrs. Hubbard is a great cook," Redd objected. "You should have tasted the dinner last night. Or any night. All of the dinners I've had here have been fantastic. But maybe they wouldn't meet your standards."

"Probably not," Stiller agreed.

The door opened, and the newlyweds arrived. So intertwined that they had to go through the door together, bumping into the frame and laughing giddily at each other. Kenzie rolled her eyes. But she kept in mind that she didn't want to seem just as dismissive and supercilious as Stiller, so she gave them a warm smile, even if she did look past them rather than into their moonstruck expressions.

"Good morning."

"Good morning," they chorused together.

And then, "Isn't it a beautiful day?" asked Mrs. Andy Collins.

"A little brisk," Stiller pointed out.

"You should have felt it last night." Redd gave a mock shiver. "That wind coming down the mountain... brrr."

"We stayed warm," Mrs. Andy Collins declared, looking into the adoring face of her husband.

"I'm sure you did," Raven muttered, just loud enough for Kenzie to hear. Kenzie gave her a small smile.

Kenzie was not enjoying the barbs and attitudes being thrown around, so she made short work of her pastry and fruit, and picked up the napkin-wrapped muffin to take back down to Zachary.

"Hey, how is Zachary?" Redd asked. "Was he okay after last night? Seemed like he isn't in the best shape."

"He was pretty tired last night, but good this morning. He has good days and bad days, and last night with the candles and every-thing..." She shrugged. "It was difficult, but he's tough. He'll be okay."

"He was really in a fire when he was a kid? That was a pretty nasty scar."

"Yes. And not his only scar. It's understandable that he doesn't like fires, even candles. *Especially* candles."

"So don't expect the two of you down at the bonfire."

"No."

K enzie presented Zachary with his chocolate chip muffin at the cabin. He looked at it, surprised. "I didn't think you'd actually find one."

"Well, there you are. Do you think you can eat it?"

The muffin wasn't one of those greasy jumbo muffins that sold at some of the coffee shops, but a small, denser product more suited to breakfast than dessert. Zachary smelled it, and then broke off a small piece to nibble on.

"Not on the couch. You'll get crumbs everywhere, and I'm sure Dewey will not be happy if we attract mice."

Zachary sighed and got up. But he was pretty good about using plates and not eating over his computer. He'd been sitting long enough, it was probably time for him to get up and move around anyway. He found a plate in one of the kitchen cupboards and sat down at the table.

"It's good," he assured Kenzie. "But I'm not sure how much I can eat."

"Well, give it a try. It would be nice if there was more than one thing that you could tolerate for breakfast. A little variety is nice."

"How were things up there? Everyone happy and well-rested this morning?"

"If I didn't know better, I would suspect that you could hear the yelling down here. No, actually, things were pretty tense."

Zachary nodded as if unsurprised by this news. "Some strong personalities in that group. I figured this new guy would probably stir things up a bit."

"Well, stir he did. He and Mrs. Hubbard were arguing about something. I guess he thinks he should be able to order whatever he wants, not eat whatever she makes."

"He should probably have picked a different resort if he wants that kind of treatment." Zachary grinned.

"If you're right about him being here to see Brittany Blake, then he might not have had much choice in the matter."

Zachary hadn't been up to taking a walk in the woods or doing any of the other activities that were available, so they had stayed in the cabin. Kenzie had been keeping an eye on her phone, so she had expected the car that drove up to the cabin midway through the afternoon. Zachary, on the other hand, private investigator though he was, had apparently not figured out what she had planned.

"Looks like we have company," Kenzie told him as the car drove up and parked behind Zachary's car.

Zachary turned his head to gaze out the window. "Who is that?" He stood up and looked more closely. "That looks like...?"

Kenzie was grinning away, but he wasn't looking at her.

"It's Tyrrell!" he said, stunned, and hurried to the cabin door to let his younger brother in. "T! What are you doing here?"

His mouth dropped open when he saw the two children getting out of the car. "Are these your kids?"

Tyrrell nodded, smiling fit to burst. He gave Zachary a tight hug. "I've got them for a few days. They've got professional development days or something. When Kenzie asked if I could come up while you were here..."

Zachary turned and looked at Kenzie, it finally dawning on him that she had to have set this all up.

"You did this?"

"Sure. I didn't know at the time he'd have the kids. That was an extra bonus."

Tyrrell motioned for the kids to join him at the door. They hung back a little, looking nervous about meeting a new person.

"This is Zachary, my big brother. I told you about him. Come say hi."

As they got closer, Tyrrell put his arm around the girl, the older of the two, and brought her forward, cuddling her against him reassuringly. "This is Alisha."

Alisha looked about ten years old. She had dark hair like her father and uncle and pretty hazel eyes and delicate features that probably came from her mother. Tyrrell's blue eyes shone in pride as he showed her off to Zachary. He looked back over his shoulder at the younger child. "Come on, Mason. Come meet your Uncle Zachary."

The boy came reluctantly forward. Tyrrell positioned the boy in front of him, putting his other hand on Mason's shoulder. "And this is my son, Mason."

"Nice to meet both of you," Zachary said breathlessly.

Mason's eyes were dark and darted back and forth, examining Zachary, the interior of the cabin, and Kenzie. He twisted away from his father and stepped into the cabin.

"Wipe your feet," Tyrrell told him, trying but failing to hold him back.

Mason stomped on the doormat and continued into the cabin. He looked at Kenzie. "Who are you?"

Kenzie guessed he was probably eight or so. She smiled at him. "I'm... your Uncle Zachary's girlfriend. My name is Kenzie."

"Kenzie? I've never heard that name before."

"You've heard me talk about her," Tyrrell reminded.

"No," Mason said with certainty, shaking his head.

"Come in," Zachary encouraged, motioning for his brother and niece to come in out of the doorway. His eyes shone in a way they hadn't in weeks. Not since sometime before Halloween.

Tyrrell and Alisha settled onto the couch, Alisha still cuddling close to her father and looking nervous of the strangers. Mason wandered around the room, looking at and touching everything.

"Come sit down," Tyrrell told him, but didn't do anything when Mason ignored him.

"It's so great to see you," Zachary told Tyrrell. "It's been too long."

"Yeah, well it's pretty hard to visit you when you're in quarantine. How are you doing? You're feeling better?"

"I'm good. Just tired, mostly. They said I'll recover quickly."

"And that's because of this virus? It must have been pretty bad."

"It's because of the treatment. I never had any symptoms. But my viral load was pretty high."

"And they couldn't just wait and see if you actually got sick?"

Zachary shook his head and looked at Kenzie for her explanation.

"There isn't a lot that we know about this virus," Kenzie said, "but we know that it is fatal within a few days of getting symptoms. They couldn't wait to see whether he developed symptoms; that might have been too late."

Tyrrell shook his head. "No, couldn't chance that."

"Is this a zombie virus?" Mason demanded, turning to Zachary and fixing him with an intent stare. "There's a virus that turns you into a zombie, you know."

"That's pretend, Mason," Tyrrell told him. "That's just in games and on TV. There isn't really a zombie virus."

"There is," Mason insisted. "Bobby told me so. It's real."

"There is no such thing as zombies. Bobby is just having fun with you. Trying to scare you."

"I'm not scared of zombies."

"You should be," Alisha told him. "It would be really scary to see a real live zombie. Or to be one."

"I'd like to be one," Mason blustered. "Because they can kill people, but it's really hard to kill them. So you would be safe. You could do whatever you wanted to."

"You wouldn't want anything," Alisha told him. "Zombies don't have brains, stupid."

"They do too!" Mason insisted, his voice rising in pitch. "Daddy, tell Alisha—"

"Zombies are not real," Tyrrell told him again, rolling his eyes and shaking his head at Zachary.

"But if they were real. They would have brains, right? People can't walk without brains."

"They're not real. Now that's enough, okay? Zachary didn't have a zombie virus. He had a virus that makes you sick. But they gave him medicine, and now he's okay."

"So he didn't turn into a zombie," Mason agreed.

"No," Tyrrell sighed. "He didn't."

Mason looked at Zachary again. "You *look* like a zombie."

Kenzie cracked up. "I don't know if I can disagree with that," she laughed. "You are looking pretty rough still. But he's getting better, Mason. He'll get better and start to look less like a zombie." She chuckled, enjoying Tyrrell's look of discomfort over his son's comments. Zachary didn't seem to be offended by the comment that he looked like the walking dead. He'd seen himself in the mirror.

H ow long can you stay?" Zachary asked, looking at the time on his phone. "There are some activities the kids might be interested in. A hayride or a hike? Or we could find something else that's more interesting for them than just sitting around listening to the grownups talk."

Tyrrell looked at Kenzie and raised his brows. "Actually, I'm told that you have a spare bedroom we could use for a day or two."

Zachary's mouth dropped open again. He turned and looked at Kenzie. "Really? You told them they could stay over?"

"I didn't think you would mind."

"No, I don't mind. That's great!" Zachary looked at Tyrrell. "I haven't slept over with family since... it happened."

"Well, I was there at Lorne and Pat's overnight last year," Tyrrell reminded him. "We sat through last Christmas Eve together. Didn't sleep, but I was there overnight."

"That's right. You did." It had been their reunion. The first time Zachary had seen anyone from his family in decades. Zachary was at his lowest point on the worst day of the year, and Tyrrell had been there to save him from being sucked into himself. "Wow. This is great. So, do the kids want to do a hayride?"

Tyrrell looked at the children. "Well?"

Alisha snuggled into Tyrrell. "If Daddy's coming."

Mason darted around the room, making airplane noises. "I could go all by myself. I'm braver than Alisha."

"We could all go," Kenzie said. "If you're up to it?" She looked at Zachary.

"Yeah." He nodded. "That would be really fun, right?"

Kenzie smiled at his question. "Have you ever been on a hayride?"

"No."

She could see how he might never have had the chance to participate in something like that as a child and youth in foster care, and frequently in a supervised facility. It was completely outside his realm of experience.

"Well, why don't we do it? Everyone bundle up, because there's a bite in the air and it will feel a lot colder when you've been sitting outside for a while. Hats and gloves for everyone. Winter coats, not just hoodies."

Alisha and the men didn't complain and went about gathering their gear together. Kenzie noticed Zachary lingering over his electronics bag, eventually pulling out a camera to take with him. Mason didn't object to the idea of a hayride, but he zoomed around the room, making noise and darting here and there, ignoring his father's instructions to get ready.

Eventually, ready to go himself, Tyrrell managed to grab Mason by the arm and to wrestle him into a coat and hat. He couldn't manage to get gloves onto Mason's hands without his cooperation, but stuffed them into the large pockets of his coat so that they would be available when Mason decided he was getting cold.

"Everybody should be gathering at the barn," Kenzie said, checking the time again. "Our timing should be perfect."

"Are there animals in the barn?" Alisha asked.

"I haven't been down there myself, but yes, there would have to be. They need horses to pull the wagon."

"Anything else?"

"I don't know. We'll have to see when we get there."

"Are there any baby animals?"

"Probably not. Animals usually have their babies in the springtime."

Alisha nodded understandingly. Kenzie locked up the cabin and they traipsed down the hill to the big barn, where some of the other guests were standing around, waiting.

A man that Kenzie hadn't seen before was getting the horses ready for the trip. He was big and broad. Husky. With a full beard that he seemed to be scowling behind. It made sense that they would have someone younger and hardier to do the hayrides. Kenzie didn't imagine that Stuart Dewey would want to get behind the wheel. Or rather, the reins.

He ignored the guests while he got everything ready, then straightened up and looked around at them. "Is this everyone?"

Kenzie shrugged, and everyone else's reactions were pretty much the same. They didn't know whether anyone else was planning to come or not.

"I am Harold Burknall," the man introduced himself. "I am the handyman around here and do a lot of the outside maintenance and activities. Everyone needs to follow the rules and do as I say, or you will not be coming to any other activities. Is that understood?"

He looked in particular at Mason, who was jumping around excitedly, looking at the horses and the farm equipment and everything else in the barn.

"Mason will follow the rules," Tyrrell said, trying to grab his son and bring him under control. "Won't you, Mason?"

"Are we going on a horse?" Mason asked, his voice falsetto. "I want to go on a horse."

"We're going to get into the wagon behind the horses," Tyrrell explained to him. "They're going to pull us around. That will be fun, won't it?"

"Can I touch the horses?"

Tyrrell looked at Burknall. "Is it okay?"

"He has to stop jumping around. Horses don't like people making sudden moves. If he wants to touch them, he has to do what I say."

Mason stopped jumping and looked at him.

"Come here." Burknall beckoned to him.

Mason looked back at his father, then advanced toward the big man, taking small, slow steps.

"That's right," Burknall approved. "Just like that. Nice and slow. You don't want to scare them." He put his hand on Mason's shoulder when he was close enough, and guided him toward the horses' heads. He patiently walked Mason through letting the horses smell him and get used to him before allowing Mason to touch them.

Kenzie was surprised. She would have written Burknall off as being crusty and impatient, but he was kind and spoke in a way that made Mason listen to him intently. Eventually, Mason was stroking the heads of the big animals. They nickered at him and sniffed at his pockets, looking for food.

Kenzie heard a series of clicks and turned her head to see Zachary taking pictures. His expression was just as intent as Mason's. Mason looked back to smile at his father. "Look at me, Dad! I'm patting them."

"You're doing a great job," Tyrrell told him. "Really good listening."

"All right." Burknall raised his voice again to address the group. "You can all get into the wagon and get yourselves settled. There's no smoking of any kind. Keep any lighters or matches in your pockets. No yelling or intentionally spooking the horses. All arms and legs stay inside the wagon, and you don't get out without talking to me." He patted Mason's shoulder. "Do you want to sit up front with me?"

"Yes! Can I, Dad?"

Tyrrell hesitated. "Are you sure it's okay? He's not going to be in the way?"

"He'll be better sitting up front with me than in the wagon."

Tyrrell nodded his agreement. "Okay, then. Mace, you need to do what Mr. Burknall tells you to, okay? Just like a teacher at school."

Mason nodded eagerly. "Yes. I will."

"Okay, good. Alisha and I will be in the wagon if you need anything."

There were a few minutes of jockeying and everybody getting into position, finding a seat on the bales of hay and getting comfortable. There were blankets, and Kenzie put one down on a hay bale, and then when she and Zachary were sitting on top of it, wrapped it up around them and snuggled. It was cozy. Zachary's arm tightened around her, and he smiled when she looked into his face.

"This is good?" Kenzie asked.

"It's good," Zachary agreed. He rubbed her back, and looked over at his brother and niece. "It's perfect."

13

Kenzie had been on a couple of hayrides when she was younger. Usually in the early autumn when it was warmer, sunny days with lots of other kids, joking around and doing all the things that Burknall had warned against. The trips were usually short, barely enough time to break out illicit drinks. And maybe that was why. The supervisors knew teenagers just a little too well to give them that much latitude.

By contrast, the hayride at the Lodge was cold and long. She was glad for the blankets and Zachary's shared body warmth. Tyrrell wrapped his blanket around Alisha, comfy in his lap instead of on the poky hay bales, and she peeked out to watch the passing scenery.

After a few minutes out, Mason climbed down from the driver's seat to get his gloves from Tyrrell. When Kenzie looked at him later, back with Burknall, Mason had the reins in his hand and was looking as pleased as punch. The horses probably knew their way through the hayride loop without any guidance, but Mason took his job very seriously. When they all got off the wagon at the end of the ride, Mason appeared to have grown about two inches.

"Daddy, Daddy, did you see me driving?" he demanded. "I

drove the horses! You won't even let me drive the car, but Mr. Burknall let me drive the horses."

"That was pretty cool," Tyrrell said. "You did a really good job."

"I did everything he said."

"I'm going to tell your mom when I talk to her. She'll be very proud of you too."

Mason looked disappointed by this. "I want to tell her!"

"Okay. You tell her all about it, and then I'll tell her later, after you, what a great job you did driving and listening. Okay?"

Mason nodded seriously.

It took them all some time to get out of the barn. Mason wanted to help let the horses out of the traces and to help care for them and feed them. Eventually, Tyrrell managed to talk him into returning to the cabin, only on promise that Mason could return to see them and Mr. Burknall the next day.

All the way back to the cabin, Mason told them the minutiae of everything he had seen and done during the wagon ride.

"Need a nap?" Kenzie asked Zachary when they got back indoors and were rubbing their hands and arms, trying to warm up again more quickly.

"Well..." He was looking tired and worn, but clearly didn't want to miss out on any time with his brother and the children.

"It's okay to take a break. They'll be here all night and for the next few days."

"Yeah. I should take a few minutes."

"Okay. Off you go then, and we'll try to keep the noise down to a dull roar."

"Maybe I should just stay up..."

Kenzie shooed him with her hands. "Go, go! You need to get your sleep. You'll crash and make yourself sick. We're here for recovery, not to make you worse."

At her insistence, he finally nodded and went back to their bedroom, after extracting a promise from Kenzie that she would wake him up after he'd had a decent amount of time for a nap.

She was not to let him sleep the whole evening away; he still wanted time with his family.

Hopefully, he would be able to sleep with other people in the cabin.

"Maybe we should put on a movie for the kids," Kenzie suggested to Tyrrell. "That will probably help keep things quiet until the others get here."

With the kids entertained, Kenzie pulled out her phone and started running through her task lists and plans, filling Tyrrell in on any details he did not know. Together, they would do what they could to ensure that the evening ran smoothly.

Kenzie turned on the outside light and peered out the window for any sign of their additional guests. There was a set of headlights just coming down the road as she watched. It was too dark out to recognize the vehicle until it was right in front of the cabin. Lorne and Pat pulled in beside Zachary's car. Kenzie opened the door to wave to them and waited there while they pulled bags and boxes out of the car to bring inside with them.

She leaned in to give Lorne a kiss on the cheek in greeting as he hobbled to the door on his cast. "Zachary is sleeping, but he'll want to be up soon. Don't worry about any noise."

"Good to see you, Kenzie." He paused beside her. "How are you feeling?"

"I'm doing pretty well. Nearly back to normal. Zachary's going to take longer, but now that he's done his protocol, it's just a matter of making sure he gets enough sleep and calories."

"We'll see what magic we can work there," Pat said, leaning close so that Kenzie could give him a kiss as well. He indicated the box he was carrying with a nod. "This will get him back on his feet."

It took several trips back and forth to the car before they had brought in everything they needed, then Pat set to work on their final preparations. Kenzie and Tyrrell helped with whatever they could, while Lorne sat down with his leg elevated and watched the movie with the children.

It wasn't long before Kenzie's sharp ears picked up the sound of the bedroom door opening. She turned around and watched Zachary walk into the living room, rubbing his eyes.

"You didn't let me sleep too late, did you?" he asked.

Then he did a double-take when he saw Lorne sitting there with the kids.

"Mr. Peterson? What are you doing here?"

It was cute how he still called his old foster father by his last name. Lorne always told him to use his first name, and Zachary tried, but when he wasn't consciously trying to call him Lorne, he always slipped back into the old habit.

"We came for dinner," Lorne said, as if that should have been obvious.

"Dinner?" Zachary looked into the kitchen area and saw Kenzie and Tyrrell working with Pat. "We're having dinner here?"

"We don't need to go up to the farmhouse every night," Kenzie pointed out. "There's a stove here. We can cook whatever we need to."

"And we're... and everyone is..." Zachary's eyes glinted with tears, and he laughed. "I can't even talk!"

"We thought we'd have an early Thanksgiving dinner," Pat told him. "Kenzie told us all about the planned vacation, and it sort of... all came together. We need a break too. Kenzie booked a three-bedroom, so there's room for all of us for one night."

"One night?"

"We're not going to stay the whole week. Just thought we'd drop in on you for a day or two. We were listening to the forecast on the way up, and it isn't good. Probably best if we hit the trail by late tomorrow, if we don't want to get caught in a storm."

Zachary's gaze shifted to Tyrrell. Tyrrell anticipated the question and raised his hand in a "halt" gesture. "We're still planning on staying a few days," he promised. "If we end up getting snowed in and have to spend an extra day or two here, it won't hurt our feelings. Will it, kids?"

They were watching the movie and not paying him any attention.

"You don't mind if you miss a few days of school, do you?" Tyrrell directed at them.

It was Mason who looked up first. "Miss school?" He grinned. "Mommy would kill you."

Everyone laughed.

"I don't think she would literally kill me," Tyrrell protested. "If we were snowed in and *couldn't* get back. That's not our fault."

Alisha shook her head. "Mommy won't be happy."

"Well, we'll see what happens. Just because there is a storm coming in, that doesn't mean the highway will be impassable. It could blow in, dump some snow, and then be gone again. I've just watched too many movies about getting snowed in at mountain resorts."

"When are we eating?" Mason asked with a hint of a whine. "I'm getting really hungry."

"We'll eat when it's ready. You be patient and polite."

"It won't be long," Pat promised. "Everything is precooked, I'm just warming up here. I didn't think we wanted to spend hours cooking the bird once we got here."

"It smells good," Zachary declared, sniffing the air. "Is it turkey?"

"It sure is. Turkey, my famous cornbread stuffing, glazed yams..."

"Mashed potatoes?"

"Mashed potatoes," Pat confirmed, smiling.

"You know what a good cook Pat is," Zachary said to Kenzie, "but until you've had his turkey dinner..."

Kenzie wondered how many turkey dinners Zachary had partaken of with his old foster father and his partner. And how many he had missed because he had been too sick or in the hospital when the special day rolled around.

"I can't wait. It smells fabulous."

"I'm a vegetarian," Alisha piped up.

Tyrrell looked across the room at her, raising his eyebrows. "That's news to me,"

"I am. Mom said she told you."

Tyrrell's brow wrinkled as he considered this. "Well, maybe she forgot to mention that."

"There will be plenty to eat other than turkey," Pat assured Alisha. "Do you still drink milk?"

Alisha nodded. "Mom said I have to. And I don't like that soy stuff."

"Well then, you can have everything except the turkey and gravy. And I didn't even cook the stuffing in the bird, so that's safe for you. Sound good?"

Alisha gave him a broad smile.

"Good," Pat repeated.

Tyrrell looked at Alisha. "So when did this happen? And why? You've never mentioned being interested in vegetarianism before."

Alisha shrugged. "I don't want to eat animals." She shot a look at Mason, who was making faces. "Would you want to eat those horses you were making friends with and driving today? In some countries, they would eat them. You wouldn't like that, would you?"

"People don't eat horses."

"Sometimes! And what about all the other animals? Chickens and pigs are really smart. Smarter than a dog!"

Mason rolled his eyes and shook his head at his sister's ridiculousness. Tyrrell didn't reprimand him.

"Well, that's fine," Tyrrell told Alisha, "but next time can you tell me? In case Mom forgets?"

"She was supposed to tell you."

"I know. I get that. But you can tell me too."

She looked down at her hands for a few seconds, then nodded. "Okay."

"You don't have to be afraid to tell me. I'm not going to get mad."

There was a heavy silence among the three of them. Kenzie turned back to the salad she was making, feeling like she was intruding on the little family. There were clearly a lot of things not being said between them. Alisha didn't immediately jump in and say that she knew her dad wouldn't get mad at her. The silence suggested otherwise. Tyrrell had mentioned, the previous Christmas, that he was a recovering alcoholic. Kenzie had thought at the time that he had probably been an alcoholic in his late teens or early twenties, and then had woken up to what he was doing to himself and sobered up. But maybe it had been much more recent than that. Recent enough that the kids could remember and were still worried that he might go into a rage over something like finding out that his daughter was a vegetarian.

"Do you need any help?" Zachary asked Pat, breaking the silence.

"I think we have as many cooks as this kitchen can handle," Pat said. "Why don't you get washed up? We'll have food on the table in a few minutes."

14
____

Unlike the dinner the previous night, there was no need to worry about things like candles. Pat knew Zachary's triggers as well as anyone, and would never have put candles out when he knew Zachary was around, much less light them.

The movie ended and Tyrrell turned off the TV to the children's moans and complaints.

"You don't have time to watch anything else. We're eating soon."

"We can eat and watch TV at the same time," Mason contributed helpfully.

"Not today, you can't. We're all eating together at the table today. Mr. Peterson and Mr. Parker have made this wonderful meal for us, and we're going to enjoy it all sitting together visiting."

"I had very little to do with it," Lorne objected. "It's all Pat."

"Well, Mr. Parker, then. I want you guys to be on your best behavior for dinner, okay? Remember your manners? No goofing off."

They gave their grudging agreements. Zachary had finished taking his dinnertime meds and washing up, so the children were sent to make themselves presentable, and by the time they were finished squabbling over the sink and had returned to the table, Pat was just setting out the finishing touches.

As they started to pass the dishes around Mason picked up his table knife and started jousting with Alisha, waving it back and forth to clink against her raised fork and jabbing it toward her.

"Mason!" Tyrrell shouted.

Mason jumped and dropped the knife with a clatter.

"What did I tell you about good manners?"

Tears welled up in Mason's eyes and started to race down his cheeks. "I was just playing!"

"No. No playing at the table. You know better than that. Does your mother let you sword fight at the table?"

Mason sniffled and shook his head. "No."

"Then you're not allowed to do it here either. Just behave yourself!"

"I'm trying!"

"Try harder," Tyrrell insisted.

Mason stared down at his plate, silent tears still flowing down his cheeks. Tyrrell spooned some of the various dishes onto Mason's plate as they went around, since Mason was making no move to serve himself.

Kenzie felt sorry for the little guy. As far as she could guess, without making any kind of clinical examination or doing any testing for hidden disabilities, he was at the upper end of the hyperactivity scale. He was clearly bright and observant, but also impulsive and constantly on the move. Even as he sat there, trying to be well-behaved for his father, he was swinging his legs back and forth and twisting his hands together in his lap. Trying harder wasn't going to help him to overcome ADHD or whatever other disabilities he might have. Medication might help settle him down a little but, as Zachary had observed in the past, there wasn't anything that worked reliably for impulse control.

Everyone was quiet for a few minutes while they dished up. Tyrrell's neck was flushed red with embarrassment over either his son's behavior or his own reaction to it. As they began to eat, they all made an effort at conversation, and gradually things returned to normal.

"This is just fantastic," Kenzie told Pat. "You've really outdone yourself. When we started to plan, I thought that maybe we could have sandwiches together. Nothing like this!"

"It's what I do," Pat said with a modest shrug. "I love to cook for people."

"And people love it when you cook for them," Kenzie declared. Everything was delectable, and she regretted that unlike Zachary, she didn't need the extra calories. She tried to eat slowly and savor every bite.

15

Zachary sat down with Lorne after supper to look at some photography he had brought with him, which inevitably led to the discussion of cameras and camera settings that could go on all night.

Getting the children to bed was not an easy affair, especially as far as Mason was concerned. Alisha was cooperative, though she got out of bed and made too many special requests and delays, but Mason was a little fireball who seemed to get more hyper the more tired he got, and Tyrrell looked exhausted by the time he finally managed to get both kids down to sleep.

"You wouldn't believe how much energy that kid has," he sighed. "I wish I had half as much as he does. Actually, I wish he had half as much too. We have a bedtime routine when they're visiting me, but being somewhere else, somewhere unfamiliar with such exciting things going on, everything just falls apart."

"Routine is everything at this age," Lorne agreed. "With a lot of the kids that we had, it wasn't worth it to do anything during the evening if it took away from the usual rituals. Change one thing, and you end up with kids who can't settle until they are literally falling asleep on their feet." He put his foot up, scratching around the top of the cast and grimacing. "With some of them, they were so hypervigilant that if you changed one thing, they would go right off the rails."

He looked over at Zachary. Zachary scratched the back of his neck. "I'm sure you're not talking about me," he said uncomfortably.

Everyone laughed. Zachary had a strong relationship with his foster father as an adult. As a child, he'd only been in their foster home for a few weeks. Zachary's own hyperactivity and other issues had been too much for them to handle. Too much for most families to handle.

"Even with night meds, you were always a tough one to get down for the night."

"I remember. I couldn't shut my brain off. Couldn't stop worrying about things. About what was going to happen. About... a fire or something happening to one of the other kids. About school and getting left back because I couldn't understand the work. Or having to go back to Bonnie Brown or go to juvie. My brain would just never settle down."

Zachary didn't usually talk about his anxieties or problems sleeping. Even in therapy, it was hard to get him to be open about what was going on inside his head. Maybe talking about his childhood gave her a little window into what it was like in there. She could picture his brain as a racing engine. Racing, racing, racing, and never slowing or stopping.

"Have you considered meds for Mason?" Lorne asked Tyrrell.

"His mom is talking to the school. They want to put him on something to make it easier on the teachers. I think we're both a little worried that it will change him. He's such a bright, inquisitive kid. I don't want them to squash that curiosity, that little spark. I remember what it was like, some of the stuff they put me on when I was his age. It didn't make me feel better. It did help my focus a bit. But I always felt like... I was swimming through wet cement."

"They've got some better options now," Zachary offered. "But even if it works without side effects, it's hard feeling like... you're defective and need to be medicated to even look like... neurotypicals."

Tyrrell nodded. "I'm just glad I grew out of that."

When they all got up in the morning, the storm was all over the news on Kenzie's phone apps. Weather warnings had been issued and they knew they could be looking at a big dump of snow. Though Lorne and Pat had been planning to stay most of the day and only head home in the evening, satellite maps showed the storm moving in much more quickly than expected, maps that were verified by the strong wind that swept in through the door whenever they opened it.

Pat had packaged up all of the leftovers of the turkey dinner and left them in the fridge for Zachary and Kenzie to use in the upcoming week if they didn't feel like going up to the farmhouse for dinner. It was nice to have something so good on hand. Better than the prepackaged stuff that Kenzie had brought with her. Pat packed up the rest of his dishes and ingredients to take back with them.

They all exchanged regretful goodbyes at the door, but they didn't hang around with the door open to watch Pat and Lorne leave. Zachary watched through the window and waved as they pulled out.

"Should we go up to the house for some breakfast?" Kenzie suggested. "You know now that they have muffins, and you were able to eat one of them yesterday. We can put in an appearance, see how the rest of the vacationers are doing."

"I think I'll stay down here. You go ahead, if you want to." His expression was frozen and his tone flat. Definitely feeling the absence of their guests.

"I think it would be good for you to come. You don't want to just mope around here feeling bad for yourself."

"Tyrrell and the kids are here. I'm not by myself."

"I know. I just think... it might help to get out of yourself a bit. See the other cabins."

Zachary sighed heavily. "Is it that important to you?"

Kenzie nodded. "Yes. Come on up with me."

Dr. Boyle had suggested that if they knew something was important to the other person, they should act on it, even if it wasn't something that they felt like doing themselves. Couples did things for one another. Made concessions. Joined them in their activities even when they didn't share all of the other's interests. It would help bring them closer together.

"Okay." Zachary said simply. He looked at Tyrrell. "Do you guys want to come up?"

"If you don't mind, I think we'll keep a low profile. I don't know how, uh... how many fragile, expensive items they might have around the place..."

Zachary looked at Mason, eating cheese strings and apple slices in front of the TV, and nodded. Maybe remembering all of the things he had broken when he was Mason's age.

He began to put on his coat and other winter gear without further objection.

16

It was a chilly walk up to the farmhouse, but the wind had died down, so it wasn't too brutal. Kenzie supposed they could have driven the car up, but Tyrrell was parked behind Zachary's car, and the exercise was good for them.

They didn't have much conversation on the way up. Kenzie sensed that Zachary was disappointed in Lorne and Pat leaving so early and was brooding over it. Having them come to share dinner with them had been a good idea. It had really helped to cheer Zachary up. But it would have been better if they had been able to stay longer.

Zachary quickened his pace slightly to reach the door of the house before Kenzie, and he opened it for her, standing back to give her room to enter. Kenzie smiled at him and went in. They shucked off the winter coats and gear and hung them up on the hooks provided. It looked like most of the other guests were there ahead of them. Kenzie couldn't help noticing the luxurious suede jacket hung next to hers. Brittany Blake's, she supposed.

They proceeded to the dining room. Zachary nodded briefly at the others already gathered there and went to the muffin dish, looking them over and picking out another of the chocolate chip muffins for his breakfast. Kenzie grabbed herself a plate and was choosing from the various offerings that had been laid out. Similar, but not identical to what had been there the day before.

"Where is Mr. Dewey?" an aggrieved voice demanded. "This really is not acceptable. I spoke to the cook yesterday and let her know my requirements."

Vance Stiller, of course. Still thinking that he could order whatever he wanted rather than choosing from what was on offer.

"I haven't seen him this morning," Redd Flagg offered. "You could ask someone on the staff."

"He's the host, why isn't he here? He should be making sure that everything goes smoothly."

"He usually does. Must be something else going on this morning. Maybe something is going on down at the barn that needed his attention. A place like this has to be maintained."

"He should have a man to take care of that. What about the one who drove for the hayride yesterday? Didn't he say that he was the handyman? He's the one that should be looking after any of the outdoor stuff. People like this just don't know how to prioritize and delegate."

"You're pretty vocal when you don't even know what's holding him up," Jack observed. "Why don't you give the guy a break? Those of us who have been here longer than you know that he's very conscientious."

"I can only judge by what I see, and he's clearly not here."

There were some more murmurs of disapproval. Kenzie couldn't tell for sure whether they were in support of Vance, disapproving of the service, or whether they objected to his casting aspersions on their host.

Kenzie was inclined to agree with Vance just a little. Their host didn't seem to be quite as pleasant and diligent as she would have expected from a place like the Lodge, which made its living off of customer service. But the man was tired, running a resort when he should have been retired. The loss of his wife had been fairly recent, and he probably didn't find it easy to run the Lodge without her. When they had run it together for decades, it would be difficult for him to pick up all of her responsibilities on top of his own.

Kenzie made her choices as to her breakfast plate and sat down at the table with Zachary and his muffin.

"What do you think?" she murmured. "You think Mr. Dewey is off dealing with other Lodge business?"

Zachary shrugged, picking at the muffin. "Could be things that have to be done before the storm blows in. He might have been here earlier. It looks like everything has been taken care of. No reason he has to stay here the whole time breakfast is available. Didn't you say it's out until eleven? He's not going to spend all morning hovering over the guests." He put a chocolate chip in his mouth. "Not with the storm coming."

Kenzie nodded her agreement. All good points.

The young woman who had helped to serve dinner, Samantha, checked on the coffee carafe and made sure that nothing else needed to be refreshed. She tried unsuccessfully to avoid Vance Stiller. He put himself in front of her and wouldn't let her pass.

"So where is Dewey? Did you talk to him? Tell him I want to see him?"

Samantha tried to get around Dewey gracefully. "I haven't seen him this morning."

"Well, what about the rest of the staff? What about the cook?"

"No, Mrs. Hubbard says that she hasn't seen him either. I'm sorry. I'm sure he'll be back... sometime. You can tell him then if you have complaints. In the meantime..." She motioned to the sideboard laden with food. "There is coffee if you want it."

"Where is he?"

"I don't know."

"Don't you have any way of reaching him? A cell phone? Walkie-talkie? You're telling me that he just takes off, and you have no way of letting him know if there is an emergency?"

"He's not answering his phone. Coverage can be spotty up here sometimes. With the storm coming in, the cloud cover might be blocking the signal."

"So you have no way of reaching him. What if there were a medical emergency?"

"The staff have first aid training. We could call the county for help. But... this is not an emergency." She raised an eyebrow at him.

"I demand to see him."

"Vance," Brittany Blake, who was prodding a few berries with her spoon, sounded as if she'd had enough. "You're being a pain. Get a coffee and sit down."

He looked at her, color rising to his face. Apparently, he was not accustomed to being spoken to like that. He was used to deference, even when he was being unreasonable. Brittany held his gaze, waiting. Eventually, Vance stalked over to the coffee carafe and put a mug under the spout.

"It's probably not even fresh," he complained. He sniffed the air as the coffee dribbled into his cup. "They don't grind their own beans, I'll tell you that. Cheap grocery store ground coffee."

"Sit down and drink it," Brittany told him.

Vance obeyed. Everyone was watching him, and he definitely did not appreciate being spoken to that way in front of the whole room. He sipped the coffee, grimaced dramatically, and set it down in front of him.

"I thought you were here to relax," Brittany said. "So why are you so uptight?"

"This isn't exactly relaxing."

"If you're going to act like a pain, then no. If you focus on enjoying the atmosphere and what they have to offer, you could let your hair down and not be so tense."

He grunted and had another sip of coffee. Maybe he just needed his caffeine fix for the day.

"You can talk to Mr. Dewey at supper or some other time today when he's not busy with other stuff. But you treat him like you would treat another business owner instead of your servant."

"I don't treat people that way."

She raised an eyebrow at him and didn't comment.

Suddenly, there was a siren-like wail that raised the hair on the back of Kenzie's neck. She and Zachary were instantly on their feet. Everybody else seemed to be frozen where they were.

"Upstairs," Zachary said.

The two of them were halfway up the stairs before anyone else in the dining room could say anything.

Kenzie and Zachary rushed to the top of the stairs just as everyone in the dining room started to talk, asking each other questions and looking up as if they might be able to see through the walls. The cries were coming from one of the bedrooms. Kenzie made it through the doorway just ahead of Zachary.

Mrs. Hubbard stood over the bed, her hands over her mouth, crying out again.

"It's Stuart. He's... I thought he was out at the barn... but then, Mr. Burknall said he wasn't, and I came up here to make sure that he wasn't sick, and..."

They could see that there was no immediate danger. No one was being attacked. Kenzie moved forward, shifting immediately into her professional persona. "Stay back, please, and let me have a look."

Mrs. Hubbard took a couple of steps back to make room for her, and Kenzie approached the bed and pulled back the blanket. Mr. Stuart Dewey was pale and stiff, clearly dead for some hours. Kenzie went through the motions anyway, checking for a pulse, pulling back an eyelid, testing for how advanced rigor was. She could hear the others approaching, coming up the stairs to see what was going on.

"Zachary, keep them out of here. Shut the door. Mrs. Hubbard, is there a doctor who comes out here? Maybe an ambulance or medical examiner?"

"I don't know!" Mrs. Hubbard wiped at her eyes. "Nothing like this has ever happened before."

"Do you have 9-1-1 service?"

"No. Not up here. You have to call the police department directly. I... I don't have the number. Maybe Mr. Dewey does."

Kenzie took a glance around the room. She didn't see a personal address book or a cell phone. "Does he have an office where he keeps a phone book or a Rolodex?"

Dewey was old school. He wouldn't have it on a computer or electronic device.

"There is... his wife's writing desk. Down the hall."

"Go check there."

Kenzie looked around for any other relevant details in the room, noting Mr. Dewey's position, the glass of water on the nightstand, a couple of pill bottles. There was no sign that anything had been disturbed. The body looked natural, with no blood or sign of violence. Pictures, personal effects, some that were probably his wife's.

Zachary finished dealing with the other guests and returned to the bedroom. "That Vance Stiller is a pain in the neck," he observed, shaking his head. "Thinks the rules don't apply to him. He can demand or buy whatever he wants. He doesn't understand the meaning of the word no." He got closer to the bed, but not close enough to make Kenzie anxious that he might disturb the scene. "How does he look?"

Kenzie shrugged. "Can't tell much from just looking at him. Looks natural. Heart attack, maybe."

"No one stabbed him in his sleep?"

"No." Kenzie lifted the blanket to visualize his back, but still couldn't see signs of anything untoward. "Nothing suspicious about the scene. He was an old man. Not happy with life. Missing his wife. Sometimes people are just ready."

Zachary nodded.

"Can you find me a phone number for the police or county medical examiner?" Kenzie asked.

Zachary pulled out his phone and started tapping. "I wonder about a next of kin. If there is some family member that we need to call. Someone will have to make decisions about the Lodge and what to do with it."

Kenzie nodded. She had been wondering what impact this would have on everyone's holidays. Was the Lodge set up to just keep running, even though the guiding hand had passed away? Or would they all have to pack up and go home? She didn't want to have to drive through what the weather bureau was saying would be the storm of the century.

Zachary found a phone number and read it out to her. Kenzie pulled out her own phone and tapped it in.

The answer came quickly. "County Police Services. Darleen Star, Officer of the Day."

"Officer Star, my name is Dr. Kenzie Kirsch. I'm staying at the Dewey Lodge, and there has been a death. I wasn't sure who to notify to take care of things."

"A death? What kind of death? Was there an accident?"

"It looks like a natural death. He didn't wake up in the morning. Maybe a heart attack."

"All the way up at the Lodge," Star murmured to someone in the background. "Doctor, what is your area of expertise? Are you a medical doctor?"

"Yes. I'm a pathologist; I assist in the Medical Examiner's Office in Roxboro."

"Well, aren't we lucky," Star laughed. "Sounds like you're the right person to have on hand. You have verified death?"

"Yes... he's definitely dead."

"We're going to have trouble getting anyone up to you in the next little while. We are overstretched right now battening down the hatches for the storm. It's going to be a doozy, if you haven't been watching the news."

"Yeah. We're aware of it."

"We will get someone up to you as soon as possible to take care of arrangements. In the meantime... if you could do what you can to secure the scene?"

Kenzie looked around to see how she was going to manage that. She couldn't exactly stand guard on it until the authorities arrived. Who knew when that would be? Probably not in the next few hours. Mrs. Hubbard returned, shaking her head at her failed mission to find a phone number for Kenzie.

"Mrs. Hubbard, does that door lock?"

"Well... yes; of course it does."

"Who has keys to it?"

"Mr. Dewey. The maid, Samantha. I really don't know if there are any other copies."

"Okay. We need to lock up until the police can send someone up here. It might be a while. Go get Samantha's key. Do you know where Mr. Dewey keeps his?"

"His keys should all be on the ring in his pocket." Mrs. Hubbard looked around and nodded to the clothes discarded on the floor. "Probably in his pants."

Kenzie bent down and picked the pants up. They were weighty and jingled, so she inserted two fingers and pulled out a key ring with a large number of keys on it. "I guess it's on here somewhere. Along with keys to every other lock on the property."

Mrs. Hubbard nodded solemnly.

"Okay. Get Samantha's. Please."

Kenzie waited until Mrs. Hubbard left again. She looked at Zachary. "If they can't get up before the storm rolls in, and it doesn't sound like they will, then it might be a few days before everything has cleared up enough for them to get here."

"Are you worried about decomposition?"

"I don't normally have to worry about it. We have refrigerated drawers. I haven't ever had to preserve a body without them."

"You could open the window."

Kenzie looked at the window and considered. It was the obvious solution. It would definitely be cold enough. Probably too cold, since she didn't actually want to freeze the body. But she would take freezing over the evidence breaking down before the authorities could reach them. And no one wanted the whole house smelling like decomp.

"Uh, yeah, I guess that will have to do." Kenzie sighed, at loose ends. "I don't have my liver probe with me, so I can't take a reading to determine approximate time of death."

"You didn't bring your liver probe on vacation?" Zachary teased.

"What was I thinking when I packed?"

"I could see if they have a thermometer we can use. Maybe one in the kitchen like you use for turkeys?"

"I think they might be a bit freaked out if I poke it into Mr. Dewey, and it won't be calibrated properly. It's meant for much higher temperatures. I guess... I'll need to make a determination based on rigor mortis and external temperature. Can you see if someone has one of those digital ear or forehead thermometers? And I'll need the current room temperature as accurately as possible. I'll write down all of my observations and the County Medical Examiner can make a determination based on that."

"I'm sure that will be fine. It isn't like we're trying to figure out who had an opportunity to murder him. He died sometime between going to sleep last night and when he would normally rise this morning. The staff should be able to give you the outside parameters."

Kenzie nodded. Zachary departed to find a thermometer. Kenzie pulled out her phone, tapped the notepad app, and started making observations. Rigor appeared to be complete, so Dewey had probably been dead for a minimum of three to six hours. Kenzie took a number of pictures of Mr. Dewey and the scene. Mrs. Hubbard gasped in shock when she returned.

"What are you doing?" she demanded, aghast.

It took Kenzie a minute to realize what Mrs. Hubbard was so upset about. Most people didn't go around taking pictures of dead bodies. Mrs. Hubbard probably thought she was ghoulish or maybe that she would post them to social media for everyone to see.

"No, no, it's okay." she assured the cook. "I'm just trying to get a record of everything for the authorities. They'll take their own pictures when they get here, but we don't know how long that will be, and I want a record in case anything changes between now and then."

She was careful not to mention that she wasn't sure how much Mr. Dewey might decompose before then. That might just do Mrs. Hubbard in.

Mrs. Hubbard sniffed. "I don't know about all of this," she said, shaking her head. "Mr. Dewey wouldn't like it. Guests in his room taking pictures. Acting like they own the place."

"I don't mean to upset you, Mrs. Hubbard. I'm just trying to make sure that everything is done the right way. You wouldn't want the police accusing us of wrongdoing, would you?"

"No! Heavens, no. I wouldn't have anything to do with such... behavior."

"Of course not," Kenzie agreed. "So this is for your protection. I can show them that nothing has been touched or moved. You won't have to defend yourself against accusations that someone was in here and... moved the body or went through Mr. Dewey's possessions. If anything of value were to disappear, you would want me to be able to show them that it didn't happen on our watch, wouldn't you?" She said it in a confidential tone.

Mrs. Hubbard drew a little closer, nodding. But then her eyes dropped to Mr. Dewey's corpse, and she looked away again, trying to keep control of her emotions. She dabbed at the corner of her eye with a handkerchief. "I just... don't understand it. Poor Mr. Dewey. I didn't even know he was sick."

Kenzie leaned closer to read the labels on the pill bottles on the nightstand. "It looks like he had high blood pressure and depression."

"Yes," Mrs. Hubbard wept some more, pressing the handkerchief to her eyes. "Yes, but he was in good health. He never expected to go now..."

"Well, he's with Mrs. Dewey now, isn't he?" Kenzie comforted. Not that she believed in heaven or loved ones awaiting the newly departed. But it gave comfort to many people.

"Yes," Mrs. Hubbard agreed, with more sniffling. She looked at the picture on his dresser, a much younger Stuart Dewey with a woman of about his age. And a son, a dark-haired older teen or young adult standing between them. Possibly a son. "He loved her very much. He hasn't been the same since she passed."

"Yeah. It's a mercy that he didn't have to suffer through a protracted illness and now he can be with his wife."

Mrs. Hubbard nodded. Zachary returned. He hovered just inside the door frame, looking at Mrs. Hubbard. "Did you find that key, ma'am?"

"Yes, of course I did," the older woman snapped. "I'm not incompetent. There's no need to 'ma'am' me."

"Uh..." Zachary looked startled at her response. "I was only trying to be polite."

"I don't need your kind of polite. Looking down your nose at me."

"No. Nothing like that," he protested. "You've been very professional while we've been here. Trying to get through this..." Zachary motioned toward Mr. Dewey's body. "I can't imagine what it must be like for you. You have been with the family for a long time."

Mrs. Hubbard's shoulders relaxed. She nodded. "Yes... they've been my family for the last ten years. Longer than that, I mean, but since I've been on my own, all of my own family dead and gone." Her eyes misted again. "We were both alone, Mr. Dewey and I." She dug into her pocket and produced the key. She handed it to Kenzie, giving Zachary a look that told him she didn't trust him with it.

"Thank you so much," Kenzie said. "We'll just finish up in here, and then we'll lock it. No one else will be able to disturb things in here until the authorities arrive."

18

Mrs. Hubbard left them again. Zachary stepped forward and handed Kenzie the ear thermometer he had found.

Another man might have disparaged Mrs. Hubbard after she left, calling her an old bat for the way she had reacted to his polite inquiry. But Zachary wasn't that kind of guy. He shook his head. "Poor woman."

"Yes. And depending on what the arrangements are for the Lodge, she might be out of work now. I'd hate to be looking for a new job at her age."

"Yeah. Maybe she already has enough to retire on. She might just have stayed on with the family because of her attachment to them."

"I doubt it. Working class women like her... She probably lives paycheck to paycheck. She has room and board, so her expenses probably are not too much, but even things like medication can be expensive at her age without some kind of plan."

Kenzie took a temperature reading of Mr. Dewey's body and recorded it.

"Thermostat downstairs is set at 72 degrees," Zachary advised. "This room is a few degrees cooler."

Kenzie tried taking the room temperature with the ear thermometer, but it gave an error. Not what it was designed to do. Kenzie added the information they had to the notes.

"Do you need to do anything else?" Zachary asked.

If she were in the morgue, Kenzie would have at least performed a gross examination of the body, checking for needle marks, bruises, or any other signs. But she couldn't see Mrs. Hubbard allowing them to strip Mr. Dewey down, even if they did tell her Kenzie's actual profession. And more than ever, Kenzie wanted to keep that a secret. If she let on now that she was a pathologist, there would be no end to the questions and speculation. It would be like being a performing monkey.

"I suppose that's it," she sighed. She went to the window and released the catch. She was glad to note that there were screens in the windows, so they wouldn't allow the snow in, unless the wind were blowing directly against that side of the house. On sliding the windows open, they were immediately assaulted by the chilly air.

Zachary walked out of the room ahead of Kenzie and waited. Kenzie pulled the door shut behind her and locked it with the key. She continued to stand there, looking at the door.

"What else?" Zachary asked.

"I'm just thinking of police tape."

"We don't have any. And I'm not sure it would do any good. Everyone knows that this is where the body is, and I think they will stay away."

"Maybe. But I would still like to have a bit more certainty. Where did Mrs. Hubbard say that the writing desk is?"

Zachary pointed down the hall.

"Would you see if there is some masking tape and a pen?"

Zachary didn't demand an explanation, he just went ahead and tracked down the items she needed. Kenzie tore strips off the roll and taped them flat along the door jamb and the door, sliding her fingers over them to press them down firmly. She scribbled her initials over each one.

"I don't think it would be easy for someone to get all of those off without breaking any of them."

"Looks good," Zachary confirmed.

"I suppose now we need to go explain to everyone else... and to tell them why they should listen to us when we're just a lowly accountant and..."

"Unemployed bum," Zachary provided.

"I'm sure you're not a bum. You're recovering from cancer. You're just temporarily out of work."

Zachary grinned.

Everyone immediately wanted to know all the details of what had happened. Kenzie did her best to be vague and yet impart to them that no one could or would be allowed to go into Mr. Dewey's bedroom until the authorities had cleared it.

"This is outrageous," Vance Stiller objected. "I've never seen such a shoddily-run inn before—"

"I'm sure Mr. Dewey didn't plan to die," Kenzie told him, her voice heavy with sarcasm. "I suppose you already have your death date picked out?"

"I'm certainly not going to die like that—" Stiller gestured toward the room.

"In your sleep? No, I don't imagine so. Someone will shoot you or stab you in the back."

Jack laughed, making no effort to cover up his enjoyment of Kenzie's response like the rest of them were trying to do. Everyone seemed to be at the farmhouse now, having heard about what was going on and wanting to get more details, maybe even get to see the dead body themselves.

"Not that any of that matters right now," Kenzie said. "The main thing is the police said we were to lock up the room and stay out of there. No one is allowed to go in. I think everyone is here, so you all understand, right? I don't think there's even any reason for anyone to go up the stairs. It was only the Deweys' living quarters up there? No common areas?" Kenzie looked at Mrs. Hubbard, Samantha, and Burknall.

"No common areas," Samantha repeated. "But there are supplies up there. I need to get my cleaning things, and it's my responsibility to keep it all clean, up there and down here."

"Well, you don't need to do Mr. Dewey's room," Mrs. Hubbard told Samantha. "That is out of bounds."

"It's probably best if you don't do any of the upstairs," Kenzie said. "Just leave everything as it is, in case the police want to look at any of the other rooms too. Mrs. Hubbard can go with you while you gather your cleaning things, and you can keep them in the kitchen or somewhere else on the main floor."

Mrs. Hubbard nodded her agreement to this.

"And no one else needs to go up there," Kenzie repeated. "We all need to do what the police said."

"How do we know that you even talked to the police?" Vance asked, making a face at Kenzie. He did not like to be told what to do by a woman, that was clear. It was one thing when Brittany, who Kenzie assumed was his girlfriend, told him what to do. It was quite another to have to listen to some random guest who thought she had the right to be giving him instructions.

"If you want to, you can look up the phone number and call yourself," Kenzie said crisply. She assumed that Vance would not. Hoped that he wouldn't, because she didn't want Officer Star to give away Kenzie's actual profession. "Then you can confirm that I called and they told me to secure the scene for them. They are overworked right now because of the storm, but if you want to bother them with your questions about whether you *really* have to stay out of the dead man's room..."

Vance shifted. "I'm not saying I would break into his room. I'm just saying I think it is a bit much to tell us that the entire upstairs is off limits to use, just because you want to act like a big shot and boss everyone around."

"There is not anything for you in the upstairs anyway," Mrs. Hubbard insisted.

"How do I know that? What if I need something that is up there? What if the main floor bathroom is occupied and I need to use the facilities upstairs? There are dozens of reasons I might need to go up the stairs."

"No, there are not," Mrs. Hubbard insisted. "No guests ever go up there. Only Mr. Dewey."

"And the maid," Vance reminded her, looking at Samantha.

"And she will only go up to get her equipment, and then she will stay downstairs. You do not need the cleaning equipment. *You* are not going to clean anything, are you?"

Mrs. Hubbard darted at glance over at Kenzie, proud of herself for standing up to the rich man or checking to see if Kenzie approved of her response. Kenzie nodded and smiled.

Kenzie's stomach rumbled. She put her hand over it and looked around. She had forgotten all about breakfast, but her body clearly had not. She needed to eat, and then they could go back down to their cabin where she didn't have to deal with know-it-alls and the tension that permeated the house with the news of Dewey's death.

"I need breakfast. I suggest that we all eat so that Mrs. Hubbard can get things cleaned up. Do you have everything you need for the next few days, Mrs. Hubbard? I mean... with the storm coming in, we might not be able to get out for a supply run for a few days."

"We always have plenty in storage here. I can make do."

Several heads turned back toward Kenzie. They had been relaxing and getting ready to go their separate directions, but Kenzie's words had stopped them.

"What do you mean, we won't be able to get out?" Raven asked.

"Haven't you been watching the news?" Brittany demanded. "There's a big storm coming in."

19

S o?" Raven didn't seem to be able to comprehend this. "So there's going to be a big storm. Why wouldn't we be able to get out of here? There are roads all the way here, we can just drive out any time we want."

"No!" Brittany laughed. "Haven't you ever, like, been out of the city before? If we get snowed in here, the cars won't be able to get to the highway. And if they do get to the highway, it isn't going to be plowed for a few days. We are isolated here. That's why everyone chose the Lodge, isn't it? Because you wanted to be by yourself, away from all the stress of civilization? Well, here you are. If we get a huge dump of snow like they're predicting, it might be a week before we are able to get out."

Guests looked back and forth at one another. Redd Flagg shrugged. "Well, it's a good thing I don't have anywhere I'm supposed to be. I guess anyone who does had better get in their car and get away now while they still can."

Kenzie wanted to protest that everyone should stay there until the investigation into Mr. Dewey's death was complete, but of course that was silly. Police said that on TV, not in real life. Everyone could leave if they wanted to. And if they did want to, it was best to get on their way as soon as they could, otherwise they would get stranded.

Jack looked at his watch. "When is it supposed to hit? I only need to throw my crap into a bag, and then I'm out of here."

"It's supposed to be here within a couple of hours," Kenzie said, checking the time on her phone. "I would hit the road as soon as you can. It might already be too late. If you get into the teeth of the storm and it's too bad, turn around and come back here. There isn't anywhere else to get help anywhere close by."

Jack swore under his breath and agreed.

The newlyweds spoke to each other in whispers, and Kenzie thought that they were also going to see if they could beat the storm. So much for the honeymoon.

Kenzie sat down at the table with her breakfast. She was glad she didn't have to rush to get away from the Lodge. She didn't want to pack in a hurry or throw everything into the car and try to get down the mountain at a breakneck pace in order to beat the storm. It was much better to sit back and wait it out. They had everything they needed. She nodded toward Zachary's muffin, barely touched.

"Are you going to eat?"

Zachary sat next to her, perched on the edge of his seat, looking as if he were ready to jump to his feet at any moment. Though he had acted calm and focused during the moment of crisis, he was now too wound up and hypervigilant to relax. He didn't even touch the muffin, looking from one guest to the other as they sat down to eat or left in their various directions. Mrs. Hubbard returned to her kitchen and Samantha followed her. Burknall grabbed a couple of danishes and went outside, headed back to the barn or wherever he lived on the grounds. He probably had a small cabin of his own, either with the guest cottages or somewhere else on the property.

It was difficult to eat slowly and enjoy herself with Zachary looking like a jack-in-the-box ready to pop, but Kenzie tried not to let him rush her. When she was finished and picked up her plate to put in the tub Mrs. Hubbard had left for the dirty dishes, Zachary sighed audibly. Kenzie didn't say anything to him about it as they moved to the clothing hung by the door and got their winter gear back on. Then they were out the door and into a very cold wind.

"Sheesh!" Kenzie wrapped her arms around herself. "It wasn't like this when we came up. I should have driven."

"Then you would have to warm the car up."

"But at least it would be out of the wind. Have you ever felt it so cold?"

He was hunched against the wind and she wasn't sure whether he shrugged at her question or just ignored it. They both hustled down the hill much more quickly than they had climbed up it. It was practically a race to the door, and they both burst into the cabin at the same time, laughing a little in breathless relief.

It wasn't until then that Kenzie even remembered about Tyrrell and the kids being there. All thought of them had been driven out of her mind when she had run up the stairs at Mrs. Hubbard's shrieks.

"Oh, Tyrrell!"

From the look on Zachary's face, he too had forgotten about his brother being there.

Tyrrell looked at the two of them, bemused. "What? Did you run all the way here?"

"Pretty much," Kenzie agreed. "It is *cold* out there!"

"As cold as a witch's behind," Zachary said, reminding Kenzie of the fire chief who had been in charge of the rescue from the wreck Zachary and Kenzie were in on New Year's Eve a couple of years earlier. Zachary hadn't been able to remember much about the accident that had nearly taken both of their lives, but he remembered the fire chief's colorful expression.

Mason giggled loudly and Alisha covered her mouth, primly shocked and entertained. Tyrrell rolled his eyes. "How many more times do you think I'm going to hear that expression on this trip?"

"Well, maybe a few," Zachary admitted, grinning.

"It must have been a good breakfast up there, you took quite a while. Did you bring anything back with you?"

"Well..." Kenzie sat down near Tyrrell. "No. But we have some news."

"Do you think we should stay here or try to get home?" Tyrrell asked, after hearing about the developments up at the farmhouse.

Kenzie looked at the time, though she didn't need to. She already knew it was too late to leave. It had probably been too late when they had discussed it at the farmhouse. With the wind that had already blown in, she wasn't sure they were going to be able to get anywhere before running into the snow.

"I think we'd better batten down the hatches here. I don't think we have much hope of getting home. I'd rather not be battling the blizzard."

Tyrrell nodded. "Okay, good. And you think... it's safe?"

"Safe? I think it's safer here than out there. We have everything we need here."

"I mean... you don't think that Dewey died of anything that might be contagious, or that someone..." Tyrrell cleared his throat and glanced at the children. "Helped him along?"

"No!" Kenzie laughed. "I think he just passed away in his sleep. Heart failure, probably. Even if he was in relatively good health, it's not unheard of, especially for someone who has recently lost a loved one. When they open him up—"

Tyrrell cleared his throat again. Kenzie was not used to having children around when discussing medical examiner stuff.

"You said that it's been a couple of years since he lost his wife, though," Tyrrell countered.

"Yes, but that's really not long. And he was on medications for depression and high blood pressure."

Tyrrell shrugged and nodded. "Okay. If you're comfortable with that."

"I don't think you have anything to be worried about. This is not a TV murder mystery. Just a natural death."

"I just wondered, with all of the stuff you had to do to determine time of death and preserve the scene. It sounds like you thought it might be something else."

"No. Those are things we do all the time. There may not be any evidence to protect in this case, but if someone else discovered a bo— discovered that someone had passed and our ME's office had to attend, I would want them to do everything they could to preserve the scene just as it was too. It's just best practices."

Tyrrell nodded slowly. "Okay, then. Is there anything that we should be doing to prepare for the storm?"

There wasn't much that they could do to prepare. It wasn't like a hurricane, where they boarded up the windows to prevent them from breaking. The cabins were meant to be used year-round, so they were weathertight and had forced air heating already. There was a fireplace if they needed it, but of course they weren't likely to use it with Zachary's issues. The Lodge had a handyman on site, and he hadn't said that he needed anyone to help with arrangements to be made up at the main house. They had plenty of food on hand. Entertainment by way of the TV and the other devices they all had. They would be able to get through the storm easily enough.

The wind picked up until it was howling around the little

house and, despite Kenzie's assurances that the house was well-sealed and weatherproof, she could still feel the wind through the cracks around some of the windows. They didn't have any way to seal them better, so everyone donned extra clothing. The furnace hummed and the fan blew warm air throughout the cabin. The snow started to come down outside, blown at a sharp angle by the brisk winds, until they couldn't even see the cars in the driveway or the shape of the next cabin over.

The kids stared out the window oohing and ahhing to start with, but quickly grew bored of watching the snow fall and went back to the TV.

Until the power went out.

Alisha gave a little shriek of surprise. Mason went barreling across the room to his father, nearly knocking him over when they collided. Tyrrell didn't scold Mason, but put his arms around him and held him close.

"It's okay, bud. It's just the power. Sometimes a storm like this makes it blink off. You've seen the power go out before."

Mason held on to his father fiercely. "Turn it back on," he insisted. "Go find the box thing and flip the switches."

"I don't think it's the breaker box." Tyrrell shuffled over to the window with Mason glued to him. "You see, there aren't any other lights on. It isn't just our cabin. It's probably everything in the resort and for miles around."

"You said it blinks." Mason blinked his eyes several times. "It's not blinking. It's not going back on."

"I can see that. But you're okay, Mason. Daddy's here. We just need to find something else to do until it comes back on."

"Like what?"

"Like... see if we can find some board games. It would be fun to play some games, wouldn't it?"

"In the dark?" Mason challenged.

"It's not that dark. It's still daytime; it's just a little bit dark because of the storm. We can still see well enough to play a game, can't we?"

"I saw some games," Alisha offered. She went into the bedroom that Lorne and Pat had used overnight, and pulled a stack of boxes from the closet. "Look. There's lots of them."

Kenzie hadn't even thought about the power going out. That was going to throw a wrench into things. The storm would last for a few hours, and then, hopefully, someone from the County would be able to get out and fix whatever lines had gone down. In the meantime, there was no electricity to blow the heated air through the house, to keep the food cold in the refrigerator, to heat the food, or to light the house.

She looked over at Zachary.

He avoided her eyes.

While Tyrrell and the children chose a game and started to set up the pieces, Zachary started to pace. At first, it looked like he was just making sure that everything in the cabin was in order, but after the first couple of circuits around the rooms, it was obvious that he was just moving to try to keep his anxiety under control.

Mason had run straight to his daddy for comfort. Although he was a grown man, part of Zachary was still just a little boy. A little boy who had been trapped, terrified, in a house fire and was now thinking through the same things as Kenzie was. That they would need some alternate source of heat and light by nightfall. The power out wasn't just a blink, as Tyrrell had suggested, but could quite possibly be out for a day or more.

And the thought of having to light a fire in the fireplace or candles to see by was terrifying to him.

Kenzie approached him. She held out her arms and, after a moment of hesitation, he stepped into them, and they held each other tightly.

"Are you okay?"

Zachary cleared his throat. "Sure. I'm fine."

"What does Dr. B. say about sharing your feelings? Is saying you're fine sharing your feelings?"

He swallowed, his Adam's apple prominent in his thin neck. "No. But with the kids..." he said in a hoarse whisper, looking over at them. "I don't want to scare them or make them think there's anything to worry about."

"Okay, that's fair." Kenzie rubbed Zachary's back. His muscles were as hard as rock, knotted up in tension. "Then let's just say not fine. Do you want to call her?"

Zachary looked at Kenzie blankly.

"Do you want to call Dr. Boyle? Tell her about what's going on and see if she has some suggestions that might help."

Zachary considered this, then nodded stiffly. "Yeah." He glanced over at the children. "I'll call from the bedroom."

Kenzie released him from her hold. "Okay. Just shout if you need me."

Tyrrell watched Zachary's departure. "Is he okay?"

"This might end up being pretty rough if the power doesn't come back on. He's going to talk to his therapist."

"He brought his pills with him, right?"

"Yeah. That will help, but I'm hoping that having a meltdown and medicating to the eyeballs are not the only two choices if we have to use that." Kenzie nodded to the fireplace.

It wasn't long before Zachary was back. He didn't look much calmer, and Kenzie didn't think that he'd had enough time for a good chat with the therapist.

"You couldn't get her?"

Zachary held up his phone. "Just for a couple of minutes. Bad connection. And then it cut out." He peered out the window at the flurry of snow blowing almost straight across and the dark clouds overhead blocking out most of the sunlight, even thought it was early afternoon.

"Did you try to get her back?"

Zachary looked at her. Like he might not have tried again? Of course he had tried her again. Knowing Zachary, he'd probably tried again a dozen times.

Kenzie sighed. "I'm sorry. Did she have any suggestions in the two minutes you managed to talk?"

"Keep my distance. Positive self-talk. Meditating or saying a mantra." He ran his fingers through his short, stubbly hair. "Apparently, exposure therapy is really good for anxiety."

A choked laugh escaped Kenzie's throat. "Yeah. In this nice, controlled environment."

"At least you're a doctor. If I have a heart attack, you could give me CPR, right?"

Kenzie was momentarily distracted by his mention of a heart attack. Was there something that Stuart Dewey had been extra anxious or stressed by? Could an outside factor or situation have triggered his heart attack, if that was what had killed him?

She went over to Zachary and gave him a quick hug. "We'll get you through this. One step at a time. You can have some control over when we switch to... alternative heat or light sources."

She wanted to say that the decision was his alone, but decided she couldn't put it all on him. He might decide he'd rather freeze than light a fire. Or he might feel pressured to make the decision for everyone else's comfort as if his own didn't matter. It was better if they all decided together.

Tyrrell had played with the kids until they were too bored to attend to it anymore. Kenzie made some sandwiches with some of the leftover turkey, and everyone had eaten a quiet supper together. It was too dark to see much after that, so their options were limited to going to bed, a game that could be played in the dark, such as hide and seek or murder, or lighting some candles or the fire.

There was a knock at the door. It sounded more like a mule kick than a knock, making them all startle or shriek. The sudden noise breaking the silence of the cabin was alarming. It was a minute before Kenzie could steel herself to go to the door. Who would be out and about when the weather was still so nasty? They had watched the snow piling up outside. It was getting pretty deep and would not be easy to slog through. She wondered whether anyone had made it out before the storm hit. Were the newlyweds getting home now? Getting tucked into a warm, cozy bed?

Kenzie opened the door, holding it tightly to keep it from banging open with the wind. A large shape shouldered its way into the room, putting down heavy equipment with a clang. Kenzie jumped back, unable to tell who it was or why he was nearly dropping the hardware on her feet. She pushed the door shut behind him.

Burknall unwrapped the scarf around his face and pulled down his face mask to speak. Kenzie felt a little better being able to see who it was.

"Space heater," Burknall declared, giving the big piece of machinery a kick. "Could see that you folks didn't have your fireplace lit." He gave Zachary a look.

"Oh." Kenzie felt a sudden, warm rush of gratitude toward the big, curt man. "Thank you so much!"

He grunted, took a moment to stomp most of the snow off of his big boots, then lugged the heater over to the fireplace. "We'll vent it up the chimney. That will help keep fumes from building in the room."

"Thank you."

She watched him get the heater set up, attaching a tube that led to what she assumed was a propane tank. She moved in closer to him. "You have to light a burner, though...?"

He glanced at her. "Just a pilot light, like the furnace. It's got an auto-igniter." He tightened up the connections and pressed a button in a few times. "There. Just like that." He stripped off his gloves and held his hands in front of it to feel the warmth from the heater. "Got all kinds of safety features. Tip over protection, oximeter. It will stop if there are any problems."

"That was very thoughtful," Zachary spoke up, his voice hoarse. "I really appreciate it."

"Don't let the kids play near it," Burknall said, ignoring the thanks. "It does get hot enough to burn you if you touch it." He dug through several large pockets, looking for something, then pulled out a long, flat box, which he tossed on the floor. "Don't use those all tonight. I don't have any more."

Kenzie picked up the box and opened it. It was filled with long plastic cylinders filled with chemicals.

Glow sticks.

"You run into any trouble, I'm in the barn and Mrs. Hubbard is in the main house. Phone lines are down as well as power, so we are cut off from the outside." Burknall stood and looked out the window. He gestured to the last piece of equipment that he had left by the door. "Camp stove. If you need to heat something up. The dining room up top is still providing meals, but if you want to take your meals here..." He shrugged.

Kenzie assumed that the Lodge would be lit with candles, so it was probably a good idea for them to eat on their own.

Burknall went on. "Strange things going on tonight. I suggest you stay in your cabin." He went back to the door and started to gear up to go outside again.

"What does that mean?" Kenzie asked, confused. "Strange things going on tonight? You mean something about the weather?"

"No. People. Acting squirrelly. That little Raven tore up one side of me and down the other, said that she saw me stealing from her cabin. The newlyweds—they didn't make it more than a mile or two down the main road—they are..." he paused, considering his words. "They go from arguing and acting like they're going to kill each other to flying as high as kites, if you know what I mean."

"You think they took something?"

"Oh, they took something, all right. And who knows what they'll do before they come back down. You can never predict. Keep your door locked. Don't let anyone in."

With that, he pulled his scarf around his head, pulled on his gloves, and departed.

Kenzie locked and latched the door before turning to face the others.

It was dark, so she couldn't see their expressions, just the shadows across their faces. Zachary looking even more skeletal than usual, though she was sure that he would be feeling a lot more relaxed knowing that they weren't going to have to light a fire.

"Well, that was nice of Mr. Burknall, wasn't it?" Kenzie said cheerfully. She walked closer to them and handed a glow stick to each of the children. "You know how to use these, right?"

"I like Mr. Burknall," Mason declared. He took the glow stick and began to snap it down the length. He shook it vigorously and it started to shine. They actually threw a good amount of light. The room immediately felt warmer and more cheerful.

"He comes across as an old grouch," Kenzie said, "but he really is very thoughtful, isn't he?"

"He let me drive the horses," Mason reminded her.

"Yes, he did. Let's sit closer to the fireplace and warm up. Now that we can see, we can play another game or read a book."

"But no TV," Mason said sadly, as if missing a departed friend.

Kenzie smiled at him. "No. No TV."

Kenzie noticed that the kids started to act ready for bed much earlier than they had the night before. Maybe because there were no devices to keep them entertained. They had all shut off their phones, tablets, and games to conserve batteries until they used them again or the power came back on. Zachary had a couple of battery packs that he used for charging devices when he was out on surveillance for a long time, and they held those in reserve. With no TV or internet access, once the children grew tired of playing board games or reading books, they were ready for sleep.

It probably helped that it wasn't the first day in a strange place and that there hadn't been a big dinner with more strangers, as there had been the night before. Mason put up a little bit of a fight over going to sleep, but it was nothing compared to the difficulty Tyrrell had with him the night before. Tyrrell stayed up for a bit longer, enjoying a chance to talk with the grown-ups, and then he headed off to bed as well.

Kenzie put the glow sticks into the snow out the back door, as freezing them was supposed to preserve the glow, and she turned the heater down to a lower holding temperature for the night.

They all had plenty of blankets and each other to help keep them warm for bed.

Zachary moved around the bedroom slowly, seeming reluctant to settle in for bed. There wasn't really anything to do to get ready for bed. No staying up catching up on social networks or working on his computer.

"Do you want something to read?" Kenzie suggested. "I could help you find something you like. There's a pretty good selection on the shelves here."

"No." Zachary shrugged. "I've never really been able to read for pleasure."

"Maybe now, with no other distractions...?"

He shook his head vigorously. "There are plenty of distractions here."

"There are?" Kenzie thought that without the electronics, he would, like the children, be bored. He would go to bed earlier than usual because there was nothing else to do.

"Yeah." Zachary looked out the window, putting his face close to the glass and cupping his hands around his eyes to see better. After a minute he withdrew, apparently not seeing anything of concern. "Mr. Dewey dying. The snowstorm. The power and phones being out. Worrying about how long it will be and whether we'll run out of fuel for the heater. People acting squirrelly."

"But we're in here, safe and sound. We have heat and light for now. Everything is good."

"For now. But it won't last forever."

"You're worrying about things that you don't need to worry about yet."

"I thought I would get a head start."

Kenzie smiled at this. "Really, though. Dr. B. has talked to us about catastrophizing. Thinking that the worst possible things are going to happen and blowing everything up out of proportion. The snow is slowing. By tomorrow it will probably be stopped. The plows will clear the highway and Mr. Burknall will clear the

Lodge's roads. The power will be fixed and the cell phones won't be blocked by the clouds. It's only temporary, and by this time tomorrow, you'll probably be wondering what you were so worried about."

"I've never wondered why I was so worried."

"Maybe you should worry about that," Kenzie said flippantly. "That's not normal." Then she held up her hand. "Forget I said that. Don't worry about not wondering why you were worried…"

Zachary sat down on the edge of the bed. "What do you think Burknall was talking about with weird things going on? It's normal for people to be stressed at a time like this. Was he just overreacting or being dramatic? Like telling ghost stories?"

"I don't know. I get the feeling that he doesn't joke around a lot. But sometimes really serious people still have a good sense of humor, they are just understated or keep it to themselves. He might think that it would… make things more entertaining for us."

"Yeah. You don't think there's anything to be concerned about?"

"I think that everything is under control. We're safe in the cabin, so it doesn't really matter what everybody else is doing. And I'm sure that with this storm, everyone else is going to stay inside too. Who would want to be out wandering in weather like this?"

"And the newlyweds? He said they were high as kites?"

"They might just be tipsy. Or giddy with the stress. Some people get like that, just a little hysterical and out of control. Or they might have taken anxiety meds. Sometimes those can make people a little loopy."

"It could be something else. Illegal drugs. Something that could make them dangerous to us. Bath salts or PCP…"

"They didn't strike me as the type of people to experiment with that sort of thing. I think that Mr. Burknall was probably just overstating. Raven was extra stressed, so she took it out on him by getting angry and accusing. The newlyweds are feeling jittery, and they argued and were a bit silly. You know how it is when people are stressed."

Zachary rubbed his jaw. Kenzie could hear his fingers rasping across the whiskers in the dark, and it set her teeth on edge.

"Maybe we should have stayed at home. Maybe coming here was a bad idea," Zachary said

"Well, it was my idea, so if it was bad, then I'm the one who should be beating myself up about it, not you. Let's get into bed."

"I'm too restless."

"Just try. Once you're in bed, maybe your body will decide it is safe to relax and sleep."

Zachary began to undress, not arguing with her logic. It was something she had said before, and while it never really seemed to work that way for Zachary, she persisted. She was convinced, despite the evidence and everything she knew about anxiety disorders, that he could relax if he just did normal, relaxing things, and focused on clearing his mind instead of worrying over everything.

She had her delusions too.

Kenzie took off her day clothes and pulled on some soft flannel pajamas. Not sexy, maybe, but they were warm and comfy, which was exactly what she needed on a night when they were snowbound. She slid in under the covers, with several more blankets on hand if she got cold in the night. Zachary climbed in. He put his arms around her and explored her curves under the pajamas.

"This is cozy."

Kenzie snuggled up to him. "It is." She put her arms around his bare back. "I should get you some too. They're very fashionable," she teased.

He jerked suddenly, turning to look at the window. Kenzie waited, watching his dark shape against the slight glow from the window.

"What is it?"

"I heard a noise."

Kenzie breathed slowly, regulating her response. "I didn't hear anything. What did it sound like?"

"It sounded like someone is out there."

He got back out of bed and looked out the window again. He stood there for a long time.

"Don't see anything?" Kenzie surmised.

"No." He finally turned back around and returned to the bed.

"Did you take something for anxiety tonight?" she asked. Normally she didn't prompt him about his meds. He was a big boy and knew what was best for his body and mind. But she was afraid that his anxiety was getting the better of him and he would never be able to settle down for the night without an aid.

"No."

"Have you thought about it? You are still recovering from your treatment; your body needs the rest."

"Not tonight." He turned his head and looked toward the window again.

Kenzie cuddled, trying to get comfortable and to distract him from his hypervigilance. But he turned away from her, lying on his other side so he could watch the window. Kenzie spooned against his back and breathed slowly, drawing her breath out long to see whether he would unconsciously match her slower rhythm and allow himself to relax. He had been still for a long time, and she was wondering if he were drifting off when he sat up abruptly and slid his feet back out of bed again. Kenzie stifled a groan and rolled onto her back. She watched him check the window once more and then moved toward the open bedroom door.

"What is it? Do you need something?"

"Just checking the doors."

Kenzie knew she had already checked the doors before going to bed, and so had Zachary. The house was very quiet, and she heard him checking not only the front and back doors of the cabin, but also going quietly into each room. To check the windows, she assumed. They were all properly latched, and probably frozen shut as well. Which might actually be a problem for

Zachary, if he started to worry about how they would all get out of the house if the heater started a fire. But the children were in the room with Tyrrell, not sleeping on their own, so if there were a fire, Tyrrell would know to break a window rather than trying to get it unstuck. He'd been trapped in his bedroom the night of the fire when Zachary was ten and Tyrrell was just four. The fire-fighters had needed to break the window from the outside to get him out.

She continued to listen, but despite herself was almost asleep again by the time Zachary returned.

"Everything okay?" Kenzie murmured.

Zachary got back into bed again. The third time now? Kenzie was losing track. "There are people out. I can hear them walking back and forth." His body was tense, and his muscles did not relax when she rubbed his back, shoulders, and neck.

"It's okay if there are people out," Kenzie told him calmly. There was no point in telling him that there were not people out. He had already decided that there were. "We are safe in here. No one else can get in. We're snug as a couple of bugs in a rug."

"Five bugs," he corrected immediately, taking his brother and family into account.

"Snug as five bugs in a rug," Kenzie agreed sleepily. "Don't worry about what anyone else is doing."

"Uh-huh."

Kenzie closed her eyes. Maybe Zachary wasn't going to get any sleep, but she was. She was warm and cozy in the bed and it had been a busy day.

23

K enzie was awakened by a loud crash. She jolted awake, and her first thought was that the noise had been caused by Mason, or Mason and Alisha together. Jumping off of the bed or playing Jenga or getting into something they were not supposed to. She tried to hold back her anger and get reoriented to time and space. She reached out for Zachary but, as she expected, he was not beside her. If he had gotten any sleep, he had risen before her, which was his usual practice.

Kenzie rubbed her eyes and looked around. The room was light, so the sun was up and was forcing its way down through the clouds. Maybe they would have some cell reception. She climbed out of bed. There was a braided rug beside the bed, but when she stepped off of it, her feet hit icy wood floor that made her want to get right back into bed. She forced herself to keep going. Zachary had probably not thought to turn the heater back up, and she would have to do it herself.

She walked out to the living room and looked around. She had expected to see the children, but they weren't there. Maybe they had gone out and it was the door slamming behind them that had woken her up?

Zachary was sitting in one of the easy chairs, facing the main window, very still.

"Was there a noise?" Kenzie asked. "Something woke me up."

"The door."

"Did the kids go out?"

"No. Someone at the door."

Kenzie looked pointedly at Zachary sitting there like a statue. "Why didn't you answer it, then?"

He didn't respond. Kenzie rubbed her arms. Her toes were going numb on the cold floor.

"Can you at least turn the heater up?"

She hated the anticipation of opening the cabin door and letting all of the cold air in. Her skin was covered with goosebumps already. It was cold as a witch's behind out there.

Kenzie reached the door and put her hand on the latch.

"Burknall said not to let anyone in," Zachary reminded her.

"That was last night. When he thought weird things were going on. But everyone will be asleep now. Anybody with any sense is still in bed."

With that, she flipped the latch and unlocked the door. She didn't even have time to turn the door handle when the door flew open, pushed by someone outside. Kenzie stepped back to avoid getting hit, her anger rising the second time in two minutes. Or the third time, counting her irritation at Zachary for not turning up the heat or answering the door himself.

Redd Flagg stepped into the room, and he shut the door quickly, blocking out the cold air. He swore and slapped his hands against his arms. He was wearing leather gloves that didn't even look as if they were lined and an autumn jacket. What was wrong with men who couldn't dress themselves properly for the weather?

"Is it ever cold out there!" Redd declared.

"Yes, it is. What are you doing up already? I thought writers sleep in."

"Something has happened."

Kenzie had been looking at Zachary to see whether he were

going to turn up the heater. Her head snapped back around to look at Redd.

"What?"

"Cabin four. I don't know what's going on; I can't get a coherent answer out of anyone. Did you hear or see anything last night?"

"No. I mean, I didn't. Zachary said he could hear people going back and forth. What time? Mr. Burknall said that... people were acting strangely last night. I assume it was just the stress, but..."

"I don't know what it is, but you should probably get dressed. There's not even anyone in charge now, with Mr. Dewey dead. I don't know who is supposed to take charge. One of the help? That doesn't seem right."

And from what Kenzie had seen of the three of them, none of them was particularly suited to leadership. Burknall seemed the best bet, but he was brusque and more likely to tackle a job alone than to lead anyone else.

"Okay, I'm going to get dressed."

Redd nodded, looking relieved. Zachary followed Kenzie to the bedroom. He was already dressed. Of course he hadn't been sitting around in the cabin in his skivvies. Even if he had been distracted, he was bound to notice sooner or later he was cold and put some clothes on.

"What do you think it is?" Kenzie asked. "Could you tell what was going on from what you heard last night?"

"No. It was all pretty confusing."

"You said you heard footsteps. People walking."

"Yes. You would think that in the middle of cold weather like this, people would stay indoors. But they were back and forth all night."

"Who was?"

"I don't know."

"I imagine people were probably uncomfortable. Hyped up. Maybe Burknall had to build a couple of fires or take care of frozen pipes or flooding. Or just calm people down."

Zachary nodded, making no suggestions.

Kenzie changed as quickly as she could, both so that she didn't have to deal with the cold air on her skin and so that she could get out and see what was going on. Redd was right. Someone would have to take charge until Dewey's replacement got there. And it was better for everyone if that someone were not Vance Stiller.

Zachary left the bedroom. When Kenzie finished and headed back to the living room, he was just coming out of Tyrrell's bedroom. "Just letting him know that we were going out," he explained.

"Oh, are you coming too?"

Zachary looked taken aback. "If there's trouble, I'm not letting you go on your own."

Was there trouble? Or was Redd just being overly dramatic, as she'd suggested Burknall was the night before? Kenzie's brain was coming up with random ideas of what could have happened to upset Redd so much. And why Burknall had been so worried about the lovebirds the night before.

Kenzie and Zachary put on their boots, coats, and the rest of their winter gear in silence. It wasn't far to the next cabin. The newlyweds'. Kenzie joined the little cluster of people around the door.

"What's going on?"

Raven just shook her head. Only her eyes were showing through her ski mask, and to Kenzie they looked abnormally wide, her pupils dilated way too much in the morning sun. Mrs. Hubbard was there, and shushed Kenzie as though she had been talking too loudly in a library. Kenzie was about to protest, then realized that the others were trying to hear what was going on behind the closed door. She cocked her head and waited, ears pricked to hear whatever she could. Two male voices. Mr. Andy Collins, of course, and she thought that the other was the curt, abrupt cadences of Mr. Burknall. Certainly not Vance Stiller's. She hadn't paid much attention to Jack and the way that he spoke, but it sounded too low and measured to be the younger man.

The door opened and Burknall stood there, looking at them all, caught eavesdropping. Kenzie refused to be embarrassed by the fact. Of course she had been trying to overhear them and figure out what was going on. Anyone would have. Everyone was.

"We have a missing person," Burknall said briefly.

Kenzie looked around at the group around her, but she already knew who it had to be. She hadn't heard a female voice behind the door. "Mrs. Collins?"

Burknall nodded.

"Oh dear." Kenzie looked around. Trails had been trampled up and down the front of the cottages, and there were several inroads going between them to the back yards which bordered on the woods. There had been too many people back and forth to simply follow Mrs. Collins's footprints away from the cabin. And Zachary had said that people had been coming and going all night. How long had it been since Mrs. Collins had disappeared? With the temperature so low, she wouldn't last very long outside. "Are you sure she's not up at the house? If they had a fight, then maybe she just went somewhere else to cool down. *Calm* down, I mean. She might have fallen asleep on a chair or something and doesn't even know anyone is looking for her."

Mrs. Hubbard and Samantha looked at each other. "I didn't see her at the house," Mrs. Hubbard said, "but the door was left unlocked all night. She could have come and be asleep in one of the spare rooms..."

"I'll go look," Samantha said immediately.

A bundle of furs that had to be Brittany spun in a circle, looking all around. "Where could she have gone if she didn't go to the house? Where else is there to go? She didn't come to my cabin. Raven?"

"No, not mine either," Raven provided.

Zachary looked down at the trails trampled through the snow. "We'd better check out each trail that has been broken. Even if only one person has walked through a certain place. We should divide into teams of two so that no one else can get lost."

Kenzie had a sneaking suspicion that the suggestion to go in pairs was not just so that people didn't get lost in the snow. The whole world outside seemed to be white, but she didn't think anyone would go far enough afield to get lost.

Zachary didn't want anyone to be alone where they could do mischief.

Kenzie's stomach clenched.

Something had happened. Mrs. Andy Collins had not just gone out for a morning constitutional.

24

Zachary and Kenzie helped organize the search. Of course they paired themselves up.

"Where do you think we should look?" Kenzie asked.

Zachary gazed around, looking at the trails that had been trampled into the snow. It was surprising how many people had been walking around since the snow had fallen. Or even while it was still falling, as she could see that some footprints had been partially filled in after they were made. She had assumed that everyone would be bundled up cozy and warm in their cabins, like she and Zachary and Tyrrell's family had been. She had written off Zachary's claim that he could hear people walking around outside as paranoia. Hearing things because he was anxious.

But clearly, people *had* been wandering about when they should have been in bed.

Zachary pointed toward their own cabin. "Let's circle around ours and see if there are any trails branching off from there."

Had he heard anything else the night before? Voices? Snatches of conversation? She didn't ask in front of the others. There would be opportunities for private conversation later.

Kenzie started walking along the trampled trail that led behind their cabin. Zachary followed close behind her. She liked that he didn't act all macho and insist on going in front of her. He didn't think that she was weak or less able to handle whatever they encountered than he was.

Directly behind the cabin, almost leading from their back door, was a trail leading back toward the woods. Kenzie wasn't surprised that Zachary had been right about that. He said he had been up all night listening to them. He would know that they had been behind the house, then fading off into the distance.

"Into the woods?" Kenzie asked.

"Yes," Zachary said gruffly.

Kenzie took the branching pathway and led the search into the woods.

The snow wasn't as thick on the ground under the trees. There were bare patches where there was thicker foliage overhead catching the snow. But the trail was still easy to see. Kenzie stopped and studied it. The snow wasn't trampled down as much as it was around the cabins. She could see the distinct treads as people had gone into the woods and returned. Three different treads, she thought. If they'd had a tech team there, they could have taken casts of the shoe prints.

Kenzie took out her phone and powered it up.

"You won't be able to get a signal in here," Zachary said.

"I don't need a signal."

Kenzie waited for the phone to boot up, then took off her glove to unlock it with her fingerprint and tap the buttons. It was too cold to go without gloves for long, but she would have to put up with it for a few minutes. She crouched down and took pictures of the various footprints. They didn't come out very well.

"Try more of an angle and turn on the flash," Zachary suggested. "That will cast shadows that will show the print better."

Kenzie obeyed, and got a few shots that were reasonably good. She put her own foot next to one of the prints to use as the scale for the picture. One of the distinct treads was smaller than hers. The other two were bigger. Two men and a woman?

"Okay." Kenzie put her phone back in her pocket and put her

gloves back on, then tucked her hands under her armpits to warm them up faster. She continued along the trail, the dread growing in her belly.

They didn't speculate about what they were going to find, if they were to find anything. A missing woman in a snowstorm? Kenzie hoped that Mrs. Hubbard found her sleeping in the main house, unaware that people were concerned about her.

The trail didn't take them far. A few twists and turns through the woods. Not as far as they had gone on their hayride. Kenzie could see a shape in the snow ahead, and picked up her pace, hoping she wouldn't find what she did.

Mrs. Andy Collins lay crumpled in the snow. There were footprints around her. Someone had been there, knew where she was and what had happened to her, but hadn't told them so. More than one set of footprints. Kenzie tried to avoid them as she got closer to the fallen woman to examine her.

She had on a coat over her nightgown; boots, but no gloves or hat. The coat had not been buttoned up, maybe just thrown on as she tried to make her escape from whatever had caused her to leave her cabin the night before.

Freezings were a tricky thing. The heart slowed and the mammalian cold response could kick in, preserving life at a level undetectable to medical professionals. A person wasn't dead until they were warm and dead, as the aphorism went. Mrs. Andy Collins would have to be brought inside and warmed slowly to see whether she could be revived.

But even as Kenzie stooped to check for a pulse and evaluate the newlywed's condition, she saw the blood on the front of Mrs. Collins's nightgown. Kenzie stripped off her glove and felt for a pulse anyway. Ice crystals crunched under the rubbery skin. No detectable pulse.

In the cold, that didn't mean that she was dead.

But the stab wounds down the front of the woman's torso told her that there was nothing that could be done for the woman, who was almost as pale as the snow in which she lay. Kenzie's anatomy classes, the dissections she had done, and the autopsies she had attended told her that Mrs. Andy Collins had sustained at least one stab wound directly to the heart. And no mammalian cold response would save her from that.

"Nothing?" Zachary asked, as Kenzie stepped back.

"No sign of life. She's been here a few hours, or there wouldn't be ice crystals forming. She's been stabbed multiple times." Kenzie surveyed the holes in the victim's nightgown, each with a blot of blood around it, some of them spread out and merging. "By my count, about nine times." Kenzie paused. She took out her phone again, took off her gloves to operate it, and turned on the video recording. She took a long shot, then zoomed in on the injuries, dictating her observations again for the record. She panned over the footprints that went all around the body. None of the footprints continued into the woods; they stopped at the body and returned again along the same path they had come on. Except for the set of footprints which didn't return.

Kenzie dictated the time and date and her and Zachary's names. She needed to record everything for the medical examiner who would eventually get the case. Make sure that he had all the details he would need. The police would also need the footprint evidence to interpret the story it told.

"What do we do?" Zachary asked, his voice low, almost reverent.

"The practice should always be to leave the body *in situ* until the medical examiner can get there, and to preserve as much of the scene and forensic evidence as possible. But we don't know how long it will be until someone can get up here, and we can't leave the body subject to predation." Kenzie pondered what to do next. "I think that we should get a couple of blankets. Wrap the body and create a sling to carry her in. Take her up to the house where her body can be preserved. Like Mr. Dewey's."

"Is there any connection between what happened to Mr. Dewey and... Mrs. Collins?"

"The two deaths couldn't be more different. I don't see any

connection between the two except that they were proximate in time and place."

Zachary didn't say anything to disagree, but Kenzie knew that he did. He was looking for the connections, analyzing everything he knew about both deaths. He was a trained investigator. He wouldn't be satisfied until he had the answers.

Maybe there was no connection between the two deaths. But maybe there was. Could it really be a coincidence that both people had now died at the Lodge?

25

hey made their way back to the cabins. Zachary stopped at the edge of the woods.

"I'll wait here. I want to make sure that no one else touches the evidence while you're getting help."

"Yeah. Good idea. I'll be as quick as I can."

She hurried on and returned to cabin four, where the others were starting to gather again. Apparently, none of the trails had led very far away.

"No luck," Redd Flagg called to Kenzie as she got closer. "No one has seen her."

Kenzie drew up closer to them. "We found her," she said, her tone somber, letting them know that it was not happy news.

"You found her?" Raven repeated. "But... she's okay, isn't she? Where is she?"

Kenzie shook her head. "No. She's not okay. I need a couple of blankets, and someone to help me to... transport her up to the house."

Andy Collins came out of the cabin, his face white. "What is it? Do you have news? Did you find her?"

Kenzie looked down at Andy's hands, but he was wearing

118

winter gloves. "You should wait in your cabin. You don't need to see this."

"What does that mean?" he asked in a confrontational tone, then repeated it, voice breaking, "What does that mean?"

"It means you should go inside," Kenzie told him firmly.

"I want to know what you mean by that!"

Kenzie looked around the group for help. Burknall would be of the most assistance to her, she thought. Jack? Redd? She chose the author. "Redd, could you go in with him? Look after him until we get everything taken care of?"

"I don't really know what to do."

"Just keep him company. Listen. Don't... don't ask him a lot of questions, try to just keep him calm and in one place."

Redd's eyes widened a little in surprise. Kenzie couldn't see the rest of his face because it was obscured by a scarf. Redd nodded his head and took Andy by the arm, turning him in a circle back into the cabin.

Kenzie waited until the door was shut before saying anything. She then nodded to Burknall. "I could use some help. I'm used to moving—uh, things," she caught herself before revealing that she had occasion to move dead bodies with regularity. "But I need a way to get her up the hill to the main house. We can wrap her in blanket and then use another blanket as a sling-style stretcher between two of us. It's a fair distance up the hill, carrying a weight like that."

"I have a snowmobile with a freight sled. Will that work?"

Kenzie raised her hands palms-up, uncertain. "I've never seen one, so I can't picture how big it would be. It sounds as if it might work."

"I can fit a deer carcass on it."

"Well then... that would be perfect."

Burknall nodded and, without another word, walked back toward the barn. He was a man of few words, but intuitive and efficient.

Raven moaned and covered her eyes. "Why did she do it? Why didn't she come see me? I told her about the monsters."

Kenzie looked at her uncertainly. "The monsters?"

"I told her. I told her they were out last night. I saw them out the window. Shadows in the trees. They were waiting. Watching us and waiting..."

"What did these monsters look like?"

"I don't know." Raven dropped her hands from her face and peered around. "Are they still out? I thought they would go away when the sun came up. I told her about the monsters. I told her."

"Are you feeling okay, Raven? Have you taken something? Some pills?" Burknall had said that he thought that the newlyweds had taken something the night before, and Raven was acting as if she were hallucinating. It could just be the shock, but hallucinating or having paranoid delusions were not typical reactions to emotional shock.

"I'm not on anything! Just my meds. I don't do anything illegal!"

"Okay. I believe you. Have you had a fever? Achy joints?"

"Maybe. I don't know. It's so cold out."

"Yes, it is," Kenzie agreed. She put her hands under her armpits again to try to keep them warm. Her gloves were good for casual winter use, but they were not good for working outside for any length of time in sub-zero temperatures. Kenzie looked over the faces of the others. Vance Stiller was still not in evidence. Was he just sleeping in? Or had something happened to him too? Maybe he didn't care that something had happened to one of their number. He didn't think he was one of them. He thought he was better than everyone else. He probably had some sort of morning routine that could not be broken under any circumstances. Winter storms and sudden deaths were no exception. "Brittany, do you think you could take Raven inside and make sure she is okay? Maybe something to eat...? I don't think she should be on her own, but staying out here in the cold isn't helping anything."

Brittany's eyes slanted up, seeming pleased to have been given an assignment. "Of course! Come on, sweetie. Let's get you inside and warmed up."

That left Kenzie with Jack Fowler, Samantha the maid, who had returned from the house after a fruitless search for the missing woman, and Mrs. Hubbard, her bare face red with the cold. Kenzie shifted uncomfortably. She didn't want to answer a lot of questions about what kind of shape Mrs. Andy Collins's body had been in, and she thought Jack was just the type of character who would ask.

"I'm going to go back and meet up with Zachary. When Mr. Burknall comes back, just have him follow this trail into the woods. That's where we will be."

Zachary and Kenzie trekked back to the place where they had left Mrs. Collins's body. Zachary looked around carefully. "No one came by here while I was watching."

Kenzie also scanned the snow for any new footprints or any other disturbances. "I don't see anything. I think we can rest assured that nothing has been touched in the time we've been gone."

He nodded. "Good."

"Burknall should be here any minute, I doubt it will take long for him to get his sled hooked up to the snowmobile and to get here."

Zachary nodded. They both stood in silence, watchful. It wasn't as windy as it had been the day before, and while snow was still falling, Kenzie could hear animals in the woods around them. A chickadee. Rustling in the leaves and bushes. Maybe a rabbit out foraging for something to eat. And deer. Burknall had said that there were deer. As long as the wind wasn't too strong, Kenzie imagined the deer would go out to search for food. They were used to the snow. It felt as if they were all alone in the world, isolated from the rest of civilization. Kenzie would not have guessed, if she had been dropped there, that there were people only a few minutes' walk away.

In a few minutes, the silence was broken by the sounds of Burknall's snowmobile. He came alongside the trail, skiing in the fresh snow beside the footprints rather than over them. He climbed off the snowmobile and walked over to have a look at Mrs. Collins without a word. He looked her over, observing the bloodied nightgown. He shook his head.

"It's a crying shame."

"It is," Kenzie agreed. "I have no idea what happened last night. If she and her husband got into a fight, or if someone else came upon her here. Or even chased her. The police will have to analyze the footprints, compare them against everyone's boots to see who else was here. I can't believe that something like this could happen just a few yards away from our cabin. It's frightening."

Burknall went to his sled and pulled a couple of blankets off. He stretched them over the undisturbed ground near Mrs. Collins, one on top of the other, then approached her to pick her up.

"Let me help," Kenzie told him. "It's always easier to move a body with two people."

She took the woman's ankles and let Burknall handle her shoulders. That gave him more weight, but he was bigger than Kenzie was and had better upper body strength. They lifted her carefully from the ground and laid her down on the blankets. Kenzie wrapped her up like a taco with the top blanket. The woman's limbs were in rigor or frozen, so she wasn't a long, thin package like a body bag, but closer to a ball shape.

Then they used the corners of the bottom blanket to lift her and carry her over to the sled. There was plenty of room. They folded the outer blanket loosely over her, disguising her shape a little more, and Burknall pulled several straps over her to secure the cargo. They certainly didn't want her flying off the sled as they went up the hill.

"Thank you," Kenzie said. "This is really helpful."

He gazed at her, his eyes unwavering. "Who are you really?"

"What do you mean?"

"You're not an accountant."

Kenzie opened her mouth to protest, but he shook his head, looking grim. "You might be able to fool the others. But probably not for long. Who are you really? Are you police?"

"No," Kenzie sighed. "I work with the medical examiner in Roxboro."

Burknall nodded. "That makes more sense."

"You don't think a forensic accountant would have that much experience in moving bodies?" Zachary asked wryly.

Mentioning that might have been a mistake.

"That and other things," Burknall agreed. Kenzie thought she detected a twinkle in his serious eyes.

Kenzie shrugged, embarrassed. But it wasn't surprising that she would be caught out in a situation where there had been an unexpected death. How many other people would be used to dealing with such a situation? And what was the point in continuing to hide her identity? She was no longer worried about people asking her unwelcome questions. Now that there had been a homicide, it was probably best that everyone know who she was and that she had special expertise in the unusual situation.

"Things have changed," she admitted. "We thought we would both be able to take a vacation from our jobs and avoid talking shop the whole time we were here. But now..."

Burknall looked at Zachary, his brows raised. "And what about you? Just some stiff she brought along from the office?"

Zachary chuckled. "Not quite. A stiff from home. I'm a private investigator. But I don't know if anyone needs to know that yet."

"People have already been speculating."

"They have?" Zachary's voice went up a few notes. "What have they said?"

"Hit man. Leg breaker. On the run for something or other."

"They think he's a criminal?" Kenzie asked, amused. She looked Zachary over. He did have a certain grim look to him. Like he was prepared to do whatever was necessary.

Zachary nodded, accepting their suspicions. He looked back down at the body on the sled. "We'd better get her up to the house. Then Kenzie can examine the body more closely."

"You want to ride on the sled?" Burknall asked. There was still plenty of room around the corpse. But Zachary shook his head and Kenzie was inclined to agree. It might be more work to walk up the hill, but it seemed disrespectful to ride with the body.

"No, we'll join you up there. Just wait when you get there, I'll help transfer the body again."

"I can do it myself," Burknall offered. "She's not that big. Where do you want her?"

"One of the upstairs rooms. She doesn't need to be in with Mr. Dewey, but we'll preserve the body the same way. Leave a window open to keep her cold and prevent decomposition until the medical examiner or other authorities can get here to transport her."

"I'll take her upstairs."

Kenzie wasn't too sure about that. "It's more awkward to handle a dead body than you might think. Especially a frozen one. And if you drop her, something might break."

"I'm not going to drop her. I move deer carcasses. I can handle a small woman."

"I'd still prefer that you wait."

He shrugged and climbed aboard the snowmobile. He raised a hand in farewell, turned the snowmobile in a wide circle away from the pathway, and then returned over the ski tracks he had already made.

Kenzie looked over the ground where Mrs. Collins had lain, looking for any evidence that they needed to preserve. She didn't find the murder weapon or letters written in the snow to identify the name of the woman's killer. There wasn't anything that provided any more clues than the footprints in the snow that they had already observed.

Kenzie opened up her phone again and made a brief recording of the ground where the body had lain. Then they turned around and walked out of the woods, past their cabin, and up the hill to the farmhouse.

26

At the top of the hill, Kenzie saw Burknall's snowmobile pulled to the side of the driveway, but there was no bundle of blankets on the sled behind it. Burknall had ignored her suggestion and had taken the body into the house by himself. A spurt of anger and irritation shot through Kenzie. Just like a man to think that he knew better just because she was a woman. He should have listened to her as an expert in the field.

But she didn't have the time or energy to waste being angry with him. It was what it was. She wouldn't win that battle anyway.

She and Zachary entered the house without a word. Kenzie stood there for a moment, just letting the heat soak into her. They'd been outside for a long time. She didn't think she had been outdoors in weather like that for long since she was a child, building snow forts and snowmen. She'd come a long way from childhood battles and snow angels. She remembered playing with Amanda...

Kenzie quickly shut these thoughts off. She would not think about Amanda and the times they had shared together. Times that were gone and lost forever. She wasn't ever going to make snow angels with Amanda again, and there was no point in pining over it. Kenzie began to take off the winter gear with deliberation. It would be nice to get some circulation back into her fingers.

They hung up their coats and pried off their boots and headed upstairs to where Burknall had placed the deceased on the bed in a spare bedroom. Kenzie was glad to see that she was still wrapped in the blankets. Burknall had not pulled them open to examine Mrs. Collins's body.

"Thank you." Kenzie tried to treat him with the same professionalism as she would have one of the workers in her office who had helped to prep a body for Dr. Wiltshire. "Zachary, would you shut the door, please?"

Zachary put his hand on the door and looked at Burknall. Burknall didn't move. "Do I have to leave?"

"It would probably be best," Kenzie said. "This is my job. You don't need to see this."

"I really don't know you two or anything about you. Maybe I should observe so that I can be a witness to the fact that no one tampered with or destroyed evidence."

Kenzie looked at him steadily, but he didn't back down. Finally, she nodded. It was true, she and Zachary really couldn't alibi each other. Anything either of them said would be suspect. Burknall, an unrelated third party, would be a better witness if called on to verify what procedure had been followed.

"Do you know where the thermometer we used for Mr. Dewey is?" Kenzie asked Zachary.

"I put it back where it came from. Let me go see."

He walked out of the room, shutting the door behind him to keep unwelcome guests from just wandering in. Kenzie pulled back each of the corners of the outer blankets, and then unwrapped the taco folds she had made, exposing the woman's body to view.

The blood and the holes in her nightgown seemed even more pitiful in the light filtering into the room through the windows. How could anyone have done that to her? How could anyone have any excuse for killing this woman, a lovestruck newlywed on a snowy honeymoon? Especially—Kenzie hated to even consider the thought—her new husband. Had they had a fight? Had he done this to her because he was high? Delusional? Or had it been something even more base? Jealousy or a life insurance policy? Who would do such a thing to a defenseless young woman?

Kenzie examined each of the stab holes more carefully, pulling the nightgown this way and that to see the size and shape of the wound and the skin around it. She took another video with her phone, getting in several close-ups. With Burknall there observing, she didn't dare undress the body. That would be for the proper authorities to do. And Kenzie was not the proper authority in this case.

When would they have cell coverage again? Kenzie looked for any signal bars on the display of the phone, but there was still a little "no service" notation there instead. Zachary returned with the thermometer. Kenzie tried taking the body's temperature. The numbers on the thermometer counted down, and then 999 and ERR alternated on the LCD screen. A fever thermometer was not calibrated to read temperatures that low. Kenzie sighed. "That didn't work. I'll have to go with other signs I can see and feel, then."

Neither of the men said anything as she repeated the exercise of searching for a pulse, pulling back an eyelid and shining the phone's flashlight LED into her eye, and feeling the stiffness of the limbs and the ice crystals formed underneath the rubbery skin.

"You think the stab wounds killed her or the cold?" Burknall asked.

"The stab wounds."

"There is a lot of blood."

Kenzie shook her head. "No, there really isn't. There's some, but not a significant amount. And the flow differs between the earlier stab wounds and the later ones."

"Because the blood pressure dropped as she bled out?" Zachary suggested.

"No. Because the heart was no longer pumping. It's only seepage. Postmortem blood loss."

Kenzie examined Mrs. Collins's hands, which were cut. "Defensive wounds on the hands. She fought off her attacker before she was stabbed."

"So she saw it coming."

"Yes. She knew what was happening. It didn't take her off guard."

Kenzie continued her examination, but there wasn't much else to find. She would leave any trace to the medical examiner whose job it was. Looking for hair, skin under Mrs. Collins's nails, testing the blood to ensure that it was all hers and there hadn't been a contribution from the killer. Eventually, Kenzie sighed and wrapped the blanket back around the body loosely.

"That's about all I can do here."

"What's next?" Zachary asked.

"Nothing. Go back to our cabin."

"We have to find out who did this, though."

"It's really not our jobs. Leave it to the police to investigate. We don't want to mess anything up."

"Who knows when the police will get here. In the meantime, there is a killer at the resort."

Kenzie held Zachary's gaze as she turned her phone off and slid it back away. "It's not our job. Our job is to keep ourselves and your family safe. If we go bumbling around getting involved in something like this, you don't know what could happen. I don't want to be in this guy's crosshairs."

After opening the window to keep the room cold, they moved out of the room in a group. Kenzie still had the house keys and locked the bedroom door. Zachary had already retrieved the masking tape, and she sealed the room and initialed the tape as she had with Mr. Dewey's room.

"You think whoever did this has motive to kill anyone else?" Zachary asked. "You don't think it was just... passion or being high?"

In other words, he too figured Mr. Andy Collins was the most likely suspect. Women were killed by their husbands. It was an unfortunate fact. There were rare occasions where it was a stranger, but in the majority of cases, it was an intimate partner. And Zachary was right, Collins would not have a motive to kill anyone else. But Kenzie wasn't sure that meant it was a good idea to confront him with their suspicions. Cornered, he might do whatever was necessary to preserve himself.

"It might have been. But that doesn't necessarily make it safe for us to investigate. I think we should just stay out of it. In a couple of days, the police will be here, and they can handle it."

They went back downstairs, each thinking their own melancholy thoughts. Kenzie could hear Mrs. Hubbard in the kitchen and went to talk to her, to make sure she knew about the body in the second room upstairs and that she shouldn't open that door either. As if she wouldn't be able to figure that out herself by the tape sealing it and Kenzie's initials on the tape.

Mrs. Hubbard was sitting at a small table in the kitchen, her face buried in her hands, supported by elbows on the table. She was sobbing.

"Mrs. Hubbard... it's okay. I know this is really hard on you, but everything is going to be okay," Kenzie told her lamely.

"Gladys," Mrs. Hubbard sobbed.

"What?"

"Call me Gladys." Mrs. Hubbard sniffled and drew in a long breath, then let it out in a controlled stream. Her body shuddered. Kenzie rubbed her shoulder and neck.

"Gladys. I'm sorry. It will be okay."

"I don't know how. I don't know what's going to happen to me or to the Lodge. And we've never had such a thing happen to a guest before. Once we had a heart attack, but he survived, and the ambulance took him to the hospital. He was back two days later to get his things. Said they put a stent in, and he was good to go."

"It must be shocking to you, I know. But we have to make the best of what we've got."

"What we've got? I've got nothing. I've got decades of employment at a place where there is no one to give me a reference. I am an old woman and I have to find another job. I don't want to still be working at this age, let alone looking for a job."

"I know. But we'll get it sorted out." The words were empty platitudes, but Kenzie had to try to cheer the woman up.

Gladys Hubbard just continued to cry, sobbing as if her heart were breaking.

It was difficult to separate herself from the crying woman in the kitchen but, eventually, Kenzie managed to get away, although she felt guilty for leaving Mrs. Hubbard alone with no one to comfort her. Burknall looked into the kitchen at her, but he didn't go in to talk to her. Whether it was because he didn't know how to deal with a woman crying—something that was a challenge for most men—or because of something else, Kenzie didn't know. They seemed to know each other well, but he was still not inclined to go to Mrs. Hubbard's aid.

Kenzie was reluctant to get her snow gear on again and brave the elements. But if they wanted to go back to the cabin, they needed to dress and walk down the hill again.

"I could give you a lift," Burknall offered, noticing Kenzie's slow movements.

"Maybe that would be a good idea," Kenzie admitted.

They got dressed and went back out into the frigid air. Kenzie shivered, even though most of her skin was covered. Burknall gestured to the sled. He pulled a strap tightly across it. "Sit down and hold on to that. I'll go slowly."

Zachary and Kenzie climbed on board. Burknall did as he had

promised, and there was no trouble staying on the sled. He stopped in front of their cabin.

"Thank you," Kenzie called to him.

He nodded and gave a brief salute, then sped off down toward the barn. Kenzie intended to go straight back inside. Her work on the case was done, as she had told Zachary. The best thing for them to do now was to stay well out of the way and leave the rest for the trained law enforcement officers to deal with.

But as she reached for the doorknob, the door to cabin number four opened, and Redd stood on the threshold.

"Are you coming in? What are we supposed to do now?"

Kenzie looked at him in consternation. She had asked him to stay with Collins. But for how long? Until the police got there? Was he just supposed to leave Collins and go back to his own cabin? Or was he supposed to stay there keeping an eye on things? Kenzie wasn't usually involved in that side of the homicide business. Bodies were her thing. Dead ones.

"Uh..."

Brilliant.

Kenzie looked at Zachary. His eyes were bright. He was an investigator. He was often involved, privately, in cases that law enforcement had investigated. He came in and reviewed the evidence, re-interviewed suspects and witnesses, brought in his out-of-the-box thinking to come up with new theories of the crime. He was a good investigator, dogged and determined.

"Uh... I guess maybe we'd better have a talk with him. Just to reassure him that everything will be handled when the police get here," Kenzie suggested.

Zachary nodded his agreement.

Kenzie swore under her breath. She really did not want to talk to Andy Collins. She did not want to be facing a man who might be a murderer. Pretending that she didn't suspect him, or that everything would be okay, as she had told Gladys Hubbard.

Kenzie let out a long sigh, and she and Zachary walked over to the door of cabin four. Redd stepped back and let them in, looking relieved.

Collins's cabin was similar to theirs, but not identical. Kenzie got the feeling that they had been built at different times and that an effort had been made to make each cabin unique rather than cookie-cutters.

Kenzie had made an effort to keep their cabin tidy, which wasn't easy with other people there, especially a couple of bored children who didn't like to clean up after themselves, and the usual differences between what Kenzie considered acceptable and what Zachary did. Their big dinner had been cleaned up and Kenzie had tried to stay on top of the random dishes produced by meals and snacks of five people throughout the day. The inside of Collins's cabin, however, looked like a hurricane had hit.

There were dirty dishes piled in the sink and on the counter, clothing strewn on the floor, and the furniture all seemed to have been bumped out of position, looking disrupted from their proper groupings. A kitchen table had been tipped over and not set upright again. There were not, to Kenzie's relief, any blood spatter or handprints on the walls. Mrs. Collins had, most likely, been killed where they had found her body. Despite the mess around them, it didn't look as though the attack had begun in the cabin and then carried on outside as Mrs. Andy Collins fled her murderous husband.

Collins was sitting on the couch. When Kenzie entered, he looked around the cabin, as if he were unsure what he was supposed to be doing. Kenzie was equally unsure. What was her role? Just to break the news to him about his wife? It couldn't very well wait until the police managed to make it through the storm. He had to be told something. And she would have to observe his reactions, to be sure she could tell the police every nuance when they eventually began their investigation. Kenzie looked at Zachary for reassurance. He was the one who was used to dealing with members of the public, whether clients who had lost loved ones or suspected cheating husbands, or whether suspects themselves.

Zachary smiled reassuringly and nodded. He motioned to the seating around Collins. "Let's all sit down."

Redd hovered nearby. Not wanting to participate in the discussion, but wanting to observe it. Kenzie and Zachary sat down. Zachary pulled an oblong silver box out of his pocket, pressed a button with his thumb, and laid it on the occasional table beside him in a practiced, casual movement. A digital recorder. Good idea. Collins didn't seem to notice.

"Mr. Collins," Kenzie began. It sounded too formal. He would know it was a death notification. "Andy. How are you doing?"

"I don't know. I don't understand what's going on. I'm so worried about Brooke. When I woke up this morning and she wasn't here. And the cabin looking like this..." He looked around himself. Kenzie allowed her eyes to travel over the disarray. Books and throw pillows on the floor. Ornaments that should have been on the shelves and side tables tipped over or on the floor. What should have been a tidy, homey cabin looked instead as if a burglar had ransacked it.

"What happened last night?"

"I don't know." Andy shook his head and rubbed his eyes. He looked haggard, as if he had only managed to get a couple of hours of sleep the night before. Which was probably true.

There were people coming and going all night.

"What do you remember?" Kenzie prompted. They had to have somewhere to start, She couldn't just tell him baldly that they had found the body of his wife, brutally stabbed to death.

"Nothing. We must have had dinner up at the house," Collins looked over to Redd for confirmation of this fact, and Redd nodded his agreement. "But I can't remember that, or anything afterward. That doesn't make any sense. Why wouldn't I remember?"

"How much did you have to drink?" Kenzie scanned the detritus around them for empties. They must have had a significant amount for so much disruption and for him to have a memory blackout.

"It couldn't have been very much. We had packed everything to go home. But then... we only got a few miles down the mountain before we ran into the storm. We knew that we weren't going to be able to make it through, so we came back here. Like you said. Thought we would have to stay another night or two... better that way... at least we knew we would get home in safety. If we tried to make it through that storm, there's no way. We got back here for dinner..."

"How much did he have at dinner?" Kenzie asked Redd.

"Not a lot that I noticed. A glass of wine or two. Maybe one before the meal and one with."

Collins nodded. "We're not big drinkers."

"And then you came down here to your cabin and...?" Kenzie waited for Collins to fill in the rest.

He just looked at her blankly. "I told you; I don't remember. I can't remember anything from last night."

"Mr. Burknall said that the two of you were fighting. Did you have an argument?"

Collins looked at everything scattered on the floor. "We never fight."

"You must have had one last night. You don't remember what it was about?"

"No. That doesn't make any sense."

And Burknall had suggested that they were high. "What about drugs? Medications? Maybe you took something for anxiety because of the storm?"

"No. I don't have anything like that." His eyes flicked toward the bedroom.

"Nothing?"

"Well... maybe Brooke had something in her bag. To help her to relax. But I don't know. I didn't take anything."

Kenzie was pretty sure that it was a lie. So what had he taken? Something had made him forget what had happened. And someone had killed Brooke Collins. The most likely suspect had to be her husband.

"Did you find her?" Collins asked, begging for a happy ending. "What did she say? I don't know what happened last night, but whatever it was, we can talk about it. Neither of us was in the best mood. We can go back, start over, whatever it was we had a fight about. What did she say?"

"How do you know that neither of you was in the best mood if you can't remember what happened?" Zachary asked.

Collins made a motion to take in the state of the cabin around him. "All of this... Brooke not coming back last night... things must have been pretty bad, right? We were both grumpy when we had to turn around to come back. Pretty tense. I need to apologize. To tell her that it doesn't matter. We can't let one night derail everything."

Collins looked from Zachary to Kenzie.

"Please."

A ndy..." Kenzie was not practiced in delivering such news, but she dealt with people who had recently found out about the deaths of loved ones. She knew the right pitch of her voice, the language around death and loss. "I'm so sorry to have to tell you this. But we found your wife. We found... Brooke's body."

"Her body," Collins repeated blankly. "But she's okay, right? I mean... she has to be. Tell me she's okay."

"I'm afraid... she didn't make it. She's dead."

"How could that be true?" Andy Collins's voice rose angrily.

Wasn't that the first step? Denial? Anger? Kenzie couldn't remember what all the stages of grief were supposed to be. She could remember, though, when her sister Amanda had died. How hard it had been to accept that they hadn't been able to save her, even when they had known that she might not survive. She had faced the specter of death so many times and escaped it. It didn't seem possible that Amanda had finally succumbed.

"Brooke was just here," Collins insisted. "She was just here last night. We just got married. Nothing could happen to her!" He covered his eyes with his palms, fingers digging into his hair.

Redd was pale too, his eyes wide with shock. He surely must

have suspected something, or he would not have been concerned enough to rouse Kenzie and Zachary to have them help with the trouble. And he had probably watched them take the snowmobile up to the house with something on the sled and return without it.

"I'm so sorry, Andy," Kenzie told him. "I really am. Are you sure you can't remember anything from last night?"

"No!" He shook his head. "I don't know what happened. It's all just... blank."

"Did she..." Redd licked his lips. "Was it the cold? Hypothermia?"

He had to ask that, didn't he? He couldn't let Collins just get to that point on his own. Couldn't let him have a little bit of peace before realizing that his bride hadn't just wandered off and died in her sleep or succumbed to the cold. He had to know the reason.

"No," Kenzie said shortly. "Something happened to her."

Collins removed his hands from his eyes and looked at her. "What happened? What do you mean?"

Kenzie looked away from him, looking out the window. She was getting deeper and deeper into something that she was really not qualified to investigate. She wasn't a cop. She didn't interview suspects.

"I think maybe we should leave that to the police."

"The police? What do the police have to do with this? It was an accident."

Kenzie raised her eyebrows. She wasn't sure how he could decide that it was an accident if he claimed not to remember what had happened.

"No, it wasn't an accident."

"Of course it was," Redd said. "Wandering off in the middle of the night like that. It doesn't really matter what she died of, it was obviously an accident. She didn't go out there intending to get killed."

"What do *you* remember?" Zachary asked. "You were out last night, weren't you?"

"No. Well, yes. But that was... I was just checking on the

weather. And I did hear a bit of the commotion. I just wondered... A person can't help what they overhear. I wasn't eavesdropping. It wasn't as if I was listening with my ear pressed to the door."

Collins looked at Redd. "What's that supposed to mean?"

"The two of you were pretty loud," Redd said defensively.

"Loud?" Collins's face flushed. "We're not loud enough for the neighbors..."

"You were arguing," Redd explained. He made a gesture to indicate the room. "Look around you. What do you think happened here? You were yelling at each other, throwing things around." He shook his head. "I've never seen anything like it."

"You were here?" Collins asked. "In our house?"

Redd shifted uncomfortably. "I knocked. You guys were... I thought maybe someone had broken in. Attacked you. Or you were trying to chase out a burglar. A wild animal. I don't know." He shook his head. "Weird stuff was going on. I thought I saw something outside... I thought... I don't know what."

"You saw what outside? You were in here? How did you get in?"

"You left the door unlocked. I just... you know... opened it to see if everything was okay. I knocked, but you didn't hear me, with all the noise you were making. So I just opened the door to have a look. It was unlocked," he repeated.

Collins looked at the front door as if he might be able to prove Redd wrong. Kenzie remembered Burknall telling them to lock their door. Had he seen Redd go into the Collins's cabin uninvited?

"So what happened?" Zachary asked. "We're trying to figure it out. You're the one who seems to know something, so why don't you tell us what it was you saw or know?"

Redd paced back and forth and ran his fingers through his hair. He tried to compose an answer, but obviously he wouldn't be able to come up with something that would suit everyone. Collins, at least, would be embarrassed. A woman was dead. Redd had already admitted to walking into the cabin through an unlocked door, knowing that he hadn't been invited in. He was guilty of that much, if nothing more.

"I just wanted to see what was going on, see whether anyone needed my help," he repeated. "They were being really loud. Yelling and throwing things around. So I opened the door; I thought there might be an intruder."

"And...?" Zachary prompted.

"There wasn't anyone else there, just the two of them, screaming at each other. Pushing, throwing things, acting like... wild. I don't know. You don't see people behaving like that. Grown adults. A married couple. After all of the mooning around, making out, ignoring everyone else and pretending to be in love..."

"We *are* in love," Collins insisted.

"They were behaving like wild animals," Redd repeated, not meeting Collins's eyes.

"Okay," Kenzie said, trying to keep her voice calm and nonjudgmental. Neither one of them needed to hear how she felt about their behavior the night before. Or her suspicions. "So you saw that they were fighting. Did you know what it was about? Did you stay and talk, or leave again? What happened next?"

"I just kind of stuck my head in the door, and I saw what was happening. I thought maybe it was an act. They were pretending, or doing it for a video, or role playing. I don't know. But they seemed to be really... both of them really angry, like none of it was put on."

"And..."

"And I left. I couldn't do anything about it. I couldn't stop them, could I? I didn't want to get in the middle of something and end up getting hurt, or maybe someone else getting hurt because... I made things worse." He gave a sort of a shudder, standing still in one place.

Kenzie saw the motion mirrored by Zachary, sitting on the other side. It was very small, and if she weren't so attuned to his emotional state all the time, she would probably never have noticed. But what Redd had said had caused an emotional reaction in Zachary. Kenzie closed her eyes briefly, and she could see Zachary, a little boy, peeking around a doorway at his parents in a drunken fight. He had told her that they used to fight. Not just yelling and arguments, but hitting and shoving each other and throwing things. Probably leaving the house in much the same state that the Collins's cabin was in now. He knew the feeling that Redd was talking about. Knowing that if he made a sound, if he put himself into the middle of the fight, he would get hurt or make it worse for one of his parents.

"So you left," Kenzie said. "You thought that was the best thing to do."

Redd nodded. "Yeah. I'm sorry I didn't know how else to handle it. You can't get into the middle of something like that. One person can't stop it. Sometimes... several people together can't stop it."

"Did you go to get help?"

"I saw Mr. Burknall. He was coming out of Raven's cabin. She must have had trouble getting a fire going or something. He was all over this place, trying to make sure everyone was comfortable last night. He was probably up half the night."

And so were several others, apparently.

"And you tried to get him to help?"

"Kind of... I told him that something was going on... that I thought they needed help."

And then ran the other direction and hid behind his own door.

"I'll talk to him later about what he did," Kenzie said. "But I know he said that the two of you were... acting strangely," Kenzie addressed this to Collins, who was looking bewildered by Redd's description. "Later, when he came over to our cabin."

"It was a spooky night," Redd said. "All of that wind and snow. The whole world looked different. And then it was suddenly quiet, the wind gone, like we were in the eye of a hurricane. Everything was... too still. And there were things..." Redd scratched his arms and shook his head, looking small and afraid. "I don't know what. It doesn't make much sense when I look back at it now. But last night, when it was all going on... I could see things."

"What kind of things?" Kenzie asked.

"I don't know. Shapes in the dark. Shadows. Maybe they were animals. But with weird shadows."

Kenzie had to shake her head at that one. She had no idea what it was Redd had seen. But it didn't seem to be anything to do with Andy and Brooke Collins.

"And that's the last that you saw of Brooke last night?"

Redd paced to the window to look out. "No."

Y ou saw her after that? Doing what?"

"She and Andy were outside. I guess... I don't know if the argument spilled outside, or she wanted to go to one of the other cabins to get away from him. But she ran out. And he ran out, and they were still talking, arguing, going back and forth, around the cabins..."

Creating at least part of the trampled-down snow trails outside. Like a bizarre game of fox and geese, a tag game she used to play in the snow at school.

"Did you see either of them... hurt each other?"

"Just chasing around. Arguing."

"I don't remember any of this," Collins insisted. "It doesn't make any sense."

"No." Redd lifted his hands up helplessly. "It didn't."

"So did they eventually go back inside?" Zachary asked.

"I don't know. They were all over the place, I had a hard time keeping track. And I was trying to watch the other shapes. Worried that the storm would come again when we had passed through the eye. If I went out there, I might get stuck in the blizzard or caught by one of the monsters. So I didn't... I didn't go back outside again. And I don't know... what happened eventually, if they both went back inside."

But of course, they knew that she hadn't gone back inside. Or if she had, initially, then she had soon left again. Going off into the woods. Being stabbed to death and dying out there of a stab to the heart.

"None of this makes any sense," Collins said. "We love each other. I would never do anything to hurt Brooke. She must have gone off and... did she trip and fall? Or maybe a wild animal...?"

"No." Kenzie decided she would have to be up-front about it. She couldn't very well keep the truth from Andy Collins. They were going to keep asking questions and guessing and making up bizarre excuses and explanations until it was all out in the open. The police might have made a different choice in their interrogations, but the police weren't there. And who knew how long it would be before they were. "Andy, I'm sorry to have to tell you, but your wife was stabbed."

"Stabbed." He looked at her with wide eyes. "What do you mean, stabbed?"

"With a knife or another blade-like instrument. In the chest. Somebody intended to kill her. And they succeeded."

"Who would do something like that? What kind of monster could even consider..." Collins shook his head in disbelief.

His choice of the word monster echoed what Redd had just said about being afraid of being caught by a monster outside. What the heck had been going on the night before? Weird stuff, Burknall and Redd had both said. But something must have triggered it. Some animal shape or noise? A person with a mask? Brittany in her furs?

What could Redd have mistaken for a monster? Or what had he taken to trick his brain into thinking that he had seen one? Collins claimed that he and Brooke had not taken anything, but she was pretty sure he was lying. Had they shared with Redd? Or had he taken something on his own? Or just had too much to drink and his writer's fertile imagination had taken over? How much of what he had seen in the night had been real and how much had been imaginary or a nightmare when he had nodded off to sleep?

"I don't know who it was," Kenzie said. She slid her chair an inch or two closer and leaned toward him. "I wanted to make sure that you don't have any injuries. I thought maybe if the two of you had fought off an intruder, like Redd suggested, or if you were both attacked in the woods... maybe you hit your head and you don't remember."

"No. I don't have any injuries," Collins said doubtfully. He ran his hands over his head, searching for a goose egg. He patted his body lightly. His chest in case, like his wife, someone had stabbed him and he had somehow failed to notice. He didn't appear to have sustained any injuries in his fight with Brooke or in the aftermath of that fight.

"Maybe I could take a closer look?" Kenzie offered. "I have some training in first aid." No need to tell him that she was actually a doctor. He would probably be more comfortable if he thought she was a nurse or had just taken a corporate first aid class. She stood up and approached him.

As soon as Collins nodded, Kenzie looked at Zachary to make sure that he had seen the man consent, and then moved in. She touched his head lightly. "I'm just going to make sure there are no bumps or bruising."

She took longer than he had to examine his scalp to make sure he didn't have any sign of a head wound. There wasn't anything. There was a scratch down one cheek that she hadn't noticed from farther away. A scratch that could have come from a stray tree branch on the trail. Or his wife's fingernail.

"One scratch here," Kenzie murmured, hopefully loud enough that Zachary's recorder would pick it up, "high on your left cheek. Let's see your hands."

He offered them to her palms-up. Kenzie checked for any cuts on his palm that might indicate he had been the one to stab Brooke, his hand slipping off the handle and running down the blade. She turned them over, checking the knuckles for bruising or split skin. "No marks on your hands."

She didn't lift up his shirt or make any examination of his torso. "And you don't have any injuries anywhere else? Any tender spots that I should check?"

"No." He moved experimentally, feeling his range of motion. "Sore muscles, that's all. As if I had worked out or slept on an uncomfortable bed."

Or the couch or the floor where he had eventually collapsed.

Or maybe he was sore from a physical altercation with his wife.

I can't understand what happened," Collins said. He dropped his head into his hands and held it as if it were throbbing. Depending on what he had partaken of the night before, he might have a pretty nasty hangover. Maybe things would get clearer when he was feeling better. But for the time being, she didn't think she was going to be able to get anything more out of him. The previous evening did appear to be one huge blank for him. There was no indication that he remembered anything that had happened after dinner, however bizarre it all seemed. "It doesn't make any sense. I can't believe that Brooke is dead. How could she be dead? Are you sure?"

"Yes, I'm sure."

As difficult as it was to call a death in the freezing temperatures Brooke's body had been exposed to, Kenzie knew that she wasn't going to revive when her body thawed out. Not with a stab wound through the heart. Kenzie gave Collins a smile that was as sympathetic as possible. "I'm so sorry. I think... you probably shouldn't be alone. Someone should stay with you."

She looked at Redd, who immediately understood. Redd looked at Zachary. "Maybe you could stay with him? I've already been with him... I should probably get breakfast. Get to work. I am here on a writing retreat, not just to relax."

As if anyone would relax sitting with the man whose wife had just been murdered.

"I need to stay with Kenzie," Zachary said. "Make sure nothing happens to her."

"She can just go back to her cabin. Or she can stay here with you. You can both stay here," he said brightly. "That would be better, wouldn't it?"

"We need to go find Vance Stiller," Zachary explained.

Kenzie's heart sank. She didn't want to deal with the man again. No matter what kind of mood he was in or what had happened the night before. She didn't want to ever speak to the insufferable man again. Especially not when she was feeling so tired and raw from everything that had already happened that morning.

"We need to," Zachary repeated softly, reading Kenzie's expression.

"I know."

"Sorry."

"Why do you need to go find Vance Stiller?" Redd demanded. "I can do that."

"We need to do it. But before we go..." Zachary looked at Kenzie, raising one eyebrow.

Kenzie was uncertain what he was trying to impart to her, what he expected her to say. She shook her head slightly. *What?*

"We should probably make sure that you're not hurt either," Zachary explained. "With everything that happened last night, all of that disruption and the weird stuff that happened. You could have gotten hurt too."

"I didn't hit my head," Redd insisted. "And I didn't fall asleep and dream this whole thing up, I'm telling you that."

"No, of course not," Kenzie agreed. "And Zachary's right. With all of that weird stuff, you'll want to know that you're okay."

He seemed far less certain of this than Collins, but when Kenzie approached him, he gave a shrug and let her take his hands, examine both sides and his forearms, and then his face. "No marks," Kenzie said for the recorder. "Face and hands are fine." She ran her hands over Redd's head, fingers light, alert for anything that was not as it should be. He was very warm. Did he have a fever? That might account for the claim he had seen monsters the night before. And it might account for anything he had seen of Andy and Brooke Collins, too. His was the only eyewitness testimony they had so far, but that might be tainted if he had a fever.

"Maybe a bit warm. Are you feeling okay?"

Redd felt his own forehead as if this might help him to answer the question. "I don't know. I feel strange, but I don't think I'm sick. I haven't been throwing up or anything. I don't have those usual 'flu-like symptoms' they're always talking about." He gave a small laugh. "Why is it so many diseases start with flu-like symptoms?"

"I don't know," Kenzie said, shaking her head. "It's a mystery, isn't it? Do you hurt anywhere else? Do you have sore muscles or joints?"

"No, all pretty much the same as usual. A little writer's elbow, maybe," he said, rubbing the back of his right elbow. "But that comes with the territory."

"Really." Kenzie knew that repetitive stress injuries for workers who used computers all day tended to be in the wrists and shoulders. But who knew what kind of posture he used at the computer? Maybe he did have writer's elbow.

"Okay, we better be going then," she told Zachary. "Let's see if Mr. Stiller is in his cabin."

Zachary nodded. He picked up the recorder and slid it into his shirt pocket without turning off the recording. They both went to the door and started putting on their warm-weather gear again. Kenzie was not excited about going out into the cold again. She had just started to thaw out.

"Do you know which cabin is Stiller's?" she asked Zachary.

"Farthest one back, I believe. He needs his privacy."

"Yeah, acting like he's better than any of the rest of us," Redd sneered. "That guy has got to be the biggest—"

"I agree," Kenzie headed him off. "And I don't usually say that about people. You know, a person can be wealthy and powerful without acting like a giant butthead. People like him give wealth and fame a bad name. I've met plenty of people who were very gracious and humble about a lot more fame and fortune than he probably has."

"He's got an inferiority complex," Redd agreed. "The ones like him always do. It doesn't matter how much they get what they want, they're always afraid that everyone else is better than they are. Or that someone else is better than they are. And they have to trample everyone down to prove it."

Kenzie nodded. "You're probably right about that." She lowered her voice and leaned closer to him. "Thank you so much for helping out with Andy. I just don't think he should be alone right now. You're being a really good friend. A really good human being."

Redd smiled, straightening to stand a little taller. "Of course. How could I leave him alone after something like that?"

Kenzie nodded. "Yeah. But thanks."

She turned back toward the door and, in doing so, tripped over the two pairs of boots standing to the side on the doormat. She set them back up carefully after a glance at the soles. Both were very similar to each other, maybe even the same brand and model, in slightly different sizes. Both similar to the treads of one of the pairs of the boots that had walked the same path as Brook Collins on her way to her death.

They went back out into the cold. Kenzie walked as quickly as she could to the farthest cabin away. They were all within easy walking distance. In the summer. In the cold temperatures, it was brutal. Kenzie held her hand up in front of her mouth and nose to keep them a little warmer, tucked her chin in, and hunched into the wind, looking down at the snow trail she was following. She had to look up every now and then to correct her course, but in a few minutes, they were outside of Stiller's door. Zachary raised his hand and knocked on it hard. The knock was muffled by his glove. They waited for a minute to see if Stiller had heard. When there was no response, Zachary took the glove off and knocked on the door as loudly as he could. He shook his smarting knuckles out and they waited again.

31

D o you think... he went out?" Kenzie suggested. "Maybe he went up to the farmhouse while we were talking to Collins?"

"No, I haven't seen him all morning. He didn't walk by the cabin while we were talking."

Kenzie didn't know how he had been able to keep an eye on what was going on outside and keep up with the conversation and everyone's faces and body language inside of the cabin at the same time. She felt exhausted from trying to read everyone's faces for any tells as she conducted the questioning.

"Then maybe... he could be in Brittany's cabin? If the two of them are together...?"

"Why would they rent separate cabins if he was planning to stay with her?"

"Maybe so that he had a place of his own to work. Or they might not have planned to spend the night together, but he fell asleep while they were at her place, so she just let him sleep there."

"It's possible," Zachary admitted. "He wouldn't have had to walk past our cabin to get to Brittany's."

"Maybe we should knock on her door?"

Zachary tried the doorknob. It didn't turn under his grasp. "Okay, we'll check hers. But if he isn't there..."

"We'll come back. I still have Mr. Dewey's keys."

"Yeah, okay." Zachary led Kenzie to one of the other cabins. She knew he was a private investigator, but it still amazed her how he knew which cabins were whose when it had never been discussed. When they had all introduced themselves at the dinner that first night, they hadn't introduced themselves by cabin number. Zachary had just paid attention. Kenzie had been so wrapped up in her own plans that she hardly even noticed who was next door to them.

Zachary knocked on the door. This time, there was an answer. Brittany opened the door and looked at them. "What is it? It's cold out there."

"Can we come in, then?"

She looked as if she would tell them no, but then took a couple of steps back and let Zachary and Kenzie in. She didn't indicate that they should make themselves at home. "What is it?" she asked, crossing her arms in front of her and rubbing her arms to warm them up.

"We were looking for Vance," Kenzie explained, assuming Brittany would probably be a bit warmer toward another woman. "There's no answer at his cabin, and we thought that maybe..."

"Why would he be here?" Brittany asked.

"I just got the feeling that... you two knew each other. Isn't that why you were both here?"

Brittany shrugged. "Maybe."

"But he's not around?"

"Not here. He's got his own cabin, that's probably where he is."

"Does he sleep late? I assumed he would be the type who was up before dawn to get a head start on making money."

"Yeah, he's usually an early riser," she admitted. "But he was up late last night, so maybe he decided to sleep in for once."

"Was everything okay last night? I mean... with the storm...? And the two of you didn't see anything unusual?"

"Unusual? Like Mrs. Andy Collins wandering off in the middle of the night? No. Why would we have seen anything? They wouldn't have to go by our cabins to get to the house. Maybe the barn, but why would they go to the barn? No hayrides in the middle of the night."

"Maybe there was something they needed. Help with a fire or finding candles when the power went out. I think Mr. Burknall was at the barn all night."

"I didn't see them," Brittany said, making a wiping-away gesture with her hand. Not something she was concerned about or wanted to talk about anymore. "There were a lot of strange sounds last night. Heard voices and howling. Maybe owls. They can be very creepy at night. Or wolves. Even a mountain lion. They make this screaming noise..."

Kenzie was a little surprised. She had pictured Brittany as the quintessential city girl. Someone who wouldn't know anything about mountain lion screams or owls that sounded like ghosts.

"You're right, yeah. So you heard a lot of noise. But you didn't think it was human."

"Animals can make sounds that you think are human. I just figured they were animal noises."

"Did you see Mrs. Collins at all last night? Were you at dinner at the house?"

"Yes, of course I was. You guys have guests, so maybe you don't want to socialize with us, but the rest of us... part of the reason we come here is to have a little fun. Do a little socializing outside of our circles, with people that we wouldn't have a chance to meet otherwise. People who aren't all starstruck and who have interests that extend beyond getting a celebrity's picture or autograph."

Kenzie nodded understandingly, even though that was never something she'd had to contend with. While people sometimes knew her by her parents' reputation and her family wealth, she hadn't had to worry about celebrity status and people always wanting something from her. She'd been able to be her own person, though she was expected to put in appearances.

"So after the dinner... did you all stay up at the house visiting, or...? I don't imagine there was a bonfire last night."

"Too windy and wet for a bonfire. Unless you want to soak the whole thing in gasoline." Brittany gave a short laugh. "No... we talked for a while, but everyone was feeling kind of restless and hemmed in by the weather. We wanted to get back to our cabins before it got so bad that we couldn't see them or get through the snow drifts."

"So you came back here. You and Vance?"

"No." Brittany gave Kenzie a hard, cold look. Then she finally thawed a little. "I went to his cabin. For a little while. I didn't spend the night. I wanted to be back in my own space. Everything just seemed... *off* last night. I thought it would be romantic to be caught in the storm. Power out, a fire and candlelight, cuddling under a blanket on the couch... talking half the night..." She shook her head. "But it wasn't like that. With the wind, and the noises... it just all seemed so wild and disjointed, and we were both out of sorts and couldn't agree on anything. Ugh. I hate it when you just can't... connect with someone."

Kenzie nodded.

"So after a while, I just said I wanted to come back here to get some sleep. It took me a long time to get settled in, but eventually I did get to sleep, and I didn't wake up until my alarm went this morning."

Kenzie must have shown her surprise that Brittany would set a wake-up alarm when she was on vacation. Brittany chuckled.

"I still vlog when I'm on vacation or traveling. I generally do it first thing in the morning so that it is done and I can work on other things the rest of the day. It's my job, so I am professional about it. I didn't turn my alarm off last night because I didn't think about it. Not having any power or internet capabilities today, I mean. So my alarm still went off. I did a recording anyway, and I'll post it when we have internet again. People will think it is exciting that I shared my blackout experience with them."

"And then you noticed that something was going on outside?" Kenzie suggested.

"Yeah, lots of voices. They carry when it's cold like this. So I put on my coat and went out to see what was happening."

"And you haven't seen Vance yet this morning?"

"No. I figured he's still in bed. He's usually an early riser too, but we were both pretty wrecked last night, so maybe he decided to sleep it off."

"Do you... want to check on him? I'm just worried with everything that has happened here that something could be wrong. It's possible that he's not just sleeping. He could be sick or need assistance."

Brittany looked uncertain of this. Her lips pursed and she considered, studying Kenzie and then Zachary. Apparently, she decided they weren't just paparazzi out to get a good shot of Vance. She nodded.

"I'll see if he's okay. That means that I'm going in there, not you."

Kenzie would have to be satisfied with that. "If there is anything wrong... I have some medical training."

"So do I." Brittany gave Kenzie a challenging stare. Kenzie had no idea what Brittany did in the real world before she had become famous. Or what she did now that she was. The woman was obviously intelligent. She could be a doctor, nurse, or first responder. Or maybe just someone who took first aid and felt qualified to make an evaluation when she went in.

Or it could be a lie and she had no training, and just didn't want anyone else near her boyfriend.

Her gaze held steady. Kenzie didn't know whether she was telling the truth or was a very good liar.

32

"Great," Kenzie said, forcing a smile. "I really appreciate your being willing to do that. We just want to make sure that Vance is safe and well. It's important for us to take care of each other, when we're isolated like this. There isn't anyone else he can rely on, no matter how much money he has."

"Yeah, well, money doesn't make people any more inclined to help you. It just means you pay a premium price for it."

Brittany sighed and reached past Kenzie to grab her coat from the peg by the door. She slipped her arms through the thick fur sleeves and pulled it around her. She pulled the hood over her head, almost obscuring her face. She drew leather gloves out of her pocket and pulled them on. Then she opened the door, letting in the frigid air once more, and they all stepped back out into the cold.

Even though they moved quickly, Kenzie was already feeling the cold by the time Brittany put her key in the lock. Her toes were numb. She hadn't had enough time inside Brittany's cabin to get thawed out.

Brittany knocked on the door a few times. Much more quietly than Zachary had. Then she turned the key and opened the door. She gave Kenzie and Zachary a look that clearly said they were to stay outside, not even standing just inside the door to get warmed up.

Kenzie wrapped her arms around herself and tucked her hands under her armpits. She stomped her feet, trying to get the blood circulating again, but they stayed numb. They were going to hurt when they started to warm up again.

"Vance?" They could hear Brittany calling him before she shut the door all the way.

"Do you think he's okay?" Zachary asked.

"Yes... probably. It sounds like he's maybe just sleeping off whatever they had to drink or any recreational substances that they enjoyed last night. I have to say, everyone certainly seems to have gone a bit overboard last night. Do you think it's just the idea that they were isolated? They wanted to escape their troubles with a little chemical assistance?"

"Maybe. It could have triggered a lot of fears... claustrophobia, being out of control, fear of death... maybe the kind of people who come here to escape are more likely to escape through others means as well."

"Yeah." It seemed strange, though, that she and Zachary would be the only ones to break that mold. They had booked the Lodge to get away from the stress in their lives, but neither of them was inclined to take drugs to escape.

They waited, stamping their feet and trying to stay warm. Kenzie started to relax. If Brittany had found Vance badly injured or dead, she would have come back for help. But since she hadn't, that hopefully meant that all was well. It still seemed like forever before Brittany came to the door again.

"He's fine," she said curtly.

"Can we come in and talk to him?"

"He doesn't need you. You can go back to your own cabin and warm up."

"I'd like to be able to see that he's okay," Kenzie said. "Forgive me for being so untrusting, but with everything else that has happened around here and two people dead, I think it is important for me to check. And we need to know if he saw or heard anything to do with Brooke Collins's death."

Brittany rolled her eyes. She blew out her breath and eventually nodded, gesturing them in. Once more, they were forced to stand just inside the door, not invited in to get comfortable. But at least it was warmer. Kenzie kept shifting her feet, trying to get the blood circulating again.

Vance was in his kitchen, heating what Kenzie supposed was instant coffee in a pot over a camp stove. Zachary tensed at the sight of the flame and watched it intently.

"Mr. Stiller," Kenzie said. "I'm glad to see you're okay. I just wanted to ask you about what you remember from last night. We're trying to get a picture of people's movements and to see if anyone saw Brooke Collins during the night."

He tapped on the side of the pot, as if that might encourage it to heat up faster. He was probably desperate for his caffeine fix. "Which one is that? The maid?"

"The newlywed," Kenzie told him crisply. He could at least have paid enough attention to his fellow vacationers to know who was who.

"Oh, her." He shook his head, rolling his eyes. "Not like she had anything to do with anyone but her husband. I don't think she even looked at anyone else. The rest of us might just as well not have been there."

Kenzie might have said the same thing about him. But apparently, he had noticed her behavior, even if he hadn't remembered her name. Even Kenzie hadn't known that her first name was Brooke until after she died. But Kenzie had known she was Mrs. Andy Collins.

"Did you see her?"

Stiller rubbed his temples. "I have no recollection of last night. I haven't the foggiest idea. I don't even know how I slept for so long. I never do that. But I feel like..." he squinted at her, his head obviously painful. "I don't know if it's the flu or what. I feel like I could sleep for another full day. Or two. I can barely focus."

"Would you mind if I have a look at you? If you have a fever or other symptoms..."

"Why would I want an accountant to examine me?"

He had, at least, remembered that much.

"I'm actually not an accountant. That was sort of a... misdirection." Kenzie smiled apologetically at Brittany as well. "I'm actually a doctor."

Stiller studied her balefully. "Sure you are."

"We're just supposed to take your word for that?" Brittany demanded. "After you have apparently lied to us already?"

"I'm sorry about that. We never foresaw that we could get into a situation like this where it could be important." Kenzie shrugged. "I just wanted to avoid getting asked to look at everyone's weird moles or hearing all of their other medical complaints."

"Then why would you want to know now?" Stiller asked.

Which was a good question.

He apparently decided that the coffee was warm enough. He wasn't going to wait any longer for his caffeine fix. He took it off the burner and poured it into a mug. He turned off the cook stove and Zachary relaxed visibly.

"I'm concerned by the deaths that we've experience already. Especially Brooke Collins's death. Mr. Dewey's looks like natural causes, but Brooke's... was not."

"What do you mean? Because she went outside and got hypothermia? That's natural enough. If she's stupid enough to go outside in the middle of a storm like this and to stay out until she's in trouble..."

"It was not hypothermia."

"I'm sure it contributed," Stiller argued.

"No. I don't think it did," Kenzie told him firmly.

He took a sip of the coffee and grimaced, either because it was still too cold, or just due to the fact that it was instant. Assuming it was instant.

"What was it, then?"

"Do you remember seeing her last night? If you think that she was outside and got hypothermia, then you must remember something."

He glanced over at Brittany. "Just something someone said."

"It wasn't hypothermia. It wasn't because she was outside."

"What happened then? A fall? I don't have a clue what everyone was doing outside. We weren't. We were inside where it was nice and warm and safe."

But it hadn't been particularly safe in the Collins cabin. Things had actually been rather dangerous.

"How do you know that you were inside when everyone else was outside?" Kenzie asked. He was clearly remembering some details. Or at least, some impressions.

"Why do you keep asking questions instead of answering them?" he shot back. He stared at her fiercely, challenging her to face him and discuss what exactly was happening.

Kenzie relented. "Brooke Collins was stabbed to death. She was murdered."

Vance's mouth fell open. Kenzie looked from him to Brittany, waiting for the woman's reaction. Brittany looked impassive. Maybe she had already guessed that part. Or maybe she didn't care.

"Murdered," Vance repeated, stunned. "Who killed her? Her husband?"

"We don't know yet." Kenzie looked at Zachary, gauging how much they should tell Vance. The fact that he had immediately assumed that it was Andy Collins who had killed his wife was telling. Zachary gave Kenzie a slight frown, indicating she shouldn't tell him too much. "No one saw what happened, and we are trying to find out where everyone was last night... even if you only saw her for a few minutes. It could be helpful."

"What would help is if I could remember anything at all about yesterday," Vance said, pressing the knuckles of his left hand into his forehead. "But the whole thing is a blank."

Kenzie frowned. It was the same line as Andy Collins had

given, though he only said he couldn't remember anything since supper. Had they both had too much to drink? Or had one particular choice of drink produced an amnesiac effect? She had assumed it was something that Andy and Brooke had taken together, to enhance their evening, but where was Vance in that equation? Unless they had bought something from him or sold it to him. She couldn't see them all just sharing illicit drugs out of friendship and goodwill. They didn't seem to have anything in common and Vance in particular was not the friendly type. He got Kenzie's hackles up every time they spoke.

"Did you take anything that might have contributed to this loss of memory? Have you ever experienced anything like this before?"

"I'm not the type to take recreational drugs," he said stiffly, which was exactly what Kenzie would have expected him to say, whether it were true or not. "I may occasionally have a drink or two for social occasions, but I do not drink to excess. I feel like... like I'm coming down with something. Or maybe I got food poisoning. I got roofied once in college; some stupid fraternity prank, and that felt very similar." He shook his head. "It's not a natural feeling."

Roofied. Food poisoning. There was one commonality among the other guests, and that was that they had all eaten the evening meal together. Kenzie turned this over in her mind.

What could have caused the symptoms that they had been encountering? Unusual anger, high, amnesia. There were many possibilities. Many substances, taken to excess, could cause one or all of those symptoms.

"Roofied," she repeated, looking at Zachary and Brittany. "That makes some sense. And if that's the case..." she looked back at Vance. "I wonder if we could get a sample... for later testing, when the police get here. It may be a few days, and we would want to preserve any evidence until then. If you took something or were given something, it will be gone from your system in a few hours or days."

"A sample? Like what?" He frowned. "You may be a doctor, but I still haven't seen any proof of your qualifications. I'm not letting any random person stab me with a needle."

"No... I was thinking more along the lines of... a urine sample."

"You want my pee."

Kenzie's face heated. She should have been professional enough for it not to embarrass her, but the circumstances were bizarre. She wasn't in a hospital or clinic setting. She was in some guy's cabin, trapped by the snow, asking for his pee. And what was she going to do with it? She needed a container. And then to keep it somewhere secure and cold. Somewhere cold wasn't a problem, but somewhere secure might be.

"If you've been roofied, you would want to know about it, wouldn't you? You would want to catch the person who did it."

He considered this, but didn't immediately say yes or no. Kenzie could understand that it would be a difficult thing for a man to admit to. Men were not the ones who were supposed to be targeted by such drugs. If a man were drugged, then of course that didn't make him weak or helpless, but it might make him feel that way. Society didn't give him a script to follow.

Stiller looked at Brittany, and at first Kenzie thought that he was seeking her opinion about whether he should try to find the culprit or not. But the look lasted, and Kenzie finally twigged onto the fact that *she* had been his date. She had been the one who was close to his drinks and who had gone back to his cabin with her. If someone had had clear access to his food and drink, it had been her. Kenzie looked at Brittany, weighing the possibility.

Brittany flushed red. She shook her head. "You think I would do a thing like that? Why? I can get whatever I want. From you or any other man. I have no reason to drug anyone." She wrinkled her nose. "Certainly not you."

Stiller chuckled rather than being offended by her declaration. He motioned her closer to him.

"You don't," he agreed. "Certainly not me."

Brittany held back at first, trying to maintain the same level of disdain, but she failed. She walked up to Stiller and he put one arm around her to snuggle her up close against his side, and then he nuzzled her cheek and kissed her.

"No need at all."

Kenzie looked away, waiting for the two of them to come back down to earth. Zachary caught her eye and raised an eyebrow at her. She just shrugged and shook her head. It certainly didn't look like there were any problems between Stiller and Brittany.

But that still left the question open. If someone had drugged Stiller, then who? And why? And had they drugged everyone at the dinner?

33

Eventually, Stiller and Brittany returned to the conversation. Brittany had a mischievous sparkle in her eye that hadn't been there before. Stiller was looking a little wider awake, but he still had a certain lethargy in his movements, and he didn't answer questions as quickly as Kenzie expected him to. As if he had to think them through and compose his answer carefully, which she hadn't seen him do before.

"So where does that leave us?" Stiller asked. "You can't think that I had anything to do with Mrs. Collins's death. Why would I? I didn't have any motive. And I have my own issues. Obviously, I can't swear that I never saw her. I could have had an hour-long in-depth conversation with her, but I haven't a clue. I can't tell you anything about last night or yesterday. Maybe she told me she was afraid her husband was out to kill her for her life insurance policy. But we'll never know now. If someone roofied me, if that's what happened, then they wiped that all out."

"Where we are now is, I want you to be tested when the police get here. And that means giving a sample now, before it all metabolizes."

"When do I have to decide?"

"Some drugs are out of your system pretty quickly. I would do it right away, to ensure the best results."

"I don't know. I don't think that's something I want to do. I have a reputation to maintain. People like me don't go around getting roofied. It just doesn't happen."

"And what if a video showed up of you doing something that you don't remember? Something worse than being targeted by another person. What if you did something or said something or hurt someone when you were under the influence? Under the influence of a drug that you didn't take voluntarily?"

Again, he looked to Brittany before answering.

"I think... that I'm better off keeping quiet. No one has any internet access here. If something comes to light... then I can work the story. But that will probably never happen. This was just... a weird night. Nothing criminal happened."

"Something criminal did happen," Zachary pointed out. "A woman was killed. And you were possibly drugged. Maybe others were too. Maybe to cover for the perpetrator of the murder. Maybe for some other reason. If you're being set up..."

"I didn't have anything to do with any of that."

"You don't remember."

"I don't remember," Stiller agreed, an edge to his voice. "And no one is going to convince me otherwise. So, no. You're not getting any piss or any other bodily fluids from me. And you're not getting any more cooperation. I'm done. I'm going back to bed."

"Sorry to have bothered you," Kenzie said. She stepped forward, off of the welcome mat. Onto the wood floor and across to the kitchen where Stiller and Brittany stood, separate from each other, just as they always were. A different class from everyone else. Lone wolves. Kenzie offered her hand to Stiller in a show of good sportsmanship and peace. He looked at her for a moment, then finally reached out his hand and shook hers. A firm shake, just a little bit harder than it needed to be. Showing her the edge.

That he had the upper hand. Kenzie smiled and released, withdrawing from him. "We'll see you around."

She stumbled over his boots at the door and set them upright again. They didn't look like a match for either of the treads she had seen, but they might not be his only pair of boots.

She and Zachary left the cabin, back out into the biting cold. They had seen almost everyone, and Kenzie hoped that meant that she could go back home. There was still Jack. They had talked to him earlier, but had not had a personal interview with him. Did they need to? And did they need to conduct interviews with the staff? Or could they leave all of that for the police to review? They had talked to the most likely suspect. They had done their best to preserve all of the evidence. They had made sure that Vance was okay and hadn't been another victim of violence. If he had been drugged, he wasn't going to allow them to test him. By the time the police got there, then whatever was in his system, if anything, would be gone.

Surely that meant that now she could go home and just relax for a bit. Warm her bones and have a little nap to regenerate.

"No marks on his hand?" Zachary asked as they walked back toward the cabin, the wind at their backs now.

"No marks on his hand," Kenzie agreed. "I'm pretty sure that he's right-handed, and there were not any blade marks or defensive wounds on his hand or wrist."

"So he isn't the culprit."

Kenzie nodded. She thought about it as they walked back to their cabin. "Or else whoever stabbed her was wearing gloves."

Zachary considered this. "Not just any gloves. Something pretty tough. Leather. Work gloves. Not just wool mittens."

"Yeah. And maybe the gloves have knife marks on them."

They both glanced around as if they might find a pair of leather gloves lying right there at their feet, as if it were a TV police drama and the clues would show up at exactly the right time.

"Might have burned them," Zachary said. "Or tossed them out in the woods. Or in the pond."

"The pond is frozen."

"Not the pond, then. Maybe buried under the bonfire wood. Or sliced into little bits and flushed."

"Maybe. Or maybe they didn't realize the gloves are cut. If they didn't get cut all the way through, maybe they don't even know."

"Maybe. Maybe we'll still be able to find them."

"Do you think Stiller was drugged?"

They reached the door to their own cabin. Zachary slowly twisted the knob to open the door. "Yes. I think he was."

"Yeah. Me too."

The kids were setting up games on the floor in front of the fireplace where it was warmest. They seemed resigned to loss of their electronic devices and the fact they would have to entertain themselves. People said that kids didn't know how to entertain themselves anymore, but Kenzie saw that they were quickly adapting. They had been at a loss the day before when plunged into the dark ages, but they seemed engaged now, discussing new games, rules, and possibilities. If it warmed up a little, they could kick the kids outside to play in the snow awhile. Make snowballs and snow angels and forts to defend themselves.

It was amazing how quickly she could forget about the real horrors that had happened not that far from their own back door. Would it even be safe for the kids to go outside to play? Would it be safe for the adults? How long would they have to stay inside before the police would arrive and take over the investigation?

"You guys have been a while," Tyrrell remarked. "I thought you would be back before now. I take it you found the missing lover?" He munched on a sandwich. Peanut butter, by the smell of it.

"Actually, we did find her," Kenzie admitted. "But..." A glance at the kids to make sure they were not listening too closely. "Things were not good."

Tyrrell's eyebrows went up. He looked at Zachary, seeking out the older brother whom he could communicate with more naturally than Kenzie, seeing whether he had interpreted her words and manner correctly or whether he had jumped to the wrong conclusion. "What?"

Kenzie began to divest herself of her outdoor gear. She wasn't going to go out there again for a very long time. Maybe not until spring. She was cold to her bones.

"Yeah," Zachary agreed, nodding, confirming that Tyrrell had understood correctly. "About as badly as possible."

"Oh, no. That's terrible. What are we going to do? Is someone going to get the police?"

Mason looked up from his game, alert to the mention of police.

"We can't get anybody right now," Zachary said. "The roads are not passable. We'll have to wait until the highway is plowed and Mr. Burknall clears the roads here. And that might be a few days. It's not snowing right now, but this storm is supposed to last at least another day, maybe more."

"Why do we need to call the police, Daddy?" Mason piped up. "They can come even if they can't drive on the roads. They could come in a helicopter."

Stiller had come in a helicopter. But the weather conditions had been far more favorable. "When the clouds clear and the winds die down," she agreed. "They can't get a helicopter here in this kind of weather. But you don't need to be worried. Everything is just fine."

Mason looked at Kenzie and immediately discounted her opinion. She could read it in his face. Which meant that there was something to be worried about and they needed the police to come.

"What are you talking about?" Alisha took longer to realize

that there was another conversation going on around her. One that she should pay attention to because it impacted her daddy and maybe others too. "What's wrong?"

"We have to call the police," Mason told her. "Where's your phone, Daddy? Why don't you call?"

"You know that we don't have any electricity right now," Tyrrell said. "I can't charge my phone. And I can't make a call without a signal. We'll have to wait until the storm is past."

"You have to try," Mason insisted. "Maybe if you hold it up high." He held his hands up in the air, looking up at them. "Sometimes if you go up high, you can make it work."

"Yes. Sometimes. But today I need to stay in the cabin and just wait. When the storm passes, then we should be able to make phone calls again."

"There's no storm right now."

"It's not blizzarding like it was. But there is still lots of cloud cover and trying right now would just run down my battery."

"Use the internet then," Mason directed. "Or send them a text."

"I know all the things to do. But I can't do them without a cell signal or a charged battery."

"A text doesn't take any battery. And Mommy says there is no charge for them because they are so small." Mason looked at Tyrrell with all the superior knowledge of an eight-year-old born into the technology age. Silly adults didn't always know how things should be done. But kids did.

Tyrrell looked pained. He pulled his phone out of his shirt pocket. "You can use it for five minutes," he said. "You show me how I can get ahold of the police."

Mason took it from him. Kenzie watched him hold down the power button to boot it up. She wouldn't have given in. She would have told him that it simply wasn't possible. He was wrong and simply didn't understand the situation. But Tyrrell didn't want the argument. He didn't want to be harassed about it. So he had given in.

Mason tinkered with the phone for a few minutes. He tapped the screen angrily.

"Daddy, there are *no bars*, and the text says, 'not sent.'"

"Yes. I know. That's because there is no signal."

"But there has to be a signal." Mason held the phone up over his head. He went into the kitchen and stood on a chair and held it over his head. He stepped onto the table and held it as high as he could reach. Zachary went over to the table and put his arms out. Mason looked at him for a moment and then allowed Zachary to pick him up and put him on his shoulders. Zachary wasn't tall, but Mason could almost touch the ceiling with the phone as he strained to get it higher. "We need to go outside. I could climb a tree."

"You can't climb a tree in weather like this," Tyrrell told him. "It's cold and icy. Very dangerous."

"You climb it then."

"No. Not me either. I'll fall on my a— on my backside. Maybe I'll break it. You want me to break my backside?"

Mason giggled. He finally gave up on being able to reach anyone by phone. He reached toward his father with the phone. Zachary walked over so that Mason could hand it to him. Mason kicked his feet as if Zachary were a horse that needed a good kick to get going. He bent down to speak in Zachary's ear.

"There's no signal."

"No," Zachary agreed.

34

It took a long time for Kenzie to get warmed up again. She sat as close to the heater as she dared and toasted her feet. She warmed her hands, rubbing them together. She rubbed her toes. She wrapped a blanket around herself and stayed under it until she was sweating. It was not going to be easy to get her back out there. She was done. Enough investigating. She would wait until the police got there. They would relay everything they knew to the police and let them sort it out.

Zachary had a granola bar without prompting and made Kenzie toast. He didn't actually toast it, but he put bread and marmalade on a slice of bread and served it to her sitting in front of the heater. He sat at the table watching her.

As the kids went back to their games and argued noisily with one another, Kenzie and Zachary gradually imparted all the details to Tyrrell. He kept shaking his head in disbelief.

"What is going on in this place?" he asked. "This is all so bizarre. Like reading a murder mystery by Agatha Christie. Everyone being picked off one by one, you know?"

"They're not," Kenzie said firmly. "Mr. Dewey died of natural causes. There has only been one homicide." Kenzie glanced at the children and then went on. "The most likely suspect is the husband. He didn't have any marks on his hands, but maybe he was wearing gloves and didn't get any cuts. They had an argument, things got out of hand, and..." She shrugged. "The same thing happens in the city. Believe me. I know."

"Of course it does," Tyrrell agreed. "But how do you know that's what happened here? It sounds like everybody was hopped up on drugs."

"It does," Kenzie admitted. "I wonder about what they ate at the dinner last night. Maybe there was something in it... some mold or fungus that is hallucinogenic."

"I doubt it was anything like that," Zachary disagreed. "For all of them to have symptoms, they all had to be dosed. If it were just a few spores of some mushroom, then one person, maybe two would get enough to have an... experience. But for all of them to be acting strangely? There had to be enough to dose everyone. Or maybe it was in all the drinks." He closed his eyes, thinking about it.

"How could it be in all of the drinks?" Kenzie challenged. "No one could know what everyone was going to drink and put it into all of the drinks being served. What about the person who decides that they just want a glass of water? From a pitcher or straight from the tap?"

"It could have been dissolved into each of the glasses," he suggested. "Dissolved and then the water evaporated, so that the drug was already in each of the glasses. It would mix with whatever was poured into them."

"And just what do you suggest it was? And why would anyone do such a thing? I think it must have been an accident. What about carbon monoxide? There could be a problem with the furnace at the farmhouse. Everyone got dosed with carbon monoxide. Just enough to affect their moods and thinking, not enough to cause physical symptoms like vomiting or passing out."

"Maybe. A gas would explain a lot. That would be easy for someone to release in a room, without anyone noticing or tasting anything."

"I didn't mean intentionally. I meant a faulty furnace."

"I know. I'm just thinking."

"But there's no reason to do something like that. Was this just... a prank? Like when Stiller was roofied in college? Someone just thought that it would be funny to contaminate everyone here, to see whether they did anything funny? Saw flying pink elephants?"

"I've never hallucinated flying pink elephants," Zachary said, cocking his head and looking at Kenzie.

"That was just an example."

"But why do they show things like that on TV? Funny, silly, safe things? They make hallucinating look like... a fun party game. When it's nothing like that. At least... I've never had any hallucinations like that."

"Uh... how many times have you hallucinated?" Kenzie asked. She wasn't sure she wanted to know the answer. Things had been bad for Zachary as a teen and a young man, and she would be the first to admit that she didn't know what kinds of things he had gotten into during that time. He could have been into all kinds of illegal drugs and activities.

"I don't know," Zachary shook his head. "More than I can count."

"Oh...?"

He laughed at her expression. "Reactions to meds. Fevers. Stuff they had me on when I was recovering from my burns. Meds that they aren't supposed to prescribe together." He shrugged. "It isn't like I wanted to hallucinate. Like I said... I never saw flying pink elephants. Some of it was innocuous. But usually... it was pretty scary."

Kenzie chuckled along with him, relieved. She wouldn't judge him if he had experimented with drugs when he was a kid. Lots of people did, and he'd certainly had a crappy enough life to have wanted to escape from it however he could. But she was happy that he hadn't been taking hallucinogens intentionally. Some of those could really mess up a person's brain, and

Zachary had a hard enough time without doing that kind of damage.

"Well, maybe you've got a point there. Maybe it was someone who bought into the TV image of hallucinogens. That it's just a fun time, silly and harmless. Maybe it was just someone who wanted to spice up the dinner hour."

"Jack?" Zachary suggested.

Kenzie shrugged one shoulder, tilting her head to the side as she considered. "Maybe. He's the kind of guy I would expect to stir the pot. To want to see what would happen if he tried something like that."

"But we have no evidence."

"What we really need to do is to find whatever they were given. If Jack or someone else put something into the food, then there must be a pill bottle or something around as evidence."

"Yes." Zachary didn't say anything for a while and Kenzie thought that the conversation was over. Then he tapped his fingers on his knees, restless, and leaned forward to talk to her. "You're absolutely sure that Mr. Dewey's death didn't have anything to do with this?"

"How could it? He died the day before."

"I don't know. If someone is intentionally poisoning the guests with some hallucinogen, then why couldn't they have poisoned him the day before?"

"But... that would imply that they wanted to kill everyone else," Tyrrell objected. "If you poison one person, and they die, then if you poison half a dozen other people... you do it knowing that they could all die."

Kenzie was inclined to agree. But Zachary shrugged.

"Some people wouldn't care about that. Or it could be someone who knew that he had a heart condition and that it wouldn't do the same kind of harm to someone who didn't."

Kenzie shook her head slowly. "I don't know, Zachary. It doesn't seem likely. Like Tyrrell said, it isn't exactly logical."

"In my experience, people who intentionally hurt and kill

other people aren't logical. They don't think the same way as you do. My question is *could* it be the same substance? Could the same thing kill Dewey and cause the others to have a bad trip?"

"Yes," Kenzie admitted. "There are a number of substances that could cause both heart problems and hallucinations."

Zachary sat back, looking satisfied.

"But I still don't think that's what happened," Kenzie warned.

"It's your job to be skeptical. You can't advance any theory on a death unless there's some evidence to back it up. I don't need evidence or proof to speculate."

Kenzie looked at Tyrrell, who shrugged. "He's got a point," he pointed out. "You guys are coming at it from two different backgrounds."

Zachary got up and started to pace. "I do think we should go to dinner tonight."

35

W hat?" Kenzie was floored. "Why would we go to dinner if you think that everyone was poisoned there and whoever did it has not been caught? What's to stop them from doing it again?"

"Well, I wouldn't suggest eating anything you didn't watch being prepared. But I think we should see if we can get everyone to buy in on a search of the cabins for any medications that might have been used to do this. And the knife, for that matter."

Kenzie blinked, thinking about it. "If someone did this intentionally, why would they agree to a search of their cabins? Why would anyone agree to a search?"

"Because if the majority agree, they would look guilty for arguing against it. Whoever did it... they probably didn't come out here with the intention of poisoning everyone. They probably have a legitimate reason for having whatever it is, whether it's medical or recreational. They can say that someone else got into it. We can't prove who actually had access to it."

"Then what's the point in doing a search?"

"To secure the poison. To make sure that they can't do it again tomorrow. The police can sort it all out when they get here, but that doesn't mean we have to be sitting ducks."

"I doubt whether everyone will go to dinner tonight. They'll probably all be too spooked."

"I don't think everyone else realizes that they were all poisoned. Stiller and Collins can't remember what happened. The others just know that Andy Collins and Brooke had a fight and Brooke ended up getting killed. They don't all have the big picture, that they all had symptoms. I think they'll still want to get together to find out more about what happened to Brooke, or at least to gossip about it if they can't get any facts."

"He's probably right," Tyrrell agreed. "Whenever something bad or shocking happens, people want to talk about it. They are isolated and can't even post about it on social media. The only social group is the rest of the vacationers. Maybe Collins will want to stay home and won't go to dinner, but the rest probably will. With us, we've got our own little group here," Tyrrell made a motion that took in Kenzie and Zachary and the children. "But most of the others are on their own. They won't want to be totally isolated for days."

Kenzie didn't relish the idea of trying to convince a group of vacationers to let other people search their belongings. It was, as Tyrrell had said, like being stuck in the middle of an Agatha Christie novel. Except the sleuths in those mysteries always seemed to be in charge and to know exactly what they were doing. Kenzie didn't have any authority and didn't even want to be involved in the whole mess.

"But we're not all going to go up for dinner, right?" Kenzie looked at the children. "I don't think... probably just Zachary and I..."

Tyrrell nodded. "Yeah. I don't want my kids anywhere near this psycho."

They spent most of the day resting and staying warm. Napping, playing with the kids, grazing on their snacks and leftovers. Tyrrell and Zachary had moved the perishable leftovers from the fridge to a snowbank outside, hoping that there were sealed well enough that the animals would not smell them and get into them. The little cook stove worked well for heating up small amounts of the leftovers at a time, though Zachary disappeared every time it was in use. Kenzie thought it was progress that he wasn't having a meltdown over it, just moving to where he couldn't see the flame.

They talked about the strange night once or twice more, puzzling over some of the details. But they didn't come to any conclusions. They didn't have enough clues to point them in the right direction, and too many suspects. Too many, and not enough, because while pretty much everybody had opportunity, no one really had a motive to kill Brooke. Aside from Andy, who might have regretted his decision to marry her or have been after her life insurance. No one else had any reason to kill her. It was probably just the unfortunate effect of whatever hallucinogen they must have been exposed to.

As the dinner hour approached, Kenzie changed her clothes, tried to finger-comb her hair into some order, and gave up on applying makeup by the green light of a glow-stick. She was just going to do more harm than good, and who cared whether she had made herself up for a dinner that was going to be held in near darkness?

They grabbed a few glow sticks for the dinner, hoping they'd be able to prevail upon the others to forgo candles, put on their heavy winter gear, and trudged up to the farmhouse at the top of the road.

It had started snowing again. It wasn't blowing like the night before, but big, fluffy flakes floated gently to the ground, and Kenzie suspected it would pile up pretty quickly. How long was it going to take them to dig out? When the weather system eventually passed over, would the rescue be immediate? Or would it take several more days for them to plow the highway? What other jobs would take precedence over the road? If there were power and phone lines down, people trapped in various farms throughout the county, and possible medical emergencies to deal with, how far down the list would the Lodge be?

When they reached the house and let themselves in at the front door, Kenzie glanced over at Zachary. He began removing his coat and other gear, a grim expression on his face. He was probably wondering exactly the same thing. How much longer?

Inside, the mood was a bit giddy, even celebratory. Not the kind of gathering one would expect when two people of their company had died. But death was like that sometimes. People had to escape the grief and pain however they could, often with inappropriate jokes, comedic movies, or loud carousing. There was a reason they had a term for gallows humor.

"Kenzie! You decided to join us today!" Raven gave Kenzie a dazzling smile, as if they were best friends, and leaned close to buss both cheeks. "How was your day?"

"Well, I'm glad we have the kids around to help keep us entertained. When you're trying to keep someone else engaged, it doesn't leave much time to be bored."

"You should have brought them up! I would have liked to meet them. They're your niece and nephew?"

Raven had seen them on the hayride. She hadn't seemed very interested in them at that point. But that was then. They lived in a whole different world now.

"Zachary's. Tyrrell is his brother."

"And remind me their names?"

"Mason and Alisha."

"What great names. They seem like fun kids."

Kenzie nodded. "Like I said, it's nice to have someone else to worry about. And they keep the atmosphere light."

"Zachary, good to see you again." Raven shook his hand, touching his elbow with her other hand as if they were old friends and she was extending her sympathies to him. "How are you holding up? I wondered, with the power being out and you having to deal with F-I-R-E."

"You don't need to spell it. Mr. Burknall brought us a

propane-fueled heater, so we don't have to have a fire. And we have these." Zachary showed off a couple of the glow sticks. "To replace candles. Hopefully, no one here will mind so much…"

"What a great idea. I didn't even know there *was* a propane heater."

Zachary shrugged. Why would she? Burknall had known, and he'd known what to do about it.

They were welcomed into the small circle of vacationers. Because they were bored? Because Kenzie and Zachary were fresh meat? Kenzie excused herself from the gathering.

"I just wanted to see how Mrs. Hubbard is doing. I'll be back in a few minutes."

She felt awkward going back to the kitchen, where she hadn't been invited and probably wasn't welcome. But she had a job to do, and she'd just have to bluff her way through as if she belonged there.

"Knock knock," she called out as she walked through the archway into the kitchen. There was no door to knock on to announce herself, and she didn't want to sneak up on Mrs. Hubbard and give *her* a heart attack.

The older woman startled anyway. She turned around and looked at Kenzie. "Oh. Hello, dear. Can I get you something?"

"Oh, no. I'm not back here to make any special requests. I just wanted to see how you are doing. I know it hit you pretty hard, losing Mr. Dewey like that."

"I don't want you to think that there was anything between us," Mrs. Hubbard started. "It wasn't like that."

"I didn't think it was. You've worked with him for years. Of course you would be upset and shocked by the whole thing."

Mrs. Hubbard nodded. "Yes, that's right. You don't know what it's like. Even if we weren't that close, it's still like losing a family member."

"I'm sure it is. I guess maybe you heard from Mr. Burknall that I'm not actually an accountant…"

Mrs. Hubbard gave her a sideways look, then nodded. "That's what he said."

"I work at the medical examiner's office. So I know what it's like, how shocking it can be to lose someone."

"Yes." Mrs. Hubbard gave each of the pots on the stove a stir.

Kenzie stepped closer to have a look, surprised to see the stove in use. Mrs. Hubbard smiled.

"It's propane. This isn't the first time we've had a snowstorm."

"I guess not! I didn't even think about it until now. I guess I pictured you working on a little camp cook stove like we have been."

"Not for a big meal like this. Wouldn't be practical. We can pretty much carry on here like usual, power or not."

"That's great." Kenzie smiled and hovered, trying to think of a way to segue into the subject she wanted to bring up.

Mrs. Hubbard eyed her, then hummed as she moved around the kitchen.

"Umm... I wondered if you get lonely in here, working all by yourself all day," Kenzie offered.

"No, I don't mind working by myself. And I'm never alone for long. The staff come and go. Samantha is in here and helps with the serving. Sometimes she gives me a hand if there are a lot of dishes to assemble. Mr. Dewey, he was always in and out, checking on things, testing new dishes, just shooting the breeze." She looked pensive. "He was lonely after Mrs. Dewey passed. It was hard for him. They'd been together for so long, he wasn't used to doing it all on his own. And even if he had all of the help that he needed, there was still... he still missed her. And he was too old to start up with someone new. Maybe folks do remarry when they're old these days, but Mr. Dewey wasn't part of the social scene. There aren't many people to visit with up in these parts. We're pretty isolated. He always liked it, before. Anyway..." Mrs. Hubbard tapped a spoon on the edge of one pot to shake the sauce off and set it to the side. "He was around a good deal. And Mr. Burknall, he is the same. He'd be up at the house to talk to

Mr. Dewey, and he'd drop in to say hello and see what was cooking. You might think this is a lonely place, but it isn't."

As if proving her point, Samantha appeared in the doorway. "Natives are getting restless. Can I give you a hand with anything else?"

"No, we're done. Just the serving now."

"What about guests?" Kenzie asked.

"What about guests?"

"Do *they* ever stop in? Or are they banned from the kitchen?"

"Oh, nobody is ever banned," Mrs. Hubbard shook her head. She and Samantha started to get out serving bowls and to transfer the contents from the pots on the stove and some plastic storage bowls in the fridge. "Guests don't have the run of the place, but they're welcome to stop in and say hello, see what's going on. People are often very interested in all of the work that goes into running this place." She smiled. "Some of the women are so used to doing all of the cooking at home that they don't know what to do with themselves after a day of vacationing. They're in here, looking for some way to help out."

"And everyone who is here now? Have any of them been into the kitchen?"

Mrs. Hubbard shrugged. "Yes. Of course. I can't think of who has been in and out, but some of them have been around to talk or see how the sausage is made, so to speak."

"You must have a lot of patience, to put up with all of that coming and going. I thought you would be lonely, but maybe it's the opposite. Maybe you wouldn't mind having some time to yourself for a while."

She smiled pleasantly. "It's been a good job. I don't know what I'm going to do if they decide to shut the Lodge down. I don't know where I'll go."

Kenzie nodded and excused herself, returning to the others before they could start to wonder what was taking her so long. Mrs. Hubbard certainly wouldn't have any motive to want Mr. Dewey out of the way, seeing how it had put her job at risk. It wouldn't be easy for her to find something else if she found herself out of a job now.

She returned to the dining room to find everyone assembling around the table. She found that she and Zachary didn't need to part with their last few glow sticks, as the table was lit by an LED lantern. Mr. Burknall seemed satisfied with the arrangements and left via the kitchen, presumably getting his own dinner on the way out.

Kenzie and Zachary followed the plan they had worked out that afternoon in their cabin, dishing up the meal as if they were going to eat with the other guests, so that they would fit in and not make anyone feel uncomfortable. But then they would broach the rather uncomfortable topic of searching everyone's cabins.

36

Jack was eyeing Kenzie as she dished up her food and passed the serving bowls around the table. She tried to ignore his looks, but she could feel him watching her even when she turned away from him.

"I assume everyone has heard the latest news about our lady accountant," Jack said, looking around the table to make his announcement.

Well, that was one way to break the ice.

"What about her?" Raven asked.

"That she's not an accountant at all. She's been pulling the wool over everyone's eyes. Pretending to be one thing when she is actually another."

Raven raised her brows, looking bored with his dramatics. She clearly recognized his need for attention and would not play into his hands. She continued to dish up the meal.

"She is a doctor," Jack announced. Trying to get her attention back. He looked around the table self-importantly. "Not just a doctor, but a medical examiner."

There was a crash as Samantha put a bowl down too hard, rattling all of the silverware and china on the table. Kenzie laid her palms on the table, trying to stop the vibrations.

"Sorry," Samantha apologized. "It's the lighting. I missed the edge of the table."

Or had it been something else? Kenzie watched her, interested in her reaction. She, at least, had not heard the gossip about Kenzie's real profession. After everyone stopped reacting to Jack's announcement, Kenzie corrected him.

"I am not a medical examiner. Not yet. I assist in the medical examiner's office."

Jack sat back in his seat, smirking. "You're certainly no accountant."

"No, I think anyone who looked at my check book would agree about that," Kenzie said. Though she was really no slouch in the financial department. "As I said to Mr. Burknall... I was just hoping to avoid having to look at everyone's weird moles or to discuss other medical issues and diagnoses." She shrugged. "I'm sure that anyone who has a doctor in the family has heard it all before. A doctor is never off duty. Everyone is always looking for special advice."

The guests looked at one another, sorting out who had known this fact before Jack's announcement and who had not. Looking around the table, Kenzie was glad that both Andy Collins and Redd Flagg had made it to the dinner. Even Vance Stiller, who had sounded as if he would be in bed the rest of the day, had managed to make it to the farmhouse for the dinner. Probably because he didn't want to have to scrounge his own. She doubted he had brought a bunch of snacks or ready-to-eat meals for himself.

"So you can tell how Mr. Dewey died. And... you know... Mrs. Collins," Raven said, with a sympathetic nod to Andy Collins, acknowledging his loss and apologizing for bringing her death up.

"I only know a limited amount," Kenzie said. "I obviously can't do a full autopsy here at the Lodge, and it wouldn't be my place to do so. All I've done is make observations and to preserve the bodies the best I can for the authorities when they are able to make it here. Just like we told everyone already."

"But you didn't say that you knew all that stuff before. That you are trained."

"No. I didn't. But we decided to share it now, because I think it is important for everyone to know." Kenzie smiled at Jack to show that she had been planning on sharing that news at dinner anyway. Stealing his thunder. He didn't smile back.

"Why does it make any difference now?" Stiller demanded. "Like you say, you're not doing an autopsy. You're not here as a medical examiner." He made a face when he looked at her, maybe remembering how she had told him she was a doctor earlier in the day, offering to examine him and suggesting that he preserve a sample of his urine for testing. The fact that she was the kind of doctor who worked on dead people did not make him well-disposed toward her. Kenzie had encountered that reaction before. As if she were some kind of vampire or zombie and her touch was unclean. Despite the fact that she nearly scrubbed her skin off every time she had been assisting in autopsy.

"Well... I have been thinking about... what happened here last night. And I have some concerns."

They just looked at her blankly.

"Several of you have talked about hallucinating or not being able to remember what happened last night. Or about others being aggressive."

Looks were exchanged, but no one jumped in to either confirm this observation or to deny it.

"And I wonder whether there was something in the food or drinks last night. Something that caused those symptoms."

Raven stopped with her fork raised, ready to take a bite. The others reacted in various ways, some of them stopping and putting down their cutlery, and others continuing to eat as if they didn't have any concerns about the food.

"What do you mean? Who would put something in the food?" Jack asked. He smirked. He gave a bit of a muffled chuckle before stifling it. Kenzie wondered whether he was intentionally giving off signals to make her think him more suspicious, or if he could possibly be stupid enough to gloat over the thought of what he or someone else had done. She decided to assume that he was not stupid at all, but just trying to get her riled up. That made it easier to stay calm and collected.

The others at the table were thinking about the question. Who would have put something in the food? And why? Had their symptoms been caused by a foreign substance, or was Kenzie just being paranoid? She was a medical doctor, or so she now claimed.

"What makes you think that someone put something in the food?" Redd asked.

"Because you all had symptoms, one way or the other. Hallucinating. Seeing monsters or thinking you could see or hear something weird and out of place. Noises in the night. People fighting who wouldn't normally fight with each other." Kenzie didn't look at Andy Collins, but let everyone draw their own conclusions. "And those of you who can't remember what happened since dinner last night. Or even for all day yesterday. You all agree that weird things were going on last night, and that you didn't feel well or feel like yourself this morning."

There was silence around the table. No one was eating any longer. Kenzie saw that Mrs. Hubbard and Samantha were hovering in the doorway, listening and not serving or preparing anything else.

"And then there was what happened to Mrs. Collins," Kenzie said gently. "You have to admit that her death was not something that could have been expected or predicted. A healthy young woman. No one expected her to die. No one would have expected her to run out into the snow in the middle of the night. And no one would have expected her to be attacked and killed in the woods. None of that is normal. And if you have been paying any attention to the media, you know that certain drugs can cause hallucinations and violent behavior. They can make people do things that they would normally not have done."

"We aren't exactly in New York," Jack Fowler sneered. "Exactly where do you think someone got these drugs? There isn't a drug dealer on the corner as you drive in. We're out in the middle of nowhere."

"People may have brought medications or recreational drugs with them. Maybe never planning for them to end up in the meal, but... it is a possibility."

"No one *accidentally* put drugs into the food," Jack pointed out. "If this really happened, then it was intentional. You're telling us that someone intentionally put drugs in our food that could have killed someone. That maybe *did* result in someone getting killed."

Kenzie nodded. She had hoped to gloss over that point. To say that the food had been tainted without dwelling on the fact that someone had intentionally poisoned it. Because then the guests would be looking at each other exactly the way that they were now, with suspicion and disbelief. It was almost too bizarre for anyone to believe. They would rather categorize it as something that was too bizarre to have happened than to protect themselves further.

"What I would like to do," she said slowly, "is to check each of the cabins, and of course the house and the outbuildings, and to gather up any medications or other substances that could be used that way. And by doing that... prevent it from happening again."

"You're saying that one of us is a killer," Brittany said baldly. "You think that someone killed Mrs. Collins, and that whoever did that might do it again."

"Someone *did* kill Mrs. Collins," Kenzie said. "I don't know whether it was premeditated or if it was just the result of someone being high on whatever substance might have been administered to the food. But whether it was intentional or not, I don't want it to happen again." Kenzie looked around the table at the food still on everybody's plates. No one was eating any longer.

"Why should you be the one to do this search?" Redd asked. "What makes you more qualified to do it than, say, me?"

"The fact that I am a doctor means that I'll have a better idea whether any particular medication could lead to hallucinations and some of the rest of the stuff that went on last night."

"And you're going to do this by yourself? You could frame anyone you wanted to. You could be the one who poisoned everyone, and you just want to shift the blame to someone else."

"Actually. If you think about you, you'll remember that we were not at the house yesterday. Not at any time. We had no opportunity to poison the food. We were never in the house, let alone the kitchen."

"Could have snuck in," Redd said petulantly.

"I think if we had been here, someone would have seen us."

No one jumped in to say that they had seen either Kenzie or Zachary at the house the day before. Everyone was quiet.

"You can talk to Mrs. Hubbard. She can confirm that we were never in the kitchen or anywhere near it."

Heads turned toward the kitchen, where Mrs. Hubbard and Samantha were listening. Mrs. Hubbard shook her head. "No, they were never around." Her eyes went around the table to the rest of them. Mentally checking off who she had seen at the house the day before and who had stopped into her kitchen for a chat or to smell or taste the dishes on the stove? Thinking about just who'd had the opportunity to tamper with the food?

"Well, if anyone might have poisoned us all at dinner last night, you know who the most likely suspect is," Vance Stiller announced, fixing his gaze on Mrs. Hubbard. "There's only one person who has unlimited access to the food."

"I did no such thing," Mrs. Hubbard snapped. "After all these years, why would I decide to poison my guests now? You think I'm crazy? What happens to my job if I do that?"

"The same thing that happens to you if Mr. Dewey dies," Jack said. "You lose your job. Is it any coincidence that right after he dies, this happens? Maybe he knew she was a poisoner and he's the only thing that kept her from murdering everyone before."

It was a ridiculous accusation. Jack looked away, as if it had sounded false even to his own ears.

But of course Mrs. Hubbard had to be a suspect. Anyone who had access to the food had to be a suspect and she was the one with the most access. Anyone else would have had to get past her.

37

I don't think that any of us have all the information that we need to make any accusations," Kenzie pointed out. "The fact is, practically anyone here could have tampered with the food at some time yesterday. But what's done is done, and the police will have to do what they can to sort it out. My concern is to prevent anything from happening again. We don't want anything to happen to anyone else here."

Raven reached for her drink, then pulled back her hand and just stared at her glass. If the alcohol had been poisoned, they had already had their cocktails. Was it possible that every bottle had been tainted? Or every glass, as Zachary had suggested to Kenzie earlier? Kenzie thought it more likely that the toxin had been put in the food.

"So you want to conduct this search on all the cabins," Jack said. He spread his hands wide. "Well then, have at it. Why not?" He looked challengingly around the table, daring anyone to argue with him.

"I don't want anyone going through my things," Redd objected.

Stiller nodded. "Absolutely not. I'm not having anyone pawing through my possessions either. I have some very... high-end arti-cles. I don't want anyone near my things."

There were murmurs of agreement around the table.

"So," Zachary spoke up, "you're good with either being poisoned again or not eating here for the duration. Until the plows get through and the police can begin an investigation." He shrugged. "Okay."

"Why not let people bring their own medications here?" Redd suggested. "Anyone who has anything can declare it, and Kenzie can say whether it could have caused these hallucinations, and if it could, we flush them."

"What an idiot," Andy Collins said flatly, voicing what pretty much everyone around the table was already thinking. "You think that whoever intentionally poisoned everyone else is just going to bring forward the poison because we ask him to? Or *her*? And *flushing* everything to get rid of the evidence? Just what do you have in your cabin that you're so worried about them finding?"

Redd's eyes darted around the room, landed on Kenzie briefly, and flitted away again. "Look..."

"Of course you have to search the cabins," Collins said. "Start with mine. Whenever you want. Go ahead and look through all of my stuff and all of my wife's things. Because I want to know who did this. I want to prove to everyone here that I did not kill my wife. I know that's what you're all thinking, so there's no point in looking so shocked. Go ahead. Search my cabin."

Kenzie nodded. That was two down. She looked around the table, waiting for other volunteers.

"You can search mine," Brittany agreed. "I've got nothing to hide."

Kenzie looked at Jack Fowler, waiting for his offer. When he didn't say anything, she moved on to Raven. Raven rolled her eyes and laughed. "Well, you're going to find a whole pharmacy of pills in my cabin. I'll admit that straight out. I've got pills to put me to sleep and pills to wake me up. And for just about anything else you can think of. Could any of them cause hallucinations?" She shrugged. "I have no doubt. So go ahead and look, and confiscate whatever you think is dangerous. As long as you'll dispense them to me whenever I need them." She laughed, bringing out several smiles around the table.

Eventually, everyone agreed. The naysayers were outweighed by those who had already agreed, and peer pressure did its thing. Eventually, they got everyone's consent.

The prevailing opinion was that Kenzie and Zachary would need to be accompanied by someone else to ensure that they were not planting evidence, and that their cabin would need to be searched as well. After some discussion, Raven was nominated to accompany them.

Kenzie tried not to think about the long night before them. Even if they only took fifteen to twenty minutes on each cabin and building, it would be hours before they were finished. It was already dark. People were hungry and grumpy, afraid to eat anything that had been prepared, no matter how much Mrs. Hubbard tried to convince them all that it was safe. How could she possibly know that, when she didn't know how the food or drinks had been tainted the day before?

"You must have canned food in the pantry," Zachary suggested to Mrs. Hubbard.

"Yes. Of course. All kinds."

"How about everybody gets a can of something that doesn't have to be prepared, and everyone opens their own can and eats it without anyone else touching it?"

"Yes!" Raven said with relief. "I'm starving, but as good as this smells, I can't eat it. Not now. There is no way someone could get poison into a sealed can, right?"

Kenzie couldn't think of a way, unless they had a canning machine of their own, and that would be rather elaborate. No one else offered any objections to this plan, and Mrs. Hubbard took everyone's orders for what food they wanted brought from the pantry.

"Kenzie and I have already eaten," Zachary said, "so I think we should get started on the search while the rest of you have your dinner. The sooner we get done, the sooner you can be back in your own cabins."

Raven was given a can of peaches and after opening it, dipped her spoon in. She drank off some of the juice so it wouldn't spill, and was ready to go with Kenzie and Zachary to supervise their search.

38

"Who do you want to start with?" Kenzie asked.

Zachary didn't need to stop and think about it. "Redd," he said immediately. "Big old Redd Flagg."

Kenzie laughed. "What do you suppose made him pick that as his pen name? And what do you think his real name is? Is it something that we would recognize, or that no one has ever heard of?"

"Probably five syllables and Polish or Russian."

Kenzie nodded. "That would make sense."

The three of them hurried to Redd's cabin as quickly as they could. It took Kenzie a few minutes to find the right key on Mr. Dewey's key chain. Zachary was watching her, trying not to look impatient. He could probably have picked the lock in half the time it took her to find the right key. But maybe not with thick winter gloves on.

The cabin was much warmer than the weather outside, but the fire that had been burning in the fireplace had died down to embers. Zachary looked at it, swallowed, and looked around the cabin to analyze the space that they would have to search.

Raven took off her gloves, but didn't remove the rest of her gear. She just stood on the welcome mat slurping her canned peaches.

Kenzie looked at her. "When I was little, I used to try to swallow sliced peaches whole, pretending that I was in one of those goldfish swallowing contests. Is that weird, or what?"

Raven laughed. "Doesn't that take all the enjoyment out of it? You would hardly even taste them."

"I guess not. But little-kid me thought that it was pretty fun."

Raven shook her head. "That's hilarious."

"Let's start in the bedroom and bathroom and work our way outward," Zachary said. "If he has anything, it's most likely to be close at hand."

Kenzie agreed and, armed with flashlights from the farmhouse, they started with Redd's bedroom, searching through his suitcase and night table first, then quickly checking the rest of the bedroom and the bathroom. He had a number of over-the-counter medications in the bathroom, nothing too surprising. Mostly headache or stomach ailment remedies. He had some alcohol in his bedroom. Not surprising for a writer, Kenzie supposed. If one were to believe all of the TV tropes about struggling writers. "Write drunk, edit sober," Hemingway had said.

Zachary returned to the bedroom after the bathroom search and looked around, frowning.

"I thought we were going to work our way out," Kenzie reminded him. "Shouldn't we check the living room and kitchen now?"

"Yes," Zachary agreed. He looked around the bedroom once more as if he had lost something. Then he followed Kenzie out to the living room. It didn't seem like Redd had touched anything there. It was all the furnishings that the Deweys or their decorators had picked out. Zachary pulled a few books off of the shelf and looked behind the rows of books, but there was nothing hidden there. Likewise, the kitchen didn't appear to have been touched. Redd was taking all of his meals at the farmhouse. There weren't even dirty dishes in the sink.

Kenzie figured they were finished with Redd Flagg's cabin.

Zachary, however, went back to the bedroom. Kenzie followed him.

"What are you looking for? We should get on to the next cabin or we're going to be all night."

"Something isn't right."

Zachary took a quick look at the night table that they had already searched. He moved things around in the suitcase and pointed out a tear in the lining to Kenzie.

"Okay. Why does that matter? Is there something in there?"

He shook his head. "No. But I think there was. What was he trying to hide?"

"Maybe it was just torn. Something snagged on it."

"No. It's one of those things... people think they're being clever, not realizing that it's what everyone else is doing and that customs or the police or whoever he is trying to hide things from are going to see it immediately."

"Drugs, you think? He's smuggling something?"

"It's not very big. So whatever it is, he's not muling for someone else. It's just for personal use. Unless it is something really high-priced, like diamonds."

"Somehow, I don't see Redd smuggling diamonds."

"No. Me neither."

Raven stood in the door of the bedroom, watching them but not offering any comment. Zachary started to go through the room more carefully, checking under the mattress, inside the lamp shade, and feeling the backs of the drawers. He pulled a small screwdriver from his pocket and unscrewed the plates over the light switch and the electrical outlets.

"Ah-ha."

Kenzie watched him pull a small baggie out of one of the electrical outlet holes.

"What is it?"

Zachary held the baggie close to his eyes, examining it. Then he took it over to Kenzie and offered it to her for her opinion. Kenzie looked at the gray-brown dust. It was difficult to tell what organic substance had been crushed into powder, but she had an idea. She opened the top of the bag and passed it under her nose. She didn't inhale, but just let the scent waft up into her nose. It had a musty, earthy smell. She zipped the bag closed again.

"I would guess mushrooms."

"Ah." Zachary nodded. "So, we found our first hallucinogen. You think this is what was used?"

Kenzie hesitated, looking at the baggie. "I'm not familiar with the dosing. If I had internet access, I could look it up to be sure, but I don't think this is enough to affect everyone like they were last night. This is a pretty small amount, so unless he has a larger stash somewhere else... I think this is just enough for personal use. One dose or several microdoses."

They looked around the room. Zachary went back to the electrical outlets and unscrewed the rest of the cover plates. There were no more baggies.

"Looks like that's it."

"Okay." Kenzie put the baggie into her pocket.

"You're going to take it?" Raven asked. "Even though it isn't enough to poison everyone?"

"We said that we would take anything that could be used to poison everyone. This could be combined with something else. And we want to treat everyone the same way, not to show any special consideration."

Raven didn't argue the point. They got their outdoor clothing back on and exited Redd's cabin.

He was waiting outside the door, pacing back and forth. The snow was all trampled down; he had been there for a while. He looked at Kenzie and Zachary, shoulders tense and hunched up inside his coat.

"All done?" he asked, attempting to mask his anxiety and look casual.

"All done," Kenzie agreed.

He looked relieved and moved toward his door.

"We did find your mushrooms," Kenzie advised. "They'll be locked up with everything else."

"What?"

"Your mushrooms."

He shook his head, a crease appearing between his eyebrows. "I didn't have any mushrooms. Where were they?"

"No one would leave them there and forget about them," Zachary said. "Don't assume we're stupid."

Redd considered this and changed his approach. "Okay. Yes. But they were just for... they help me to open my mind, make it easier to write. I have friends who have had a lot of success with—"

"You can save it," Kenzie said. "I know all of the arguments. When you take something like this," she patted her pocket, "you have no idea how much of the active ingredient you are getting from one dose to the next, you could end up on a really bad trip when you think you're taking a safe dose. You can't tell."

"If you're experienced or have someone who is experienced to help you—"

"You still can't control it," Kenzie asserted.

Redd's eyes flicked to the side, over Kenzie's shoulder to the dark woods behind her. She automatically looked behind her to see what he was looking at, then looked back at Redd's face. His pupils were widely dilated.

"You're hallucinating right now!" she accused.

"I didn't take anything," Redd insisted. "I haven't had anything in two days. I swear it."

"Right." Kenzie shook her head in disbelief. "After all that went on last night, I can't believe you would still want to take hallucinogens."

"I didn't. You're right, after last night... I wouldn't take anything. And I didn't. Is it possible that whatever I got is still affecting me...?"

Kenzie didn't believe a word he had said. He'd probably been high ever since they had arrived. His talkativeness... who knew what he was like when he wasn't on something?

"We're doing you a favor by taking this away, then. You wouldn't want a repeat of last night."

He looked for an argument to this, but gave up, shrugging and shaking his head at the same time. "Can I go back in my cabin?"

"Yes. And if I were you... I'd stay put for the night. Sleep this off."

He didn't say anything to that, just opened his door and disappeared into his cabin.

39

C ollins's cabin next," Zachary suggested.

They walked past their own cabin. Kenzie suspected that Raven would want to search their cabin as well, but that hadn't been discussed, so they would just leave it and see whether she pressed the matter later.

Somehow, Zachary had ended up with Dewey's key ring in his hand, and he was faster at figuring out which was the proper key for the cabin. He pushed the door open, and they all went in.

It looked pretty much as it had that morning. It didn't look like Redd or Andy Collins had made any attempt at cleaning it up. Raven looked around at the disorder with wide eyes.

"Wow. They really did have a knock-down blow-out fight, didn't they?"

Kenzie nodded. She was relieved, once again, that there were no blood spatters. Brooke had, at least, not been attacked there. Kenzie had not been to many crime scenes. Most of her exposure to dead bodies had been confined to the morgue. Dr. Wiltshire had only taken her out to crime scenes a couple of times, and they had not been horrific bloody scenes. He was pretty good about preparing her for each new procedure and experience, and Kenzie knew they would work their way up through the least disturbing scenes first, until she was gradually prepared for the worse ones.

"Okay. I guess we'll need to go through all of this," Kenzie said, looking at the litter of objects on the floor.

Zachary shrugged. "I doubt there's anything there. Let's check the most likely places first."

So they again started with the bathroom and bedroom. Unlike Redd, Mr. and Mrs. Collins had not bothered to hide their stash. There were small packets of white powder on the nightstand beside the bed.

"I would guess that's not sugar," Kenzie said.

"I would guess not," Zachary agreed.

"I don't have a field test kit. And despite what you see on TV, I'm not going to taste the stuff. We'll just confiscate and let the police sort that out later. I assume it's coke."

"More than likely," Zachary agreed.

Kenzie shook her head. "Why do people have to do things like this? They're newlyweds, they're supposed to be on this wonderful natural high just from being with each other. Why would they feel the need to... add chemical enhancements?"

Raven, standing in the bedroom doorway, tilted her head slightly. "I take it you haven't ever tried it?"

"Well..." Kenzie couldn't help feeling a little embarrassed. But she had never been tempted in college or society life to try a little coke to see what all of the fuss was about. She had never felt the need for it. "No, I haven't."

"If you haven't tried it, then you can't really knock it, can you? What does a coffee drinker say to someone who's never tried it? You drink coffee?"

"Sure. Yes."

"How do you explain to someone how that first cup of coffee in the morning makes you feel? The smell of it percolating? Wrapping your hands around a warm mug and taking your first sip. And the clarity and energy boost that you get when it kicks in? You can describe it all you like, but if it's not an experience they have shared, then they really aren't going to understand it like a fellow coffee drinker does."

"No. I guess not."

"Well... the same with coke or other drugs. If you've never tried it, you can't understand the feeling you get. The way it can enhance other experiences."

Kenzie put the packets into her pocket, considering. "But on the other hand, it could lead to what happened last night. Instead of the high you're looking for, you could react violently to the coke or whatever else it is adulterated with. You could end up having a psychotic break or hurting someone you love." Kenzie looked at the bed, where Andy and Brooke had slept in wedded bliss and to which Brooke would never again return. Two had become one, and not by merging with each other.

"You can't predict," Raven said. "But that's life. You never know what effect your actions are going to have."

"You can have a pretty good idea."

"Maybe. Maybe more for some people than for others. But you could also... get hit by a bus. Be poisoned by someone. Die in a snowstorm." Raven gazed out the window into the blackness outside. "You can make all of the right, sensible choices, and die just like the person who took all of the risks."

She was right, of course, but Kenzie had to believe that most people who lived safely did not die violently, and those who took risks were more likely to lose their lives. It didn't hold true for every person, that was true, but overall.

"Let's see what else we have here," Kenzie sighed. She looked through the pill bottles beside the bed and in the bathroom, trying to identify each one and how dangerous it would be if used as a weapon. "This is really tough," she told Zachary. "I'm so used to being able to look medications up. Remembering what everything is for and what all of the side effects are... I don't have as much of the information stored in my head as I would like to think."

"Just do your best. If you're not sure, assume it's dangerous. A lot of them say stuff like 'keep away from children' or 'contains enough to seriously harm a child.' Or the maximum dose is really low."

"Right," Kenzie agreed.

There was a noise outside, and Kenzie and Zachary both turned toward the window at the same time. Kenzie rolled her eyes at her own reaction, but nonetheless... how could she not be concerned about the possibility of someone lurking outside the cabins? It could be an animal or someone going about their own business. But they had to consider the threat real. Two people were already dead, and one of them by violence.

"There are three of us," Zachary said in a low voice. "That makes us less vulnerable than one person off on their own. We should be fine."

"*Should* be," Kenzie agreed. "But that doesn't mean that we will be."

Raven's words echoed in her head. *You can make all the right, sensible choices, and die just like the person who took all the risks.*

Just because they were trying to keep themselves and everyone else safe, it didn't mean that they would succeed. And someone out there might be ready to take a big risk to prevent Kenzie and Zachary from uncovering his—or her—secret.

Zachary walked closer to the window and looked out at an angle, pressed close to the wall.

"You see anyone?" Kenzie asked.

"No. Might just have been an animal. Or the wind. Everyone should be staying up at the house until their cabins are cleared."

They should be. But Redd had been hanging around outside his waiting for them to finish, and Collins was probably out there now, waiting for them to be done with his cabin. And he had a lot more to lose, if he had killed Brooke. No one else really had a motive to kill her, so unless someone had been so off their head that they thought she was a threat, it didn't make sense that it had been anyone else.

"Is it Collins?"

"I don't know," Zachary asserted, his voice taking on an edge. "Can't see anything clearly through the frost on the window, the dark, the glare of our flashlights, the snow outside... You might as well ask me to use my x-ray vision to see through the solid wall."

"Okay." Kenzie was a little hurt by his sharp retort. He hadn't said all of that the first time; how was she to know?

Zachary let his breath out slowly. "Let's keep going. I want to be out of here. I don't like this cabin."

Was it really any different from any of the others? Kenzie too felt more anxious being there. Maybe it was just because Brooke had lived there and her presence still clung to the place. Her clothing and empty suitcase were a reminder that her life had been cut short very suddenly. And all of the stuff that had been thrown around in the living room made it feel like a war zone. Someplace unsafe.

Their search of the living room was cursory. The kitchen hadn't been used much. There was nothing in the fridge and only a few dirty dishes in the sink. "Okay. Let's get out of here."

40

Collins was waiting for them, but he was waiting farther from the cabin than Redd had. He didn't want to talk to them. So they didn't bother to tell him that they had taken his coke. He would figure that out pretty quickly.

The next closest cabin was Raven's. Kenzie approached it awkwardly. They should probably have gotten someone else to supervise them while searching Raven's cabin. She shouldn't be allowed to be in the cabin while they were searching it, just like the others hadn't been allowed to be in there until they were finished. But there was still an issue if Kenzie and Zachary searched it alone, the accusation that they had planted something.

Raven produced her own key and unlocked the door. She pushed it open and stepped back to let them in first. Kenzie and Zachary entered and looked around. Once they had again shed their outerwear, Zachary reached into his pocket and pulled out his digital recorder. Showing it to them both, he pressed the record button, announced the date and time and who was there, and slid it back into his shirt pocket. There would be one unbiased record, at least.

"Do you want to wait for us outside?" Kenzie asked.

Raven shook her head. "I'm not standing around outside.

You're taking at least half an hour to forty-five minutes to check each cabin. I'll be a Popsicle in that time."

"We should stay together then, so that... everyone knows what everyone else is doing."

Raven rolled her eyes. "I trust you."

Kenzie didn't know what to say to that. It wouldn't exactly be friendly to tell Raven that they didn't trust her. But it was the truth.

"I'm going to get the fire going," Raven said. "I know you don't like fires, but it's cold in here and I want to get it warming up."

Kenzie looked at Raven, then at Zachary. Zachary was, Kenzie thought, getting more accustomed to the fact that fires had to be lit while the power was out. He was starting to get desensitized, but that didn't mean he wanted to be in the same room as a fire or would be able to watch her.

"Why don't you get started on the bedroom, then?" Kenzie suggested. "You can see whether there is anything in there, and I'll keep Raven company for a few minutes. Once the fire is going, we'll join you."

Zachary nodded. He swallowed, looked as if he were going to say something, then walked out of the room without another word.

Raven watched him go. "He really does have a problem with fire, doesn't he?"

Kenzie was getting tired of everybody's interest in this fact. They had told everyone that it was a problem. They had said why. Zachary had shown off one of his scars. Wasn't it time for them to all just get over it?

"He was trapped in a house fire when he was ten," Kenzie informed Raven yet again. "He couldn't get out. He was burned. It would be a big deal for you, too."

"I know... but for so long. I mean, there were things that happened to me when I was a kid... but I got over them. You have to go on with life. Spending your whole life being afraid of something like that... it seems like such a waste."

Raven gathered her fire-building materials together, setting lightweight materials over the glowing embers, topped with larger sticks and logs. In a few minutes, she had a roaring fire going. Kenzie looked for another way for Zachary to get out of the house. Whether he went out the front or the back, he was going to have to go past the fireplace. Was that why Raven had built it so large? Just to see how Zachary handled it? To see if she could send him into a panic attack?

"Pull the screen over it and let's go join Zachary," she told Raven.

Raven looked at her for a moment, as if she weren't sure whether she was going to do it or not, then she pulled the screen over the fireplace to keep embers from flying out and got up. She and Kenzie went to the bedroom.

Raven hadn't been kidding when she had said that her cabin was a virtual pharmacy. Zachary gestured to the side table where he had staged everything he had found. There had to be a dozen bottles, a combination of prescription and over-the-counter aids. Kenzie started looking through them. She had half-expected to find heavy-duty prescriptions that would indicate that Raven was under treatment for cancer, an immune disease, or some other big issue that they were trying to suppress or cure with a wide range of experimental treatments.

But they were mostly psychotropic. Meds for depression, anxiety, mood control, sleep, along with a variety of painkillers and stomach ailments. Raven had said that bad things had happened to her as a kid and she had gotten over them. Kenzie suspected that she hadn't actually gotten over anything. She was just medicating heavily enough that they didn't bother her as much anymore. If she stopped treatment, those demons would come galloping back full-force. Kenzie started separating out the drugs that she knew could have hallucinations and mood changes as side effects, which was the majority of them. Raven watched her, eyes shut partway, acting as if she didn't care what Kenzie left and what she took away. If it had been Kenzie, she would definitely have been panicking over someone taking half of her "pharmacy" away. She had promised to dispense whatever the guests needed as they needed it, but Raven was pretty trusting to just take them at their word.

"A lot of these could be a problem," Kenzie said, unnecessarily, she was sure.

Raven shrugged. "So does that mean you think I'm a killer? I'm the poisoner?"

"I didn't say that. I'm just saying that many of these could be a problem if they got mixed in with people's food."

"Accidentally," Raven said sardonically.

"Well... okay, I know it isn't something that happened accidentally. I actually don't know what to say about that."

"I didn't poison anyone."

"Okay."

"You believe me? Just because I said it?"

"It isn't my place to figure out whether you did it or not. Just to prevent anyone else from getting hurt."

"This isn't going to stop anyone from getting hurt."

"What do you mean?"

"I mean... it will just necessitate whoever it is changing their method. If they actually want to kill someone else. Maybe they don't want to. Maybe it was just a joke. But if they actually want to kill someone else in the group... anyone else, some random target... then they'll have to find another method. A different kind of poison. A gun. Knocking them over the head with a fireplace poker and leaving them to freeze to death outside." She smiled sweetly. "I've read Agatha Christie, you know. There are lots of ways to kill someone who gets in between you and what you want."

Kenzie looked at Zachary and didn't say anything. She tried to pick up all the pill bottles, then realized she wouldn't be able to carry them or shove them all into her pockets, even with the large pockets of her outdoor coat.

"Do you have a bag I could put these in?"

Raven went over to her suitcase and pulled out a large zip-top plastic bag. Probably what she had transported the pill bottles in in the first place. Kenzie filled it up with the pill bottles. She looked at Zachary. "Is that it? Anything else?"

"I haven't checked the bathroom yet."

Kenzie sighed. She headed toward the bathroom. "Do you have anything else in there?"

Raven shrugged. "I don't know what else you'll want to take."

Kenzie entered the room and found more pill bottles on the counter around the sink. As well as the pills, she also found eye drops.

"Seriously?" Raven asked. "I have contacts. I can't wear them without my drops."

"You should have artificial tears. This particular kind of eye drops can be very dangerous if taken internally. Squirt a bottle full of these into someone's food, and there would be serious problems."

Raven shrugged. "Why would I waste the stuff in someone's food?"

Kenzie worked in silence, gathering up the rest of the potentially dangerous items and putting them into the bulging bag. "What else have you got around?"

"Booze in the liquor cabinet. Some of it mine, some not. I don't know what else. If there is rat poison in the kitchen, it's not mine."

Kenzie walked down the hall back out to the living room. The fire was crackling away, throwing waves of heat into the room. Kenzie appreciated being nice and toasty, but was still worried about how Zachary would handle it. She stood in front of the fireplace to help screen Zachary from it, and looked back.

He proceeded down the hallway slowly, sweat glistening on his face that wasn't just from the warmth of the fire.

"Anchor," Kenzie suggested. "Five things you see?"

He looked at Raven and clearly didn't want to do the exercise in front of her. He pushed himself onward, the sweat gathering at his temples and dripping down his face. He walked past Kenzie without looking at her or stopping for a kiss as he often did when they passed each other in the hall.

"You're doing good," Kenzie encouraged.

He said nothing, putting on a burst of speed and going into the kitchen, where he started opening and shutting cupboards loudly. Kenzie looked around for the liquor cabinet and started going through it. She wasn't sure why she was bothering. Liquor in abundance could be found at the farmhouse. She didn't think that was what had caused everyone's symptoms. There could be something that was more likely to cause hallucinations. Absinthe was supposed to. But she didn't find any in the cabinet, and she didn't find any other pills or substances wedged in with the bottles. She put them back away and closed the liquor cabinet.

While Zachary continued to check the kitchen, Kenzie looked for any other hiding places in the living room. Behind books or cushions, in the boots at the door. She didn't find anything else unexpected. Raven hadn't expected her cabin to be searched, and she hadn't made any effort to hide any of the many medications that could have been used to poison anyone. Kenzie suspected that if Raven had wanted to kill someone with poison, she would have done it easily. She was certainly the best equipped out of all of the cabins they had searched so far.

Kenzie realized that there was no more noise coming from the kitchen, and looked around the corner to make sure Zachary was okay. His face was still shiny with sweat and, having apparently finished his search, he was frozen, staring off into space. Kenzie went to the door and pulled her coat on, then took Zachary's from its peg. She went into the kitchen and touched his arm.

"Come on. Here's your coat. Get it on and then we can get out of here."

He didn't move, didn't look at her. Kenzie pulled one sleeve on over his hand, and he automatically went through the motions of pulling it on the rest of the way and putting his other hand back to feel for the other sleeve. Kenzie helped him to get it on, then put her hand behind his back and guided him to the door. She put on her boots and indicated Zachary's to him.

"Boots. Let's get your boots on, then we'll go."

He didn't move. His eyes were glazed, far away from the cabin. Stuck in a flashback to the fire, unable to break free from it. Kenzie opened the door, letting in a gust of frigid air. Zachary put his arm up in front of his face to fend it off, blinking and grimacing. He coughed, his intakes of breath between the deep coughs sounding strangled. Kenzie kicked one of the boots over onto his toes.

"Get those on."

Zachary looked down, and with fumbling fingers was able to get them set upright again and put his feet into them. Raven took her coat from the peg beside the door, groaning.

"Just when I get it nice and warm, you have to do that. Come on, everyone out so it can warm up again. I want it to be nice and warm when I get back."

They still had several more cabins and the outbuildings to search. Kenzie's head hurt. She wasn't sure how long they could keep going. They would need rest and sleep. Zachary especially would be wiped out after a flashback. He always was.

41

Zachary was still coughing and wheezing in the cold air outside, nearly doubling over with the wrenching coughs. "Are you okay?" Kenzie asked, bending over and trying to get close enough to see and hear if he responded to her. "Do you need an inhaler? What's going on?"

As far as she knew, he didn't have asthma and didn't use an inhaler, but sometimes people hid things from each other. Especially things that made them look weak. Kenzie already knew many of Zachary's weaknesses and perhaps he had tried to keep at least one thing a secret.

Zachary shook his head. "The smoke," he croaked, dragging the cold outside air into his lungs in loud wheezes.

"There's no smoke. It's okay. Try to slow down. Look around. You're not there. You're safe. There is no smoke."

Though, of course, the tang of woodsmoke filled the air as everyone used their fireplaces to keep their cabins warm. But it wasn't enough to impede Zachary's breathing. She knew he was still caught in the past, a ten-year-old rescued from a burning house. She knew about the burns he had suffered. And the most dangerous thing about a house fire was not the burns, but smoke inhalation. Tyrrell had said that he and the other kids had suffered from smoke inhalation, and they had been away from the fire, behind closed doors. Zachary had been right in the middle of it. When they had pulled him out of the house, they would have put an oxygen mask over his face to help him breathe.

With one arm around his shoulders to keep him in place, Kenzie brought Zachary's scarf up to his mouth and nose to help to warm the air that he was pulling in. He would end up with inflamed and congested lungs if he kept breathing the frigid air so deeply. With the scarf over his mouth and nose, she cupped her hand loosely around them, imitating the shape of an oxygen mask.

"You're safe. You feel that? You can breathe. Nice warm, filtered air. Slow down and feel it. Just try to breathe normally. You're safe. You're out of the house. Just take a few minutes to breathe."

Raven was stomping her feet, impatient for them to go into the next cabin. But Kenzie didn't feel bad for making her wait. It was Raven's own fault that Zachary was dealing with a flashback. She had, Kenzie was sure, fully intended to trigger Zachary's anxiety with the fire. She wanted to know just how far it would tip him over the edge. So Raven was going to have to wait until he was ready to go on, and she could get nice and chilly while she waited.

Zachary's breathing started to slow down, the coughs and choked gasps smoothing out. Kenzie kept her hand over the scarf to keep it in place. He needed the warm air, not air that was so cold it would freeze the moist lining of his lungs. His body started to relax under her other arm, shoulders releasing, neck and back straightening a little as he looked around, locating himself in space, getting reoriented.

"Where...?"

"We're just outside Raven's cabin. We're finished with hers."

"And we should get on to Jack's," Raven encouraged, arms wrapped around herself, stamping her feet to keep the circulation going.

Zachary looked around, studying Raven's face for a moment, then looking around slowly to cement all the landmarks in his mind. Pulling himself out of the past and remembering where he was and what he was supposed to be doing. He took long, slow breaths. He touched Kenzie's hand over his mouth, then gently nudged it away, continuing to breathe slowly and evenly. He held the scarf against his mouth and nose himself.

"Okay. I'm okay."

"Are you ready to go on?"

Zachary looked at Jack's cabin, then turned and looked longingly back at their own cabin. "I need... a break."

"If we take time out now, this is going to take all night. I'm not sure how we're going to get done as it is." Kenzie rubbed her head, pounding from lack of sleep.

"Maybe it's too much, tonight."

"But we need to check the cabins before people can go home and go to bed. To make sure that everyone is safe. If we don't, whoever did this can just go back to their cabins and hide the poison and we'll never find it."

"I need a break," Zachary insisted. "You... keep going. I'll send Tyrrell, he can help for a while."

Kenzie didn't like it. She wanted to work with Zachary. He was the trained investigator. He was the one who had cultivated his ability to observe and remember tiny details. To know in his gut when something was wrong, and be able to look until he found it. Tyrrell... he would be an extra witness and a deterrent from any attack, but that was all. He didn't have the same skills.

But people had limits, and apparently Zachary had reached his. She knew he would push through if he could. He often pushed himself too far, so if he was saying that he was done, she needed to listen. She didn't want him curled up in a ball on his bed for the rest of the time they were at the Lodge.

"Okay, send Tyrrell over." She tried to keep the frustration out of her voice. "I'm going to get started."

Zachary opened his mouth to argue about her starting on her

own, then closed it. He turned away from her and went back to their cabin.

Kenzie motioned toward Jack's cabin. "Let's go," she told Raven.

She managed to find the key before her fingers froze, and opened the door.

Kenzie wasn't sure what she had been expecting from Jack Fowler. He had given her the creeps since the first day. She supposed she had expected to see squalor, maybe a shrine or a pinboard with lengths of red yarn connecting various newspaper articles, like they always had on TV when the police finally got to the serial killer's private lair.

But there was no sign that he had been plotting the murder of anyone in the group at the Lodge. No pictures or newspaper articles pinned up, taped to the wall, or hanging from the ceiling. Kenzie had thought maybe he would have a bunch of candid shots of Brittany showing that he had stalked her there.

The living room was neat and cozy. There was a paperback book lying on the couch. Not some serial killer horror book, but a thick tome by a Russian author. One of those ones that Kenzie always thought she should get around to reading one day, but didn't have the inclination to actually begin.

There was no clutter. No beer cans on the floor. No duffel bag of suspicious objects.

Kenzie walked through to the bedroom, and again looked around in something akin to wonder. Jack was not just a neat man. The room was obsessively neat. At first glance, the room was empty. Like an unoccupied hotel room. No personal effects, no suitcase out or clothes draped over a chair as she had seen in the other cabins. Nothing on the night table. No vacation sloth.

Kenzie checked the closet, wondering if Jack were even staying in that cabin at all. Maybe she had walked into a vacant cabin. Or he was registered there but was staying with one of the other guests. Maybe Raven herself. Or Samantha, the maid. Or even Vance Stiller—Kenzie couldn't make assumptions.

There was an empty suitcase in the closet, and a few items of clothing neatly hung from the rod. The suitcase was entirely empty. Jack wasn't living out of it. He hadn't taken out just the items he needed right away and left the rest stowed there for when he would need them another day. It was spotless, as if she were looking at it in a luggage store. Kenzie went through the pockets of the clothing that was hung in the closet, but she already knew they would be empty. He would empty everything out of his suitcase and then leave something in his pockets when he hung his clothes up? Not likely. The creases in the clothing were crisp. Not like they had been mashed into a suitcase, but as if he had taken the time to iron them before hanging them up.

"This guy is something else," Raven murmured.

Kenzie nodded. "I've never seen anything like it."

She went to the dresser and opened the drawers. They slid smoothly out and, as she had expected, his underwear and other non-hangable clothes were neatly folded and stacked. In the top drawer were a few other sundries, all laid out in the sections of a collapsible organizer tray.

No medications. Those would be in the nightstand or the bathroom. She closed the drawers, making sure they were all pushed in all the way, the fronts perfectly flush. She didn't want Jack to feel like she had tossed the place. Everything that he had taken such care to put in its place should be left just as she had found it.

She opened the drawer of the nightstand. It was empty. Kenzie looked at it for a minute, frowning. She had expected pill bottles, probably something to help Jack to calm his obsessive brain in order to be able to sleep at night. Or at least a bottle of Tylenol. Maybe reading glasses, chargers for his watch and phone, a few other things that he would want close to his bed. Earplugs and an eye mask to shut out world.

She closed the drawer, again making sure that it was shut tightly.

"Nothing?" Raven asked.

"No. Nothing." Kenzie went on to the bathroom. There was a small toiletries kit on the counter. Kenzie opened it to find Jack's brush, comb, razor, and toothbrush, along with anything else he needed to get himself ready for the day. But again, no medications. Not so much as an aspirin, vitamin, or sleeping pill. Kenzie looked at the bottles of shampoo, conditioner, and soap. They all appeared to be exactly what they were labeled. "I've never seen someone as neat as this."

Raven shook her head. "The sign of a sick mind for sure," she joked. "Why would someone like this even come out here? I mean... nature is messy. And having someone else do all of the cooking for you, the cleaning being done in a substandard way... You would think someone like this would want to stay in his own house and never leave it."

Kenzie nodded her agreement. "Yeah. And I would never have guessed that's the kind of person he is. He seems very... casual. Undisciplined. I never would have thought it was just a mask."

Thinking about Raven's comment about the cleaning, Kenzie checked under the bathroom sink for cleaning products and found some travel-size bottles of bleach and cleansers. She went out to the kitchen and found the same.

"Are you going to take those?" Raven asked.

Kenzie shook her head. "I don't think it was anything like this. They might be toxic, but this isn't what was put in the food. Besides, you would know. You would taste it. It would smell strongly. And it would burn."

"So you're not going to take it? Even though it could be poisonous?"

"No. You don't think you would smell this if he put it in your food?"

Kenzie held one of the bottles, still screwed shut, under Raven's nose. Raven reared back, nostrils flaring. She shook her head.

"No. I guess not."

Kenzie did one more sweep of the cabin and didn't find anything else worthy of note. She and Raven got their coats back on again and stepped out of the cabin.

4 2

Tyrrell was coming the opposite direction and nearly collided with Kenzie.

"Oh! Sorry, Kenzie." He looked over her shoulder. "Are you already finished?"

"Not much to see in this one. We can go to the next cabin, which I guess is... Brittany's."

They were all quiet as Kenzie sorted through the keys to find the one for Brittany's cabin. Kenzie wondered what it would be like. She had been totally wrong about Jack. Maybe she had misjudged Brittany as well. She hadn't taken much in when she had gone there looking for Vance Stiller. She had only stood inside the door and hadn't been able to see the rest of the cabin. She didn't remember it being untidy, like the Collins's cabin, or extra neat, like Jack's. Somewhere in between. Like she would expect from someone on vacation.

She managed to find the right key and twisted it in the lock. They went inside and took off their boots and other winter gear. Kenzie looked around, assessing the cabin. It was a larger one, like the one she had rented. More than just a single bedroom. And that meant it was going to take longer to search.

She wasn't lingering and doing a detailed search anymore.

222

There was too much to be done. Her stomach felt tight and heavy at the idea of having to search the barn and outbuildings too. How could she be expected to do that on her own, at night, in the freezing cold, when she was already bone tired? For the time being, she had to focus on the guest cabins. Even the residences of the staff would probably have to wait until the next day. It would be easier when it was light out and she'd had a few hours of sleep.

It wasn't likely to be the staff anyway, was it? If they'd had murderous feelings toward guests, they wouldn't have lasted there as long as they had. They would have been fired for having a bad attitude or would have already poisoned someone and been arrested. The Lodge couldn't have a history of poisonings, or it would never have lasted.

Kenzie started with the bedrooms, as before. The first room was not being used as a bedroom. The furniture had all been pushed to one end of the room, with the mattress leaning up against the wall, to make room for a small seating area surrounded by lights and camera equipment. A recording studio for Brittany's vlog. Kenzie took a quick look around, but there were no pills, food, or chemicals there. Just expensive-looking electronic equipment.

They went to the next bedroom. Half of it had been set up with an exercise mat and various elastic bands and other light-weight exercise equipment. Brittany's computer equipment had been set up at a writing desk on the other side of the room. Kenzie couldn't identify all of the electrical components. It was a more sophisticated system than she would have been able to deal with. Brittany was clearly experienced in taking her show on the road and setting things up in a way that allowed her to work efficiently and maintain her lifestyle.

The last bedroom was Brittany's sleeping room. Her clothes were unpacked, the nightstand full of miscellany, and the bed hadn't been made. Kenzie went to the nightstand and looked through the pill bottles there. Nothing but Tylenol and an herbal sleep aid. Nothing in the drawers. Nothing illegal.

"You can take another look through here," she told Tyrrell. "Just make sure I haven't missed anything."

"Okay." Tyrrell looked a little lost, but he nodded and looked around.

Kenzie stepped into the bathroom, where there appeared to have been an explosion of cosmetics, jewelry, and other feminine detritus. Kenzie smiled and started looking through it for pill bottles. She fished a few out from the mess and pocketed only one of them. The cabin was a fascinating behind-the-scenes insight into the celebrity. Kenzie didn't know a lot about Brittany, but the general perception of such successes was often that they were totally lazy and had hit it big for doing nothing. It was pretty obvious from Brittany's set-up that she was a professional who worked hard to achieve the success that she had. Still setting her alarm to get up early and record a session, even while she was supposed to be on vacation.

Kenzie looked around for anything else she might have missed, then went on to do a cursory review of the living room and kitchen.

Brittany had a number of prepackaged snack foods in her kitchen. Unlike the others, she was not completely reliant on the meals up at the farmhouse. They were mainly portioned diet foods. Like Brittany's exercise mat, they were a testament to the fact that she had to work at maintaining her image. She had to watch what she ate and make sure that she exercised if she were to keep her audience. The Bambas wouldn't be very forgiving if she ballooned up three sizes.

Tyrrell joined Kenzie. Raven was standing at the door, not even putting on a show of supervising Kenzie. After having watched Kenzie search all of the other cabins, Raven had probably concluded that she was not out to frame anyone by planting drugs. Like Kenzie, she probably really wanted to get back to her own cabin and get to sleep. It wasn't as though she had volunteered for the job in the first place. She had been nominated by all the others.

"Nothing?" Raven asked.

Kenzie held up the one pill bottle she had taken. "Just this. Pretty clean." She cocked her head at Raven. "I thought you would be really interested in seeing how a famous vlogger like Brittany lived. Not your thing?"

Raven rolled her eyes and shook her head. "No. Why would it be? I get that she has a big audience, but I'm not one of her fans. I have better things to do with my life than just to watch some inane monologue about how Brittany the Bombshell lives her life every day."

"I've never met someone like her before."

"How do you know? She's not that different from anyone else."

"Well, I mean... I've met people who were wealthy or famous before. But not that much of an icon. Or doing whatever it is she does." Kenzie motioned to the room full of recording equipment. "I just thought it was interesting."

"Not very."

Kenzie nodded. "Okay." She turned to Tyrrell. "Anything?"

"No, I didn't see anything else. I'm not exactly sure what I'm looking for. You already saw the pill bottles beside the bed, right?"

"Yes. Nothing I'm concerned about there."

"I wasn't sure about the herbs." He shrugged. "You can never tell what the side effects might be. Or even if it's the same thing in the capsules as it says on the bottle. I saw this one study where they tested a bunch of herbal supplements, and a lot of them were just grass clippings."

Raven snorted. "Wouldn't that serve them right?"

"Serve who right for what?" Kenzie asked curiously. "Someone who is trying an herbal remedy for their health isn't that different from someone who is taking a medication. Sometimes they work. A lot of the medications we use now originally started as folk remedies. Scientists distilled down the active ingredients, and..."

"People who take all of that homeopathic junk are always so virtuous about it. Like they don't take drugs, because that would be wrong or it would mean there was something wrong with them. But if they can cure their problems with herbs, that's different, that's just living in harmony with nature or some stupid thing. I hate people who get all high and mighty and say you should be able to solve any illness without medications."

Kenzie nodded, understanding. "Yeah, I see what you mean. I wouldn't want to put up with that either. If you need a medication, there's nothing wrong with that."

"That's right. And people who think that everyone should just 'go natural' or whatever they want to call it, they should think again. They should have to go through everything that the person they're criticizing goes through. Seriously. Maybe then they would stop being so superior."

"Sorry that you went through that."

Raven looked at Kenzie for a minute, then nodded. "Yeah. Fine."

Kenzie didn't know what Raven had been through, but from the looks of the pharmacy that had been in her room, life hadn't been very easy for her. Kenzie looked at Tyrrell.

"How was Zachary?"

"You probably know that better than I do. All I know is how he looked when he got back, and that he said he was done. He needed a break, but he wanted me to keep an eye on things in case you needed a hand. Make sure that nothing happened to you." Tyrrell spread his hands apart. "I'm not exactly a fighter. I don't carry and I'm no karate expert. So if push comes to shove..." He grinned, his cheeks getting a little pinker. "Well, pushing and shoving I can manage. But if it's something serious... I'm not much of an asset."

"I think it's just the safety in numbers that he's concerned about," Kenzie said. "Three of us, one of whoever else might be out there. It isn't like anything is going to happen. Everyone is supposed to stay up at the farmhouse until we finish with their cabins."

Kenzie finished getting on her winter gear and opened the

door. Brittany was stamping her feet in the snow, waiting for them.

"You're getting faster," she commented.

"We're tired," Kenzie admitted. "And most of these cabins are the same design, so we already know where everything is going to be."

She didn't tell Brittany that they were not checking electrical outlets or light switches for hidden contraband. If they were that thorough with every house, they would never get to bed.

"Well, glad you're done." Brittany covered a yawn. "That means that I can get to bed."

"Have a good sleep."

"Oh, I plan to. I'll be up bright and early tomorrow."

"Are you going to shut off your alarm tonight, or still get up at the usual time?"

"Well, I'll probably still get up the same time as usual. I like to be able to get my routine done early, even if I can't upload everything right now. I just feel better if I can get my workout and video and everything else done."

"Have a good sleep. I guess we'll see you sometime tomorrow."

Brittany raised her face to look up into the dark sky. There were no stars out overhead. Thick clouds still covered the area, blocking out any light from the moon and the stars. Snowflakes still drifted down in thick flakes, gathering on the trees and drifting around the ground. "When will it finish, do you think? Tomorrow?"

"I don't see any sign of it clearing yet. I don't know. I hope it's soon, so that we can get some reception and hand this investigation off to the police."

"Not much of a vacation for you either, is it?"

"I guess not. But I did plan for it to be. I fully intended to have a nice relaxing holiday."

Brittany laughed and entered her cabin. "See you tomorrow."

She shut the door and Kenzie heard her slide the bolt to secure it.

Funny, Brittany had said that she had medical training, but she hadn't shown any curiosity about what Kenzie might have found so far. Had that just been a line? If she did have medical training, what area was it in? Was she laughing at Kenzie's attempts to sort out what had happened at the Lodge? Or was she just as confused about the situation as everyone else?

43

V ance."

Kenzie looked at the next cabin. She had already seen inside once, but like with Brittany's cabin, only from the front door. She didn't know what kind of a person he was behind closed doors. What secrets or indulgences he might have. She had not found anything in any of the other cabins that pointed the finger at one particular suspect. Several people had substances or medications that could have caused hallucinations, if used in fairly large amounts, but Kenzie didn't know how they tasted or how much would have been needed to cause the effects that they had seen.

And had the perp intended to get the results that he or she had? Was it just about making people hallucinate and lose control? To make them forget what they had done? Or was it intended to hurt someone? To cause an overdose death? As much as she kept telling everyone that Mr. Dewey's death was just a natural death and was completely unrelated, she couldn't help but wonder. Had he been given the same drug, and it had caused a fatal heart attack? Or had he been given something else? Was he the test case and the poisoner had been disappointed that everyone else hadn't died?

If everyone was supposed to die, then who was the poisoner? Was it Mrs. Hubbard, who no longer had a job or cared what happened to her? Was it attempted murder or murder-suicide? Could it had been Burknall? Maybe he wanted to steal valuables from the wealthy guests and disappear into the wilderness, never to be heard of again.

Kenzie found the key for Vance Stiller's cabin. She pushed the door open and took a deep breath, steeling herself for one more search. Just one more, and she could be done for the night. She couldn't go on and do the searches of the staff's quarters. That would have to wait until the next day. If one of them were the poisoner, then it would give them a chance to get rid of the poison. Kenzie admitted that. But the point was to keep everyone safe.

If the poisoner got rid of the poison, then they didn't have to worry about being dosed again. And they could all eat canned foods again the next day if there were any concerns. Everyone could keep eating canned food that they themselves had opened until the police got there and everyone else could get out and go home. Maybe the poisoner would never be found, but she was so tired, she just didn't care. She wanted to finish with the search and go to bed. Whose idea had it been to search everyone's cabins, anyway? She didn't feel like they were any further ahead than they had started.

Vance's cabin looked the same as it had when they had seen it earlier. Other than the fact that it was dark. Kenzie played her light around the interior, and headed for the bedroom, as they had with every other cabin.

And like with Jack's cabin, she couldn't help being a little surprised that the bedroom looked as ordinary as any other bedroom in a cabin or hotel. Nothing to indicate the dark workings of Vance's mind. Nothing to indicate that he was a selfish jerk who didn't care about anyone else. No way to tell whether he was a psychopath and a poisoner, taking this vacation just to give him an opportunity to kill his girlfriend, or one of the other guests, or everybody there.

He probably was a psychopath. A lot of people like him were. Wealthy, famous, ready to push everyone out of his way in his climb to the top. That was how some people succeeded; they didn't have the moral compunctions that others did. Some people were worried about how everyone else would feel, about who they stepped on on their way to the top. A psychopath didn't have all of those things to worry about. They had a goal, and as long as they reached the brass ring, it was all good.

There was nothing in Vance's room that suggested he was out to poison or hurt anyone. His computer sat on the bed, where he had probably reviewed his emails when he was finally awake enough to focus on them. Kenzie wondered if he were feeling back to one hundred percent, or whether he were still under the weather. He hadn't said one way or the other. There was a safe in the bedroom closet. One that took a key, not a combination. It was hefty, but small enough for one person to carry. Kenzie wondered whether she should ask Stiller to open it for her. She suspected the results of such a query would not be favorable.

There was a glass on the nightstand. Water or alcohol? Kenzie picked it up and sniffed it. She couldn't detect anything. Probably water. She opened the nightstand drawer and found several pill bottles. She picked up the prescription bottles first. Diabetes, blood pressure, a statin. Vance was not in particularly good shape. He was still a relatively young man, but his lifestyle was catching up to him already. Too many rich foods, too much stress, not enough exercise. She picked up the non-prescription bottles. A painkiller. A sleep aid. Vitamins. An herbal remedy for men's health issues.

Kenzie made a quick search through the rest of the room, the dresser, the closet, the writing desk. She looked through the books on the shelves but couldn't see anything that appeared to have been touched recently. Everything was lined up flush and there was a light sprinkling of dust along the front of the shelf in front of the books. Kenzie checked the next room down the hall. Like Kenzie and Brittany, he had rented a multi-bedroom cabin. But there wasn't anything in the next bedroom. No sign that anyone had used it, or that Stiller himself had used it for any other purpose as Brittany had. Everything was still and untouched. Maybe he had expected someone to join him later. Or maybe he'd just wanted to rent the most expensive cottage there so that he wouldn't be shown up by Brittany or anyone else. Kenzie checked the other rooms and ended up in the bathroom, which was quite a bit larger than the one in Kenzie's cabin, with both a shower and a hot tub, his and hers sinks, and a sauna. Not bad for a little cabin in the woods.

She looked through Stiller's toiletries bag, which was not organized as neatly as Jack's had been. Kenzie pricked her finger on something and pulled her hand out quickly, sucking on the tip of her finger. She looked back into the bag and carefully moved the contents around to see what she had poked herself on.

There was a razor blade in the case. Not in a protective plastic case or even a folded paper. Just loose, a straight edge, bound to cut someone who put her fingers into the bag unaware. Kenzie carefully pincered it out, grasping the back instead of the sharpened side, and put it onto the edge of the counter. Had he used it for something and then forgotten it was there? Kenzie bent down and studied the rusty edge, glad she was up to date on her tetanus shots.

"What's up?" Tyrrell asked, poking his head into the room. He had finished with his search of the living room and kitchen.

"This," Kenzie said, pointing to the edge of the blade. "I don't think it's rust."

44

Tyrrell frowned and leaned forward, getting his eyes close to the razor blade and staring at it steadily. "Well, it could be... but I don't think it is. It looks more like blood." He switched his attention to Kenzie, her finger in her mouth again. "Did you cut yourself on it?"

"Well... poked myself. Nothing serious."

"But if this is blood, it isn't yours. It isn't fresh."

Kenzie nodded slowly. "No, it's not," she agreed.

They both stared at it. Raven was in the hallway, and she too came to see what they were looking at. She didn't need to look as closely as Kenzie and Tyrrell to see it for what it was. She drew her breath in sharply.

"Is that...?" She shook her head, eyes wide. "That's not the murder weapon, is it?" She continued to shake her head. "He couldn't have killed Mrs. Collins with that."

"No. It's not consistent with the blade that killed Mrs. Collins. This is not the murder weapon. But it is... somewhat concerning."

"Especially since you just cut your finger on it," Tyrrell pointed out. As if Kenzie wasn't already thinking that. "Can you get AIDS from dried blood? Or does it have to be fresh?"

Kenzie stared down at the little rectangular blade. It looked so harmless, and yet wickedly sharp. "I don't think that a virus could survive like that for long. I'm pretty sure it has to be fresh blood or bodily fluids. I don't think it's anything to worry about."

"Then what...?" Raven asked. "He cut himself shaving? Why isn't the blade actually in a razor?"

That was a very good question. Kenzie thought about Mr. Vance Stiller, revising her opinions of him. A psychopath? Someone who didn't feel anything? No. She thought not. If she were right about Stiller, then despite his mask of apparent indifference, he actually felt things very keenly.

"I don't think he cut himself shaving," Kenzie said. "But I think he cut himself."

Raven frowned. She looked at Kenzie and shook her head. "Men don't do that."

"Men can cut too. It's not solely limited to teenage girls."

"No," Tyrrell said, "I've known of a couple of guys who cut. Usually in the name of body modification, but you still know... you just know with some of them, exactly what's going on."

"Why would Vance Stiller cut?" Raven asked. "That doesn't make any sense. The man has more money than he has a right to. He can buy anything he wants. Do anything he wants. So why would he cut? What reason would he have to do that?"

"It isn't about having money. It's about pain. And feeling." Kenzie shook her head slightly. She had misjudged Stiller too. She would never have guessed that he was troubled by anything. But how likely was it that the man would have gotten through life without the same trials as anyone else? Maybe more. Maybe he pushed so hard because of what had happened to him in the past. Or maybe a privileged upbringing had actually put him in harm's way, raised by nannies or other servants, not by parents who kept a close eye on his well-being. Whatever had happened, the man she had thought was just a jerk, rude because he figured having more money than anyone else gave him the right to be rude, was not as indifferent as she had believed.

She remembered the way that he had looked at Brittany,

wondering whether there was any possibility she had been the one to roofie him. Wondering whether she had taken advantage of him, drugging him to get whatever it was she wanted. It was just for a few seconds, a moment in time, but for a moment he had been naked, his emotions visible for everyone to see.

Kenzie looked down at the razor blade. What to do with it? Put it back in his bag and pretend they hadn't seen it? Throw it out or take it with her so that he couldn't use it to cut himself more after she had gone? She didn't want him getting an infection from using a dirty blade. He might have more razor blades around, but at least he would have to open a fresh one and maybe not poison his system with whatever bacteria clung to the old one just thrown carelessly in his toiletries bag.

She eventually decided that she couldn't leave it there. Maybe he would think he had just lost it. Maybe he would guess that she had taken it. But she couldn't leave it as if she hadn't seen it. She was a doctor, and it was her job to try to protect people from further harm. Maybe she would take him aside quietly and give him some resources for those who self-harmed. Maybe no one had ever reached out to him that way before and he didn't know where to go.

"Can you grab me a piece of paper or cardboard?" Kenzie asked Tyrrell. "Maybe in the writing desk?"

"I doubt he writes anything longhand."

"No, but the writing desk is stocked by the Lodge, so there should be some kind of writing paper in there. It doesn't matter what it is. I just don't want to put this in my pocket without wrapping it first."

"You're taking it with you?" Raven demanded.

"I think I have to. I don't want him getting an infection."

Raven rolled her eyes and shook her head. "He probably uses a lighter to sterilize it."

"Maybe. But I can't assume he's following any safety measures. So... I'm taking it with me."

Tyrrell went back to the bedroom to see if he could find a

piece of paper for Kenzie. He returned a minute later with a sturdy sheet of writing paper. Kenzie folded the blade up in it before putting it in her pocket.

"Okay. What did you find in the kitchen and living room? Anything I need to see?"

Tyrrell shook his head. "No. Not really. Alcohol, but Raven said you don't care about that. Some notebooks and stuff. No more pill bottles." He shrugged. "No bloody knives."

Kenzie shuddered. She was glad that she hadn't found any bloody knives in any of the cabins. Coming across the blood-encrusted razor was bad enough, even though she had known immediately that it could not have been the blade that had killed Brooke Collins.

"Okay. Let's call it a night. I really can't do any more tonight."

Tyrrell nodded. They donned their winter gear and Kenzie let out a deep sigh. "That took a lot more out of me than I expected it to. We should have started in the early afternoon. I never even thought... how dark it would be after dinner. That's not the time to start a search like this."

They left the cabin, heading back toward their own. Kenzie saw Stiller walking down a pathway created by a truck or piece of machinery that had been driven down the farm road. She raised a hand to wave at him, but he didn't wave back. Like she, he was probably tired. And he probably didn't want to talk to anyone else. Especially someone who had just gone through all of his personal stuff. He needed distance.

Kenzie expected Raven to turn off to her cabin, but she didn't. She kept walking with Kenzie and Tyrrell to their cabin door. Kenzie raised her brows. "You don't need to come all the way with us. You must be tired too."

"There's still one more cabin to be searched."

Kenzie looked at her blankly for a minute before realizing that Raven meant theirs. "Oh... yeah, I guess so. Do you want to get someone else to search it with you...?" Kenzie was awkward. Of course, the others would want to be sure that they were not the ones who had poisoned the meal. On one hand, they shouldn't be suspects because they hadn't been up to the house and hadn't taken part in the meal. But on the other hand—they hadn't partaken. They had not been affected like everyone else had. Maybe because one of them had been the perpetrator. Maybe Raven would want to have Brittany with her.

"I don't need anyone else. I can do it myself," she asserted.

Kenzie let everyone in. She was happy to be taking her coat and gear off for the final time. Putting it on and taking it off half a dozen times left her feeling sweaty and clammy. She was too warm as soon as she put it on, and as soon as her sweaty skin was exposed to the cool air of the room or outside, she was immediately shivery and uncomfortable.

She hung her coat and took Tyrrell's gear from him to hang up as well. Zachary had left his coat flung to the side even though the pegs were right there within reach. Kenzie picked it up and hung it on an empty peg.

She felt like she had been away from home all day. It had only been since supper, but that felt like a long, long time ago. And by the looks of the living room, the children had been bored. The game boxes had been pushed to the side, but there were still cards and game pieces and spinners left here and there. Like maybe they had been making up a game of their own, bored with playing the same games over and over again. The room was a little cool. Warmer than the cabins that had been left with their fires burned down to embers. Cooler than Raven's cabin with its blazing fire.

Kenzie still couldn't believe that she had lit such a large fire with Zachary in the cabin, knowing how it would affect him. She must have realized how much it would bother him, if he couldn't even stand to have a candle burning at the table when he ate. For someone who appeared to have as many mental health issues as she did, Raven was pretty ruthless.

I'm going to check on Zachary."

Raven looked at her, frowning. "You should stay out here while I do the search."

Kenzie was irritated by the suggestion, but knew that Raven was right. They had told the others that they needed to stay out of their cabins until the searches were complete. She wouldn't have wanted one of them hovering over her while she completed the search, or to worry about them going into another room and hiding or taking something before Kenzie had had a chance to find it. It had been awkward to search Raven's cabin while she was there.

"Come in with me," she told Raven. "Then you'll know I didn't touch anything. After I make sure Zachary is okay, I'll wait in the hallway so I'm out of your way. We've got Tyrrell's kids, too. It's not the easiest, having to search around everyone here."

"There are too many of you," Raven agreed. "I'd rather you were out here. Both of you."

Kenzie looked around. Maybe Raven figured that if they had anything toxic, they wouldn't have left it out where the kids were playing. Or around the food in the kitchen. Logically, the least likely place for a poison to be stored was out in the front rooms of the cabin where everyone congregated and where people might see it if they came to the door. In all of the cabins they'd searched, medications and possible poisons had been in the bedroom and bathroom.

"Okay," she agreed. "Tyrrell and I will stay out here. But can I please check on Zachary first? If he's up to it, he can come out here too, where he won't be in your way while you are searching."

Raven rolled her eyes. "Fine. Go ahead."

Kenzie walked back to their bedroom. Raven followed her and stood in the doorway to keep an eye on her. While Kenzie chafed at the idea that she or Zachary would do anything to hurt any of the other guests—they didn't even have any motive—she knew that she needed to be okay with Raven doing what she had to in order to protect herself and the other guests. Zachary and Kenzie had to be watched like anyone else. Their cabin had to be searched like any other cabin.

Kenzie tried to block out the distraction of Raven being there and to act just like she would if she and Zachary were alone. Zachary was curled up in a lump under the blankets of the bed, pulled up right over his head. Kenzie sat on the edge of the bed in the dark room and tugged the top blanket back to expose his face. She didn't turn on her flashlight, not wanting to shine it in Zachary's eyes, but that meant that all she could see was his shape by the slight glow of the window.

"Zachary. Hey, how are you doing?"

"Not yet," he mumbled. "Just need a break."

"I don't need you to search any more cabins. We're done for the night. I just want to know how you're doing."

He groaned and didn't answer.

"Can you come out to the living room so that Raven can search this room?"

"No."

"Come on. It's warm there, and you can visit with me and Tyrrell. It will only be a few minutes, and then you can go back to bed if you want."

"Don't want to get up."

"I know. But it will only be for a few minutes. You don't want to be in here while she's searching, and she wants us out of the way."

And it would give her a better opportunity to evaluate Zachary and whether she needed to be concerned about his mental state.

"Don't want to." Zachary attempted to drag the blanket up over his head again. Kenzie pulled the blankets away from his body instead. He would be more likely to get out of the bed if she made him uncomfortable. If he couldn't snuggle under the blankets there, and it was warmer near the heater in the living room, he would be more likely to go with her without her having to insist or drag him by force.

"Bridget..." Zachary protested.

Kenzie's breath caught in her throat. *Bridget?* After the length of time he had been separated from Bridget, it should not have been her name that had come to his lips. Kenzie pulled the blankets back harder, frustrated and angry.

"Not Bridget," she told him tightly. "Kenzie. And you are getting out of bed and coming with me. So quit being such a—" She caught herself before she could say something really damaging. As much as she wanted to retaliate for the hurt he had caused her, she didn't want to *be* Bridget. She hated the way that Bridget treated Zachary, for the anger and disdain that she had for the man she had once been married to and had claimed to love.

Kenzie could be kind and understanding of Zachary's limitations and challenges no matter how frustrating they were. She had not entered into the relationship with the intent to change or cure him. She had known how difficult his behavior could be and had vowed not to turn into Bridget.

"Come on," Kenzie told Zachary, her voice neutral. "We need you to come to the living room." She swiveled his legs around to the edge of the bed and pushed his feet to the floor, bringing him up into a sitting position. Zachary was still fully dressed. He held his fingers against his temples, moaning. "I know you just want to go back to sleep, and you can soon. Just come out and let Tyrrell know that you're okay. It won't take long for Raven to search the room."

She put her hand under his arm and behind his back to encourage him to get up. He rose unsteadily to his feet and she stabilized him. He didn't lean his full weight on her, but shuffled and was wobbly as she walked him out of the bedroom, past Raven, and down the hall to where Tyrrell waited. A blanket had been left on the couch, so Kenzie encouraged Zachary to sit down, then pulled the blanket over him. He hunched over, holding it against his face but not pulling it over his head.

"Hey, bro. How are you doing?" Tyrrell asked.

"Fine." Of course he wasn't fine, and if he had told Kenzie that, she would have reminded him that "fine" was not an acceptable answer when she really wanted feedback on how he was doing.

"You need anything? I could get you a drink—of water—or if you need one of your pills...?" Tyrrell suggested.

Kenzie didn't like to ask Zachary. It was better if he decided what he needed and asked her for it.

"No." Zachary rubbed his eyes. "Sorry... just... tired." He directed it at Kenzie rather than Tyrrell. An apology for resisting getting out of bed or for calling her Bridget?

How many times had Bridget berated him and forced him to get out of his protective shell to go to a party or event with her? How many times had she told him that his feelings didn't matter, only his attendance at her side?

"I wouldn't normally force you to get up," she explained, "These are special circumstances."

"I know."

Kenzie thought that rubbing Zachary's back might be a good idea and help him relax, but he was sitting just a little bit apart from her and might not want to be touched. "I don't think she'll take too long."

Zachary leaned with his elbows on his knees and his hands covering his eyes, as Kenzie might if she had a migraine. Kenzie listened for Raven's movements. She didn't know how thorough Raven would be, since this was the only cabin she was searching. She would want to be thorough enough that she could tell the others she was sure Kenzie and Zachary weren't hiding anything. The time ticked past slowly. Kenzie was glad for the gentle heat of the propane heater. Grateful to Burknall for making sure they had a way to stay warm without having to light a fire. Despite Dr. B's statement that exposure was the best way for Zachary to desensitize himself from his anxieties, Kenzie wouldn't have wanted to try several days with him in a cabin with a fire blazing in the fireplace. That might be a bit much, if his reaction to Raven's fire was any indication.

Eventually, Raven came out of the bedroom. She had her hands full with both prescription pill bottles and over-the-counter and herbal remedies. She shook her head. "He's got as many as I do."

"Yeah." Kenzie shrugged. "But there aren't very many pills there. Not enough to poison a group of people."

"Not now. I don't know how many he started out with. And maybe if a few of them were mixed together...?"

Kenzie raised her hands in a surrender. "Probably not, honestly. But you would have to take my word for it."

"Yeah," Raven agreed. "And I'm not inclined to do that."

Zachary pulled his face up from his hands and studied her. "You suspect me?"

"It doesn't matter if I do or not. If one of the others does, and I didn't check carefully and take all of the precautions, then they're going to blame me."

"But you don't."

"Seeing how sick you are?" Raven looked down at the pile of bottles in her hands. "You got trouble, dude."

Zachary didn't argue the point.

"Are you finished?" Kenzie asked. She knew Raven wasn't and

wanted to move the proceedings along. There was no point in their chatting about what she had found. They all knew what Raven had found and what all of the medications meant. As Raven had said, Zachary had his troubles. If someone were looking for a man with mental health issues for a scapegoat, Zachary was an easy target. There was no evidence that he had done anything to poison the other guests up at the farmhouse. In fact, they had all agreed that no one had even seen him at the house. But that wasn't proof.

"No. This is just the bedroom." Raven shook her head. "Do you have a bag I can put these in?"

Kenzie tracked down a zip-top bag, similar to the one they had put all Raven's medications into. If the quantity of pills were any indication of guilt, then Raven was just as much a suspect as Zachary. And she *had* been up at the house.

Raven sealed the top of the bag and kept it with her while she went back to check the room that Lorne and Pat had vacated, and then the one that the children were sleeping in. No one told her that she shouldn't be checking the children's room. Kenzie knew from her time talking to law enforcement officers that criminals were not above hiding contraband in their babies' diapers or carriers. There wasn't anything hidden in the children's room, but Raven had to check anyway, before she could confirm to the others that she had been thorough. Then, finally, Raven moved on to the bathroom and took her time going through their toiletries and the additional pill bottles she found there.

Eventually, she came out. "Okay. I'm done in there, if you want to go back to bed."

Zachary stayed where he was. Kenzie was a little relieved that he didn't go straight back to bed. Maybe since he'd been forced to wake up, he was more himself.

Raven looked around the living room, but mostly just moved around the kids' messes and didn't find any contraband. Then she checked the kitchen and took a long time going through the food. She opened the fridge and frowned. "Nothing in here?"

"No electricity. It's not cooling anymore," Kenzie pointed out. "We put the food outside. I'll show you."

She took Raven to the back door, opened it, and showed her where she would find the leftovers from Pat's Thanksgiving dinner feast.

"It's no wonder you guys didn't come up for the dinner," Raven commented.

"No. We had plenty here."

"Why did you have so much? Was that planned?"

"Well... in a way, yes. You can see Zachary needs to put on some weight, so we're always looking for ways to tempt him to eat more. I didn't know how much of the food provided by the Lodge he would eat, so I needed to make sure we had enough to eat without it. And our friends who visited—not Tyrrell, but Lorne and Pat, who were here the first night—they made the big dinner. Pat loves to cook, and it was a surprise for Zachary." Kenzie closed her eyes briefly. She was tired. She felt as though she had been awake for a week. All of her plans for the vacation had been turned upside-down. She had planned everything so carefully, but that was the way things went in life. She could never plan everything and have it all work out. Life was too messy. "It was nice, but they had to leave early the next morning to beat the storm. I'm glad they did, but... it would have been nice to have had them for longer like we were expecting."

Raven shrugged as if it didn't matter. But Kenzie knew that these points would all be brought up with the rest of the guests. Zachary had a lot of medications on hand, many of which, Raven would know from experience, were psychoactive drugs. They had brought lots of their own food and had not planned to eat all their meals at the farmhouse as the others had. It wasn't proof of anything, but in the face of the lack of evidence pointing to anyone else, it looked at least mildly suspicious.

"How are we going to secure everything we found?" Raven asked. "All of the stuff that you took from the other cabins, and this stuff?" She indicated the bag of Zachary's medications.

"I'll need you to leave a single dose of Zachary's night and morning pills here. Then tomorrow, we can get a second dose."

"Same with me," Raven agreed.

"Right. I guess you'll need yours too. And the rest... we need to secure them in a way that no one else can get into them."

"And that you can't by yourself," Raven pointed out.

"Right..."

They were all quiet, considering possibilities. They could take them up to the farmhouse and lock them in one of the rooms, but a single key would open the door. Who were they to trust it to? Kenzie? Raven? One of the house staff? None of them could be beyond suspicion.

46

It was Zachary who worked out the method of securing all of the pills. Kenzie had counted him out, assuming he was too tired to be coming up with a solution.

They imposed on Stiller to borrow his safe. It was just large enough to hold everything they had confiscated from the cabins and a few of Stiller's possessions which he insisted be locked up. Hopefully, there wouldn't be much more to take from the staff or the outbuildings the next day, or they were going to have to come up with an alternate solution. They placed the safe in the trunk of Zachary's car. The keys to the car were given to Raven, as was Dewey's key to Raven's cabin.

Kenzie ticked off the safeguards in her head. Raven was the only one who could get into her cabin, so the only one who could get into Zachary's car. Vance Stiller had the only key to the safe. The other guests would not know where the pills were stowed, but even if they did, they would have to break into either Raven's cabin or Zachary's car to be able to get at the safe, and into Stiller's cabin to get the key to the safe. With three levels of security, the pills were out of play. Everyone would be safe from any further tampering with the food, which had been Kenzie's initial goal.

Of course, there were still the staff quarters and outbuildings to be searched the next day. But they could be reasonably sure that the food would be safe. The vacationers could either eat food from the cans of food in the pantry, or they could watch Mrs. Hubbard cook. Maybe she wouldn't like being watched, but they were talking about something that might be life and death, not just someone having privacy and her own space.

Kenzie's head hurt. She and Zachary needed to go to bed. In the daytime, when they were all fresh and feeling better, they could decide if there were a better way to secure the medications. And maybe the snow would stop and there was a chance that the police might make their way out to the Lodge to take care of Mr. Dewey.

But that was wishful thinking.

———————

Raven left. Kenzie shut the door behind her and was relieved to finally be alone with Zachary. And Tyrrell.

Kenzie gave a long sigh. "Got your night meds here," she offered Zachary.

He didn't always take everything. In fact, he rarely did, but she had grabbed a dose of everything he might need, because once they were locked up, it would be impossible to access them until morning. Zachary put his hand out, and Kenzie transferred the pills to him. He stared down at the capsules in his hand.

"You remember that first day they prescribed me meds?" he asked Tyrrell. "I was so embarrassed that I had to take all of those pills. And I wasn't used to taking pills, I couldn't swallow them."

Tyrrell shook his head, frowning. "No. Was that while we were at home? I don't remember any of us having meds then."

But he had only been four years old at the time of the fire, so maybe he had forgotten about it.

"Oh." Zachary continued to stare at the pills in his hand. "Maybe not. I guess it was at Petersons'. I forgot you weren't there."

Tyrrell glanced over at Kenzie. It wasn't like Zachary to forget any details about where he had been or the fact that he hadn't seen any of his siblings after the fire. He had not gone into foster care with any of them, but had been kept separate the entire time he as in foster care. He hadn't been reunited with any of them until Tyrrell had sought him out a year earlier.

Kenzie shook her head and shrugged. It wasn't usual for Zachary, but after his big flashback due to Raven's fire, she couldn't be surprised by any lapses. He was probably still struggling to keep his head in the present. He needed rest. A good night's sleep would help him to reset. Tyrrell seemed to sense this. It would not be a night where he and Zachary sat up together talking and reminiscing.

"You going to be okay, bro?" he asked in a cheery tone, slapping Zachary on the shoulder.

"Yeah, I'm fine," Zachary assured him.

"Okay. You take care of Kenzie. I'll see you in the morning." Tyrrell made a face. "I'll try to keep the kids quiet so you guys can sleep in if you need to, but I'm warning you ahead of time, that's kind of like trying to stop a stampede of wild horses..."

Zachary gave a small smile. "If I'm still asleep by then, I don't want to be."

"You need to get what you can. It's been a brutal day."

Zachary shrugged. Tyrrell gave him a brotherly hug goodnight, clapping him briskly on the back. He went to the second bedroom to join the children in dreamland.

Zachary picked through the pills in his hand and gave several of them back to Kenzie. She bit her lip when she saw that he wasn't taking a sleep aid or anti-anxiety pill. It would probably have been better for him to take both. But it was up to him to decide what was best. Maybe he was tired enough from his flashback and the day's events that he would just fall back asleep once they lay down.

"Okay? You want some water?"

"Yeah."

Kenzie went to the kitchen and cracked a water bottle open for him. He tended to get a dry mouth from some of the meds. He swallowed the pills he had chosen with a few gulps of water, then rose unsteadily to his feet, keeping the blanket wrapped around him like a robe and taking it and the water bottle with him to the bedroom. He didn't follow his usual bedtime routine and brush his teeth, but headed directly to bed. Kenzie left him to get settled in and performed her own evening ablutions, running a cold washcloth over her face and brushing her teeth. It had been a very long, difficult day, and she thought she was doing well to not skip brushing her teeth as Zachary had.

She went quietly into the bedroom. Not tip-toeing, exactly, but being quiet to avoid waking Zachary if he were already asleep. He didn't move. Kenzie slid in under the blankets and lay down behind him, wrapping her arms around him to cuddle. He didn't make any movement or snuggle into her. Already fast asleep. That was good, he certainly needed all the sleep he could get.

Kenzie started to drift herself, her brain winding down and the sleepiness welling up like a tide until she was nearly asleep.

"Who do you think it was?" Zachary asked quietly. Maybe not addressing her, but just the quiet, dark room, or maybe his own subconscious. "Who would do a thing like that?"

Kenzie didn't answer.

47

The herd of elephants that were Zachary's niece and nephew awakened them in the morning as it began to get light outside. Kenzie shifted and groaned. Her muscles were cramped, as if she had been holding herself tense all night, even in her sleep. She felt Zachary move beside her. It was so rare he was still in bed when she awoke, she was startled. She put her arm around him and moved in close to kiss his cheek.

"Hey, handsome. Good morning."

Zachary grunted. He didn't kiss her back, but one arm wound around her and he squeezed her against him, then released her, and he just lay with her, their bodies lined up with each other.

"Feeling better this morning?" Kenzie asked. She rubbed his back, making him purr in appreciation.

"Bit better."

"A bit?" Kenzie propped herself up slightly on her elbow. "You're still feeling the aftereffects?"

He nodded and rubbed his eyes, not looking at her, lids still lightly closed.

"Maybe you should take a Xanax today."

"No. Be fine."

It was harder than usual not to give him her advice. She might be a medical professional, but she wasn't his doctor, and he was far more qualified to know what his body and brain needed at any time than she was. But Kenzie wanted to be in control of something. To gradually gather the lost threads in her life and to bring them back into order. She took a few deep breaths, letting them out slowly.

"You sound anxious too," Zachary observed.

"Yeah. I guess I am. I don't like the uncertainty. Feeling like I'm supposed to stop this runaway train, but not being able to do it. I want my own lab and computer and law enforcement officers investigating and telling me what's going on. All the things I normally have. This... chaos is really unsettling."

There was a shriek, and the bedroom door burst open, and two little cannon balls landed on the bed, nearly sending Kenzie straight up to the ceiling.

"Whoa! Take it easy," she protested, reaching for the two troublemakers and trying to corral them.

"Alisha! Mason! You're supposed to be leaving Zachary and Kenzie alone!" Tyrrell shouted from across the cabin. Probably in the kitchen, preparing their breakfasts.

Kenzie tried to get control of them so she could send them back to their father with a stern word. But beside her, she heard a strange, unexpected noise. Zachary chuckling. He managed to catch the smaller whirlwind and pinned him to the bed, tickling Mason and making him shriek with laughter for his father to come rescue him. Tyrrell didn't. Alisha dove in to try to stop Zachary and pull Mason away, but Zachary managed to get her too, somehow holding on to both children and causing fits of giggles as they tried to escape. Kenzie blinked and shook her head at the sight.

Zachary, often so grim, drowning in his depression lately and still suffering from the previous evening's flashback, laughed as he tickled and wrestled with the two children. Kenzie's heart filled with affection at the sight of him happy and enjoying himself with his niece and nephew. Her eyes filled too, and she swiped at them, not wanting Zachary to see her tearing up.

Eventually, the three of them collapsed on the bed, all exhausted by the game and breathing heavily. Tyrrell stuck his head in the door.

"Is anyone listening to me?"

Zachary shook his head. "No. No one."

"It's time for breakfast. Come on. I made you food. I am your provider; you need to eat the food I bring home to you."

"You didn't bring any food," Alisha declared. "Kenzie did."

"Still, I'm the one who assembled it into some semblance of a meal. You're supposed to show me your immense gratitude."

"Thank you, Daddy," Mason said sweetly, not moving. "Can you bring it here?"

"This is not breakfast in bed! You need to come to the kitchen and eat there. What would Kenzie say if you got crumbs in the bed?"

"She'd say, 'you got crumbs in the bed,'" Mason informed him.

Kenzie couldn't help laughing at his deadpan response.

"Don't encourage him!" Tyrrell protested. "Come on, everyone out of bed."

"But I don't want to get out of bed!" Kenzie protested.

"If you guys are going to encourage them to be wild, you have to get up too."

"But I didn't. That was Zachary."

Tyrrell brandished a wooden spoon at Zachary. "Zachary, is this true?"

Zachary chuckled again. Kenzie shut her eyes and basked in the sound. That was why she had arranged for their vacation. That was why she had planned for Loren and Pat to be there. Why she had invited Tyrrell to join them. To surround Zachary with family and hope that it helped to turn him around. Even if it only helped to lift the depression for a day or two, he needed the break so desperately. The antiviral regimen had taken away everything extra he had in him. He needed to regain some of the ground he had lost.

"Everyone up," Tyrrell repeated. "Kenzie, Zachary..."

Kenzie opened her eyes and sat up. She held the blankets against her body. "I need some privacy to get dressed."

"Come on, kids," Tyrrell ordered. "You heard her."

Neither one moved. Zachary sat up and started to log-roll them, until he'd pushed them both off the bed. Alisha and Mason giggled and, tickling each other, eventually crawled out of the room.

"You've got five minutes," Tyrrell told Kenzie, and shut the bedroom door. "If you're lucky!"

It took Kenzie longer than five minutes to dress and make herself presentable, but Tyrrell managed to keep the kids away from the bedroom until she was finished. She and Zachary wandered out, stretching and yawning without covering their mouths, to join Tyrrell and the children at the table.

Tyrrell had managed to toast a few slices of bread on the camp stove. Kenzie helped herself to one and put it on her plate. The marmalade and jams were out, and she helped herself to her usual morning marmalade.

"I don't like that kind with peel in it," Mason observed. "It's gross."

"A lot of kids don't like marmalade," Kenzie told him. "They are more sensitive to bitter flavors, so they sometimes don't like things that taste good to adults."

"It is bitter," Alisha agreed, wrinkling her nose.

Zachary stood near the kitchen sink and downed several pills, the morning meds that they had kept back from the stash that was locked away. Kenzie looked toward the front window of the cabin. She couldn't see the car from where she sat. Zachary's quick eyes caught her glance, and he stepped forward. "What is it?"

"Nothing. Just wanted to make sure that the car is still there, safe and sound."

Mason looked at the window. "Where else would it be? It's stuck in the snow."

"Yes, it is," Kenzie agreed.

Zachary went over to the window to look out. He rubbed at condensation and frost on the inside of the window and peered through the small patch he had cleared. "Yep. Still there." He leaned closer to the window, and Kenzie saw his body language transform from relaxed and happy to anxious.

"What?" she asked.

Zachary walked to the door. He pulled his coat off the peg and slid into it as he put his feet into his boots.

"Zachary?"

"I can't see very well through the window."

But Kenzie knew it was more than that. There was no reason for him to be so concerned that he just couldn't see the car well. She tried to decide whether to get up and see what was wrong or to pretend that everything was okay and just eat her breakfast. Her concern won out, and she went to the window as Zachary darted through the door and slammed it shut behind him.

He went to the driver's side door. Kenzie pressed her nose against the window glass and saw, as he had, a dark place on the car's window, where all the others were white with frost and snow. As she watched, Zachary opened the car door. The door that was supposed to be locked with the key Raven had kept, shut away safe in her cabin. And Kenzie could see that the dark spot wasn't a place where the glass had been cleared of frost and snow for someone to look inside, but a hole where the glass had been broken.

Zachary reached into the car to hit a button below the dash. The trunk popped up a couple of inches. It didn't go all the way up like usual because of the weight of the snow holding it down. Zachary went around to the back of the car and brushed the snow off the trunk with his arm. The hatch opened the rest of the way. Kenzie held her breath. *And the safe?*

Zachary reached down with both hands and retrieved it. Using his elbow to shut the trunk, he retraced his steps, kicked the car door shut, and hurried to the front door of the cabin. Kenzie left her place at the window to open the door for him. Zachary hurried in, snowflakes flying from his coat. He put the safe down on the floor with a thud.

"What's that?" Mason demanded.

"Is it okay?" Kenzie asked, looking down at it. "It's still locked?"

Zachary stared down at the heavy metal box. He shook his head grimly.

"What?" Kenzie looked at it, trying to process what she was seeing. Vance Stiller was the only one with a key. But they had tried to ensure he couldn't open it either, putting it in the locked car, with the car key in Raven's locked cabin.

But the place where there used to be a keyhole, there was now a large, round hole. Kenzie looked at Zachary for an explanation, feeling her eyes go wide, unable to believe what she was seeing.

"They drilled it," Zachary said. He looked back toward the door and the car. "Someone broke into the car and drilled the lock while we were sleeping."

Kenzie bent down and swung the door open, her stomach queasy. It was empty. The items that Stiller had insisted had to remain locked in the safe were gone, as well as all of the medications and other items that Kenzie and Zachary had gathered in their search of the cabins the night before. Kenzie sat on the floor, unable to believe it. She looked back at Zachary.

"But no one knew. The only people who knew how we had secured everything were you and me, Raven, and Vance." Which one of them had broken into the car? Raven? Would Vance have drilled his own safe? That didn't make any sense.

"Anyone could have been watching us out their windows. We put a safe in the trunk of the car. They knew we wanted to protect something. It had to be something valuable or something danger-ous. Or both."

Who had the contents now? Burknall had access to all the tools he would need. Not that he needed anything other than a rock to smash the door and a drill for the lock of the safe. Presum-ably everything in the barn wasn't locked down, and any guest could have walked over there and taken what they needed, then returned it or thrown it into a snowbank.

"I can't believe it," Kenzie moaned. "After all that work last night." She held her arms over her stomach, feeling sick.

"But why?" Zachary mused. "Why would anyone take the contents? They can't be out to poison everyone again. They know that there are enough canned goods in the pantry to keep everyone safely fed until the police get here."

"No..." Kenzie agreed. "You're right. It would have to be..." She rubbed her forehead, thinking. The headache of the night before was returning. Everything from the night before was returning, as if they had gone back in time. All they had done had turned out to be a waste of time. The searches, Zachary's flash-back, Kenzie's headache and exhaustion. "I suppose... because the police will be able to identify the toxin once they get here. That would have to be it, wouldn't it? Whatever it is, it doesn't metabo-lize fast enough, and it might still be in their systems when the police get here. In Brooke's system, at least. Then they'll know what the poison was, and they'll know whose prescription or... recreational aid it was."

"But you know what came from each cabin. If they tell you what the toxin was, you can tell them whose it was."

"Well, more or less. Sometimes more than one person had the same thing. You and Raven had a lot of similar medications. More than one person had the same sleeping pills or tranquilizers."

"But the culprit doesn't know that. The only person who knows what you know is... you."

"Oh, this is crazy." Kenzie ran her fingers through her hair, tugging at it, trying to get her brain to engage. She couldn't sort it out quickly enough for her satisfaction. "Maybe it was just someone after Stiller's valuables. He had documents and written records in there. We don't know what was in the zip-up deposit case in there. Silver or gold or currency. Bearer bonds. Do they even make bearer bonds anymore?"

Zachary shook his head. "We have to protect *you*. Your knowledge of pharmaceuticals could solve this case. Either now, when you figure out which drug was used, or when the police run their tests and tell you what it was."

Kenzie was too stressed and nauseated to eat her breakfast. She could empathize with Zachary. She couldn't imagine even being able to stomach one of the granola bars. There were some applesauce cups in with the other snack foods that she had brought, and she thought she might be able to tolerate one later, but not right away.

"What are we going to do?" she asked as they sat down at the table again, though Kenzie knew she would not touch her toast.

"We have to be careful," Zachary said slowly, thinking things through. "I think we'd better stay here as much as we can. I don't want something to happen to you if whoever broke into the safe realizes that you know what was in there and can still implicate them. Any time we leave the cabin, it puts you at risk, so we can't do that."

Kenzie hadn't been too worried about being stranded until then. Yes, they were snowed in, but they had a warm, safe place to stay and, sooner or later, the snow would stop, and the authorities would get there.

But knowing that she couldn't leave the cabin made her feel claustrophobic. She hadn't wanted to leave. She'd just wanted to stay there and relax and have a good visit with Tyrrell and

Zachary. Cocoon and play with the kids and make some camp meals. An adventure that would be over in a few days. Something that they would look back on with fond memories in the future.

That vision had already been eroding away as people died and she had to consider the fact that there was a killer in their midst. But she'd still been able to hold on to it.

But if she *had* to stay inside, that was different.

Being afraid and being forced to barricade herself against the rest of the guests was different. And she didn't like it.

"We have to keep you safe," Zachary said, watching her face, reading her expression.

"I get it... but I feel like you're overreacting. I don't like the idea of being forced to stay inside."

"You didn't want to go out in the freezing cold, did you? It isn't like we were going to be out there making snowmen."

"No. I'm tired of the cold. I had to go outside and inside so many times last night, going from cold to warm to cold again, I don't want to have to go out. But I want to *be able* to."

Zachary nodded sympathetically.

"Can we go outside and make a snowman?" Mason demanded.

Tyrrell looked at Zachary, who shook his head slowly. "I don't think it's a good idea. I think the kids are safe, but... I wouldn't want anything to happen."

"We want to make a snowman," Mason insisted. "Daddy, you come outside with us."

"Zachary doesn't think it's a good idea, Mason."

"He doesn't know," Mason said scornfully. "He just doesn't want to make a snowman."

"No, he wants to keep everyone safe. You don't know what things might be dangerous outside."

"Yes, I do! I'll wear a hat and everything. Even the one with the mask!"

Kenzie had gathered from previous conversations that Mason was very sensitive about having something touch his face and was resistant to having to wear a ski mask even with the weather being so cold. They had been lucky that up until that point the children had been happy to stay inside and play games there. The weather outside had been so inhospitable, they hadn't even asked to go out. But now that Zachary had mentioned snowmen...

Zachary rolled his eyes, realizing that he'd made a mistake they would all regret for the next few days.

"Sorry."

Tyrrell shrugged. He looked at his watch. "Maybe if it warms up a bit later, we can take a few minutes and build a snowman in the back. But we can't be out for long, and if Uncle Zachary or I say that you can't go out, then you can't. We're the grownups, and we have to make the decisions about when it is safe or not."

"It's safe," Mason insisted. "We'll wear gloves and hats."

"I know you will. Because you know how to take care of yourself in cold weather, don't you? But there are other things going on too. Zachary and I have to make sure that there isn't anyone around who might bother you. You have to listen to us."

Mason clearly didn't approve of this course of action. "We can go out later, right? In the afternoon. When it's warmer."

"Maybe. It will depend."

Mason rolled his eyes, oozing attitude. Kenzie had to grin despite herself. She was worried about the missing medications and the possible danger, if Zachary was right. But Mason's attitude was so classic, so over-the-top dramatic, she couldn't help being amused.

"Why don't you guys find something to play with now," Tyrrell told them. "And I'm going to have some jobs for you to do later on. We all need to help in keeping the cabin clean and tidy, right?"

"We didn't make a mess," Alisha said, looking around the kitchen and what she could see of the living room.

"There's a lot of stuff out right now. The grownups don't want to be stepping on spinners or playing pieces."

"Then you should watch where you're going," Mason advised.

"And you can help me to make the beds and put the clothes away," Tyrrell said, ignoring the smart comment. "And we need to think about what we want for lunch. Do you want to help to cook something on the camp stove?"

Mason looked at the camp stove set up on the counter. "Yeah, I want to cook something!"

"Good. Think about what you want to cook. Remember, we can't go to the store, so we have to make do with what we have. It's like a cooking challenge."

"What do we have?"

"You can look in the cupboards. And we still have some leftovers from when Lorne and Pat were here. Turkey, potatoes, stuff like that. We just have to thaw it out."

Mason got down from the table and went to work, looking through the cupboards and whispering to Alisha about the possibilities. Apparently, their special lunch was to be a secret from the adults.

"How much can you remember about what you found in each cabin?" Zachary asked Kenzie.

"Well... I was getting pretty tired. I don't remember all the specifics."

"Maybe you can write down what you remember and fill in more as you can."

"Do you think that will help us to figure out who took the contents of the safe?"

"I hope so. We need to compile all of the information we can, see whether we can figure it out." He nibbled at his granola bar. "And if you have to testify in court, it's better if you have something written down the day after, rather than relying on your memory months later, when you might have been influenced by the questions and revelations in between."

Kenzie nodded. All of that made sense. She and Dr. Wiltshire always wrote everything down and dictated notes as they worked for exactly that reason. Notes written at the time were far more reliable than memories which could change and fade over time.

"Okay... I guess I'll do that now. There's paper in the writing desk?"

Mason looked up from his discussion with Alisha. "There's paper in the desk," he confirmed. "Alisha and me were using it to write down scores and rules."

"Thanks, Mason." Hopefully, they hadn't used it all. There was sure to be more writing paper in the other cabins, but she didn't relish going to one of the others to say that she needed paper to write down the notes about who might be guilty of what. Zachary was already making her feel a bit creeped out over the idea that someone might want to silence her to make sure that she couldn't tell what she knew. Was that the reason Zachary wanted her to write down everything she knew? So that if something happened to her, they would still have a record of what she had discovered?

Kenzie stood up from the table and looked through the writing desk. There was, thankfully, a good supply of stationery and pens. She grabbed a sheaf of paper and sat down on the couch, where she could wrap a blanket around herself and get comfortable while she racked her brain, trying to remember all the details of what she had discovered the night before.

The morning was quiet. Kenzie had expected Raven and others to come knocking on the door to ask about the contents of the safe and the fact that there was a hole in their driver's side window. Someone was bound to be wondering if they had figured out who the poisoner was. And the staff would know that their quarters had not been searched and had to be wondering if she were coming to do them next or if she had found something that made it unnecessary.

Everyone would have questions, and Kenzie anticipated trying to turn them all away at the door to keep herself safe from any potential attack.

But it was all quiet. If anyone was wondering what had happened to their car or the safe, they didn't let on. Even Vance Stiller didn't come over, and he would have been concerned about what happened to his valuable papers and articles if he realized that the safe had been compromised.

For the first little while, Kenzie worked on her lists, keeping a separate sheet of paper for each cabin and adding to each one as she remembered more details. She talked it through with Zachary, and he contributed what he remembered and any little things that he thought might help her to remember what pills she had found in each cabin. In the end, Kenzie had a pretty good list. She thought it was generally representative of what had been found in each cabin, though she didn't remember all of what had been in Raven's pharmacy, or the exact details, brands, or dosages of most of the medications.

How valuable would the list be if she ever had to testify in court about the various pills and substances they had found? Kenzie wasn't sure. She supposed it all depended on what the authorities decided Brooke and Mr. Dewey had died from. If Kenzie could point the finger at who had been in possession of that substance... it wouldn't quite be a lock, but it might help.

She was drowsy after spending a couple of hours concentrating on the lists, with all of the activity that was going on inside the cabin. While they hadn't been disturbed by a bunch of questions from the other guests, the children were bored and restless, alternately whining about having nothing to do and getting too wild doing it. Kenzie rubbed her temples. She still had some over-the-counter painkillers. Maybe if she took a couple of pills and had a short nap, she would feel better. She would catch up on her sleep from the night before and feel more like herself.

"Stay there; what can I get you?" Zachary offered, seeing her prepare to stand up.

"Just a Tylenol."

"Sure. One or two?" He got up and stepped toward the bathroom.

"Two," Kenzie decided.

As Zachary disappeared into the bathroom, Kenzie made a sudden realization. Her heart sank into her stomach, filling her with a feeling of dread and causing bile to rise in her throat.

She tried to keep her face impassive so that Zachary wouldn't read anything in it when he returned with the pills.

They had taken all of Zachary's and Raven's pills and put them into the safe so that they couldn't be used to cause further harm. Psychoactive medications that could not be stopped cold turkey.

She didn't know how Raven would react to the sudden withdrawal of her medications, but Zachary would destabilize within a day or two, and they might not be able to get him back on track even if they restarted the regimen as soon as they were able. The chemicals had to remain at a consistent level in his system if they were going to do their job. Disrupt that, and there was going to be trouble.

Both Raven and Zachary might respond as the others had to a new toxin being introduced into their bodies—with hallucinations, mood swings, and irritable, unpredictable behavior.

And then there were the guests who were taking medications for blood pressure, cholesterol, and other ailments. They wouldn't go into immediate withdrawal. Probably, they would be okay until they could get back onto the medications that had been seized. But it was also possible that they wouldn't. That the process had already begun and without their daily meds, they could be looking at heart attacks, strokes, seizures, and all kinds of other issues.

Zachary returned from the bathroom and handed Kenzie a couple of white Tylenol capsules and a glass of water. Kenzie swallowed them down without comment.

"Do you want to go lie down?" Zachary asked. "You probably didn't get enough sleep last night."

"You're probably right. But... I hate to bow out on the two of you."

Zachary looked over at his brother, who looked quite relaxed, sitting with a glass of Tang in one hand, watching the children play. "I think everyone is fine. Things have been quiet. Why don't both of us go stretch out for a while...?"

Nothing could possibly sound better than lying down in a warm, soft bed and cuddling with Zachary until she fell asleep. "That sounds like heaven."

Zachary's eyes crinkled at the corners. "Come on, then. Let's get you into bed."

"Lock your door," Tyrrell warned, "if you want any privacy."

It wasn't the kids who woke Kenzie and Zachary up an hour or two later, it was Tyrrell. He pounded hard on the door to wake them up, and Zachary was on his feet and to the door before Kenzie could even wake up enough to know what was going on. Zachary quickly unlocked the door and pulled it open.

"T? What is it? What's wrong?"

Tyrrell's face was white as a sheet. "Mason. He went outside. Just for a minute. He's not there. I don't know where he went. I called him, but he didn't answer me—"

"Is Alisha with him?" Zachary shouldered his way past Tyrrell into the hallway. Rubbing her eyes, Kenzie forced herself out of the bed to follow.

"Alisha is here. She said she doesn't know where he would go. She was going to go out with him, make a snowman in the back where no one could see that they were out, but when she got out there, he wasn't there."

Kenzie followed the two men out to the living room. Alisha was there, tears running down her red face.

"I don't know where he is!" she wailed.

Kenzie hugged her around the shoulders. "It's okay. No one is blaming you. Do you know where he might have gone? Was there something he said he wanted to do?"

"Just building a snowman. He wanted to build a really big snowman. And then he wanted to make lunch. We planned it all out."

"What did he want to make for lunch? Was there something he was missing?" Zachary suggested.

"I don't know. We were going to make it with just what we have here. Like Daddy said." Alisha sniffled. "Just like Daddy said to do."

"It's okay, Alisha," Tyrrell assured her, though it was clear he was struggling to stay calm. "We just need to find him. You know how your brother is. He gets distracted. He wandered off to do something and forgot to let anyone know first. That's all. It's happened a million times before."

Alisha nodded. She sniffled again and hiccupped. "I know, but this time, it was dangerous. You said it was dangerous and he's gone, and what if something happens to him like that lady?"

Kenzie hadn't realized that the kids had heard about Brooke's death. She had thought that they had refrained from talking about it in front of them. But one of them had said too much, or the kids had been hanging around with their ears open when the adults thought they were out of the way.

"Alisha, it's okay. We want to protect you guys, but no one is out to hurt you. Nothing is going to happen to Mason. He'll be okay."

It wasn't like it had been with Brooke. People had been hallucinating. They had been fighting. It was just an accident, someone overreacting to an argument or a vision. Striking out at a nightmare. But it wasn't like that now. It had been more than twenty-four hours since they had been exposed to the toxin, whatever it was, and no one posed a danger to the children. The biggest danger was Mason himself. That he would wander off and end up too far from the Lodge or fall into a pond and catch hypothermia. It was the environment they had to worry about, not the other guests.

But Kenzie didn't immediately suggest that they raise a search party to go looking for him.

"We need to think clearly," she said. "Not to rush into this. Think about Mason. What he was interested in. What he might do if he wandered away. He was distracted or he remembered something that he wanted to do and didn't think it would take that long. He just did something without thinking. What was it?"

Zachary already had his coat on. He looked at Kenzie, then around at the others. If there was anyone who could put himself into Mason's shoes, it was Zachary. He had been a kid like Mason. Always in trouble because of the way his brain was wired. Too distracted, too quick to make the wrong choice. Hyperactive. He could get himself into trouble much faster than it would take them to figure out what he had done.

"Check the back," he told Tyrrell. "That's where he was supposed to be, so that's where you should start."

"I already checked the back—"

"Look for footprints. Check the perimeter, his footprints have to lead off somewhere, unless he was snatched. And then someone else's footprints will give them away."

"Where are you going?" Kenzie demanded as Zachary reached for the doorknob of the front door.

"I've got a few places to check out. You guys be methodical," he told her and Tyrrell firmly. "I'll be impulsive."

Kenzie nearly laughed. Zachary was out the door and slammed it shut behind him. Tyrrell went to the back door as instructed. He put his boots back on.

"You stay here with Kenzie, Alisha. I don't want you wandering around too. We need someone to be here in case Mason comes back, and I need you to look after Kenzie. She can't be out here searching, understand?"

Alisha looked at Kenzie, baffled. "What?"

"Just do what I say. You stay here with Kenzie. The two of you need to stay inside. Don't let anyone else in. Keep the doors locked."

He left out the back. Alisha and Kenzie looked at each other. It was clear that Alisha didn't understand why her father had told her to take care of Kenzie and not let anyone into the cabin. But Kenzie did. Zachary had said that the poisoner might target her. He or she would see Kenzie as a threat because of her knowledge and might try to remove her from the equation.

Now Kenzie was stuck in the cabin by herself, except for Alisha. Someone could have taken Mason just to get the men away from the cabin. It might all be a ruse to get Kenzie alone or to persuade her to leave the cabin to join in the search.

"Okay," Kenzie said calmly. "Let's lock the doors."

Alisha nodded solemnly. She reached out to the back door and locked the handle and then the bolt. She looked out the window of the kitchen, watching her father as he walked around the yard, looking down at the markings in the snow. Kenzie and Alisha couldn't see much from inside. Kenzie hoped he would be able to find Mason's trail and find him quickly. Kenzie went to the front door and did the same there. She looked out the living room window, but couldn't see Zachary. He was already out of sight. She wondered where he had gone. Where would she have gone to look for Mason?

One of them would find him. She was counting on it.

I don't know what else to do," Alisha told Kenzie.

And what could they do? If they weren't allowed to leave the cabin, there wasn't much they could do. Even if they had an idea, even if Alisha suddenly realized where her brother had taken off to, they wouldn't be able to call Zachary or Tyrrell and let them know. They had no bars. The storm was still blocking out any cell signal.

"Well... why don't we sit down and play a game?" Kenzie suggested. "I know it won't help them find him any faster, but it will help us to distract ourselves so that we don't worry as much."

Alisha put her hands on her hips. "I don't want to not worry!"

"Well... okay. What do you want to do about it, then?"

Alisha looked around, trying to find an answer. "We'll clean up," she said finally. "Daddy told us that we needed to clean up. So we'll do that, and when we get done... he'll be back. And he'll have Mason with him."

"Okay," Kenzie agreed. She was willing to buy into Alisha's magical thinking. They would clean. And when they were done, Mason would be back.

They picked up game pieces and matched them to the appropriate boxes, then stacked the boxes back in the closet where they had been stored. They picked up various wadded-up and torn papers and threw them out. There were dishes from breakfast that had not been cleaned, so they washed them and put them away. Kenzie looked around again. There had to be some way for them to occupy themselves. There was always more work to do.

There was a knock at the door. Her heart in her throat, Kenzie looked out the front window. She had known that it wasn't Zachary's knock, but she'd been hoping that it might be Tyrrell's. Burknall stood there, looking back at her through the window, waiting for her to let him in.

What if he were the culprit? He had tools, he'd lived at the lodge for a long time, he was clearly smart and able to think things through. What if he'd been the one who had decided they didn't need any more guests at the Lodge? Or that if he got rid of his boss that he'd be able to get some sort of benefit. Did the Lodge go to Dewey's next of kin? Did it get divided among the staff? Did he leave something to his loyal workers to make their lives more comfortable? Kenzie stood there, not opening the door.

Burknall knocked again, insistently. "Kenzie!" he shouted through the door.

Kenzie finally went to the door and unlocked it. She opened it a couple of inches.

"What is it?"

"You need to come out to the barn."

Kenzie shook her head. "I'm supposed to stay here."

Burknall was looking down. He could see the safe on the floor by her feet. He probably knew that it was empty. Maybe he was the one who had emptied it.

"Come on. You want the kid, don't you?"

Kenzie frowned. "Mason? Of course. Is he in the barn?"

Burknall rolled his eyes. "Where else would he be?"

He sounded so genuinely irritated, Kenzie didn't doubt him. She reached for her boots and her coat. Alisha grabbed at Kenzie's coat as she tried to put it on.

"Kenzie, no!"

"I'll just be a minute. I'll go get Mason, and I'll be right back."

"Daddy said no. He said to stay here."

"Well, he didn't know that anyone else would find Mason while they were gone. You want me to bring Mason home, don't you? You want him to be home safe."

"Yes..." Alisha drew her answer out, looking unconvinced.

"You can lock the door behind me, right? And only open it for one of us?"

"Yes. But I don't want to be here by myself."

"It will only be a few minutes. I'll be right back."

Kenzie finished pulling her winter gear on. She promised once more to be right back, then left the cabin.

"Come on," Burknall told her, and strode toward the barn.

His stride was much longer than Kenzie's, and he broke through the snow that wasn't yet trampled down much more easily than Kenzie did. She wasn't used to getting around the grounds, especially with all of the drifted snow, and she kept taking the wrong paths, tripping and stepping into holes and off the sidewalk into the gutter, neither of which she could see in the snow. She wanted to ask Burknall to slow down and wait for her, but she didn't want to look like a helpless woman either. She was as competent as the next man.

By the time Burknall reached the barn, Kenzie was well behind. She could see her destination, but she was no longer within calling distance.

"Come on," she muttered to herself. "City slicker here. Give me a bit of a break."

But he didn't. He was into the barn and out of Kenzie's sight.

The last couple of minutes it took Kenzie to struggle through the uneven snow into the barn were worse. She could no longer see Burknall and reassure herself that she was doing the right thing. All that she could think of was that she had done the wrong thing. The opposite to what Zachary and Tyrrell would have told her to do.

What if Burknall were the poisoner? What if he were just trying to lure her to where he could dispose of her out of sight of all the other cabins? No one would know what had happened to her. Alisha was the only one who even knew that Burknall had come to the door and that Kenzie had gone with him. She was the only one who knew that Kenzie had gone to the structure. After dealing with Kenzie, Burknall could go back and take care of the last witness.

But Kenzie couldn't think of a reason he would go through all of that. She couldn't think of any motive he had to poison them all or to kill Brooke. It just didn't line up.

She entered through the big doors of the barn and looked around. It was warmer in the barn than it was outside, despite the big doors being open. There was some sort of furnace or heater running to keep it warm. That, and the warm animals helping to heat it with their body heat. The big horses that Mason had been so proud of making friends with and of driving during the hayride.

"Mason? Are you in here?" Looking around, Kenzie couldn't see Burknall, which made her even more anxious. Why wasn't he standing there waiting for her? He had said that he would take her to Mason. Why the disappearing act?

"Kenzie?" A small voice called back.

"Hey. Where are you?" Kenzie looked around, trying to pinpoint the sound.

"I'm up here."

Kenzie looked up and kept raising her gaze higher until they reached the top of the hay loft, where she could see Mason looking tentatively down at her over the edge.

"What are you doing all the way up there?"

"I was climbing." Mason's voice was thready and uncertain. Had he figured out how much trouble he was in for taking off? Where was Zachary? Kenzie figured the barn would be the first place Zachary would have looked for him.

"Is your Uncle Zachary up there with you?"

"No." She could see Mason's head shake. "It's just me..."

"Why don't you come down now. You still want to help make lunch, don't you? Alisha said that the two of you had it all planned out. You don't want her making it all herself, do you?"

"No! It was my idea. She has to do what I say!"

"Come on down, then. Let's go back to the cabin and make lunch."

"Me and Alisha. Not you."

"Okay." Kenzie waited for him to decide to come down from his high perch. Had he imagined climbing Mount Everest to get there? He was several stories high. Kenzie tried to avoid thinking of what would happen if he slipped and fell. Unfortunately, she knew way too much about those kinds of accidents. The kind of tragic case that made them all shake their heads and say how they would never have let that happen. The parents must have been crazy to let the kids get away with climbing so high or taking part in other risky behavior.

Yet when it happened, there really wasn't anyone to blame. Parents did blame themselves, and so did the public, but Kenzie knew that if there was any way they could take back what had happened, they would. They would give up anything to have the child back safe and sound.

Mason's head disappeared, which meant that he had backed up and was on his way to picking his way down, climbing back over the mounds of hay and the ladders or ropes or whatever else he had used to climb to the pinnacle. She waited, trying not to be impatient with him. If he thought that he was going to get punished for his little adventure, he would be far less likely to come down and go back to the cabin with her. She needed to act as though it were nothing.

"Kenzie?"

She tried to follow Mason's voice, but she could only hear him, not to see him. "Yes?"

"Are you my auntie?"

Why would he be concerned about such a thing while

climbing down from the loft? Kenzie rolled her eyes and tried to keep her voice relaxed and soothing.

"If you want to call me auntie, you can. Zachary is your uncle. We're not married, but we're together, and I don't think anyone minds."

"Auntie Kenzie." Mason tried it out to see how it sounded and felt.

"Yes?"

Mason giggled. "I wasn't calling you."

"Did you see Zachary? He was looking for you."

"Yes," Mason admitted. "I saw him."

"Did you talk to him? Did he find you?"

"Well... no..."

"You hid from him?"

"Well... not exactly."

"We'd better let him know that you're found. Do you know where he went after he looked here?"

"Yes. Into the woods."

Kenzie's throat felt tight. "Into the woods? Why would he go there? Did you go into the woods?"

"Yes. That's where the knife is," Mason said quietly.

Kenzie walked to the back of the barn, craning her neck to see up into the loft where Mason should be. "What knife, honey?"

"I found... I was going to build a snowman. I was looking for sticks. You need sticks for the arms, and rocks or something for the eyes and mouth."

"And a carrot for the nose," Kenzie said lightly.

"Yeah. I was looking for sticks, but I found the knife."

"Where are you, Mason?" Kenzie called softly.

"I'm here!" Mason jumped down from somewhere above Kenzie, tumbling into a pile of loose hay. Kenzie was so startled that she let out a shriek.

Mason laughed. "Auntie Kenzie!"

"Mason!"

He laughed again.

"We'd better go back to the cabin now," Kenzie said.

"I want to stay here with Mr. Burknall."

"Where is Mr. Burknall?" Kenzie asked. "He brought me over here, and then... he disappeared."

"He didn't disappear. He just went to check on the animals. There are lots of animals, and he has to take care of them all."

"So where is he?"

Mason shrugged. He waved in a random direction. "Maybe looking after the pigs."

"There are pigs?"

Mason nodded. "There are lots of animals. I always thought that pigs were little. Like in that book about the spider. And Templeton the rat."

"*Charlotte's Web?*"

"Yeah. The pig in that was just really little. But Mr. Burknall's pigs are big."

"Okay." Kenzie's mind went to the stories she'd heard of pigs and how good they were at disposing of dismembered bodies. Something she didn't want to be thinking of and certainly didn't want to talk to Mason about. "We need to get back to the cabin. Unless... maybe you should show me where you found the knife, on the way back. Did you tell Zachary where it was?"

"No."

"You just hid from him."

Mason looked down at his feet. "Yeah."

"You should have told him."

Mason nodded.

"You should have come out from hiding and told him where to find the knife. That was important."

"I'm sorry."

"Okay."

"Do you want me to show you where it is?"

Kenzie hesitated. She knew she should get back to the cabin. That was where Tyrrell and Zachary would go when they failed to find Mason. And that's where Alisha was waiting, all by herself, where Kenzie had abandoned her. She shouldn't have left the little girl there alone, but when Burknall had come calling, it was the only thing she could think to do.

"Yes. You'd better show me."

Mason led Kenzie out the back door of the barn, through a couple of muddy, trampled paddocks, into the woods that the cabins backed onto. Whoever had killed Brooke had probably thrown the knife away, hoping no one else would find it.

Mason looked around as they walked into the woods, his head swiveling back and forth. Kenzie hoped that he knew where the knife was and could find the cabin again. The last thing they needed was to get lost in the woods. Everything looked alike to Kenzie. She didn't know how he would be able to navigate through it.

"Do you remember where it is?" she asked.

"Yeah."

"Okay." She let him lead the way.

Mason looked down at the snow as he tromped through the trees. "That's where Zachary went." He pointed at a footprint.

Kenzie looked down at the zigzag pattern in the footprint. It looked about the right size, but she hadn't noticed the tread on the bottom of Zachary's boots. If Mason said it was one of Zachary's footprints, he was probably right.

"But he went the wrong way," Mason said after a minute, looking at the footprints as they diverged to the left.

"Maybe he saw something. Or someone."

"Maybe," Mason said doubtfully. "But I think everyone is in their cabins."

"Not everyone!"

Mason chuckled, nodding. He rubbed his face, red with the cold. "Was Daddy mad?"

"No, not mad... but he was worried about you when he didn't know where you went. You weren't supposed to go off on your own."

"Yeah... I forgot. Kind of."

"And kind of wanted to go off even though you weren't supposed to."

Mason looked at her sideways and didn't answer. After a couple of minutes, he motioned to the underbrush. "Over here. I thought it would be a good place to get sticks."

Kenzie bent down and looked where he pointed. She could see

a long, thin-bladed knife. A kitchen knife of some sort, not something that was intended to be used as a weapon. She could not see any blood on the blade, but it might have been wiped off. The police would send it to the lab to see if they could find microscopic amounts of blood.

"Did you touch it?" she asked Mason.

He shook his head. Kenzie continued to look at him. After a minute, he dropped his eyes.

"Yes, but I put it right back where it was."

Kenzie hadn't brought her phone with her to take any pictures. She hadn't even thought about it when Burknall had knocked on her door. Kenzie looked around.

"Are we close to the cabin now? I'm turned around."

"It's just over there." Mason pointed. He smiled proudly. "Mommy says I have very good visio-sp..." He struggled to remember and form the word.

"Visual-spatial memory?" Kenzie suggested.

He grinned. "Yes!"

"I bet you hardly ever get lost."

"Nope. I can always find my way home. Daddy plays this game, where he asks us how to get home when we're out in the car. I always know how to get home. Alisha doesn't. Sometimes she does, but not always."

"You're very lucky. That's a great skill to have. If we can go back to the cabin, then I can get my phone to take some pictures, and a bag or something to put the knife into, so we don't destroy any evidence. That would be a big help to me."

"Okay. This way."

Kenzie followed her small guide to the back door of the cabin. They knocked and called out to Alisha.

It was a few minutes before Alisha finally opened the door, cracking it open and peering out at them. Mason pushed on the door. "Let us in, Alisha!"

Alisha finally stepped back from the door and let Mason open it the rest of the way.

"Where were you, Mason?" she demanded, as Mason bent over to pull off his boots. Her face was still red and visibly tear-streaked. "Daddy was really scared."

Mason tried to put on a brave face. "I was just over at the barn. I didn't do anything wrong."

"You weren't supposed to go anywhere. You were supposed to stay in the yard."

"But I just went to the barn. Dad should know that I would go to the barn."

"You hid from the people looking for you," Kenzie reminded him. "So you knew it was wrong and you tried to keep anyone from finding you."

"I didn't hide from you."

Kenzie admitted this was true. "No. You were good about telling me where you were and coming down. But you shouldn't have hidden from Zachary and your dad. You should have stayed in the yard like you were supposed to. Someone out there... could have wanted to hurt you."

"I can run really fast," Mason protested. "If anyone tried, I would run away."

Kenzie made sure that the back door was shut and locked. "If I was you, I wouldn't give your daddy those excuses when he comes back."

Mason bit his lip, looking away from her. Kenzie wondered again about Tyrrell's past relationship with his family. He seemed stable now, a loving father, patient with the children most of the time, but what had he been like when he had been married? When he had been drinking? Was Mason afraid of him because of the way he had been before he sobered up? Or was it just the natural reaction of a child to a parent who was in authority, knowing that he was going to be in trouble for having broken the rules? The fact that he had come down for Kenzie and not for Tyrrell or Zachary suggested that he was more comfortable with women than with men, which was natural for most children.

"Let's see if we can see them outside. I want to get back to that... spot... to take pictures."

Mason nodded wisely, looking at Alisha and not telling her about the knife.

"And maybe you and Alisha can make that lunch, once your dad is here to supervise."

"We're going to make—"

"Alisha!" Mason shouted her down. "You're not allowed to tell! It's a surprise!"

Alisha closed her mouth and didn't give it away. Mason glared at her fiercely to make sure she didn't think about opening her mouth about it again.

"What about Uncle Zachary?" Alisha asked. "If he comes back, we can cook, right?"

"Well... I think you'd better wait for your daddy."

"Zachary doesn't like to cook," Mason said with authority.

"He doesn't mind cooking. But it is hard for him. And with that camp stove... he doesn't like it. He'd rather use an electric stove, when we have the power back again."

"He was in a fire when he was little," Alisha offered, surprising Kenzie. She hadn't known that the children were aware of this.

"Yes, that's right."

"Like Daddy. But he got burned. Daddy's not scared of fires, but he didn't get burned."

Kenzie nodded. "Different people are afraid of different things. Fire makes Uncle Zachary very nervous. He might be worried about you getting burned, even if you were being careful and safe."

Alisha and Mason both nodded understandingly.

Kenzie opened the front door, looking around for either of the men.

Kenzie spotted Tyrrell coming out of the trees on the other side of the road. She waved at him.

"Tyrrell! Tyrrell! Hey!"

He looked up and saw her. His face was still a frozen white mask. Worried and angry and trying not to let it all out.

"He's here," Kenzie shouted at him. "Mason is back."

Tyrrell looked at her for a minute as if unable to process what she had said, then headed toward her at a quick clip.

"He's back?" Tyrrell demanded. "Mason came back?"

"He's here," Kenzie confirmed, nodding in an exaggerated way to make sure he could see it. "Come on back."

Tyrrell made his way across the snowy road to the cabin. "Where was he? I'm going to tan that boy's hide!"

"He was at the barn. But he's back and he's safe."

"I checked the barn."

Kenzie nodded and didn't reveal that Mason had hidden from them. "He's kind of worried about being in trouble, so..."

"He should be," Tyrrell agreed.

"I'm just saying that maybe..."

"Don't try to tell me how to parent. He knows he's not supposed to take off like that."

Kenzie stepped back to let Tyrrell in, then shut the door against the cold.

"He's hoping that he and Alisha can make lunch now," Kenzie said, hoping that would distract Tyrrell from a focus on punishing Mason. "They've got something all planned out. I'm going to go up to the farmhouse, see if Zachary is up there. He'll be relieved to know that Mason is safe."

"I should go up there," Tyrrell suggested. "He didn't want you to be out on your own."

"I'll be okay going that far. I'll be visible the whole time. And there will be people up at the house. I won't be alone."

She didn't mention that she and Mason had just been off in the woods alone. She would have to find a way to tell Zachary about that without upsetting him too, which might not actually be possible. She was all right. Nothing had happened to her. Like Mason, she hoped to avoid censure by pointing out that the outcome had been good. Nothing had happened, therefore she hadn't been in danger, therefore she hadn't made a bad choice by leaving the cabin when she had been warned not to.

"I'll just be a few minutes," she told Tyrrell. "Why don't you get the kids started on lunch, and then Zachary and I will be back in time to eat it?"

<hr>

Kenzie climbed the hill to the farmhouse, thinking about Mason. She hoped that Tyrrell wouldn't be too hard on him. He had disobeyed and walked into a situation where he could have been hurt—both into the woods where Brooke's killer had disposed of the knife, and up into the barn loft where he could have fallen— and she could understand why Tyrrell was upset about that. But Mason hadn't intended any harm and hadn't been hurt, so it had worked out okay in the end.

She knew that Zachary had dealt with parents who were abusive when he had broken the rules or been distracted due to his

ADHD. Both his and Tyrrell's biological parents and foster families that he had lived with. She could see how parenting a kid like Mason, who couldn't conform to the rules, could become a power struggle, with a parent trying to force his compliance. And a power struggle could quickly lead to being too harsh physically or emotionally.

Even trying to get Zachary to stick to a short set of rules for their relationship and the upkeep of the household frequently failed. He was an adult and he was willing to do whatever it took to keep their relationship on the tracks, but the way that his brain was wired, all of the good intentions in the world did not result in his being able to stick to the program. He would forget to tell her about something. Abandon a job right in the middle. Forget how she had told him something was to be done a hundred times before. Not because he didn't care what she had to say, but because he frequently didn't have the executive skills to follow through. And that was something he couldn't control, no matter how he tried to focus or to remember the simple steps she had given him.

She sighed. Maybe Mason would grow out of the worst of his symptoms. Scatterbrained or willful children could still become adults with good jobs and family relationships. It was impossible to tell how their brains would mature and how their interests might lead to success. Despite all his challenges, Zachary was still a good investigator, photographer, and partner. He nurtured a number of friendships and professional relationships, and he was very close to his siblings.

She reached the house and paused for a moment for a breath. "Okay."

She knocked briskly on the front door and entered. It was not yet time for lunch to be served, but Raven was sitting reading a book, a glass of wine at her side, and Jack was fiddling with the blinds, presumably trying to get them at the right angle to take the best advantage of the sun, weak though it was through the clouds. Kenzie smiled.

"Hey. Is Zachary up here?"

They both looked at her as if surprised to see her there. Eventually, Raven replied. "He was. Check the kitchen; see whether he's with Mrs. Hubbard, I guess."

Kenzie nodded. "Thanks." She paused, hesitating. "Is Mrs. Hubbard still making meals? Even though...?"

"Do you really think that we believe she was trying to poison us?" Jack asked. "Or that someone else here was? It's pretty ridiculous, when you get right down to it. Doesn't make any sense. So a couple of people had a bit too much to drink one night." He shrugged. "That doesn't mean that we were all being given some mythical hallucinogen."

Kenzie blinked in surprise. They had all been more or less onboard the night before. But she supposed that after a good night's sleep, they had shaken off their anxiety and decided that skipping meals or making their own until the police got there was unsustainable. If it were impossible to avoid a danger, people eventually accepted it, even if it were something that would previously have seemed untenable. The other guests had to eat, so they had to accept it in spite of any warnings.

"You don't even like to take over-the-counter medications," she pointed out to Jack.

Maybe it was a mistake to use something she had learned about him during the search the night before as an argument against him. Her mother would certainly have frowned on it.

Jack narrowed his eyes at her. "What does that have to do with anything?"

"You already confiscated everyone's medications," Raven said. "So even if someone was trying to harm us, they can't now. So it's safe to eat here."

Kenzie closed her mouth and kept her lips pasted together. It would not help her to argue with either of them. Pointing out that Mrs. Hubbard's possessions and the kitchen had not been searched would just make both of them antagonistic toward her.

Kenzie shook her head and went to the kitchen. She knocked on the door frame as she entered, trying to give Mrs. Hubbard notice that she was there and not to just walk into her domain as if she had the right to be there.

"Good morning, Mrs. Hubbard."

Mrs. Hubbard turned. She raised her brows at Kenzie and didn't look pleased to see her there. Kenzie figured she had probably already made enough of a disruption for the cook. Telling people that the food was poisoned was not exactly likely to endear her.

"Sorry to bother you. I was just looking for Zachary. Is he around?"

Mrs. Hubbard nodded, turning back to her stove. "He went downstairs to make sure that boy didn't end up down there somehow."

Kenzie walked over to the stairs and looked down. She didn't think that the farmhouse had a full basement. Probably just a dugout for some preserves or wine to be stored where they would be cool and out of the sun.

"Zachary?"

"Kenzie?" Zachary appeared at the bottom of the stairs,

twisting his neck for a good look at her. "What are you doing here?"

"We found Mason. I wanted to let you know."

"You found him!" Zachary began to climb the steep, creaking stairs. He kept one hand on the wooden stair rail, the other hovering an inch from the wall next to him, as if the whole thing might collapse and he needed to be ready to catch himself or to hold it up. "Where was he?"

Kenzie waited for him to get to the top of the stairs. She touched his arm, but he didn't move closer to embrace her or give her a kiss.

"He was in the barn, up in the loft. Way up the top. Mr. Burknall found him and came to the cabin to let me know."

"I checked the barn."

"I know. So did Tyrrell. But he hid from you. He didn't want to get caught or to be in trouble."

Zachary rolled his eyes. "Well, I'm sure that helped."

Kenzie smiled. "Not so much. I didn't stick around for the fireworks, but Tyrrell was pretty steamed when he got back to the cabin."

"T won't be happy."

"No. I hope he's not too hard on Mason, but..."

"He'll be okay," Zachary assured her. "Kids are tough."

"Yeah. But I don't want him to have to be tough. I want Tyrrell to be..." Kenzie searched for the right word and shook her head. "To be easy on him."

"Well, I guess we found him," Zachary told Mrs. Hubbard, though of course she'd heard the conversation and already knew that for herself. "So we can all stand down. Are you expecting everyone up for lunch and supper?"

"I expect so," Mrs. Hubbard agreed. "Other than you folks."

"Yeah. We still have plenty at the cabin to eat. I wouldn't want it to go to waste."

Kenzie caught Zachary watching Mrs. Hubbard very carefully for her reaction. Did he suspect her? Think that she had been the one to put something into the food? She was the one with the best access, but Kenzie could not think of a reason the woman would have to hurt anyone. She was sure that Mrs. Hubbard was not the kind of person who would do something like that out of pure mischief.

Though Kenzie's searches of the night before had shown her that her assumptions and judgments of others were not always right. She had been very wrong in some of her conclusions.

"If you get tired of it, you know you can always come here," Mrs. Hubbard told him. "It's our Thanksgiving night. Turkey, potatoes, a couple of salads..."

Zachary's expression did not change. "You're a very good cook. I'm sure it will be delicious."

Mrs. Hubbard nodded her agreement.

"I'll see you tomorrow, then," Zachary said pleasantly. "Maybe the weather will have cleared by then and we'll actually get some company."

Mrs. Hubbard's eyes rolled up toward the ceiling. "I certainly hope so. Mr. Dewey and the young lady will not improve with age."

Kenzie grimaced. At least she didn't have to work in the house, in the company of a couple of corpses. She wasn't sure how she would feel living under those conditions.

But then she realized that she did work under exactly those conditions, and it had never bothered her. But then, that was what she had signed up for. She didn't suddenly just find herself in the middle of a situation where she was required to put up with bodies being stored in her workplace.

Zachary nodded to the back door. "Let's go out this way," he invited.

"I... my coat and things are at the front door."

"Oh." He paused to consider her. "I guess they are. Why don't you grab them and come out this way, then?"

"I'll just go out that door. I can walk around the house and meet you out back, if you like."

Zachary nodded. "Yeah. Do that."

Kenzie wasn't sure why he wanted to go out the back instead of the front. Clearly that was where he had taken off his outerwear, but he could have grabbed it and gone out of the front with Kenzie, where it was a clear shot down the road to the cabin.

"Okay, see you in a minute."

Zachary exited the kitchen through the other door, which Kenzie assumed led to some kind of mudroom or porch. She said a quick goodbye to Mrs. Hubbard, which wasn't returned, and she returned to the front door to get her winter gear. Andy Collins and Vance Stiller had joined Raven and Jack in the living room. No one seemed particularly interested in or happy to see Kenzie. She supposed she had made enemies of all of them by going through their private belongings. It wasn't nice to have someone pawing through your personal, private things, even if you didn't have anything that was really secret to hide. People just didn't like it. Raven's search of Kenzie's things the night before had seemed like the ultimate imposition. She hadn't been worried about Raven learning her deepest, darkest secrets, but she hadn't felt good about having someone go through all their things.

"Couldn't find him?" Raven asked.

"Oh, I did. He just went out the back door."

"I saw that kid of yours messing around by the barn," Vance Stiller commented, fixing his gaze on Kenzie. "You should keep him in the house if he isn't being supervised."

"He's not my kid. But thank you for keeping an eye on him. We found him and he's back at the cabin now. He wasn't supposed to take off like that."

"Kids." Stiller shook his head. He looked like the thought of having kids around, of starting a family himself, was repulsive. *Why would anyone want to have children?* "This isn't really the kind of place to bring them."

"Actually, they provide a lot of family activities," Kenzie pointed out, as she slid her hands into the sleeves of her coat. "Hayrides, bonfires, board games, hot chocolate. When it isn't so cold and snowy, there are other activities for them too. It's a family resort."

"Shouldn't be," Stiller said unapologetically. "A place like this should be adults only. So that we can enjoy it properly without worrying about children and what they might say or do."

"Hear, hear," Jack chimed in. "I'm all for adults-only."

Kenzie just shook her head. She wasn't sure why they were trying to get her goat about it, but they weren't going to draw her into an argument.

"Enjoy dinner. I'll see you later," she told them blandly. She pulled on her gloves and let herself out.

There were no fences or guard dogs to get past outside; it was an easy walk around the house from the front door to the back where Zachary was waiting. He nodded as if confirming something to himself.

"What's up?" Kenzie asked.

"Nothing. I just wanted to come this way." Zachary motioned to the woods. "We can cut through this way."

"I thought you wanted to avoid me being killed by someone."

He raised his brows. "I do."

"Then shouldn't I stay where people can see me, instead of tromping off through the lonely woods?"

"No one comes through here. They all go up on the road."

Kenzie thought about the knife in the bushes. "Not everyone. Someone killed Brooke in the woods."

"Well... yes. But that's not going to happen to you. You're not alone, and you're not high on some illegal or prescription drug."

Kenzie remembered Raven's conversation with her the night before. A person could make all the right decisions, all the low-risk choices, and still end up killed. She and Zachary could only control their choices, not what happened as a consequence. Or just as a random happening. Sometimes a person's decisions had nothing to do with how things unfolded.

Kenzie let Zachary lead the way. Like Mason, he had better visual-spatial memory than Kenzie did, and his better sense of direction meant that he could get her back to the cabin way before she could sort it out herself.

"Mason and Alisha are making lunch," she informed Zachary.

"Uh-oh."

Kenzie smiled. "I just hope it's edible."

"At least with it being winter, you don't need to worry about him putting poisonous berries into it."

"Yikes! You're right. He's only allowed to choose from the food that we have. So we should be safe."

"That's one of the reasons I came up here." Zachary explained. "In case he went looking for more ingredients."

Mason going to the house for more ingredients was something that hadn't even occurred to Kenzie. And she had known that Mason and Alisha were putting their heads together to come up with something they could make for the adults for lunch.

"Well, probably a good thing that they didn't, since we still don't know where the toxin came from."

Zachary nodded. "Down in the basement, there were a lot of preserved plants and herbs. I don't know what they all were."

"Jars of fruits and vegetables?" Kenzie asked, since that was what she had pictured when she thought about the small basement room.

"Some," Zachary said. "But also lots of herbs tied into bunches." He made a movement, trying to sketch it out with his hands. "Like flower bouquets without any flowers. Tied together and hung to dry. I don't know what they all were. Some kinds of herbs and spices for her cooking, right?"

"Herbs," Kenzie repeated thoughtfully.

Zachary's brows went up as he considered her response.

"Does that surprise you?"

"No... But it does make me wonder what she might have down there."

D o you want to go back and look?" Zachary asked, turning back toward the house and gesturing.

"No... I want to get back to the cabin and get warmed up. Before the kids are finished whatever they are making. So that we don't have to eat whatever it is cold."

Kenzie could just imagine some of the bizarre combinations the kids might come up with together. And they wouldn't be better once they had cooled.

Zachary chuckled under his breath.

"But I do wonder what she has," Kenzie said. "I would say we should go back after and see... but I'm not even sure how I would know what I was looking at. I might be able to identify poison ivy, but I'm afraid that my plant identification abilities don't go much farther than that."

"Do you think there is anything we need to worry about?"

"I don't know. And without the internet, I can't even look them up. I would just have to take her word for it that everything she said was true."

They walked in silence for a few minutes, their gloved hands shoved into the oversized pockets of their jackets.

"Oh," Kenzie remembered one of the reasons she had wanted

to get Zachary right away instead of waiting for him to return to the cabin on his own once he'd run out of places to look for Mason. "Mason found a knife."

Zachary stopped walking. Kenzie halted to continue the conversation.

"A knife?"

"Well, *the* knife, I guess. A long kitchen knife. The murder weapon, I'm guessing."

"Did it have blood on it?"

"Not that I could see. But hopefully some microscopic traces."

"Where?"

"Under a bush. He was looking for sticks to use for his snowman."

"Well, that was lucky."

"I haven't told anyone or retrieved it yet. But I grabbed my phone and a bag from the cabin to preserve any evidence."

"We should go get it before whoever hid it decides to retrieve it again. If he remembers where he put it."

"It is sort of back behind our cabin." Kenzie looked around. "We're pretty close, right?"

Zachary nodded. He raised an eyebrow. "Do *you* remember where it is?"

"Uh... I sort of do. But Mason and I were coming from the barn, not back this way, so it's a little different. I don't know whether I'll recognize the exact place..."

"And you didn't happen to mark that particular bush in some way...?"

"No." Kenzie's face warmed. "It isn't like I had an evidence kit with me, you know."

"Clearly not. Do you remember what kind of a bush it was? What it looked like?"

"I don't know my bushes any better than my poisonous plants. It was about... this high..." Kenzie raised her hand above the ground, trying to convey the approximate size of the bush to him.

Zachary looked around.

"You walked close to it before," Kenzie told him. "You were coming back from the barn, and you turned off to the left, instead of back toward the cabin, which was to the right."

Zachary thought about that. "How do you know that?"

"Mason pointed out your footprints. He said they were yours."

Zachary looked down at his boots. He made a print and stepped to the side to study it. Kenzie saw the same zigzag pattern that Mason had pointed out. She looked around the ground for more footprints.

"Okay..."

"Let's try this way." Zachary pointed. "If I was coming back from the barn, then this should be the approximate path I took..."

They walked slowly, watching for more zig-zag footprints. It took a while, but eventually, Zachary spotted his previous path. "Here. This is the way I went..."

"When Mason and I came back from the barn to the cabin, we turned away from your footprints, and he found the bush and showed it to me..." Kenzie looked around. Everything looked the same. She couldn't figure out where the elusive bush was. She looked under all the nearby bushes for the knife. It had to be close by. She could feel Zachary's tension. He was trying to follow her instructions and knew that they must be close to the spot where the knife was hidden.

Kenzie's stomach started to growl. She covered it with her hand and laughed. "I don't know whether I should be hungry... who knows what they are cooking up..."

"Well, you like all the food that we brought, don't you? So it doesn't matter what they make."

"Except kids mix weird things together. I don't want ketchup on granola bars or anything bizarre like that."

Zachary made a face. "I don't want ketchup on granola bars either," he agreed. "That might put me off of breakfast foods forever."

They kept looking for the bush.

"Here!" Zachary called finally. "Over here."

Kenzie hurried over to him. Zachary pointed. "Your footprints and Mason's."

She sighed with relief. "Perfect. This will lead us right to the bush."

She let Zachary go first, leading the expedition. She had already seen the knife. He would be the better tracker. Kenzie didn't pay much attention where they were going until she saw the cabin in front of her. "Uh... this is too close. We missed it. It's back farther."

Zachary reversed and walked alongside the footprints. He stopped a couple of times. It felt like they had been following the trail for too long. Kenzie shook her head, puzzled. "Something isn't right."

"These *are* your footprints."

"I know, but..." Kenzie looked around and saw the barn. "It wasn't all the way back here. It was in the woods. You couldn't see the barn *or* the cabin." She was getting hungry and frustrated. It didn't make sense that they had lost the knife. They were in the right place. They couldn't both be that blind.

Zachary looked at her for a minute, then followed the trail back again, toward the cabin. He moved slowly, carefully. "Here?" he asked finally, pointing to a bush.

"Yes! That's it!" Kenzie agreed. She got closer, pointing to the base of the bush. "Right... there..." The words faded away. Kenzie looked at Zachary, then down again. "This can't be right."

"Are you sure this is the bush?"

"No... I think it is. They all look the same to me. But it looks like the right one."

Zachary looked around at some of the other shrubbery. He pointed down at the footprints. "You can see that this is where you and Mason stopped. Did you stop to look at more than one thing? Maybe there was a bird or an animal...?"

"No. The only time we stopped was to look at the knife. I didn't want to pick it up, because I didn't have my phone or a bag to put the knife in. I didn't want to destroy any evidence."

"Did you bring your phone with you this time?"

"Yes, but..." Kenzie shook her head. "We need to find the knife."

"It isn't here."

"I know, so we need to find it..."

"No," Zachary said firmly. "Someone has picked it up. It isn't here anymore."

Understanding dawned on Kenzie. "Oh, no."

Zachary nodded. "Yeah. I'm sorry, but... we took too long."

Kenzie looked down at the bottom of the bush. "There isn't any point in taking pictures of nothing."

"There still may be something here that helps." Zachary pointed at the footprints in the snow. "The police may be able to sort out who has been by here. Not just you and Mason. Whoever left the knife there and whoever picked it up. Not necessarily the same person, but more than likely."

Kenzie nodded. She patted her pockets to find her phone, then removed her glove in order to unlock it and launch the camera. "I can't believe someone came here while I was up to the house to get you. What are the chances that they would come right at that time and take the knife?"

"They might have been watching."

Kenzie tried to suppress a shudder. If they had been close enough to see her and Mason leave the knife and go on, or to see Kenzie go up the hill to the farmhouse, then she should have seen them. She should have known that someone was watching the house and she should have done a better job at protecting herself and the little boy. She had put him in danger and hadn't even known it. They had walked right by a murderer. Or at least, they had walked by the person who had retrieved the knife. If that hadn't been the killer, then who else could it have been? Would anyone else have picked up the knife if they had seen it? They would all want to preserve the evidence, wouldn't they? To prove that it was someone else who had killed Brooke. Nobody would want to hide the identity of the killer.

At least, she hoped not.

Kenzie took several pictures of the leaves under the bush, of the footprints. She took close-ups and shots from farther out, hoping to capture all the evidence the police would need.

"Who do you think it was?" Kenzie asked Zachary. She put her phone in her pocket and slid her fingers back into the nice warm fleecy interior of her gloves. "You think that the person who retrieved the knife is the person who killed Brooke?"

"Probably. I don't know. We'll have to see whether anyone says anything about it. They might have just been trying to do the right thing, like you. To gather evidence for when the police get here."

Kenzie nodded. She really hoped that was all it was. She felt very exposed, standing out there with Zachary, taking pictures of the bush. She hated to think of the unknown shadow watching her and Mason when they had walked through the first time. She was lucky that whoever it was had waited to see if she would pick up the knife or not. And she was probably lucky that she hadn't picked up the knife. If she had, and whoever had killed Brooke had wanted to keep it a secret, then she might not have made it back to her cabin at all.

She shuddered.

"You're cold," Zachary observed. "We've been out here long enough. Let's get back to the cabin and have a hot meal."

Kenzie just hoped it was edible.

It wasn't far to the cabin, but Kenzie was feeling tired and wrung out, as if she had a run a marathon instead of just walking around in the snow. She had walked more than she had expected to, to the barn, back to the cabin, up to the farmhouse, back to the barn again, and back to the cabin. But still, that couldn't add up to very much if one were just counting miles.

The back door was locked, so Zachary knocked and called out a few times before Tyrrell came to the door and opened it.

"You're back! I was afraid you had gotten lost."

"Goldmans don't get lost," Zachary said lightly.

"Yeah!" Mason agreed, jumping down from a chair and running over to give Zachary's legs a hug. "Goldmans don't get lost!" He grinned up at his uncle. "That's because we have excellent visio..."

"Visual-spatial memory," Kenzie contributed.

"Yeah!" Mason agreed. "We have that, right?"

"We do," Zachary agreed. "So... how are we in cooking skills?"

Mason considered this seriously. "We made pasta."

"Pasta is good," Zachary said agreeably.

"It has pieces of turkey in it. And a tomato sauce. Daddy says it tastes really good."

"Well, we should all have some, then. You know, Kenzie's stomach was growling so loud, I kept thinking that we were being stalked by a wild animal!"

Alisha giggled loudly. "You did not!"

"You should have heard it," Zachary said dramatically. He looked around, acting out how frightened he had been. "Every time we went around a corner, I was sure that it was coming..."

Kenzie put her hand over her stomach. "It growled once! And that's just because I didn't have any breakfast."

"You should always have breakfast," Mason told her, his voice taking on a lecturing tone. "It's the most important meal of the day."

"Yeah, Kenzie," Zachary teased.

Kenzie glared at him.

Alisha put bowls and spoons on the table for them, and Tyrrell supervised Mason handling the hot pot and bringing it over. Kenzie and Zachary sat down. Mason placed the pot on the table with a large serving spoon. "Do you want me to dish it up?"

"I'll get my own." Zachary reached for the spoon.

He dished up more than he would normally eat. Kenzie wondered whether he had worked up an appetite from walking outside, or whether he was taking more so that Mason wouldn't think that Zachary didn't trust his cooking. When he had dished up, Kenzie took the pot. She leaned over it and sniffed the savory steam.

"Mmm, it smells really good, Mason. What made you think of this?"

"We just looked in the cupboards to see what we had," Mason said with a shrug. He had a wide grin at her compliment. "I make pasta with Mommy sometimes. It's not hard. And we had turkey. Usually, we put ground beef in it, but I thought turkey would be okay. Sometimes we make other kinds of pasta with chicken or turkey."

"Sure," Kenzie agreed with a nod.

"We have dessert too," Alisha piped up, hovering over them. "So don't eat too much!"

"Ooh, dessert," Zachary murmured. "I'll have to leave some room. I might have taken a bit too much."

This gave him an excuse for not being able to eat all the pasta that he had taken. Not a bad plan.

Kenzie watched Tyrrell and Mason. Whatever discussion had taken place after Kenzie had left didn't seem to have resulted in any tension between them. Maybe Tyrrell had only given Mason a lecture on leaving when he wasn't supposed to, hugged him and said how worried he had been, and then moved on to lunch preparations. Kenzie hadn't been gone for long enough for much more to have taken place.

If Mason were under house arrest or facing some other punishment, he didn't seem to be upset about it. Alisha had washed her tear-streaked face and seemed to be back to her usual cheerful self.

Kenzie took her first bite of the pasta. The children had managed to cook it properly without letting it get too mushy. It wasn't underdone or overdone. The pasta sauce was a bottled sauce that Kenzie had brought with her, but she thought they might have added something to it. The turkey lent it a nice heartiness. She might actually try adding turkey to pasta at home.

"This is really good. You did a great job!"

Both children beamed, happy with her reaction. Kenzie dug in, her body ready for a larger meal after skipping breakfast. Zachary took only a few bites. He praised Mason and Alisha, but they could see how little he was eating and obviously doubted his assurances that he enjoyed it.

Zachary got up, muttering something that Kenzie couldn't make out, and started to wander around the kitchen. She didn't realize at first that he was pacing; she thought he was looking for something. She ate a little more and tried to get him to return to the table. At least for their dessert.

"What's up?" she asked. "You're thinking about something."

"Trying to figure it out... who took that knife and what they did with it. And all of the pills that you searched out and collected... where are they? I was hoping that when I looked around this morning, I would find them. Disposed of in a ditch or shoved into a pile of snow. Because... no one is going to want to deal with them, are they? They won't try to poison anyone." Zachary shook his head. "Did anyone actually put any of them into the food to start with? Or were we wrong?"

Kenzie looked at the kids, wishing that Zachary wouldn't say so much around them. But he didn't follow her glance and didn't stop talking about it.

"A lot of drugs can have the kinds of effects that we saw or heard about."

"But *did* they?" Zachary demanded. "How much would be needed to make everyone suffer the effects? And they wouldn't be able to taste them? For them all to be affected, Kenzie. Does that make sense?"

"What are you suggesting, then? That we were just being paranoid? That everyone was just... feeling their oats that day? It was a full moon? What about the amnesia? Both Vance Stiller and Andy Collins had pretty significant memory blocks."

"Maybe they drank too much? They're both drinkers, right? But we don't know how much they usually drink. If they went overboard or if they started out dehydrated?"

Kenzie tried to follow Zachary's reasoning. "So... you don't want to think that it was an intentional poisoning. It was just... a series of coincidences, and we made it out to be something that it wasn't?"

"We misjudged."

"I did, you mean. It was all my idea from the start, not yours."

"We both thought it," Zachary said firmly. "Everyone except us had... weird experiences that night. But what if it was just... mass hysteria? One person setting another off? Like kids telling ghost stories. Like the Salem witch trials. A couple of people had too much to drink, maybe Redd was into his mushrooms, and between them... they managed to influence everyone, to make them see and hear things that weren't there. But in reality... it was just..."

"A couple having a fight that ended in disaster."

"It happens." He grimaced at her. "It happens a lot."

Kenzie knew that was true. She was the one who worked in the medical examiner's office. She knew very well how easy it was for a domestic dispute to turn bloody. And fatal.

"It could be," she admitted.

Zachary continued to wander around. Kenzie rubbed her forehead and thought about what he had said. Had they gone way overboard in their theory that someone had poisoned the food? Had she been that far off base? If so, then why had someone broken into the safe and stolen the drugs? Just like the knife under the bush? Someone was cleaning up, trying to sanitize the area and get rid of any evidence. They would say that Dewey's death had been by natural causes, and Brooke's was just a tragic accident. A newlywed's argument gone bad. Would there be any evidence to the contrary?

Had Kenzie just let her imagination get the better of her? Was she prone to flights of fancy without Dr. Wiltshire there to bring her down to earth?

It was true that they didn't have much in the way of evidence. There would be more once the authorities had a chance to examine Mr. Dewey's and Brooke Collins's bodies. The medical examiner for the county would be able to find a hallucinogen, if he knew what to look for.

"Are you done?" Alisha asked. "Are you ready for dessert?"

Kenzie brought herself back to the present. The children were watching, hovering nearby, eager to serve them the next course.

"Yes," Kenzie agreed, pushing her dish away. "I had a lot, but I left a little bit of room..."

"It was really good, right?" Mason asked.

"Yes, it was. I'm going to make some at home sometime. It's a really good use of the turkey and other ingredients that you have on hand. I was afraid you guys were going to come up with something really weird. I used to do experiments in the kitchen when I was little, mixing potions and coming up with some really bizarre—and totally inedible—stuff."

Alisha giggled. "Really?"

"Really. Like... mixing chocolate milk and orange soda and... brown sugar and cinnamon." Kenzie made a face. "It was not something you would have wanted to drink."

"Eww!" Both children broke into giggles, making little shrieks to express how disgusting it was and then laughing until they were out of breath.

Kenzie shook her head. "Okay, you'd better tell me what you've made for dessert, before you bust a gut."

Mason wiped at his eyes, wet from tears of laughter. "Can you really do that?" he asked seriously. "Bust a gut?"

"No. It's just an expression."

"You can break a rib laughing," Zachary contributed, walking back to the table. "Or get a nosebleed. Or... if you're drinking milk, it could come out your nose."

"Or if you're mixing together chocolate milk and orange soda," Alisha gasped. "And cinnamon!"

"Don't spray that through your nose," Kenzie said. "Trust me."

That sent them into more gales of laughter. Tyrrell moved into the kitchen, interceding. "You guys are a terrible influence!" he scolded Zachary and Kenzie. "These two are going to be in hysterics before long. Dessert!" he told Mason and Alisha sternly. "No more nonsense!"

The children's faces fell, and they went to the counter to get the dessert ready. They tried to pout and stay serious, but Kenzie could see them still exchanging looks with each other, trying to keep their expressions serious.

"We have peaches and yogurt," Alisha said, bringing over bowls of each and a couple of small dessert bowls for Kenzie and Zachary to dish up their individual desserts.

"Are we supposed to choose one or the other?" Zachary asked mischievously. "Or mix them both together?"

Alisha giggled. But she glanced at Tyrrell and quickly stifled it. "You're *supposed* to mix them. And you can sprinkle granola on top. If you like granola." She supplied a small dish of clumps of granola that had once been formed into bars.

Kenzie and Zachary dished up their desserts with solemn expressions. Once they had tasted a couple of bites, Tyrrell shooed the children away, telling them that they could play for a while and work out their silliness.

He shot a glance toward his brother that told Kenzie without a doubt that he had picked up enough of their conversation to not be happy about the way they were talking around his children. Kenzie imagined him trying to explain to his ex-wife why the children were suddenly obsessed with the idea of their food being poisoned or were talking about dead bodies at their vacation resort. She grimaced and took another bite of her peaches and yogurt.

The children were in the living room, playing, already arguing over what they were going to play and what the rules would be. If they had been disturbed by overhearing any of Zachary's and Kenzie's discussion over lunch, it didn't seem as if it were bothering them anymore. Kids were like that. Flexible. Able to switch from something worrisome to something safer in a few minutes.

Most kids, that is.

Kids who hadn't been traumatized as Zachary had been as a child. Children who didn't have OCD or other obsessive conditions that forced them to relive the conversations over and over again.

"The Salem witch trials," Kenzie said in a low voice.

Zachary raised his brows. He took a bite of the peach and yogurt concoction.

"You said that it was all mass hysteria," Kenzie said.

He looked at her. "Wasn't it? You're not contending that it was actual magic, are you?"

"No, that's not what I meant." Kenzie smiled and shook her head. "I'm not arguing for actual magic and witchcraft. There might have been some traditional herbal healing that was identified as witchcraft, I'll admit to that. It's easy to attribute malice to things that you don't understand. But I don't think it was just mass hysteria, either. That might be part of it. And the same kind of pressure to inform on your neighbors as you might have dealt with in the anti-communist era or in Nazi Germany. But it was more than that."

"What, then?"

"They think that part of it might have been ergot."

Zachary shook his head. He blinked at her, trying to make sense of it. Clearly not a theory he had heard before. "What is ergot?"

"It's a disease that rye and other grains can get. And if people eat the infected grain, then they can experience hallucinations and other odd behaviors. So some of the 'hysteria' surrounding the trials might have had to do with people having hallucinations about things that other people were doing, or hallucinations about performing magic themselves."

"Ergot. I've never heard of it before. So... is it one of those diseases that doesn't exist anymore? Like the plague?"

"It still exists, but with the commercialization of grains and regulations on care and handling, it rarely affects anyone anymore. Maybe a farmer who grows rye for himself and doesn't know what to watch for. But it doesn't generally enter the market."

"Could they have it here? Could something that Mrs. Hubbard cooked with have been contaminated with this disease? She makes bread, buns, all of that kind of thing. Whatever they need, she makes from scratch."

Kenzie thought about it while slurping down a few more bites of peaches and yogurt. It was a nice, sweet treat. Not chocolate ice cream, but something nice to have when they were separated from most of her usual comfort foods. The kids had really risen to the challenge and had produced a very nice lunch.

"I don't think they could have it here, but of course anything is possible. I would think that if Mrs. Hubbard had any diseased rye, she would recognize it and not cook with it. But if a neighbor had it and ground it up..." Kenzie shrugged. "It could be something shared between households in these parts. A farmer's market or a barter group."

"How would we find out?"

"We're just going to have to wait until the authorities can get here. They can check Brooke's body for ergot and any other toxins that we think she might have been exposed to. We can't test everyone else, but *her* metabolism stopped while she still had it in her system. Unless it's got a really short half-life, it will still be present in the body."

"But there's nothing we can do until then?"

"Just talk to Mrs. Hubbard. Ask her where she gets her flour. If she's ever heard of anyone having this in the area. But I don't know how forthcoming she will be. Not if she thinks that we suspect her of wrongdoing. It's one thing to say that someone came into her kitchen and put something into the food without her realizing it. It's another thing to say that she did it herself, either through negligence or intentionally."

Zachary nodded slowly. He stirred his peaches and yogurt around, then licked off the spoon. Sometimes he ate at a maddeningly slow speed. Like a kid who took three hours to eat Brussels sprouts, hoping that Mom and Dad would give up and not make him eat them all.

"Mushrooms, ergot, what else?"

"What else what?"

"What other plants can cause hallucinations? We were looking for drugs. Something that would have to have been intentionally added to the food to have this effect. What if it were something that was in the food by accident? Something that... Mrs. Hubbard thought was something different. There are mix-ups sometimes. Berries, wild parsnips, herbs that someone thought were one thing, but they were actually another. You hear about people being poisoned by accident because something was misidentified. So what might have caused these other symptoms? Psychedelic mushrooms and moldy rye. Anything else?"

"It's not really my area."

"But it is. How would you find out if someone ate something poisonous by accident if they came to your morgue? It happens, so there must be some kind of protocol to figure it out."

"Okay, yes," Kenzie agreed. "Of course there is. We talk to the people who were around the deceased last, find out what they were doing and if they showed any signs or symptoms. Actually, the police usually do that, but sometimes the ME's office has follow up questions. We take stomach contents and try to identify what their last meal consisted of. If it seems suspicious or poisoning is suspected, then we will take a longer time doing that. Not just observing what is in the stomach contents, but testing the various ingredients. And we do tox screens. The most basic ones just check for drugs someone is likely to overdose on, but if there is something specific we are looking for, a particular plant or drug, then we can test for those."

"But you can't do any of that here."

"The only thing I can do here is to talk to people and look for signs and symptoms of what they might have eaten. And people are not being really cooperative right now. I think everyone is tired of the questions and just wants to pretend that nothing happened. It was just... a nightmare or a drunk. Nothing more than that."

"And you don't know what other plants could cause these symptoms?"

"Which symptoms? I know a few, but I'd have to look most of them up in a database. I at least need internet access so I can look them up."

"And we can't." Zachary sighed. "Oh, well. Hopefully, it won't be very long until the weather clears up and the authorities can get here. I know we won't be first priority, but they know we already have a body here. Even if it were just natural causes, the ME is still going to want a look while it is still as fresh as possible. In three days, a body is already starting to decompose."

"Luckily, ours is in cold storage. I'm glad we ended up here in the winter rather than the summer. But yeah. They don't know that and... hopefully they're eager to get here before it decomposes too much."

Zachary went back to stirring his fruit around. Kenzie worked through the symptoms in her head. She kept starting a list and then getting distracted, so she tried to work it through out loud. "Hallucinations or delusions. Amnesia. Anger, irritability, oppositional behavior. Maybe heart attack."

Zachary's eyes sparked. He was eager to work it out with Kenzie. They both enjoyed it when they could work on a case together, bouncing ideas off each other and seeing what they could come up with. Kenzie providing the medical knowledge and Zachary making suggestions based on his observations of human behavior.

"What about fever?" he suggested. "You thought that Redd might have a fever."

"Yes... a fever can cause hallucinations, but what caused the fever? It could be a virus."

"And we know that viruses can cause a lot of other neurological symptoms as well."

"Yes," Kenzie acknowledged, and rolled her eyes. "They certainly can. And you and I would be less likely to catch a virus, staying down here away from the rest of the crowd and having just gone through an antiviral protocol."

"What else could fever be caused by? Is a virus the only possibility?"

"Bacterial infection. There are definitely drugs that can raise your core temperature as well. Ecstasy is one of them."

"Did you find any of that when we searched the cabins?"

"No, but that doesn't mean that no one had any before I did the search. Or had it on their person, since we didn't search everyone to see what they were carrying."

Zachary nodded. "What else?"

"Redd had dilated pupils as well. Very wide."

"Not pinpoint like with opioids."

"No. Opioids are out. If everyone were exposed to the same thing as Redd. His pupils were definitely dilated."

"Anything else?"

"They seemed drunk. More than they should have been for having a drink or two with dinner."

"They might have started drinking earlier, or have had more than you thought."

"Or it made them act drunk."

Zachary nodded, conceding. "So what does that tell you? Anything?"

"Death. Drunken. Delirium. Dilated pupils." Kenzie blinked, trying to put it all together.

"You sound like... you know."

"The ten D's," Kenzie said. There was something tickling the back of her brain, but she couldn't bring it to the fore. Why did they have to have no internet access? With a few searches, she could have looked up the ten D's. She could have reminded herself what the others were, so she could see whether they fit. And they would tell her, if they all fit, what the toxin was. "This is maddening! I can't think of it."

"This is something you learned in medical school?" Zachary suggested. "What class?"

Kenzie tried to picture it. Which professor or doctor had listed them? Was it a class? A case she had attended to on rounds? The emergency room? Something that had come up in the medical examiner's office? She pressed her fingertips to her forehead, trying to remember.

"Yes, but I can't remember. It's just on the tip of my tongue, but I can't remember it."

"There were ten D's? What else could there have been? What other symptoms start with D?"

"There are too many of them to count. I have to remember what those ten were. Or what they indicated. It was... it was a toxin, I'm sure of that. Not a genetic disorder. Nothing congenital."

Zachary was quiet, watching her. But despite the fact that he was respecting her process and giving her the time to think it through, Kenzie was irritated by his focused interest. It was too much pressure.

"Are you done with that?" She indicated his dessert bowl. "If you are, then get rid of it. Don't keep *playing* with it."

Zachary stood up. He picked up the bowl and took it with him to the sink. Of course he was hurt. He was trying to help, and she had snapped at him for something that wasn't even the issue. Kenzie would make it up to him later. She would thank him for being quiet and leaving her to just think about it. She would thank him for getting up and washing his dish without making a big deal of it. Once she had sorted the symptoms out and knew what it was they were looking for.

Tyrrell had heated a pot of water for washing dishes. Kenzie tried to ignore Zachary as he scraped his dessert bowl and his main course into the garbage, then splashed around in the sink, cleaning them up. He returned to the table and didn't say anything to Kenzie about whether she had solved the puzzle yet. He indicated her dinner bowl. "You're done with that one?"

Kenzie nudged it toward him. She looked down at her dessert bowl, but wasn't really interested in the fruit and yogurt anymore. The kids were both in the other room, so they wouldn't see whether she finished it off or not. She took one more bite, and then pushed that bowl to Zachary as well.

"Thanks."

He nodded and took them both away without a word.

Kenzie leaned her head back until she was staring up at the ceiling.

She was a trained medical professional. She had seen the group of symptoms that had been described to her. It might have been rare, but that wasn't any excuse for not remembering the details. Doctors had to be able to consume and retain vast quantities of information. She had been too lazy, relying on her ability to perform searches to find out what she needed to instead of on retaining the new information that she learned. She couldn't stop learning. Just because she was in the Medical Examiner's Office now, that didn't mean that she could just coast. There was far more that she could be learning from each and every case that went through their autopsy.

Zachary finished the dish-washing and didn't return to the table to check up on her and see whether she had figured out the information she was trying to remember yet. He knew, of course, that she would tell him when she remembered. It wouldn't be a secret. She wouldn't hold back to surprise him later when he least expected it. It wasn't some kind of game or power play.

They both knew that however safe they felt there in the cabin, their lives could depend on it.

It sounded melodramatic, but it really wasn't, was it?

She needed to know what it was that the guests were being poisoned with, if anything. It could be the difference between someone living or dying. Not only that, but if someone had intentionally poisoned the food or drinks, then they were not going to want Kenzie to figure it out. They would already be looking for a way to take her out. To remove Kenzie and her knowledge from the equation.

And she had seen the knife. Maybe that wasn't a key piece of evidence. She hadn't been able to see what fingerprints were on it, of course. Seeing the knife itself hadn't told her anything about who it was that had stabbed Brooke. It was just a knife. She hadn't even been able to prove that it was the knife that had killed Brooke, though she was sure it was. Why else would someone have thrown it away behind the cabins? People didn't just randomly throw knives away in the bush.

It was a matter of life and death. Kenzie's, and maybe others' as well. She couldn't afford to treat it like a case she was only remotely interested in. People could die if she didn't figure it out. Like on a medical mystery TV show—the doctors always kept looking until they found out exactly what the patient's problem was. It didn't matter how rare the disease or syndrome was or how expensive the testing or treatment were. It didn't matter how long it would have taken doctors in real life to figure out what the problem was. A TV show doctor would figure it out.

And that was what Kenzie had to do too.

She got up from the table. Sitting there wasn't bringing her any inspiration. She needed to move around, to think through what they knew again. Maybe make a written list this time. Like she had written down the drugs that she had found in each of the cabins. She should probably look at that again to see whether she could add anything to it. She might remember one or two more medications.

Not that it mattered. Not if, like Zachary suggested, it wasn't even someone's medication that had been used to poison the guests. Something that occurred naturally or had been added in. A berry? Belladonna? Wild parsnips? Something that Mrs. Hubbard had foraged and saved, thinking it was a harmless substance. It wasn't her fault. People made mistakes.

Tyrrell looked at Kenzie as she wandered through the living room. He too gave her the space she needed. Maybe he didn't know what they had been talking about and he was just tired or enjoying watching the children. But he didn't interrogate her and ask her if she had figured out what the ten D's were yet, or what they signified.

She would write down all of the D symptoms she could think of. Then she would pick out the ones that fit together. And once she had the list of ten, she would remember what it was that they were looking for. And they would be one step closer to figuring out the answer.

It wasn't just mass hysteria. She was convinced of it. The constellation of symptoms was too familiar.

Kenzie finished going over her written lists and pushed them to the side, sighing loudly. Zachary was playing with the kids on the floor and looked up at her.

"Maybe you need to distract your mind. Sometimes, when you're trying to remember something, the best thing to do is to not think about it. Distract yourself with something else, and then it suddenly pops into your head."

"I don't think that's going to happen here."

Zachary shrugged. "Well, you've written everything down, so it isn't like you're going to lose something if you put it out of your mind. Why don't you play a game with us. Distract yourself and see what happens." He looked toward the window, which was starting to get dark. "It doesn't make any difference whether you remember tonight or tomorrow. I don't think anything is going to happen tonight."

But the fact was, something had happened every night since they had arrived there. Deaths, the theft of the drugs from the safe, something had happened ever time the sun had gone down. But she'd better keep it to herself. She didn't want to upset the kids and give them nightmares.

Maybe the weather would break, and they would be able to get help the next day.

The doors were locked and, unlike in many of the houses in the city, they were not hollow core doors, but heavy, thick, hard-wood doors with bolts that sank into thick log walls. Practically impenetrable. Or so she hoped.

They were safe for the night. Help would not arrive until at least the next day. She might as well put her worries aside and do something that the kids would enjoy.

"Okay, what? What do you guys want to do?"

"Play *Clue*?" Alisha suggested.

Kenzie laughed. *Clue*. When they were trying to figure out a real murder. That would be distracting, all right.

But at least there were no poisons or toxic plants in *Clue*. It was all manual murder weapons. Knife, gun, rope, candlestick. No one could leave a poison in one room and then leave, so that their crime was not discovered until much later.

Kenzie shook her head, but she agreed. "Okay, *Clue*. You guys get it out. I want to be Mrs. Peacock."

"I like Professor Plum," Alisha said. "I like purple."

"You can't be Professor Plum," Mason objected. "You have to be one of the girls."

"Girls can be professors."

Mason looked skeptical. He pulled the box out of the pile and started going through the cards. He showed Alisha the one for Professor Plum. "He's not a girl. He's a man. You have to be one of the girls."

"No I don't. And that doesn't mean that Professor Plum has to be a man. They just had to make him a man or a woman when they drew the card. He can be anyone you want. If I want him to be a woman professor, he can be." Alisha looked at Kenzie, appealing to her. "A lady can be a professor, right?"

"Of course," Kenzie agreed. "I'm a female doctor. I had lots of professors at school who were women."

"In this game, he's a man," Mason grumbled.

"He can be a woman," Alisha asserted. "And that's who I'm going to be. What color do you want, Mason?"

Mason made a face. "Mr. Green."

"Okay. Mr. Green. Who do you want to be, Uncle Zachary?"

"Colonel Mustard."

"He's the yellow one," Mason declared, setting the figure on his square. He sounded the word out. "Col-o-nel. Why do you say it *kernel?*"

Zachary shook his head. "That's how it is pronounced. I don't know why."

Mason accepted this. "Daddy, you have to be White or Scarlet, because Alisha took Professor Plum." He lowered his eyebrows at Alisha. "See? You should let Daddy take Professor Plum. You can be one of the girls."

"It's okay, Mason," Tyrrell told him. "I'll be... Miss Scarlet."

Mason giggled.

Tyrrell tried out a falsetto voice. "Is this how Miss Scarlet talks?"

Mason guffawed loudly. He pushed Alisha over.

"Hey!" Alisha objected.

"You still sound like a girl. You have to make a voice like a man."

"No. I'm a lady professor, not a man professor, so I don't have to use a deep voice."

Alisha continued to set up the board game. Mason sighed and sorted through the cards to select out the murderer, weapon, and room.

"Kenzie?" Zachary touched Kenzie on the shoulder to get her attention. "Kenz, it's your turn."

Kenzie blinked and looked at Zachary. She looked at the game board and the clue sheet in her hand. She had completely lost track of the last few moves, when she should have been marking down each of the clues she gathered as the other players passed cards back and forth.

"Are you okay?" Zachary asked. He looked at the window. "What time is it? Do you want to go to bed? I know you didn't get very much sleep last night."

"No."

He waited. "You don't want to go to bed, or you aren't okay?"

Kenzie looked away from him. Zachary was sitting on the floor in front of the bookshelves. As with the other cabins, the books in the shelves covered a wide range of genres and topics, hopefully providing something of interest to everyone who stayed there. There was genre fiction and non-fiction, topics ranging from food to gardening in Vermont and history of the area. All kinds of things.

"Umm, I pass," she told the other players. She moved toward Zachary, who hid his cards and clue sheet.

Mason and Alisha protested that Kenzie couldn't pass on her turn. She had to roll the dice and make a guess if she could.

"Someone else roll for me," Kenzie said. "I'm going... over there," she pointed to one of the rooms the farthest away from her playing piece. "I need to find out about the Ballroom."

She, of course, had the Ballroom in her hand, but hopefully they didn't know that. Kenzie kept going. Not directly to Zachary, but to the books behind him. *Gardening in Vermont. Traditional Vermont Cookery. Wildcrafting and Backwoods Forage. Early Virginia History.*

Kenzie started to pull books off the shelves. The children protested that they were still playing the game, but Kenzie ignored them. "Someone else can take my turn. Zachary, can you play my cards?"

"That's not fair!" Mason insisted. "Then he knows all your cards too and he will win!"

Kenzie ignored the protest. They could sort it out without her. Her attention was needed elsewhere. Zachary picked up Kenzie's cards and dealt them around the table. "Now everyone has more. Let's keep going. Kenzie can't play right now."

"Why can't she?" Mason continued to whine.

Kenzie opened up the gardening book and started to leaf through it.

As she had told Zachary earlier, she could identify poison ivy, but that was about the extent of her plant identification skills. Other than the obvious. Daisies and strawberries and things that everyone grew in their gardens. But all of the different types of plants and flowers and berries and herbs... there were just too many for her to make any headway on them. She had too many other things she was trying to learn and retain as a doctor. She slowed down and started really looking at the plants and skimming through the sidebars, looking for any warnings about plants that were toxic or could cause people health problems if they were susceptible. Some of the warnings were just lore, and others had actual medical warnings on them. She stopped halfway through and picked up the cooking and wildcrafting books. She didn't know a lot about wildcrafting, but knew that the general idea was using plants that grew wild in your environment for food or other purposes. Medicine, fuel, decoration, soap making. Whatever people could think of to do with them.

She couldn't read all the books simultaneously, but she was sure going to try. She looked over the pages for keywords, skipping from one book to the other, turning each of the pages and checking again. She wanted to absorb all the information at the same time. It seemed ridiculous that people were only able to read one document at a time, when a computer could have easily searched all the books at the same time and come up with the hits for her. Old school was so slow!

Zachary continued to play the game with the children, but she could see him watching her out of the corner of his eye. Kenzie continued to leaf through the books, impatient to find something that would help. Maybe, as Zachary said, it had all been a mistake. Mrs. Hubbard had gathered some plants she thought were safe, and they were not. She had no way of knowing that they could have caused the hallucinogenic effects or that they could lead to death. She would never have intentionally killed her employer, something that might force her into an early retirement.

Kenzie turned the page in the gardening book and found that the next chapter was "A Poison Garden." Kenzie stopped and stared at the page. Would someone actually plant a garden they knew contained poisonous plants? Certainly not someone with children or animals who might get into the plants. The introductory paragraphs in the chapter referred to a garden in England that was famous for the number of poisonous plants that it contained, and how it was becoming the new trend among gardeners in the US.

There were, of course, plenty of warnings about fencing the garden and keeping it secure from children and pets. No warnings about making sure you didn't have any budding serial killers in the area. Kenzie slowly turned the pages, studying the leaves, flowers, and fruits shown on each panel and reading through the descriptions of the effect of each poison. Some of them were extremely toxic in small amounts, and Kenzie couldn't imagine growing them intentionally, knowing what heartbreak they could cause. What if your fence wasn't high enough? Or a neighbor unknowingly let a child into the garden to retrieve a lost ball or to look at the pretty flowers or berries? It would be horrifying to discover that you had made a mistake and someone had suffered or died because of it.

Kenzie stopped at one panel, reading the symptoms over again carefully. She looked at the heading. *Datura stramonium.*

"Datura," she said aloud.

"What's that?" Zachary's head turned toward her.

Kenzie scanned the common names of the plant with the purple, trumpet-shaped flowers.

"*Datura stramonium.* Jimson weed."

"What is that?"

"It's... a plant that grows all over North America." Kenzie read through the description of the areas and type of soil the plant grew in. "It is part of the same family as deadly nightshade and tobacco. Many of our popular vegetables come from that family, but it has some toxic members as well as the edibles."

"And do you think... that someone used it by accident?"

Zachary abandoned the *Clue* game, apparently not even hearing the protests of the children as he turned his back on them, completely focused on Kenzie.

"An accident... I don't know. It sounds as though it is fairly well-known. Some people smoke it for its hallucinogenic properties, but it is very toxic. Easy to overdose and kill yourself."

"Do you think it grows around here?"

Kenzie showed him the cover of the book. *Gardening in Vermont.*

"Okay, so I would guess that it does." Zachary considered. "Does it cover all the symptoms?"

"Yes. And I remember hearing about it in rounds. The doctor talking about how you don't see a lot of it, but you have to be able to recognize it. The ten D's. Dry mouth, dry hot skin, delirium, delusions, death, I don't remember all of them. I'll have to look them up when we get internet access again. This article doesn't list them all as D's, but it's all in there..." Kenzie's eyes were focused beyond her, thinking about it.

"We should go up and talk to Mrs. Hubbard."

Kenzie looked at the window. It was very dark outside. She didn't want to be wandering around so late. "We should wait until tomorrow."

Zachary followed her gaze. He shifted restlessly. "I don't think it's that late yet. She won't be in bed. We could talk to her tonight."

"Not at night. With everything else that has happened... I don't want to be out there after dark."

"We could get Burknall to take us up there. He would be a good guard, make sure that nothing happened."

"As long as he isn't the poisoner. He has access to the kitchen. He visits with Mrs. Hubbard. He could slip something into the food." Kenzie looked down at the book. "It doesn't take very much Jimson weed to cause an overdose. You can't tell how much of the active compound is in the leaves. Or the seeds. It's very concentrated."

"But why would he do that? This is his livelihood."

"Why would anyone do it? It doesn't make any sense to me. Maybe it's just... someone who likes to cause excitement. Or to see other people suffer. There are plenty of sadists out there. Of all people, you know that."

"We could sort this out tonight. Figure out what's been going on and who did it."

Kenzie shook her head emphatically. "We're not going to rush into this. We can't afford to be impulsive."

Zachary turned his face away from her. Of course he recognized that impulsivity had been his downfall in other cases, leading to him or someone else getting hurt. They needed to take it slowly. To be sure of each step so that they didn't run into a dangerous situation or start throwing around accusations that someone would be desperate to stop.

But who?

"It could be any of them," Kenzie said. "They were all here the night Brooke was killed. They were all up at the house and would have had access to the food and drink."

"This was planned," Zachary suggested. "If it was one of the guests, then they must have brought the Jimson weed with them. Because there's nothing growing right now."

He was right, of course. Everything was buried under layers of snow. The gardens, the ditches, the woods, anywhere Datura might have grown was covered.

"Mrs. Hudson could have some in the basement, where you said she had dried herbs hanging."

"Because she thought it was something else? Or did she know it was Jimson weed?"

Kenzie thought about how broken up Mrs. Hudson had been over Mr. Dewey's death. She was sure that emotion had not been fake. Mrs. Hudson really was sorry that Mr. Dewey had died, and the effect that losing her employer would have on her. That hadn't seemed fake.

"I really can't see her using it knowingly. Maybe she thought it was something else. The book says that sometimes people mistake it for tobacco."

"She doesn't strike me as a smoker."

"No. But maybe she used them in some poultice. They do that, don't they? A poultice for bruises or to draw out poisons?"

Zachary shrugged and indicated the books with his chin.

"You're the one with the medical training and the reference material. Maybe there's something in there about uses."

Kenzie nodded, flipping a few more pages. "We'll go up to the house tomorrow. See if we can find anything out from Mrs. Hudson."

"I suppose."

"And if it's not her... then someone must have planned this whole thing and brought it with them."

It wasn't a very pleasant thought.

Kenzie felt bad about the *Clue* game starting with all five of them, but ending with just the kids and Tyrrell. But Tyrrell waved off her apologies, and they did eventually finish the game, with Mason crowing about how he had figured it all out. Nothing to do with the extra cards that he had received from Kenzie's and Zachary's hands.

"You guys are trying to figure out what really happened," Tyrrell said, careful not to mention murder or killing in front of the kids. "That's important. We're just playing a game. It didn't mess anything up. We still finished."

"Well, I am sorry," Kenzie said to Alisha. Mason was bouncing around the room like a pinball, jumping and yelping and not looking as if he were getting ready for sleep. "Maybe I can read to you guys before bed? Would that be good?"

Alisha looked doubtfully at the big texts Kenzie had spread out on the floor.

"Not these ones," Kenzie said quickly. "Something more interesting. Did you guys find some books that you like?" Kenzie looked at the bookshelf, which seemed to have a bit of something for everyone.

"Well, there was one about animals," Alisha said. "I know maybe it's a little young, but it was interesting."

"That sounds good. Once you guys get settled for bed, I'll come in and read a chapter or two for you, okay?"

Alisha looked at Mason with raised eyebrows and sighed the long-suffering sigh of the big sister of a hyperactive boy. "Sure."

It took Tyrrell some time to get Mason corralled and started on his bedtime routine. Kenzie had hoped that without screens to wind him up, he would have a fairly quiet night. He seemed to have been doing better at sleeping since the power went out. But he kept bouncing around and thinking of one more thing he had to do before bed, and by the time Kenzie's story time came around, Tyrrell was having a hard time keeping his voice even. He told Mason firmly to get into bed and stay there, but he seemed to be fighting a losing battle.

"What day is it?" Mason demanded. "When are we going home? I want to see Mommy again. And to play with my games. My *real* games."

"It's Thursday," Tyrrell told him. "And we'll go home when we can. Right now we can't get anywhere on the highway. We need to stay here until it stops snowing and the plows come and clear the snow."

"But it's a school day! And I haven't talked to Mommy at all. She said to call every night before I go to bed, and I haven't called her." He shook his head, brow knitted in worry.

"Mommy knows that there was a storm coming in. She'll understand that you didn't call because you couldn't. I'll let her know, when we can get through again. Okay? I'll let her know that it wasn't because you forgot, but just because you weren't able to get through."

Mason nodded. "I really want to go home now."

"We will when we can. But you've had a good time here, haven't you? We've played lots of games, and cooked on a cook stove, and you got to go outside for a while today. Even if you didn't build a snowman."

"Can I build a snowman tomorrow?"

"We'll see. You need to be supervised so that you can't just wander off again. That was really scary. You can't do things like that."

"I was okay. And I came home."

"I know you did, and I was really glad that you were safe. I don't want to worry like that, so you need to be more careful of your decisions."

Mason considered this, but didn't say that he would. Kenzie wondered what was going on in his head. Did he understand that his impulsivity wasn't something that he could control, even if the adults in his life told him he needed to? Did he understand that it was part of a disorder? Or did he think that he did things that were dangerous and that his parents told him not to because he was a bad kid? Did he avoid promising to stay close to home and make his snowman because he knew that he'd never be able to keep his promise, or did he not promise to obey because he didn't want to and didn't think that Tyrrell's rules were fair?

"Can Kenzie read to us now?" Alisha asked.

Tyrrell nodded. He kissed each of the kids on the forehead. "You guys lay down quietly and let Kenzie read. I don't want to hear another peep from you. You stay in bed, as still as you can, until you fall asleep."

Alisha nodded obediently, and Kenzie imagined she would do just that. Mason was already looking away from his father, eyeing the window rattling in the storm. Kenzie hoped it was the last hurrah of the weather system, and that, like a tantruming child, all would be peaceful and forgotten in the morning.

Kenzie had found it difficult to settle down and go to sleep. Not because she wasn't tired. She was exhausted. But she kept trying to puzzle through everything they knew about the poison and the other people stuck at the Lodge. Was it a guest with a grudge?

One of the staff? Someone who was just out to do some mischief? She kept thinking of their personalities, their faces, and the things she had discovered when she searched their cabins. A lot could be learned about a person by how they lived or the possessions they decided to take with them on a holiday.

Look at Kenzie and Zachary. Kenzie had been concerned about having comfortable clothing, the toiletries she needed, and food she knew Zachary would eat even if he were nauseated. Zachary had been unable to pack his clothing and the other things that he would need, feeling too overwhelmed by the idea of going away. But he had picked up his bag of electronics and detection equipment. Kenzie had not brought anything work-related with her. Some of the guests brought with them all of the comforts of home or everything they needed for work—thinking of Brittany in particular—and others had brought little, expecting to be entertained and provided for by the staff at the Lodge. Some had a lot of medications like Zachary, others had almost nothing.

She didn't know as much as she would like to about their backgrounds. She didn't even know Redd Flagg's real name. And despite Brittany's fame, Kenzie hadn't really figured out what it was she was famous for. If Kenzie had been an Agatha Christie detective, she would have gathered a lot more information about everyone's backgrounds and how they were related to each other. They would all be bound to be related by different connections. People who had served in the war together, estranged family, employers, nannies—the Grande Dame always had lot of interesting ways to connect different people and their pasts together.

Zachary sat on the edge of the bed for a while, but couldn't seem to settle in. Normally, he could at least lie down with her for a while to cuddle, even if he didn't go to sleep right away. Or if he only went to sleep for a few hours and then was up again. Kenzie listened to him breathing for a while. Too uneven and too quick.

"Hey. Are you okay?" she ventured.

Zachary startled and turned toward her slightly. "Yeah," he whispered back. "I'm fine."

Fine. Which meant that he wasn't.

"What's wrong?"

He rubbed his hands down the pants of his thighs, drying his palms or smoothing his pants. He normally didn't wear pajamas, but the cabin bedroom got cold even with the heater running in the other room, so he was wearing some light gray sweatpants.

"No meds," Zachary said eventually. "I'm feeling a little... anxious."

Kenzie rubbed her eyes. She was going to suggest that it would be okay for him to take one of his anti-anxiety pills when she suddenly realized. When he said no meds, he meant no meds. Raven had confiscated everything and put it into the safe. Whoever had broken into the safe had taken the meds, hiding or disposing of them, and leaving people like Zachary and Raven who depended on them to get through the day with nothing. They had both kept a dose of night meds and of morning meds, and had expected to be able to have more dispensed the next day as they needed them. But the day had come and gone, and they were left with nothing.

Kenzie sat up, swearing as the realization hit. She pushed off the cozy blankets and rubbed Zachary's back and shoulders. "I didn't even think about that. I'm so sorry! What can I do?"

"Nothing. I'm just going to have to... take a med holiday. I've done that before. No big deal."

But she knew it was a big deal. It was always a big deal. And several of the meds he was on were not supposed to be discontinued cold turkey. He was supposed to cut down on them under a doctor's supervision, not just to stop taking them. She rubbed his neck, trying to loosen the knots of the muscles he was holding so tightly.

"What about... what other things would help? Dr. B. has given you relaxation exercises before. Meditation, progressive relaxation....? How about that?"

"I've been trying to relax."

"With her exercises?"

His head ticked to the side. Not quite a nod or a head-shake. Sort of a diagonal. Which Kenzie interpreted as *I tried.*

"How about... a soak in the hot tub." Kenzie suggested it before thinking it through, then laughed at herself. "Except with no heat, it is more like one of those polar bear dips. Sorry. What about exercise? Or a drink?"

"Yeah." A definite nod this time. Zachary usually avoided alcohol because of the contraindications with several of his meds. But if he had no way to take the meds, there was no reason he couldn't have a drink or two to help him to relax.

"Yeah? Why don't we both have a drink? Go relax by the heater and toast our feet for a while." Kenzie's feet were cold, even with the blankets and socks on. It wasn't quite like staring into a crackling fire, but the heater would keep them cozy and warm. Burknall had replaced the propane tank before bedding down for the night. Always thinking about his guests and their needs. Kenzie shook her head over thinking that he was too gruff and bad-tempered the first day there. No matter how crusty his exterior was, he was just the right man for the job of keeping things up and making sure the guests were comfortable and happy.

Zachary nodded his head. "That sounds really good."

"Okay, come on. Quickly, because I don't want my feet to freeze between here and there."

She grabbed Zachary by the hand and they skittered like a couple of squirrels over the cold floors to the rug in front of the fireplace where it was nice and toasty. Kenzie threw cushions and blankets on the floor so they could make a nest for themselves, and Zachary went over to the liquor cabinet.

Kenzie wrapped herself up, getting comfortable.

"What do you want?" Zachary asked, shining a pen light into the cabinet.

"I'm not really picky. I'll have a glass of whatever is in there."

She heard bottles clinking and liquid sloshing.

"Kenz?"

Kenzie looked over at him, detecting worry in his voice. "What is it?"

"Did you have something already? I mean, since we got here?"

"No." It was sort of a strange question. Kenzie propped herself up on her elbow, looking over at him. The pen light cast just enough light for her to see the outline of his face. "Why?"

"Because... I looked when we got here. Just to see what there was. And... more than one of the bottles are lower than they were when we got here."

"Really? Are you sure?"

Zachary fingered the bottles. "If I didn't have any, and you didn't have any..." He turned his head toward the bedroom where Tyrrell slept with the children.

Tyrrell. Recovering alcoholic. Snowbound and in close quarters with the children, stressed out trying to handle a wild eight-year-old twenty-four hours a day. One who had disappeared completely for a while.

Kenzie shook her head. "Tyrrell? You don't think so, do you? He wouldn't."

"I don't know. I don't think so, but... it must be pretty stressful."

"Yeah. I was just thinking that."

"Raven was here. She might have had a drink."

"Yeah. For sure. She was drinking like everyone else when we were up at the house together," Kenzie agreed. "And what about Pat and Lorne? They might have had something while they were here."

"Mr. Peterson doesn't really drink very much," Zachary said doubtfully. "Just on special occasions, a glass now and then."

"And it was a special occasion. It was Thanksgiving with his family. There isn't a *lot* missing, is there?"

Zachary considered. "No," he said finally. "Not a lot. Maybe a couple of drinks each, Raven, and Pat, and Lorne. Maybe." The bottles clinked again.

"Well, there's no point in worrying about it tonight. Pour us each a drink, and we'll see if we can relax for a bit."

Drinking wasn't really going to help relax him if he was worried that his alcoholic brother was hitting the bottle again. But maybe the suggestion that the others had helped themselves to moderate portions would help. He could deny that Tyrrell had had anything to drink, at least for a while, until they had to confront him about it.

Zachary didn't say anything. He poured a couple of glasses and brought one over to Kenzie. She sipped hers. A red wine. Something pleasant. She was no connoisseur. Didn't have a clue what the vintage was. But it went down easily.

"Come cuddle with me." She held up a blanket for Zachary to slide under. "I'll see if there's any way I can help you to relax..."

Zachary got comfortable next to her, but she could still feel his tension. Kenzie had another sip of her wine and set it to the side. She couldn't see much in the dark and was afraid she was going to knock it over if they moved too much.

"I can't see you."

Zachary took his pen light out of his pocket again and turned it on. He pointed it at his face, at hers, and then eventually set it on the couch behind them so that it shone toward them and shed its dim glow on both of their faces. The battery wouldn't last long if they left it on, but Kenzie wanted to be able to see Zachary's face. She needed to be able to see his eyes and read any changes in mood.

"Much better."

Kenzie leaned over to kiss Zachary gently.

He was distracted to begin with. Thinking about Tyrrell and the liquor cabinet. Thinking about having to go the next night and maybe a couple more days without any chemical assistance. Thinking about what had gone on up at the house and their agreement to see whether they could make any headway on it again in the morning. But after a few minutes of kissing and teasing, he started to focus on her, his body losing some of the tension and his face smoothing over. He still looked cadaverous in the strange lighting from the pen light, but the deeper ridges disappeared.

"This is what we needed," Kenzie told him. "Some time just to get away and get to know each other again."

"Mmm-hm."

Kenzie smiled, feeling the planes of her face against his shifting in the darkness. "We haven't had much time alone."

He broke away from her for a moment to speak. "You're the one who invited other people along."

"Well... I suppose I did. I didn't expect us to get stranded together. I thought a day or two with everybody, and then some alone time for you and me..."

"Uh-huh." He kissed her again. She could feel his fingers exploring under the blanket. Tentative, but interested. His body hadn't released all the tension, but she could work on that. She pulled him closer and just held him for a few minutes, glad for their shared warmth and the blankets and heater, but mostly for his eagerness. For a long time, they had been dealing with his dissociation during intimate moments, and with meds that, while they took the edge off of his worst anxieties and compulsions, also reduced his drive. The combination of the two was brutal, but couples therapy was helping, and they were finding more moments together without Zachary dissociating or withdrawing.

Kenzie tried to focus one hundred percent of her attention on him, pushing all the other concerns and worries away, for just a few minutes.

"Do you mind if I turn the light off?"

Kenzie shifted, opening her eyes a bare slit to remind herself where she was. In the cabin with Zachary. Enjoying some couples time in front of the heater. She was glad that Tyrrell had eventually been able to get Mason to sleep for the night.

"Yes," she whispered back to Zachary. "Go ahead."

He switched off the pen light and put it back down. Neither of them had made any move to get dressed again, so Zachary didn't have a pocket to put it into. Kenzie was barely even awake. She ran her fingertips along Zachary's arm. "Nice."

"It was," he agreed.

Maybe there was something to be said for a med holiday, or at least a reduction. If Zachary could make do with less medication, maybe they could have a drink together and some other recreation more often.

"You feeling better?"

He shifted, snuggling her body closer to his. Not that they

could get much closer. His muscles were much more relaxed than they had been. "Yeah. better."

"We'll have to add it to your relaxation tools."

He chuckled, his breath giving her goosebumps for a moment. Kenzie rubbed her arms and laughed. She felt like everything that had happened on the holiday had been leading up to this. It had all turned out better than she had expected.

She closed her eyes again, breathing in the smell of Zachary's body against hers.

When she awoke again, everything was wrong. Zachary was moving around frantically, muttering and sobbing, searching through the blankets for something. Kenzie reached out her hand to him and tried to quiet him.

"It's just a dream, Zach. It's okay."

"No, no, no! It's not a dream. Look! Look for yourself!"

Kenzie tried again to press him down and calm him. "You had a dream. It's okay. Let's cuddle some more." She rubbed her eyes. "Do you want to go back to the bed? Maybe you'd be able to settle down better there."

"No!" He said it firmly, almost angrily. "You're the one who needs to wake up." He shook her arm roughly. "Look!"

Kenzie blinked and rubbed her eyes again. She squinted at him, trying to see what it was she wanted him to look at. Sometimes his dreams were very real and it would be several minutes after waking up before he was able to get his head out of the dream and realize where he was. Being at the cabin had probably disoriented him. Waking up in a living room instead of a bedroom might have been a trigger for a dream or a bad feeling.

Zachary pulled on a shirt. He tossed clothing at Kenzie, and she tried to feel its shape and sort out what part of her body to put it on. "Zachary?"

"Look!" He tugged on her arm, trying to get her to her feet.

Kenzie tried to keep one of the blankets wrapped around her. He positioned her in front of the living room window, looking out, up toward the farmhouse on the hill.

It was lit up. Kenzie closed her eyes and opened them again. Why would it be lit up? It was too late for dinner. Everybody had finished and gone back to their cabins.

Was the power back on? Was that what Zachary was so excited about? If it were, they could finally call for help. See when the county was going to send someone to check on them and take the bodies back to the county medical examiner's office.

Kenzie realized with growing horror that it wasn't electric lights that had lit up the farmhouse.

It was a fire.

Kenzie swore. A fire. And not just the flicker of candlelight in the windows.

Blazing light in nearly every window that was visible from the cabin.

Zachary had his boots on. He kicked his way through the cushions and blankets scattered on the floor and strode to Tyrrell's room.

"T!" he shouted, voice already hoarse, "T! There's a fire! T, you have to get up! There's a fire!"

It wasn't just a flashback. It wasn't just a nightmare. It was the worst possible thing for Zachary to face. A house fire. Trying to save his brother and the children from the fire. It didn't matter that it was actually up the hill at the big house. For Zachary, it was right there; he was living through it all over again.

She could hear Tyrrell's voice through the door. Tired, trying to reassure Zachary that everything was all right. Trying, as Kenzie had, to convince him it was just a dream and he should go back to sleep.

"Tyrrell," Kenzie shouted, taking a few steps toward the door as she tried to sort out her clothes and pull them on. "Tyrrell, there *is* a fire. Get up."

"Kenzie?"

In a few moments, Tyrrell was at the bedroom door, opening it slowly, breathing hard. Probably confronting his own memories of the fire. He and the other children had been trapped in their rooms, unable to get out because of the heat and smoke, trapped and terrified until the firefighters had gotten there, broken the windows, and rescued them.

"Kenzie, what's going on?"

"It's up at the farmhouse. A big fire. You need to stay awake, reassure the kids if they wake up. Make sure that... if it spreads to the woods, you get out of the house."

She could barely make out his face in the moonlight that made its way in through the windows. Three dark holes. Two eye sockets and a mouth open in horror. Kenzie squeeze his arm.

"It's okay. You're safe here for now. It's all right."

Tyrrell's head turned to look at Zachary. "Zachy?"

Zachary sniffled. "I have to go. Take care of the others."

He turned away, heading for the front door of the cabin. Kenzie hurried after him. "Zachary? What are you doing? Where are you going?"

He already had his boots and coat on. He pulled a hat on over his head and patted his pockets for the gloves. "We have to get help."

Kenzie shook her head, not understanding. "There's no way to reach anyone. There's nowhere to go for help."

He opened the door and stepped out. Kenzie hurriedly pushed her feet into her boots and pulled on her coat. She raced after him. He moved the opposite direction from the farmhouse, yelling and banging on doors. "Get up! Get up! We need help! Come out!"

Flashlights and candles went on, people came to their doors, bleary-eyed and confused. Kenzie pointed to the farmhouse. She didn't know what to do. It was in full blaze. There was no fire department. No way to reach any help. Zachary ran down to the barn, leaving Kenzie behind. He would get Burknall. Burknall would have some idea what to do. Maybe he had a pump in there. Something that would help them get water onto the blaze.

Kenzie turned around and led the group up the hill.

"What are we going to do?" Brittany demanded, running to

catch up with Kenzie. She had her coat pulled on over a thin white nightgown.

"I don't know. Make sure there's no one inside."

"What happened?" Redd was trying to get his gloves on. Kenzie didn't even know whether she had hers. She felt her pockets, but couldn't find the flaps to open them.

"We don't know. Zachary saw it first. He went to the barn." Kenzie looked back, over her shoulder. She couldn't see Zachary or Burknall. "Maybe Mr. Burknall has a hose. Or a well. I don't know. I don't know how anything works up here."

"An ember must have fallen out of the fireplace," Redd suggested. "Or a candle got knocked over."

"Maybe a chimney fire," Brittany said, breathing hard as they climbed the hill

"Maybe." Kenzie shrugged. Did it really matter how the fire had started? There was a fire, and that was what they had to deal with. Make sure that no one was in danger. Mrs. Hubbard and Samantha both slept in the house, didn't they? They must have been woken up by the fire. The smoke detectors would have awakened them. They could still operate on battery power, even if the main power were out.

If they hadn't woken up... Kenzie wasn't sure what she was going to do. She could see fire in every window. Not just the main floor, but upstairs too. If anyone was still in there...

She ignored the other questions, from both the others and her own brain, as they hurried toward the fire. Nothing mattered except making sure that no one was caught inside the blaze and that it didn't spread to the woods.

It felt like a dream, climbing and climbing and climbing the hill and never getting to the top. But finally, they were there, and Kenzie stood staring at the house, trying to comprehend what was going on. There was no one in front of it, standing clear and watching it burn. Did that mean that they were inside?

"I'm going around back," Kenzie told Brittany, though she didn't know why she felt the need to tell anyone what she was doing. Brittany wasn't her boss. She wasn't someone that Kenzie had to report to.

Brittany nodded. Kenzie hurried around the side. She was yards away from the house and could feel the heat of the flames. It was like walking into a sauna. A dry sauna, obviously, not a steam bath. Kenzie hurried around the side, trying to see into the windows. Hoping to see something other than just flames inside. Some sign of people, or that the whole house wasn't going to burn to the ground. They would be able to save something. To salvage the structure or their valuables. She couldn't believe that the whole thing would burn like that.

Behind the house were three shadows, three silhouettes against the light of the fire. Three people, safe. Kenzie hurried toward them.

"Mrs. Hubbard? Is everyone okay? Everyone got out?"

As she got close, she could see it was Mrs. Hubbard, Samantha, and Jack. Their faces were a little sooty from smoke, but they seemed unharmed. They weren't even coughing from smoke inhalation. Kenzie took Mrs. Hubbard's hand, wanting to reassure herself that the woman was safe and sound. She was a medical professional, but not one who often treated living patients. Her hand went automatically to Mrs. Hubbard's pulse. Fast as a train engine, but hammering away nice and strong and even. Mrs. Hubbard had the constitution of an ox. She would live to be a hundred. Kenzie looked at Samantha and Jack. They both seemed fine as well.

"How did you get here so fast?" Kenzie asked Jack.

"I was up to the bathroom. Saw a reflection in the window, and when I looked out... I could see a fire in one of the windows. Thought I must be seeing things. That it was just the fireplace. But... I had to go see." He blew out his breath in a puff of white vapor. "I got up here in enough time to make sure that everyone got out."

"There's no one else in there, right?" Kenzie asked Mrs. Hubbard and Samantha. "It was just the two of you?"

"Mr. Burknall sleeps down at the barn," Samantha said, her voice a little breathless. "In case anyone needs anything."

"So it was just the two of you."

Samantha nodded.

"We should tell the others. They're out around front." Kenzie looked behind her at the dark woods. She mentally gauged the distance from the house to the woods. Far enough that there was no danger of an ember or flame reaching any of the trees? She wasn't so sure.

"Jack... you want to stay back here to make sure it doesn't spread into the woods? I need to talk to the others... then maybe we need to set up a perimeter, or get Mr. Burknall to help us make a firebreak... I don't know."

"With all of this snow?" Jack gestured around. "I don't think we need to worry about the fire spreading."

"It could, though. Mr. Dewey said it was a fire hazard. The cold dries everything out... even though it's snowy, the air and the trees are so dry..." She couldn't help thinking about Zachary, as a little boy, watching the dry branches of their Christmas tree going up in flames. She shuddered, and it wasn't because of the cold. "Just wait here, I'll talk to the others."

Kenzie returned to the front of the house. The others were spreading out, some of them starting to check around the sides of the house as well, moving toward the back.

"Everyone is out," she announced. "Mrs. Hubbard and Samantha, they're both okay."

Raven looked up at the burning building, pulling her coat tight around her. "It's so... primal. I don't know."

"It's scary," Kenzie agreed.

"Is there no way to get outside help?" a man demanded.

Kenzie turned her head to see who the query came from, but she knew before she saw that it was Vance Stiller.

He had pulled out his phone and was looking at the useless brick. He looked at the house, then down the hill at the barn. "Doesn't anybody have... a short-wave radio? A sat phone? There should be some way to reach help in the event of an emergency!"

"If there was, don't you think we would have done it in the last few days?" Kenzie asked, irritated.

"But that was just..." Stiller waved his hand. "Nonsense and speculation. This is serious. This could spread to the forest, to the other buildings on the property. It could decimate the business."

"Yes, it could," Kenzie agreed. She didn't make any comment on the fact that he thought the murder of one of the guests and possibly his own poisoning as nonsense and speculation.

Kenzie heard the growl of an engine starting and looked around. At first, she couldn't see anything, but eventually, she could see a large, dark shape coming into view down by the barn. Her spirits lifted. It was Burknall, coming to the rescue. Always competent, he knew exactly what to do.

The shape lumbered toward them. Kenzie squinted, trying to make out the shape in the darkness. As it drew closer, the light of the fire illuminated a John Deere tractor with some kind of digger attachment. Kenzie's heart fell again. She was hoping for a fire truck pumper, or something similar. She knew it was probably ridiculous to think that a resort might have their own fire engine, but maybe something used to spray chemicals on crops or on fields they needed cleared of weeds? There must be a need for such things.

The heat of the fire swelled up behind Kenzie. She turned to look at the house and saw that the flames were no longer just behind the windows, but had eaten their way through the roof and were reaching up to the sky. She murmured a curse under her breath. Without a fire hose, they had no hope of being able to save the house.

There had probably been no hope by the time Zachary had woken her up. Mrs. Hubbard and Samantha were lucky to have gotten out of the building unharmed. They were lucky that Jack had been up and around and had noticed the flames.

The tractor emitted several loud beeps, and Kenzie and the

others decided to get out of Burknall's way. He rolled up to the house, engine growling loudly, and circled around it, moving toward the back of the house. Kenzie followed at a distance to see what he would do. More horn honks to get Mrs. Hubbard, Samantha, and Jack out of the way. Then Burknall started to dig a trench across the back yard between the house and the trees. Dark clumps of dirt were piled up on the snow.

"What is he doing?" Raven demanded, watching from a few feet away from Kenzie.

"It's a firebreak. To try to keep the fire from spreading into the trees. If there isn't any fuel between the house and the trees for the fire to burn, it can't spread. As long as no embers from the fire float up over into the trees..."

"Why isn't he trying to put the fire out?"

"He probably can't do anything about it at this point. Even if the fire department was here, it would take several trucks to get this under control."

"So he's just going to let it burn?" Raven sounded outraged at the idea.

"Yes. If there's no way to put it out, then the best thing to do is to keep it confined and let it burn itself out."

Kenzie wondered if there were anything that the fire department—if there were one that served the outlying areas—would do if they had been called. There were no fire hydrants to hook their hoses up to. Maybe they would have been able to put an intake hose into a stream somewhere. But if there were one, it would have been frozen over. She supposed all they would be able to do was to watch it burn, like the rest of them were doing.

She turned away from the tractor and moved back to the front of the house where she could see down to the cabins and barn. A figure was making its way up the hill. Hunched over, moving slowly as if in pain. With his bulky coat on and slow, pained movements, Kenzie barely recognized Zachary. She walked down the hill to meet him part way.

"Zachary. How are you? Are you okay?"

He didn't answer, but kept moving toward her. Eventually, he was close enough to touch. She couldn't see his eyes in the darkness.

"Zachary." She reached out and took his arm. "Hey. Are you with me?"

"Yeah." His voice was hoarse. From calling out to everyone else to warn them of the fire? From crying? From dragging the cold, smoky air into his lungs as he tried to get enough oxygen, lost in flashbacks? "I'm here."

She pulled him close and put her arm around him. "This must be awful for you. I'm so sorry. Do you want to go back to the cabin? You don't need to go up there."

"No." He looked up toward the house, then put his head down again, marching forward like he was walking into a strong wind. "I want to go up."

Kenzie didn't argue with him. He knew what was best for him. His fear of fire was something that had plagued him for decades. If he was ready to face it now, she wouldn't get in his way.

This time... everyone else can see it."

Zachary and Kenzie stood arm in arm, watching the flames consume the farmhouse. Zachary's voice was still hoarse. She could feel how tense his body was, feel his limbs quivering from standing in such close proximity to the fire.

"You can see it," Zachary said.

"Yes," Kenzie agreed. "We can all see it." She gave him a squeeze. "Is this what it was like, watching your house burn?"

He shook his head. "No... when they got me out... I couldn't really see anything. Too many people around me. An oxygen mask on my face... people talking about me, cutting my clothes off." He clutched his coat against him, as if trying to convince himself that he was fully dressed and no one was going to cut his clothes off this time. Kenzie thought about what she knew of the fire. It had been Christmas Eve. It would have been cold outside. Snow on the ground. Being taken from the heat of the fire to the chill of the winter air outside and having the clothes cut away from his body so they could treat him, he must have been freezing. At least, the skin that wasn't burned. Maybe the cold air had helped to soothe his burns and to stop further damage.

When he had first told her about being rescued by the firefighters, she had imagined him standing outside, safe like he was now. Upset, even devastated by the fire, but walking away under his own power. It wasn't until later that she learned about the hospital stay, debriding, skin grafts, and rehabilitation he had gone through before going to the Petersons, his first foster family.

"You're safe here," Kenzie assured him. "You're not burned, and neither is anyone else."

"Everyone got out?" His voice was a little choked as he asked the question.

"Yes. Everything is fine. Jack woke up before you did and he got up here in time to make sure that Mrs. Hubbard and Samantha got out of the house."

Zachary nodded.

"And Mr. Burknall is digging a trench around the house, to keep it from spreading. Everyone will be okay. Everyone is safe."

He nodded again. He pressed his face into her knit hat and the wild, curly hair that puffed out all around the bottom edge of it. He breathed in, his mouth close to her ear and neck and making her shiver, goosebumps running down her neck. But she didn't pull away from him. He needed her there, calm and giving him strength to face the fire. To see his memories clearly and process them instead of running away from them as he had for years.

"Everyone got out," Zachary repeated. "Everyone got out."

A couple of the guests went back to their cabins when it became clear that the rest of the Lodge was safe. Kenzie couldn't imagine how they could go back to sleep. And maybe they didn't, but just wanted to be away from the cold and the smoke and the other guests huddling together and speculating on what had happened.

She had a pretty good idea that Zachary would not be going back to bed. No hope of that. Even on a normal night when he was awakened by a dream or a noise outside, he wouldn't go back to sleep. No chance he would be able to after dealing with a fire.

"What do you think happened?" Kenzie asked Burknall, when he had finished trenching around the house and parked his tractor. "A gas line? Propane leak?"

He stared at the house. The fire was beginning to settle down instead of getting bigger. Starting to burn itself out. But it would still be a long time before it was completely extinguished and the ruins cool enough to examine.

"We've had propane appliances for decades," he said, giving his head a shake. "There wasn't anything wrong with them. They were perfectly safe. Same with the boiler. It was inspected regularly, never had any problems. Fireplaces, same thing, we got the chimneys cleaned and kept everything in perfect condition."

"So you don't know what could have caused the fire," Kenzie said.

"What about candles?" Zachary asked.

Burknall looked at him, brows drawn down. "We only use candles if someone is in the room to keep an eye on them. And never sleeping with a candle lit. Mrs. Hubbard knows that. Samantha too. She didn't even like candles. That's why we had the glow-sticks."

"Something started it," Zachary observed.

Burknall nodded his agreement. "Something."

There was something more in his expression. Something that he was not saying. Maybe he had suspicions, but he wasn't sharing them. Kenzie watched the burning house. All of that history. The families that had grown up in there. Mr. Dewey's pictures and all the reminders of the wife he had lost.

It wasn't until that point that Kenzie thought about Mr. Dewey.

And Brooke.

It wasn't just Mr. Dewey's memories that had been burned up, but his remains as well. Maybe they wouldn't be completely destroyed, but all of Kenzie's efforts to preserve the scene and the trace evidence was for naught.

They couldn't even test Brooke's body now to see whether it had been Jimson weed that had caused all of the trouble that night. Brooke's remains were probably damaged past any hopes of retrieving evidence of toxins. Kenzie turned her gaze toward Zachary to see if he had twigged on to this as well. He was probably light-years ahead of her in sorting out the implications. He had wanted to go up to the house before they went to bed, hoping that Mrs. Hubbard could help them or that there would be some evidence of the use of Jimson weed. But it was too late. Now, Mrs. Hubbard was the only possible avenue. If she knew anything.

Zachary gazed back at Kenzie. He rubbed away a smudge on her face. He gave a little grimace, confirming that he understood they had just lost all of that evidence. Everything they had, other than what Kenzie had managed to record on her phone or Zachary's digital recorder. They had no remains, no scene or trace, no weapon, and no pills. Everything was gone. Kenzie held on to Zachary, for her support this time rather than his. She felt sick at the thought of all they had lost.

"At least everyone was okay," she said weakly.

Zachary nodded, holding her tight. "Yeah."

Kenzie took a few deep breaths. She looked around at those who remained, watching the destruction. She let go of Zachary and walked slowly over to Mrs. Hubbard, who was looking tired and worn, dark circles around her eyes.

"Mrs. Hubbard, would you like to come back to our cabin? We have a spare room. You could go to sleep or just have some time to yourself."

Mrs. Hubbard smiled at her. "That's very sweet of you, my dear. That would... I think that would be very nice."

Kenzie took her arm. "Why don't we walk down, then?"

The sky was starting to grow light. A column of smoke was still going up from the farmhouse.

Zachary followed, saying nothing. Mrs. Hubbard clutched

Kenzie's arm, holding tightly as if she were afraid she might fall. Or maybe just as if everything else had slipped out of her grasp and she didn't want to be left alone and anchorless. Kenzie didn't say anything. What was there to say?

"I can't believe it," the older woman said after a few minutes, as they made their way slowly down to the cabin. "I can't believe that everything I own has just gone up in smoke. All of the memories. Everything I ever owned. What am I supposed to do now? I don't have a job, a place to stay, even a spare shirt to my name. I got out of there with my life, but I don't have anything. Even my purse." She shook her head. "My ID, my bank cards. How am I going to survive?"

Kenzie looked over at Zachary, walking a few feet away from them, giving them some privacy. "Zachary might be able to help you out there. He actually lost everything he had in a fire just a little while ago. His wallet and ID too. I know it was really hard to get things replaced, but he can tell you what to do. Where to start."

Mrs. Hubbard looked at Zachary. "Really? I thought that the fire you guys were talking about happened when you were a little boy. I didn't realize that it was recent..."

"Well..." Zachary cleared his throat. "There were two fires."

"Two of them." Mrs. Hubbard looked overwhelmed by this thought, like it was too much to grasp.

"Yeah. There was one when I was ten. An accident. That's when I was injured." Zachary indicated one of the scars visible on his neck. "And... I lost everything then. My whole family too. Then... two years ago, there was another fire, in my apartment. Arson. And like Kenzie said, my wallet and everything was burned up. I had to start from scratch. Lived with a friend while I was trying to get my ID reissued and to get access to my bank accounts and everything. I didn't use any cloud storage, so I didn't have my passwords to any of the online stuff. Had to get people who could verify my identity to the government." Zachary rolled his eyes. "It's arduous... but it's possible. I can help you to sort it out."

"Oh, you're a godsend. Thank you. I don't know what I would do without you."

"Someone else would help you," he assured her. "There are a lot of helpful people in the world." He looked at Kenzie, smiling a little. "People who you wouldn't think had any reason to help you out... step up and become the best friends you ever had."

Kenzie's cheeks warmed. She blamed it on the fire, even though they were getting farther away from it. They reached the cabin and Zachary dug out his key to let them in.

"Whatever you need, just ask. In the next little while... you're going to learn how to ask for things. Even if you're a person who has never had to depend on anyone before. But we'll help out however we can."

They stepped into the warm, welcoming space of the cabin. Mrs. Hubbard took off her coat and smoothed back her hair. She was, of course, in her night clothes, a matched set top and bottom of warm-looking purple velour with flowers embroidered on the left breast and hip. "I guess... the first thing is sleep. You would think that I would be too worried to sleep, but... I'm exhausted."

"Your brain doesn't want to deal with all the trauma," Zachary told her, nodding. "Go ahead and get some sleep while you can. You can worry about other things later."

"I'll show you where," Kenzie offered, and took Mrs. Hubbard down the hall to the room that Lorne and Pat had stayed in. The sheets hadn't been changed, but Kenzie had no way to remedy that with the power out. Mrs. Hubbard didn't appear to notice or to care.

"Thank you for this, Kenzie. You're so thoughtful."

"You're welcome. I'm glad you accepted. Just lie down and rest, get as much sleep as you can. The kids might be a bit noisy when they get up, but we'll do our best to keep them to a dull roar."

Mrs. Hubbard smiled. "Oh, that's fine. I don't mind children's voices."

Maybe not when they were well-behaved children talking and playing in the distance. She might revise her position if she ended up with Mason jumping on top of her, or with both of them screaming at each other, wrestling, or fighting over a book. Kenzie helped Mrs. Hubbard into the bed and pulled the covers over her. After another murmured good night, she left, pulling the door behind her.

G ood plan," Zachary told Kenzie when she returned to the living room.

Kenzie raised her brows in query. "What do you mean?"

"Keeping Mrs. Hubbard close. Where we can talk to her and keep anyone else from getting access to her."

"Well... she might know something. And if she does... I wouldn't want her to be the next casualty."

"Her and you. We don't know how much you know that could catch the culprits either. They could come after you next, try to burn this cabin down." Zachary's eyes darted around the interior of the cabin. He turned to look out the window. It was getting brighter outside. Kenzie didn't see anyone nearby, hanging around the house.

"I don't really know anything. Nothing that can be proven, anyway."

"I think...we might know enough to figure it out."

Kenzie frowned. "What do you mean?"

"I get this feeling sometimes... when I know that I'm getting close to solving a case. When I get this feeling that I have all of the pieces to the puzzle, if I can just put them together the right way. I guess subconsciously, my brain knows I have what I need. But it can be really frustrating, if I feel like I'm at the end of a case and nothing has come together."

Kenzie sat down on the couch. Zachary sat beside her. His fingers tapped the arm of the couch, his knee, the back of the couch behind her, fidgeting and restless, his brain trying to unlock the clues he believed they had.

There was the sound of a door opening, and Kenzie leaned forward to look down the hall and see what Mrs. Hubbard needed.

It wasn't her, but Tyrrell. He blinked and rubbed his eyes. He didn't look like he'd gotten much sleep. Kenzie had told him to keep an eye on the fire to make sure that he moved the kids if it happened to move along the treeline and endanger the cabin. So he'd probably been awake until he had seen Mr. Burknall dig the trench around the house and the fire start to burn down again.

"I thought I heard voices." Tyrrell looked out the window, studying the house up the hill, then sat down in one of the easy chairs. "Everything is okay? Under control?"

Zachary nodded.

Tyrrell stared at him, studying his face closely. "And you, bro?" He cocked his head slightly. "I expected you to be... bad."

Zachary took a deep breath and let it out. "My therapist... she's talked about exposure therapy before. How if you let your brain get past the panic stage, then it will even back out, and you'll start to adjust to... whatever the trigger is."

"Yeah? And you think that this," Tyrrell made a motion toward the farmhouse, "got you past that stage?"

"I've always avoided it before." Zachary still didn't name his fear of fire. "Even... thinking about it. If I ever started thinking back to what happened, or was around candles or some other trigger, I would go straight to panic. Try to shut down my response, but if I couldn't, I'd go right into flashbacks and not be able to deal with it."

"But this time it wasn't a candle," Kenzie said slowly. "It was a house fire. With other people in danger, and your family close by. And you couldn't tell yourself that it was just a flashback."

"I had to... deal with it. To keep everyone safe, I *had* to..."

"Well, I'm sure you'll have a lot of unpacking to do with Dr. B. But she's going to be very proud of you."

Zachary smiled. That shy, little-boy smile that sometimes broke through his carefully-masked emotions when he was proud of himself. He had been criticized and humiliated by so many people in his past that he rarely allowed himself to take any pride in his accomplishments. He looked down, closing his eyes and trying to compose his expression. But the hint of a smile lingered in the corners of his mouth.

"You helped to keep everyone safe," Kenzie told him. "It was really scary for all of us too, but you were strong."

He ducked his head, partly a nod of acknowledgment, and partly hiding his face, hiding behind the mask.

"So what's going to happen next?" Tyrrell asked. "I mean... are we even allowed to be here anymore? If there's no one managing the place, then...?"

"We're still paid-up guests," Kenzie pointed out. "We still have the staff taking care of things, even if they don't have a... home base anymore." She looked at Zachary. "And then there's the food. Everything that they had stored up at the house, and their cooking facilities... they won't exactly be able to feed the guests three meals a day anymore."

"We have some food here... and there are still farm animals and their feed. It won't exactly be a feast, but there is enough to get by on, until the roads are clear. Maybe today or tomorrow the plows will be able to get through." Zachary twisted to look out the window at the iron gray sky. "If people have seen the smoke from the fire... someone will have to investigate. We'll be a priority now."

"If anyone saw the smoke. There's no guarantee."

"I think the chances are pretty good. Close neighbors might have been able to see the flames too."

"Maybe the staff can gather some roots and berries," Tyrrell contributed.

Zachary and Kenzie both looked at him. Tyrrell shrugged.

"Well, you left that wildcrafting book out. I had to stay awake, so I looked through it."

Kenzie smiled and nodded. "I don't think I'm going to eat plants anyone else has gathered," she told him. "After what happened..."

Tyrrell shook his head. "What?"

"The way that everyone was hallucinating and having other symptoms. I think they were dosed with Jimson weed."

"Jimson weed?"

"You can look it up in the book. It's pretty dangerous stuff."

Tyrrell nodded. "I'll say!"

Kenzie heard the emphasis in his voice. She tilted her head, looking at him. "You'll say? You sound like... you've seen the effects before?"

Tyrrell nodded. He looked from Kenzie to Zachary and made a movement that was meant to be casual, but looked jerky and self-conscious.

"When I was drinking... you know, as a kid... I would try anything." He rolled his eyes. "I mean *anything*. If you told me I could get high on Corn Flakes, I would have eaten a whole box. Huffing fumes, drinking vanilla or mouthwash, hand sanitizer, I would do it all on a dare. Not even on a dare, just on the suggestion that it might get me to a 'higher level of consciousness.'"

"You didn't!" Kenzie said in horror.

"Yeah, you bet. Anything I could get my hands on. Including Jimson weed. Locoweed. Some kid at a party... I don't know, like... a hillbilly. He said it was the best high ever. As long as you didn't kill yourself."

Zachary swore under his breath. "I can't believe you tried it. And...?"

Tyrrell shrugged. "I don't remember. Every now and then, I get a little fleeting recollection of it... like deja vu. Remembering the feeling of being outside myself, flying, seeing... weird, weird stuff happening. Knowing that I was hallucinating, but not caring. I felt... I liked it. Most people who try the stuff remember it as being a good high, if they survive. But it's so dangerous. It's just... do you take it again, knowing you might die the next time? The hillbilly died, and I didn't look for another source. Seemed like it would just be asking for trouble."

"Thank goodness for that." Kenzie gave a laugh of disbelief. "I feel like I should smack you just for trying it."

Tyrrell chuckled. "Yeah, you probably should. Wasn't the brightest thing I ever did. I promise I won't do it again."

"No, don't," Zachary agreed vehemently.

The hillbilly died. Tyrrell had been lucky that hadn't been him.

Tyrrell was clearly embarrassed, maybe wishing that he hadn't told them the story. He rubbed his jaw, blinking and looking up at the ceiling, trying to think of something else to say that would distract Zachary's and Kenzie's attention from his youthful stupidity.

"It's not like I cornered the market on stupid," he reminded Zachary. "Not like I'm the only one who ever did anything that endangered my life."

Zachary nodded solemnly at this. He had tried to end his own life several times in the past. Kenzie hoped against hope that he never would again, and knew that she always needed to keep an eye on him and to be aware of his mental state. She couldn't let her guard down just because of a good day or an achievement. She knew from experience that a big step forward was often followed by an even larger slide back.

"What do you think we know?" she asked Zachary, changing the subject back to what they had been discussing before Tyrrell had shown up. "You said that you think we know enough to figure out what happened. So... like what?"

Zachary scratched his stubbly chin. Tyrrell looked relieved to have the conversation topic move away from his stupid teenage exploits. Kenzie watched him for a moment longer, thinking about the liquor cabinet, before turning her attention back to Zachary to see what they could piece together.

"Well. I guess first is that you know what all of the other guests were given," Zachary said. "We followed a false trail to begin with, thinking that it was a pill or some other chemical. Rather than something like Jimson weed, that someone could gather from practically anywhere in the state."

"Right." Kenzie nodded. "The symptoms, the ten D's, all point to Jimson weed."

"The ten D's?" Tyrrell repeated.

"Delusions, dry mouth, dry hot skin, delirium, death..." Kenzie trailed off. "I can't remember them all right now, but they fit. If it's not Jimson weed, it's something very close. Some other *datura* species, probably."

"Okay."

"And..." Kenzie turned back to Zachary. "It's wintertime. So whoever it was couldn't have gathered it anywhere in the state. It's under a blanket of snow. They would have had to gather it before they came here. They had to have some kind of premeditation. Planning."

"Maybe it was just for personal use," Tyrrell suggested.

"But like you say, it's very dangerous. There are better ways to get high more safely. Just buy some weed before coming out here. Or like Redd Flagg, bring some mushrooms."

The two men both nodded, agreeing.

"So it was planned and intentional," Kenzie asserted.

65

P retty much had to be," Zachary agreed.

They were all quiet, thinking about that for a few minutes.

"Then it would have to be someone on the staff," Tyrrell said eventually. "Wouldn't it? Who else would know everyone would be staying here?"

"Well... not necessarily," Kenzie disagreed. "I would assume that they were only targeting one person, even though everyone got dosed. Wouldn't you?"

"Probably," Zachary agreed, the word slow and thoughtful.

"And if you were only targeting one person, then you only have to know that one person will be here. You don't have to know any of the other guests or staff."

"I suppose," Tyrrell said.

"Everyone was poisoned to hide who the actual target was," Kenzie speculated. "If just Vance Stiller was poisoned, then we would know that it was someone who knew he would be here and had a motive for wanting to kill him."

"But no one was killed," Zachary said, holding up his hand to stop her from interrupting. "Not by the Jimson weed. Dewey died the day before. And Brooke didn't die from the Jimson weed. She died from being stabbed."

"That could have been planned. Maybe the Jimson weed was to cover up the fact that she was killed on purpose. Make everyone think it was just an accident due to hallucinations."

"Okay." Zachary nodded and remained focused on the point. "Let's take a minute and say that's what happened. It's a simple, clear-cut situation. So who would want to kill Brooke?"

"The husband is always the first suspect," Tyrrell offered. "That's what they say on TV."

"Right," Kenzie agreed. "And I've seen that, working in the ME's office. Lots of spousal killings. Pretty common, though usually it is in a fight, a crime of passion, not pre-planned."

"Motive?" Zachary queried. "Jealousy? Insurance?"

"If it was Andy Collins, then I'd go with insurance," Tyrrell said. "That, or she had a lot of money or an asset he wanted. He marries her, she changes her will to make him her beneficiary, and then he kills her. It looks like an accident, someone off their head on a hallucinogen. Case closed, and he gets the money."

It was a neat package. But Kenzie wasn't sure it was the right answer.

"Then why burn down the farmhouse? What's the motive for that?"

"It was an accident," Tyrrell suggested. "Unrelated. Someone knocked over a lantern."

"Burknall says not," Kenzie said. "They've been without power plenty of times before. They're used to using propane and the fireplaces and candles. It's all normal for them and they haven't had any accidents before."

"That doesn't prevent one from happening," Tyrrell argued. "Or... how about one of the guests goes up to the house. They want a midnight snack. They light a candle or a lantern, but they're not used to using them and they put the candle under a towel rack. Or knock over a lantern. Or light a fire in the fireplace and forget to close the screen to keep embers from flying out."

Kenzie looked at Zachary. His eyes were closed. She took his hand. "You okay, Zachary?"

She felt his pulse. It was pounding away, twice as fast as it should have been. But there was no panic in his expression. His breathing remained even.

"I'm fine."

She wouldn't normally accept that answer from him, but he probably didn't want a big emotional discussion in front of Tyrrell, and she didn't want to be distracted from the topic of the fire at the farmhouse. So far, Zachary was holding it together. She would have to accept that he would be able to manage the discussion of how the fire might have started.

"Any of those are possible," Kenzie admitted. "But do we think that it was just a coincidence? There just *happened* to be a fire that destroyed all of the physical evidence we still had?"

Tyrrell shrugged, thinking about it. "Probably not."

"I don't think so either. So if it were just straightforward, Andy killing Brooke for her money, then why burn down the house? What evidence were they getting rid of?"

Zachary started to tick possibilities off on his fingers. "Any drugs or toxins in Brooke's body. Any other marks on her—bruises, needle marks, fingerprints. Pregnancy. Trace evidence. The same with Mr. Dewey. You didn't think that his death was related, but what if it was?" He spoke rapidly. "It could have been to hide anything in the rooms that we put them in or in the rest of the house. The cooking dishes. What ingredient was contaminated. If there was Jimson weed stored in the cellar with the other herbs. Papers belonging to Mr. Dewey or someone else in the house. Identification. Fingerprints—both marks left behind and the fingerprints of Mr. Dewey and Brooke themselves. Were they really who they said they were?" He considered. "Did I miss anything?"

"Pictures," Kenzie said slowly. "Dewey had one beside his bed of him and his wife and a young man that I assume was their son.

There could be other pictures that show some relationship to a guest or someone else at the Lodge."

"Blackmail," Tyrrell said, sounding excited. "Could have been blackmail pictures too. Poison pen letters. Tax fraud."

There were so many possibilities, Kenzie started to see the hopelessness of their ever being able to figure out what evidence might have been destroyed that they had no way of knowing even existed.

"And what if Brooke wasn't the intended victim?" Zachary proffered. "What if she were an accidental casualty?"

"Well... if it wasn't intentional murder, then what was it?" Kenzie asked. "Did they mean to kill someone who didn't die? Or did they not mean to kill anybody?"

"Or was Mr. Dewey the intended victim?"

"But he wasn't—" Kenzie stopped herself. They were brainstorming. Every possibility had to be explored. What if Mr. Dewey's death had not been accidental? What if someone had meant to kill him, and the Jimson weed poisoning the next night had just been to muddy the waters or keep everyone off-balance? Or to give the killer a chance to eliminate evidence at the house while everyone was flying high? Maybe they hadn't been able to destroy whatever evidence they wanted to and they had resorted instead to burning the house down?

"Okay," she said instead. "Why kill Mr. Dewey? He's the one who owned the Lodge, so the first obvious motivation was to acquire the Lodge. Who would have inherited it from him?"

"The son?" Zachary suggested.

"Maybe... I haven't heard anyone mention him, so I don't know if he was still around, or if he had died or been disinherited. If the Lodge didn't go to a son, then who?"

"If it went to one of the staff, then any of them might be the culprit," Tyrrell said.

"Yes... I don't think it could be Mrs. Hubbard. She's pretty broken up about having lost everything," Kenzie pointed out.

"It could be an act," he argued

"I don't think it is."

Tyrrell shook his head. "That Burknall is kind of creepy. He could get anywhere, do anything he wanted to."

He did have opportunity, Kenzie had to admit that.

Kenzie looked at Zachary. They didn't seem to be any closer to figuring it out.

"Who else knew someone who was going to be here?" Zachary asked, bringing the conversation back around.

"Well... Vance Stiller and Brittany seem to be a thing. So they must have planned to be here together."

"Could one of them have poisoned the other? In hopes that they would overdose or have an adverse reaction? Or be able to get the other alone and they just happened to fail at that part?"

"Vance had cardiovascular disease. I certainly wouldn't recommend someone like that take Jimson weed."

"It could have killed him?" Zachary asked.

"It could have killed anyone. But someone with heart disease? He would definitely be more susceptible than someone who was healthy."

"Like Brittany."

"Brittany takes pretty good care of herself," Kenzie said, remembering the exercise equipment. "So... a lot less likely than Stiller to die, if they were both poisoned. if she were the poisoner, then she could avoid eating whatever was contaminated and eliminate the possibility of overdosing herself."

"What reason would Brittany have to kill Stiller?" Zachary asked.

Kenzie couldn't come up with anything. The two seemed to like each other and to be a good match. They weren't married, but it was possible that Stiller could still have left something to Brittany in his will. "Stiller seems like he got a pretty good dose. He couldn't remember anything that happened the day before, and slept pretty heavily all that night and the next day. That's typical of Jimson weed. Brittany, on the other hand, didn't really act like she'd been dosed at all."

"So that's a possibility," Zachary said.

"But without a motive...?"

"We don't know," Tyrrell said. "Maybe he had done something to someone in her family in the past and she was out for revenge. Or he insulted her, or thought her business and fame was a sham. We don't know what went on between them."

66

There were voices outside the cabin. Kenzie turned her head and looked out the window. It was getting brighter outside, the sun up over the horizon. Raven and Jack were walking by, returning from the site of the fire up the hill. Kenzie studied their body language as they approached their cabins. She had wondered before if there were a previous relationship between Raven and Jack. They had not said so, but they seemed very familiar with each other and to have a sort of rapport between them. Sometimes, people just clicked the first time they met, but they acted like people who had shared something before they had come to the Lodge. It didn't feel like a first meeting to Kenzie.

But she could be wrong.

Raven's voice was raised as they walked near the cabin. Not just a typical talking voice. Maybe she had been affected by all of the excitement. Maybe, like with Zachary, the fire triggered some emotional reaction in her and she was agitated by it. But she seemed angry.

"What's going on with them?" Tyrrell asked.

"I don't know." Kenzie leaned closer to the window, trying to pick up their words. "Arguing about something, I think."

Watching their faces and straining for their words, Kenzie thought Raven said, "What were you doing up there?"

She frowned at Zachary. "What was he doing up there?" she repeated. She shook her head in confusion. "He went up to the house when he saw the fire. To make sure that everyone got out safely."

Zachary raised an eyebrow. "Is that what he told you?"

"Well... yes. It is. He said he got up to go to the bathroom, and he saw the fire, so he went up to make sure that Mrs. Hubbard and Samantha got out okay. And a good thing he did. It would be awful if we had lost someone in the fire. A third death, or a third and fourth, that would have been terrible."

"How did he get up there so quickly?"

"He saw the flames when he got up in the night," Kenzie repeated. "Just by luck. He was the first one to see them, so he was the first one to the house."

"And he didn't wake up anyone else? Try to get help? He just decided to run up to a burning house and try to rescue everyone himself?"

"Yes." Kenzie couldn't help the way that her voice curled up at the end of the sentence to make it sound like a question. She couldn't understand what Zachary was getting at. That was exactly what had happened.

Zachary shook his head. "No way. He was already up there. There's no way that he saw the flames and got up there before Mrs. Hubbard and Samantha woke up to the smoke alarms."

"You can't know that."

"The smoke alarms would have sounded long before the flames were visible through the windows."

"But if it started in one room and then spread, he might have seen the flames in the kitchen before they spread to the rest of the house."

"I'm with Raven on this one. What was he up at the house for?" Zachary looked out the window at them, having a heated discussion just a few feet from the cabin.

"Why would he lie? Maybe he went up for a midnight snack. Or a night cap."

"Or to see someone."

Kenzie looked at Jack. His face was red. From the heat of the fire? The cold air? The exertion? Or something else? Was he embarrassed or angry about Raven's questions?

"You think he was up there to see Samantha...?"

"It's possible."

"I suppose... but she never seemed that interested in him."

"She wouldn't have to be. Attraction doesn't always flow in both directions."

"Well, if we're eliminating coincidences... then what are the chances that he went up to the house to visit Samantha and there just happened to be a fire when he got there?"

Zachary nodded his approval of the question. "Maybe because it was no coincidence."

"Jack didn't start that fire!"

Kenzie and Zachary both startled and looked over at Mrs. Hubbard, who was standing in the hallway looking at them, her eyes blazing.

Zachary stood up quickly. He faced Mrs. Hubbard, his body language wary. "How do you know that?"

"He wouldn't do something like that. When I got downstairs, he was trying to put out the fire!"

"How?"

"He was... I don't know. He was trying to push all of the stuff that was on fire to the side, away from the furniture..."

Zachary looked at Kenzie. Using a fire extinguisher or trying to beat it out would have made sense, but trying to push burning debris to where it wouldn't spread didn't sound quite right. Kenzie saw Jack in her mind's eye, hunched over the burning materials, whirling around when Mrs. Hubbard came up on him from behind. Stammering out an explanation that he was trying to stop the fire from spreading. And then getting them all out of the house.

"He was a hero!" Mrs. Hubbard insisted. "He *didn't* light that fire! He'd never do something like that."

"Do you... *know* Jack, Mrs. Hubbard?" Kenzie asked tentatively.

"Jack is..." Mrs. Hubbard shook her head impatiently. "You don't understand! He was trying to put the fire out."

She moved to the door and jerked it open.

"Jack! Jack, come here!"

Jack turned from his discussion with Raven and looked at Mrs. Hubbard. It took him a moment to overcome his consternation at seeing her there. "What?"

"You need to tell them."

He walked slowly toward Mrs. Hubbard. He cast one worried glance over at Raven, then looked back at Mrs. Hubbard.

"You need to tell them who you are," Mrs. Hubbard insisted.

Jack hesitated, stopping just outside the door. He looked back at Raven, then at Mrs. Hubbard. He sighed. "Maybe you'd better come in too," he suggested.

Raven scowled. "What's going on? You can't just walk out on me."

"I'm not. I'm asking you to come in with me. If we're going to have this discussion... it may as well be all together."

"What discussion? I was talking to you, not to... anyone else." Raven shook her head in irritation.

"Please, Raven..."

Raven sighed loudly, then followed Jack, and the two of them entered the cabin. Mrs. Hubbard shut the door. She had eyes only for Jack, not even glancing at Raven.

"You have to tell them," she insisted.

Jack pulled off his hat and gloves and unzipped his jacket. He didn't take off his boots or his coat. He was clearly not staying. Raven pried off her boots and went directly to the liquor cabinet and poured herself a drink without asking anyone else. She glared at Jack.

"So what is all of this about?"

Jack looked at her, then at Zachary and everyone else, waiting for him to say something. He rubbed a hand across his eyes as if he just wanted to go back to sleep, and not to explain anything.

"I am Stuart Dewey's son."

There was dead silence. Kenzie tried to reconcile this to what she knew. She remembered the picture beside Dewey's bed, the picture with his wife and son. A blond boy. Fair, not dark like Jack. Their faces had not been the same, and it wasn't just a matter of hair color. He was also, Kenzie thought, younger than the boy in that picture. Too young to be claiming Dewey as his father.

"I don't think you are..."

"Not that one," Jack shook his head. "And... not by his wife." He looked at Mrs. Hubbard. "Someone else."

That explained his not having the same last name. Or there being any pictures of him around the house.

"You're Dewey's son," Zachary repeated. "Are you... his only issue?"

"His heir?" Jack asked. He shrugged his shoulders and spread his hands apart. "I haven't seen his will. But... I could be. Or I could contest it, if he's left me out of it. As far as I know, I was his only living child."

"Why are you here? And did he know who you were?"

"He knew. Didn't want to talk to me, but he knew who I was. Not that any of that matters anymore." He shook his head. "It's not like I'm going to get to know him now."

"You hadn't ever met him before?"

"Met him? Didn't even know he was my father. Not until recently."

"And you were staying here... to meet him?"

"No. Maybe. I wanted to see the place. Where... my roots were. Whether it meant anything to me."

If he had set fire to the place, Kenzie assumed that the answer to that question was no.

"That's why we're here?" Raven demanded. She slugged back a swallow of her whiskey. "Because the old man was your father?"

"Yes."

"I thought..."

It was clear what she had thought. Even if she didn't say it in front of Zachary and Kenzie, they understood. She had thought that he had invited her there on a romantic getaway.

But that still didn't explain why Jack had gone up to the house. If he knew his father was dead, what was the point in going to the house? To search for his will or some other documents? To break into that bedroom and get a good look at his deceased father?

Or to burn it all to the ground?

"I thought that you went up there to see—"

"Raven." He shook his head, trying to silence her.

"I won't shut up! Why should I? I haven't done anything wrong." Full of righteous indignation, she turned to Kenzie, her closest ally in the room. "He stole my things!"

Jack opened his mouth to protest.

"Where did they go if you didn't take them?" Raven demanded. "Clothes don't just go walking off by themselves. You were the *only one* with access to my cabin."

Jack shook his head. "Raven..."

"I couldn't understand why you would take them. Then you were up *there*. Going to *her*! So I knew you had taken them. To give to another woman as some sort of sick gift."

Jack continued to shake his head. "You don't know what you're talking about. Raven, please..."

But it was too late to stop her. A picture was already beginning to form in Kenzie's head. Why would Jack take Raven's clothing? Especially if they were lovers. He didn't need any kind of trophy.

Why had the house been burned down?

What would Jack have done with Raven's clothes? It wasn't, as Raven thought, to take them as a gift for his new love interest.

And he hadn't been trying to stop the fire from spreading when Mrs. Hubbard had come upon him.

He'd been trying to destroy the evidence. Raven's bloody clothing.

Kenzie looked at Jack. He was still shaking his head at Raven as if he could put the words back in her mouth. He pressed his hand to his forehead, focused, trying to think his way out of this one. Too many people knew. Now it wasn't just him. Zachary, Kenzie, Tyrrell, Mrs. Burton. He couldn't silence all of them. He needed to change his approach.

"Look..."

"Was Raven the one who killed Brooke Collins?" Kenzie asked, her voice flat. She wasn't making an accusation. She didn't want them getting all emotional and overwrought. If Raven had killed Brooke in a hallucinatory or agitated state because she had been poisoned with Jimson weed, then she wouldn't necessarily be guilty. If she hadn't voluntarily taken Jimson weed, but it had been administered to her without her knowledge, she couldn't be held responsible for what had followed.

Jack just looked at her, pain in his eyes. He didn't say anything to Raven to explain or defend his actions.

If he had knowingly destroyed evidence, then Jack was guilty of something. And if he had been the one to put Jimson weed into the food, then *he* might be responsible for Brooke's death to some degree. And what about Mr. Dewey? Had he killed Dewey when the man refused to acknowledge him or have a relationship with him? He could have burned Raven's clothes in his own fireplace. He'd wanted to destroy more than that.

"What are you talking about?" Raven asked.

"You don't remember everything that happened that night," Kenzie suggested. "One of the problems with Jimson weed is that it causes memory blanks. Episodes of amnesia that can cover hours or days. Sometime that night, you went out and met up with Brooke Collins in the woods. And when you went back to your cabin, or to Jack's cabin, you were covered with her blood."

Raven's eyes widened. She looked at Jack, no longer accusatory. "No."

"Jack?" Kenzie pressed.

Jack nodded, not looking at her. "Soaked with blood. And cold as ice, out there without any coat or warm clothes on. You'd just put my boots on. I... helped to warm you up. I tried to wash them, but they didn't come clean. And all of those TV shows, they say that you can never get all of the blood out."

"So you burned them. Along with the rest of the evidence. Brooke's body. Anything that might point to what Raven had done. Or what you had done."

"*I* didn't do anything," Jack shot back. "None of this had anything to do with me."

"The Jimson weed was yours. That makes you guilty of Brooke's death, even if it was Raven who had killed her."

"No! Jimson weed? I don't even know what that is. You're crazy. I don't know what happened that night. What she did," Jack looked at Raven, "but it was nothing to do with me. She has..." His eyes moved back and forth between Zachary and Kenzie, trying to identify which of them would be the most sympathetic. "She has problems. Medical problems. Something set her off. Andy and Brooke fighting. I don't know. But something happened."

Raven's whole face was a scowl. "You think I had a psychotic break that night? I didn't. I would know."

"Do you remember what happened? Do you remember coming back covered in blood? What happened before that?"

She shook her head.

"Then you had a break," he insisted.

"It wasn't just Raven," Kenzie said. "Others had hallucinations, strange behaviors, fights," she reminded him. "That's why we searched everyone's cabins."

"But you didn't find anything."

"Are you the one who stole the medications too?" Kenzie challenged. "You know, other people need those. Just like Raven needs hers."

Jack looked at Raven and didn't admit to it. But Kenzie had a pretty good idea he was the one who had drilled the safe. He had been worried about making sure that Raven got her meds. Or he'd wanted something else in there. Maybe he'd needed a tranquilizer in order to stay calm and function, knowing that his girlfriend was the one who had killed Brooke. And he'd lost his father, too. Had *that* been a coincidence? An accident?

If they weren't accepting coincidences, then why had Dewey died? Had Jack intentionally killed him? Had they had an argument? Had Jack tested out the Jimson weed on him, and then given it to everyone else to cover up what he had done?

"How did you know who Jack was?" Kenzie asked Mrs. Hubbard. "Had Mr. Dewey told you about him? Did he know that Jack was coming?"

"We knew who Jack was." Mrs. Hubbard didn't explain how they knew. "We knew he was here to confront—to talk to Mr. Dewey."

"Who is included in the 'we'? How many people knew that he was coming?"

Mrs. Hubbard shrugged. "I don't see how any of it matters," she declared. "It was just me, and Harold, and Mr. Dewey."

"Harold?" Kenzie repeated stupidly.

"Mr. Burknall."

"Oh. Sure. So it was only the three of you who knew who he

really was? That he wasn't here to vacation, but to see Mr. Dewey and to *talk* to him."

"It was a vacation," Jack said. "I wanted to bring Raven here, see what she thought about it. Relax and enjoy the atmosphere. The planned events. Meals. It was a nice retreat. I don't take a lot of vacations."

He looked at Raven, smiling at her, trying to get something from her other than the scowl she was displaying. She probably was not pleased that the romantic getaway he had planned had actually had the ulterior motive of seeing his biological father and scoping out the landscape. And that he had poisoned her and everyone else. *What kind of a psychopath did that?*

"I didn't poison anyone," Jack growled, reading Kenzie's expression.

"The evidence suggests that you did."

"What evidence? You never found anything on me or in my cabin. The only thing I'm 'guilty' of is trying to protect Raven from prosecution. I knew no one would understand. I had to take it upon myself." Jack shook his head. "I would think *you* would understand that."

What would Kenzie have done if she thought that Zachary had done something that put him in danger of being prosecuted? What if he came home with his shirt soaked with blood? How would she handle it? She would like to think that she would do the right thing, but what was the right thing? Turn him in or protect him?

She had an obligation, working in the medical examiner's office, to the truth. But did that apply to every circumstance? Or only to official evidence that came to her through her job?

She hadn't hesitated when Zachary had come to her with Madison and Noah, when Noah had been shot and Zachary wouldn't take him to the emergency room in case they put a dirty cop on to him. So she had already been tested in that arena. She knew that if Zachary came to her with something possibly unethical, she would still help him to cover for it. How could she fault Jack for doing the same?

"I can't condone the destruction of evidence," she told Jack anyway, "It would have been better if you had left it to the police to sort out. If Raven did something in an altered state... they would investigate it. Figure out how to deal with it."

"And decide to put her away for life. Come on. You know it."

Kenzie shrugged. She put her face in her hands and rubbed her eyes and her temples. "I just want... to understand what went on here. If you weren't the one who poisoned everyone with Jimson weed, then who did?"

Jack folded his arms across his chest, staring at her sullenly.

"Two truths and a lie," Zachary said.

Kenzie looked at him. "What?"

"You know, it's that game where you try to figure out which statement that someone made was a lie."

Kenzie nodded. "Sure. I know that."

"It isn't coming together because we have taken as true something that was a lie. What do we believe that isn't actually true?"

Kenzie sighed. They couldn't keep going back over everything again and again. She had already accepted everything Zachary had suggested. That there were no coincidences. That Dewey's death was somehow related.

They knew more now, with a better understanding of Jack's and Raven's roles in the events, but they still didn't have the whole picture. They needed the police to investigate it and to sort it out.

"I don't know, Zachary. What do we believe that is a lie?"

"The night that we searched the cabins. What did we accept as true?"

Kenzie closed her eyes and thought it through. "That no one could have spiked the food with their pills. That the mushrooms were Redd's. That each of the medications we found belonged to the person whose cabin it was. That we found everything that was hidden." That one clearly wasn't true, if Jack had been in possession of Raven's bloody clothes at that point. Where had he hidden them in his neat-as-a-pin cabin? Maybe outside under the snow? In the barn or one of the other outbuildings? Until he decided he couldn't hide them any longer and they needed to be destroyed.

She sighed.

"That everyone was telling the truth about their own symptoms," Zachary added. "Hallucinations, fights, amnesia, that all of that was true."

"And it wasn't?" Kenzie asked. Her eyes snapped open.

Zachary shrugged. "Maybe... maybe not. What does your training tell you?"

"What did we observe?" Kenzie mused. "The argument and people coming and going, you saw that."

Zachary nodded.

"Redd having hallucinations. He was still hallucinating the next day. I could see him... the way his eyes would move to follow something that wasn't there. Dilated pupils. Jimson weed is known for causing hallucinations for days, even weeks sometimes."

"Raven had dilated pupils too," Zachary said, giving Raven a nod. "I remember noticing that."

Kenzie thought back, nodding. "Yes. She did."

"Andy Collins said that he couldn't remember. That's another of the symptoms of Jimson weed, so—"

"But we can only take his word for that. It may be true, but he could just be covering up."

"And Stiller too," Kenzie said. "He said it felt like when he'd been roofied in college."

Zachary scratched his jaw. "That seems... like something a man of his standing wouldn't usually admit to."

"No, but it's one of the things that made me realize they'd all been given something. Not just him, but all of them."

"Did he eat or drink more than the others? Does the amnesia mean that he was given more?"

"I don't think there's a correlation. Some people get one symptom, some another."

"And if someone knew the symptoms, that would be an easy one to fake. A lot easier than dilated pupils."

"Vance Stiller." Kenzie thought about him. "Why is he even here? It doesn't seem like the type of place that a high roller like him would vacation. Brittany is known for being 'one of the people,' so I can see it in her case. But Stiller? The man came here in a helicopter."

Jack looked from Kenzie to Zachary. "He wasn't here for a vacation."

"Well, to see Brittany," Kenzie clarified. "I guess maybe she picked the venue."

Jack shook his head. "No. He wasn't here for any of that. He told Brittany about the place and she decided to come too, but *she* followed *him*, not the other way around."

"How do you know that?"

"Because he was talking with Dewey about buying the place, came to try to talk him into it, get the lay of the land."

"Buying it?" That seemed even more unlikely than his choosing to vacation there. Why would he want to buy a place like that, so far out of his comfort zone? He was a city boy, high finance, a tech guy. Not the kind of person who enjoyed camping in a cabin. And he'd been vocal about it. Why would he buy a place like that if he didn't even like it?

Jack nodded. He motioned to Mrs. Hubbard. "Tell them. He was trying to talk Dewey into selling it to him."

Mrs. Hubbard shrugged. "Mr. Dewey said he would never sell. Especially not to a man like Mr. Vance."

Kenzie nodded slowly. Her eyes found Zachary's. "There was no way he would sell to a man like Stiller. But maybe his estate or his heir would."

They both looked at Jack.

"Was that the plan?" Kenzie asked him. "Mr. Dewey wouldn't sell to him, Vance decided to go to the next in line. You."

"I never talked to him before I came here. And like I told you,

I have no idea if Dewey left me anything. You'd have to check his will."

"But you could contest it if he didn't. Make a claim on his estate as his sole living relative."

"Maybe. If I wanted something from him."

"A place like this would bring in a lot of coin," Zachary said, motioning around them. "Medical care can be expensive. Specialized therapy." He was looking at Raven. "For someone who didn't grow up with a lot of money, it would be a windfall."

"I hadn't made a decision," Jack said, keeping his arms folded in front of his chest, giving off a stubborn, belligerent air. "There was no reason to rush into anything."

"Did Stiller give you an offer? Suggest a price?"

"No."

Watching his eyes, Kenzie didn't believe it for a minute. They had been in negotiations, without Jack even knowing if he would inherit the Lodge, or a portion of it.

"And Stiller could bring down the price," Zachary said. "If it turned out the Lodge wasn't as valuable as you thought initially... if things didn't go well and it got a bad reputation..."

"If there was a death or two," Kenzie filled in, as the pieces clicked into place, finally making sense. "People going crazy there. A rumor that it was bad luck or cursed. A series of tragedies."

"*He* did this?" Jack demanded. "Vance Stiller poisoned us? Caused—" he looked at Raven, "—caused Brooke to get killed? Endangered all of our lives with his poison to get a better price on the deal?"

"Maybe," Zachary said cautiously. "It's speculation right now. But it fits the facts. He could pretend that he had been affected by the Jimson weed. Throw anyone who was suspicious off of the trail. Use anything that happened here as leverage to lower the selling price of the Lodge. And you played right into his hand, burning the farmhouse down."

68

Jack opened the door and bolted. Raven hurried to get her boots back on and follow him. "Jack! Jack, wait!"

"We'd better stop him," Zachary warned.

Kenzie got her boots on and grabbed her coat. She was out the door right after Zachary, leaving Mrs. Hubbard and Tyrrell in the dust. Jack was already pounding on Vance Stiller's cabin door, making threats, demanding that he show his face. If Stiller had any sense, he would know to keep as quiet as possible.

He didn't answer the door. Zachary and Kenzie caught up with Jack. "We need to let the police take care of this," Kenzie told him. "Another day or two, and they'll be here..."

"And by the time they can get here, he's going to be on a helicopter away from here, and I'm never going to be able to get close to him again. This is it. It all comes down to this." Jack hammered on the door, calling Vance names, trying to needle him sharply enough for him to lose control and come out of the cabin to fight Jack.

But Stiller didn't come out. The cabin was quiet. No movement that Kenzie could detect. She turned toward Brittany's cabin. Close enough to see what was going on. Maybe Brittany would know whether her boyfriend were there or if he had somehow bolted, escaping without their realizing it. She wouldn't put it past the guy.

As she turned and looked at the other cabin, she heard a noise. The soft click of a door latch between Jack's assaults on the door. The front door hadn't moved, so it had to be the back. Kenzie stepped to the side, trying to see into the back yard to see whether Brittany were making her escape. She saw Stiller, head down, moving slowly and quietly so as not to attract any attention.

Jack turned toward Kenzie. Following her gaze, he caught sight of Stiller. "Vance! Hold it right there! You're not going anywhere!"

Vance turned around to see Jack. In doing so, he revealed the fact that Brittany was with him. At first, Kenzie thought that he just had his arm around her. A gesture of protectiveness and possession. But Brittany's face was white, and it only took Kenzie a fraction of a second to realize that she was Stiller's hostage.

"Just stay back," Stiller warned. "There's no need to get all hot under the collar..."

"No need?" Jack shouted, drawing closer. "You poison us? Cause someone's death? Ruin people's lives? And there's nothing to get hot about?"

Stiller took a few steps back, trying to keep distance between himself and Jack. His arm was tight around Brittany's neck and he held a knife in his hand. Was it the knife that had killed Brooke? Kenzie wasn't sure if it was the same one, but it looked wickedly sharp and deadly. Brooke's body had been a bloody mess. Knife wounds were not pretty. A slash across Brittany's throat would cause her death within minutes. She would bleed out right there in the snow, with no chance of their saving her. Not without a trauma team on hand and a surgeon to sew her up before she bled out.

"Vance..." Kenzie tried to keep a calm, professional tone. Something that would make him feel validated. Make him feel like someone was listening to him. "I don't think we need to do this, do you? You don't want to hurt Brittany."

She could see Brittany swallow, trying to pull her throat back from the knife as she did so. "Vance," she whispered hoarsely. "Honey..."

But Vance had trained himself to be a shark. To ruthlessly go after what he wanted. No matter what personal pain it brought him. However much grief and regret it might cause him later, it would not stop him from proceeding.

For a moment, Kenzie could hear nothing but the rushing of blood in her ears. Then she looked around, puzzled by a noise outside her head. It was like the crash of an ocean. Waves of sound swallowing them up. She tried to separate them out, but they all rushed together. People shouting. Snowmobiles. Heavy equipment. A hundred voices all crying out at once. Kenzie looked around, trying to understand what it was and where it was coming from.

There was a dark flood coming down the hill. Kenzie's brain couldn't break the surge of movement into its component parts, dazzled by the sun coming out from behind a cloud and hitting the bright white snow. Overwhelmed by all the images flowing together, as if the flood were made up of a thousand moving parts.

As the flood engulfed them, Kenzie saw people on snowmobiles, some of them standing or waving shovels. Followed by ranks of tractors, everything from little Bobcats to heavy-duty plows. All coming in from the highway, down the hill, and into the middle of the stand-off.

Stiller seemed as stunned as any of them. He didn't have his sunglasses on, and a beam of sunlight suddenly broke through the clouds, causing tears to run down his face. He swiveled his head, trying to see or make sense of all the moving, shifting shapes.

There were shouts of "He's got Brittany!" and "The bombshell" and "Go Bambas!"

A hostage situation should be carefully controlled, managed by a skilled negotiator who was trained in de-escalating situations and ensuring a positive outcome. Everything should be kept quiet and calm, and nothing should be done to startle the hostage-taker.

The fence between the front yard and the back was no obstacle. Snow machines went airborne over it and, shrieking like pigs being slaughtered, the riders mobbed Stiller and Brittany, parting them with overwhelming force. Kenzie tried to get to Brittany, visions of a severed carotid filling her brain. She shoved the people in the crowd aside, insisting that she be allowed to see Brittany to give her medical care.

"I'm a doctor! Get out of the way! Let me see!"

She managed to bully her way through them, over the broken remains of the fence pounded into the snow, until she reached Brittany, stretched out on the ground.

"Let me see!" Kenzie insisted, jerking and pulling on coats and sweaters that got in front of her. "Brittany! Brittany!"

Brittany held up her hands, laughing. "It's okay, Kenzie. I'm okay! I'm fine!"

Kenzie shoved more people away. She stared at Brittany. Her throat was unmarked, though there were several tears in her coat. Kenzie held out her hand to Brittany and helped her to her feet.

"Is Vance okay?" Brittany asked, looking around.

Kenzie searched the crowd for him, but couldn't see him and wasn't sure she wanted to. "What just happened here?"

"The Bambas!" someone shouted close to her ear.

Kenzie winced. "What?"

"My fans," Brittany said, her laugh soft. "It looks like... they found me."

"How? How did they find you and how did they get here?"

"We hadn't heard anything from the Bombshell in, like, three days!" one of the men nearby blasted Kenzie. "So it was like, everybody was looking for her! And no one knew where she was. We had to follow the trail here, but there was literally no way to get here through the snow. We called out for every dang snow removal vehicle in the state, and we made our own way here!"

Kenzie blinked, trying to take it all in. "Your fans plowed the highway," she said to Brittany.

"Looks like it. And not a moment too soon!" Brittany laughed.

"I thought... I thought Stiller was going to kill you!"

Brittany forced a banal smile, keeping all the anxiety out of her face. Two minutes before, she had been as white as a sheet, begging for her life, and now she was doing her best to show that nothing had fazed her. She looked around her, again looking for some sign of Stiller, then shook her head.

"I'm not sure... what happened to him. But I guess... everything is okay now."

Kenzie heard sirens whoop and looked up the hill to see fire trucks and police cars turning in from the highway. "A little late for them now."

"We saw the smoke!" another of the fans shouted. Kenzie didn't know whether everybody just sounded loud after the isolation of the past few days, or if all Brittany's fans were just natural yellers. "We were afraid that something might have happened to Brittany!"

She nodded. "Well... we're glad that you got here when you did."

___

It was some time before Kenzie managed to make it back to the cabin. Zachary caught her arm as she pushed her way through the crowd of Bambas.

"Kenz! Are you okay?"

"Yeah. I'm honestly not sure what just happened, but I'm fine. You?"

She managed to focus on his face and saw that he had a black eye.

"Oh. We should put some ice on that. Grab a handful of snow."

They holed up in the cabin and watched as the police gradually got the fans moved out of the area. Kenzie saw a white tent go up in the yard and knew that there was only one reason for the scene to be processed that way. Somewhere under the awning was Stiller's beaten and trampled body. She was glad that it wasn't her investigation, that she didn't have to be part of that particular crime scene and to view Stiller's remains. To be an effective pathologist, she needed emotional distance, and she didn't have it in this case.

Before long, the police would be making their way to her cabin and would want to know all about everything that had happened. They weren't going to be happy with the destruction of the evidence in the fire.

Soon, there would be a lot of questions for her and the others. And she wasn't sure she had many answers for them.

69

Kenzie helped Tyrrell and Zachary load up Tyrrell's car and get the kids ready to go. They were all eager to get out of there, Mason chattering on about how he was going to see his mom again and about all the things that he would tell her.

Kenzie smiled at Tyrrell sympathetically. "I guess your ex will have a lot of questions on just what happened here this week."

Tyrrell nodded and rolled his eyes. "Uh, yeah. She is definitely going to have some words about putting them in this situation."

"It isn't as though you could have done anything to prevent it. You did everything you could to keep the kids out of the way, and they didn't actually *see* anything."

"Thank goodness! Oh, would I be in some deep trouble then. But... maybe I should have headed out when I knew the storm was coming in. I knew that we might get stranded for a couple of days, but I didn't think there was any harm in it. Even with the power and communications out, the kids were still safe and had food and everything they needed."

"Maybe even a good thing for them," Kenzie contributed. "No screens. Just books and games and finding ways to entertain themselves."

"It didn't actually go too badly, other than when Mace took off and hid in the barn."

"And he didn't fall or get hurt in there. I'm sure it's not the first time he's wandered off."

Tyrrell chuckled. "By no means. But my ex still thinks that we should be able to prevent it. If we're just vigilant enough."

Kenzie shook her head. It would take a bit more than just vigilance to keep track of everything Mason did. An ankle monitor and a body cam, for a start. Maybe one of those perimeter collars that you put on dogs to keep them from crossing the property line.

"Well, good luck."

"Thanks." Tyrrell turned back toward the car to get the children settled and to make sure they hadn't forgotten anything.

"And Tyrrell...?"

He turned back around and looked at her.

"Is everything okay with you...?" She knew that Zachary had brought up the alcohol cabinet with Tyrrell, but the younger man had denied falling off the wagon. It would have been understandable under the circumstances, but he said he'd never touched a drop.

Tyrrell nodded. "Sure, I'm fine. You take good care of this brother of mine." He grabbed Zachary, who was headed back to Kenzie's side, and gave him a fierce hug. "You did really good, bro. Really good. Take care."

Zachary slapped him on the back. "I will, T. You too."

"Let me know how you're doing. I know that this is... a tough time of year." Tyrrell looked at him for a moment, meeting his eyes. "For me, too."

"Yeah. Will you have the kids this year?" In keeping with his usual practice, Zachary didn't say "for Christmas," but it was understood.

"I'm supposed to. It's my turn."

Zachary swallowed and nodded. Kenzie knew that he wanted to say something like "We'll have to get together" or to suggest an activity they might like to do with the children. But he had a mental wall where Christmas was concerned. He could not plan anything until after Christmas Eve was past.

Tyrrell gave Zachary an understanding pat on the back and climbed into the car.

"I'll give you a call."

Kenzie finished tidying up Dr. Wiltshire's office and putting everything else back to rights, which had taken quite a bit of work after all the time she'd been away. Between the antiviral protocol and her last-minute vacation, she'd been away for several weeks, and none of it had been planned, so Dr. Wiltshire and the part-time staff that he could get in had run things the best they could while she was gone. And, she was happy to see, they badly needed her to get things straightened out again. They had managed to get along without her, but it was clear that they had struggled and that several of the department protocols had fallen by the wayside as they tried to make do without her.

They needed her. And that was a good feeling.

She had gotten there early to make sure she would have a lot of time before Dr. Wiltshire got there. She wasn't a morning person, but it had been worth it to get up extra early for one day.

She was back at her desk when Dr. Wiltshire got there, just starting to go through the accumulated email in her inbox to sort out the priorities and get started on printing and filing.

"Kenzie!" His greeting was more enthusiastic than usual. "Look at you! You don't know how much I have missed seeing your smiling face when I get in each morning."

"Well, from the state of the office, I can understand why."

"We did our best to keep things running while you were gone," he said, scratching his head, "but we have clearly come to rely on you for nearly everything around here."

He had a tray and a box from the donut shop down the street. He put them on the ledge of Kenzie's desk, and carefully removed a cup of coffee from the tray.

"For you."

"Thank you!"

"And there are donuts..." He opened the box and held it tilted for her to pick out her choice of pastries.

"Oh, I shouldn't..." But Kenzie knew that she would take one, and so did he. She'd already burned up all the calories from her marmalade toast that morning, running back and forth getting things tidied up. She was ready for something decadent after hospital food and camping food. It seemed like a long time since their Thanksgiving dinner with Lorne and Pat. Though the real Thanksgiving Day was still coming up.

"So, how was your vacation?" Dr. Wiltshire asked. "Nice and relaxing?"

"Well... it didn't turn out quite the way that I expected."

"Oh? I suppose they never do happen quite the way that we plan, do they?"

Kenzie shook her head. "No. I guess that would be asking too much."

"You'll have to tell me all about it. But right now, I should check to see what's on my desk. And I think you have a few things waiting for you in your inbox."

Kenzie nodded. "Yes... it would appear that I do."

**Did you enjoy this book? Reviews and recommendations are
vital to making a book successful.**

**Please leave a review at your favorite book store or review site
and share it with your friends.**

Don't miss the following bonus material:
Sign up for mailing list to get a free ebook
Read a sneak preview chapter
Other books by P.D. Workman
Learn more about the author

Sign up for my mailing list at pdworkman.com and get Gluten-Free Murder for free!

PREVIEW OF GENTLE ANGEL

CHAPTER 1

It felt good to be back in the morgue.

It might sound strange, but after their stressful vacation in a mountain resort, Kenzie and Zachary were both glad to be home and back into the usual daily routines. Zachary running his private investigations business and Kenzie returning to the Medical Examiner's Office where none of the bodies she dealt with were people that she had known personally. Most people considered the work of a medical examiner to be gross and depressing, but Kenzie was fascinated with the work of uncovering what the deceased had died of and found it life-affirming rather than discouraging.

Dr. Wiltshire and the part-time staff had let a number of things slide while she had been gone. She had been prevented from coming to work first due to a virus she had contracted and the anti-viral protocol to kill it, and then on a short holiday that was supposed to be a chance for her and Zachary to recover their health and rest before getting back to work. It hadn't exactly turned out that way.

There were a lot of requests and reports to be processed in Kenzie's physical in box as well as in her email queue.

A couple of bodies had been transported from the hospital,

and Kenzie reviewed the intake forms to find out the details and make sure that everything had been filled out correctly. She opened new files for each of them and checked the bodies themselves to make sure that the names and numbers matched the forms that the hospital had sent with them. Always better to catch any clerical errors early. Families tended not to like it when bodies got mixed up.

She was back at her desk printing reports when Dr. Wiltshire got in. The idea of the ME's office being paperless was a joke. They went through reams of paper.

"Morning, Kenzie," Dr. Wiltshire greeted.

"Morning, Doctor. Got a couple of intakes from the hospital today."

He nodded and took a sip of his coffee. "Anything of note?"

"One from a single-vehicle car accident. And one a request from a doctor."

Neither was particularly out of the ordinary. A doctor-attended death did not automatically go to the Medical Examiner's Office, but if the attending physician had any doubts about the cause of death or deemed it suspicious in some way, he could request that the medical examiner perform an autopsy.

"What is the doctor's name?"

Kenzie hadn't made note of it, so she brought the form up on her computer to check. "A Dr. Philemon?"

"Philemon..." Dr. Wiltshire pondered this for a moment. He frowned. "He's in geriatrics, isn't he?"

Kenzie went to the Vermont Health Network website and searched Dr. Philemon in the directory. "Yes, looks like that's his specialty. Does some general practice as well."

Dr. Wiltshire nodded. "Okay. I'll look at them today. How is your workload?"

"Still trying to get caught up. Lots of printing and filing to be done."

"Yeah... we might have let that slide a little."

"A little," Kenzie agreed. She wasn't sure anyone had done any filing during the weeks she had been gone. And since no filing had been done, she couldn't be sure what reports had been printed already. She had to keep going back and forth between the computer and the piles of printouts and the files to try to make sure everything was accounted for and that they could put their hands on what they needed immediately. It wasn't any good if there were lab results floating around that hadn't been reviewed or if they were holding onto bodies that should be moved on to funeral homes because they hadn't been cleared yet.

"Sorry about that. But we didn't want to mess up your system..."

Kenzie laughed and shook her head. "Good excuse!"

He smiled and took another sip of his coffee. "Well, we had to come up with something to explain this mess."

Maybe they could have put some of the time that had gone into thinking up an excuse into actually getting the work done.

"I'll do what I can to get it all whipped into shape... but I'll be ready for a break from the paper this afternoon, if you don't mind me scrubbing in on one of the autopsies."

"Sounds good. I'll be sure to start early enough that you can get through it and still get back to Zachary in good time."

Dr. Wiltshire knew Zachary from a couple of previous cases that he had been involved with. And he knew a little bit about the challenges that Zachary faced.

Only someone who lived with Zachary or was close to him could know the real extent of his difficulties, but Kenzie appreciated Dr. Wiltshire thinking about her and her home situation in setting his schedule for the day. Despite the amount of work she had to do, Kenzie didn't want to be there too late. She would get caught up over time. Being able to spend time with Zachary and keep an eye on his health was important too.

Kenzie was a little disappointed that the autopsy she was able to scrub in on was Dr. Philemon's patient rather than the accident victim. The accident victim would have been more interesting. She suspected that a geriatric patient who had died at the hospital wasn't going to be a particularly intriguing case. Although she couldn't make that judgment. They had recently autopsied a nursing home patient whose death had turned out to be anything but routine.

George had already prepped the remains for them, gathering any forensic evidence and washing the body off. The old man's body lay on the table with a drape over it, awaiting their investigation. Dr. Wiltshire tapped the button on the floor with his foot to start recording, and dictated the patient's name and file number, the date and time, and his and Kenzie's names. He began as usual, making note of the patient's height and weight and his appearance on gross examination. Nothing remarkable. He didn't look any different from any other geriatric patient who had passed away in his sleep.

They checked for any cuts, bruises, or needle marks, as well as making notes of livor mortis. Time of death had been noted by Dr. Philemon, and Kenzie didn't see anything that would indicate that the timing was off.

"Bruising to the chest and ribs," Dr. Wiltshire commented. "Let's get some films and have a look."

He and Kenzie donned the appropriate radiation shields and took several x-rays of the body. The images were processed and ready for their review immediately. Dr. Wiltshire called them up on the screen.

"Some inflammation and fractures," he commented. "What does that look like to you, Dr. Kirsch?"

Kenzie was the student, and Dr. Wiltshire preferred the Socratic model of leading her with questions rather than lecturing. Kenzie had seen the victim's injury pattern in textbooks and didn't have a problem coming up with the answer.

"Looks like CPR was performed."

"Would you perform CPR on an elderly patient like this?"

Kenzie looked at him. "Probably not. He's very frail and what would be gained by reviving him? Even if he could be revived with CPR, chances are he would have brain damage or his quality of life would not be good. Not with broken ribs at his age. I'm surprised there was not a DNR."

"There might have been. If it's not properly recorded and flagged, they might proceed with CPR anyway. Although with a patient of this age," he shook his head, "I'm not sure why."

"I don't remember there being anything on the records we got from the hospital about CPR being performed. They should have noted it."

"Unless this was from a previous incident. If he had a cardiac event earlier, we might not have all the relevant records. We'll need to follow up on whether there was a DNR or a previous incident that required resuscitation."

Kenzie nodded her agreement. She couldn't stop and make a note in the middle of the autopsy, but it would be on the transcript she got back from the recording. She moved the magnifier over the deceased man's arm and examined the IV catheter and tube.

"See something?" Dr. Wiltshire asked.

"No. I just wondered whether I would be able to tell whether anything was injected into the IV."

"Doubtful," Dr. Wiltshire shook his head. "Sometimes there is trace evidence. Crystals, bubbles, things like that. But if it was meant to be injected, adrenaline or some other lifesaving measure, then no. It would just mix with the IV fluid and not leave any visible traces."

Kenzie examined the tubing for another minute, but couldn't see anything unusual.

"Okay. What's next?"

CHAPTER 2

It was a little later than Kenzie would have liked when she got home, but considering how late she had worked other days, it wasn't really bad. She hadn't had to eat a sandwich from the vending machine, but she was more than ready for her supper. She pulled her baby—a cherry red convertible—into her garage and walked in through the kitchen door. Zachary was sitting on the couch with his computer table in front of him, but he looked up when she opened the door, not so focused on his work that he failed to notice her.

"Home, sweet home," Kenzie declared.

Zachary smiled. "How was it today?"

"Still getting caught up. But Dr. Wiltshire understands that I can't get through three weeks of backlog in a couple of days, so I'm not going to kill myself trying."

"That would sort of defeat the purpose. Then you'd never get out of the morgue."

"Well, I would eventually, but it would be on a gurney."

Zachary chuckled. He pushed his table away from him and stretched. "Do you want me to order something?"

"I'm too hungry to wait for delivery." Kenzie put down her bag and opened the freezer door to see what supplies they had.

Even a pizza would take half an hour to heat, and she wasn't in the mood for frozen burritos. She closed the freezer and opened the fridge, but as she had expected, there wasn't much to eat there. Some fruit, a salad that she'd made with perfectly good intentions but then not even touched. Some leftovers from Sunday that she should probably throw out. Kenzie sighed.

"You could have a snack while we wait for delivery," Zachary suggested.

"Well... maybe." Kenzie considered the fruit. She could have an apple with some cheese while she waited for something better to be delivered. That would hold her over and help to keep her calm and relaxed to visit with Zachary but wouldn't take the amount of effort that actually coming up with something and preparing dinner herself would.

Her mother would despair over the lack of culinary and home-making skills her daughter possessed. But then, Lisa Cole Kirsch had employed a cook for most of Kenzie's childhood. Granted, she'd had a sick child to take care of, which was far more impor-tant than making sandwiches. Or mini quiches.

Kenzie removed an apple from the crisper drawer. She decided she didn't have the energy to get out the cheese and cut herself a couple of slices. She sat down on the couch with Zachary.

"Go ahead and order us something."

He nodded and picked up his phone. "What do you want?"

"I don't really care. As long as it isn't something that I have to make." Kenzie bit into her apple. It had been a long time since lunch. While Zachary poked through his phone and decided what to order in, she picked up the remote control and listened to the news headlines as the local news began. As she had come to expect, there wasn't much in the way of good, uplifting news. Negative headlines garnered more attention. When they switched to a story about Brittany "the Bombshell" Blake and her recent close-encounter with a possible killer, Kenzie quickly turned it off.

She turned her attention to Zachary. "So, tell me about your day today." Kenzie mentally reviewed what she remembered of his schedule for the day. "You got in to see Dr. Boyle for therapy today?"

Zachary nodded. He suppressed a smile, looking down at his hands. "It was good. I caught her up on... some of the stuff that happened while we were on vacation."

"I guess you kind of left her hanging before, when we lost cell coverage."

"Yeah. So she's been wondering how everything turned out, but I guess since she didn't get any reports that I'd had a breakdown and was in hospital somewhere, she figured that everything was okay."

"Well, I hope you told her that you did more than just okay. For you to be able to deal with the fire at the Lodge was huge." Kenzie smiled at him encouragingly. "I hope you really bragged it up."

His pale face was turning pink. He smiled again, nodding, but not raising his dark eyes to look into hers. It was nice to see him smile, especially as they approached Christmas, the worst time of year for his depression. He ran a hand over his short, stubbly hair.

"She was impressed. She said that she knew I could do it."

"I guess it's pretty amazing what we can do if we have to," Kenzie said. "We think we know what our limits are, but then something comes that pushes us out of our comfort zone... and we don't know until we face it if we can handle it."

"I told her..." Zachary licked dry lips, speaking hesitantly, as if worried how she might react, "that I'm worried... that nothing has changed. That the next time I remember the fire again... the flashbacks will be just as bad. That I won't have progressed at all."

Kenzie wanted to jump in and reassure him that of course he had made huge progress, and he wouldn't fall right back to where he was before. But psychology was not her area, and even if it were, she knew better than to counsel someone so close to her. She was too close to Zachary to have an unbiased opinion. "So... what did Dr. B say about that?"

Zachary picked at a thread in his jeans. "She said that... I'll probably still have some anxiety around it, but now that I know I can get through it, that she doesn't think it will be that bad. She's done exposure therapy with patients before, helping them to get over phobias or anxieties." He shrugged. "I don't know. I guess... we'll find out."

"We could go to a restaurant with candles or a fireplace. See how you feel."

Zachary shook his head immediately. "No way."

"Are you sure, you don't want to take some time to think about it?"

Zachary started to protest again, then looked at her and realized that she was teasing him. He ran his hand through his dark hair again, chuckling. But it was forced. Kenzie might have pushed it a bit far.

"Sorry," she apologized. "I'm a little punchy. Long day."

He laughed again. "No, it's fine. Sometimes... I don't realize when you're joking."

"I shouldn't do that. I'm glad things went well with Dr. B. And if you didn't brag enough about how well you handled the situation out there, I'll tell her at our next couple's session too. Because what you did out there was... remarkable. It really was."

"It's not such a big thing for anyone else."

"You were the one who took charge. That would be impressive by itself. Add in the fact that even a candle flame is usually enough to break you down, and that you faced a blazing house fire...?" Kenzie shook her head. "I can see I'm going to have to brag you up more. If that's how you told her about it."

He looked away from her, but not fast enough that she didn't see his smile of pleasure over her insistence that he deserved praise for having faced his biggest fear.

Kenzie had nibbled away most of her apple. She looked down at the core. "How long before dinner is here?"

He checked his phone screen. "Fifteen minutes."

"Okay. I'm going to go get changed. I'm not wearing grown-up clothes for the rest of the day."

She disposed of her apple core and went to her bedroom to change into a pair of comfortable pajamas. It wasn't so much that she hated her work clothes or that they were uncomfortable. She just needed a transition from 'work Kenzie' to 'home relaxing Kenzie.' She would put away any worries from the office and just focus on herself and Zachary for the evening.

She had hoped, with the holiday to the mountains, that she would be able to boost his mood and help him to get to a better place before December. He had already been sliding into depression in October, before the two of them had to endure the anti-virus protocol, and his physical decline during the treatment had been much worse than hers. Maybe because she kept herself in good condition, eating and sleeping well, and he had difficulty with both. His viral load had ended up being much higher than hers, even though he had contracted it from Kenzie. And that meant that they had also hit him a lot harder with the drugs they hoped would wipe out the virus before it could affect him as it had the nursing home victims.

The holiday had not gone as expected, but she didn't think he had lost more weight at the Lodge, and he had returned knowing that he had handled one of the things he had feared the most in life. If he could beat his fear of fire, maybe he could beat the depression and some of the other challenges as well. She hoped so.

"Food's here," Zachary called out.

"I'll be right there."

Gentle Angel, Book #4 of the *Kenzie Kirsch Medical Thriller* series by P.D. Workman can be purchased at pdworkman.com

ABOUT THE AUTHOR

Award-winning and USA Today bestselling author P.D. (Pamela) Workman writes riveting mystery/suspense and young adult books dealing with mental illness, addiction, abuse, and other real-life issues. For as long as she can remember, the blank page has held an incredible allure and from a very young age she was trying to write her own books.

Workman wrote her first complete novel at the age of twelve and continued to write as a hobby for many years. She started publishing in 2013. She has won several literary awards from Library Services for Youth in Custody for her young adult fiction. She currently has over 70 published titles and can be found at pdworkman.com.

Born and raised in Alberta, Workman has been married for over 25 years and has one son.

***

Please visit P.D. Workman at pdworkman.com to see what else she is working on, to join her mailing list, and to link to her social networks.

If you enjoyed this book, please take the time to recommend it to other purchasers with a review or star rating and share it with your friends!

facebook.com/pdworkmanauthor
twitter.com/pdworkmanauthor
instagram.com/pdworkmanauthor
amazon.com/author/pdworkman
bookbub.com/authors/p-d-workman
goodreads.com/pdworkman
linkedin.com/in/pdworkman
pinterest.com/pdworkmanauthor
youtube.com/pdworkman